Dark
Sapphire

Lisa Jackson

A SIGNET BOOK

SIGNET
Published by New American Library, a division of
Penguin Putnam Inc., 375 Hudson Street,
New York, New York 10014, U.S.A.
Penguin Books Ltd, 27 Wrights Lane,
London W8 5TZ, England
Penguin Books Australia Ltd, Ringwood,
Victoria, Australia
Penguin Books Canada Ltd, 10 Alcorn Avenue,
Toronto, Ontario, Canada M4V 3B2
Penguin Books (N.Z.) Ltd, 182–190 Wairau Road,
Auckland 10, New Zealand

Penguin Books Ltd, Registered Offices:
Harmondsworth, Middlesex, England

First published by Signet, an imprint of New American Library,
a division of Penguin Putnam Inc.

First Printing, August 2000
10   9   8   7   6   5   4   3   2   1

Heartfelt and deep thanks to those whose help
was critical with this work, especially
Nancy Bush, Cecilia Oh, and Sally Peters.

Author's Note

For the purposes of this story I used a little artistic license and embellished Captain Keegan's ship, the *Dark Sapphire*, and made it slightly more grand than the vessels of the time.

Prologue

Castle Ogof, Wales
Autumn, 1369

*A*t last he would become a man.

Gritting his teeth, Keegan pulled back on his oar with all the strength of his fifteen-year-old muscles. The wind shrieked and howled with the coming of the dawn, and the sea was choppy, white caps boiling around the small craft. Keegan's heart thudded wildly. His blood lust ran hot, the thrill of a battle at hand. Finally. His fingers curled around the oars in a death grip as he saw himself, sword drawn, ready to slay any of his father's enemies who attempted as much as the hint of a fight.

Others in the small craft were not as inflamed as he.

Hollis, the old goat, was the worst of the lot. Even now he was complaining.

"Ye be on a fool's mission, I tell ye, Captain Rourke," the old man warned Keegan's father as the tiny rowboat pitched and rolled on the angry, dark waters of the bay. "There be no good come from this."

Rourke was having none of it. With a grunt he, too, rowed inland, helping drag the small craft toward the ever approaching shore. "'Tis time to face Jestin again." His eyes narrowed. "Past time."

"Ach, by the saints, ye be mad."

"I swore I'd return, and so I have. The term of the bet is up. Twenty years have passed. Now, row!" Captain Rourke ordered, and Keegan swallowed a prideful smile. His father would not be intimidated by the old man's ranting.

"For the love of all that be holy, listen to me. Ye may be the captain, but ye keep me on to be yer adviser, do ye not?"

"Not today."

"Oh, bloody Christ, why do I bother?"

Rourke's head snapped around, and he impaled the older man with his glare. "Quit worrying like an old woman. I say we meet Jestin, and we meet him. I vowed to see him in this lifetime again, and today be the day!"

" 'Tis better to forget what happened."

"And next ye'll be tellin' me to forgive as well," Rourke sneered as the wind licked at his hair.

"And ye'll not be listening to that, now, will ya?" Hollis threw up his hands as if in supplication to the stormy heavens, abandoning his oar. "I may as well be talkin' to the wind, but the fact of the matter, Rourke, is that what happened between ye and Jestin was long ago. It matters not now. Ye've got yer ship and yer son and—"

"Damn it, old man. Row!" Rourke barked as a wave splashed over the side. Salt water as cold as ice rained down on Keegan.

As one the crew threw their backs into maneuvering the craft over the rough waves. The smell of brine was thick in the dark morning air, the taste of salt settling on Keegan's lips, but his blood was on fire, his eager pulse pounding at the thought of meeting his father's old enemy. Oh, to finally be part of a battle, to embrace the fight, should there be one. 'Twas what he'd dreamed of, what he yearned for.

Hollis, true to his nature, would not stop forewarning doom. "If ye don't care about yerself, for the love of God, Rourke, think of the boy. Vengeance has no part in Keegan's life."

Keegan bristled and drew hard on his oar, nearly standing

as the little boat pitched and bucked. He spat into the sea. He was no boy. Nearly fifteen, he was almost a man. His body was testament to it. His voice now cracked and lowered, the hint of whiskers speckled his chin, the muscles of his arms and legs had become strong, and more often than not he awoke with his manhood stiff and hard as the main spar of the *Warrior*, his father's ship. Nay, he would not think of himself as a lad. As usual, old Hollis with his hook of a nose and dark eyes sunk deep in his skull, was seeing the devil in every corner.

"My son stays with me," Rourke insisted.

"Even if ye go to yer grave? Will ye be takin' him with ye at his young age?"

"I'll not be dyin' today Hollis."

"I might remind ye that Jestin is the lord of Ogof, and he might not agree. He has no love of ye, Captain."

"Nor do I of him." Rourke snorted, and Keegan's heart swelled with pride. His father was captain of his own ship, a brave man who, though sometimes a swindler, smuggler, and thief, never fell victim to cowardice. Unlike jittery old Hollis. Oh, why hadn't Rourke left the anxious, aging man back on the ship where he belonged?

"Ye be temptin' fate, Rourke, ye know ye are," Hollis worried aloud, and the aging man's concern only served to irritate Keegan further. The old goat was forever worrying about storms, and sea serpents, and witches and the like. More often than not Hollis paced the deck, praying and crossing himself and glancing with anxious eyes at the heavens.

As if God was listening to him prattle on and on. Humph!

Even now the old worrywart was muttering a quick prayer. As if in response, his hood was snatched by the fingers of the wind, exposing his balding, spotted pate. Long silvery strands of his hair whipped over his face.

Keegan swallowed back a grin and, along with the other men, a few of his father's best archers and swordsmen, rowed as one, guiding the bobbing craft over the waves and

ever closer to the rugged shoreline near Ogof just as dawn
was breaking.

Sweating despite the bitter cold, Keegan hazarded a look
at the mouth of the bay, where the *Warrior*, the only home
he'd even known, lay anchored. The sails had been lowered,
and the masts, like long, skeletal fingers, stretched upward
toward the dark clouds.

"What do ye hope to do, arriving here at the home of yer
enemy unannounced?" Hollis demanded, taking up his
litany of doom again.

Rourke's eyes narrowed. "Settle an old score."

In all of his fifteen years, through rough seas and stormy
weather, Keegan had never witnessed the glint of raw
vengeance that now possessed his father's eyes.

Hollis opened his mouth to speak, then snapped it shut as
he took up his oar again. The small craft crested a final
wave, and the men climbed out of the boat to pull it ashore.

Keegan caught his first glimpse of Castle Ogof. Spread
upon the surrounding hills, the heavy gray curtain wall
rose and dipped with the terrain and reminded Keegan of
the spiny back of a slumbering dragon, napping in the
foggy October air, ready to be awakened at the first scent
of trouble.

He pulled hard on the rowboat's line as his boots splashed
through the tide pools. Sea foam and icy water swirled
around his ankles, but he took no notice. His eyes were focused on the behemoth of a castle stretching above the bare-
limbed trees. So this was where the enemy abided. Fine.
Good. Keegan couldn't wait.

"You," Rourke said, pointing a gloved hand at one of the
Warrior deckhands, "stay with the boat."

"Aye, sir," the sailor replied sharply, as if anxious not to
face Rourke's old nemesis. Probably a coward.

Keegan himself was unafraid. He lusted for the thrill of
sword play, the exhilaration of besting another warrior. He
wore his bone-handled knife proudly strapped to his waist,
and inside one boot, another smaller knife with a wicked lit-

tle blade, was hidden. If there was to be trouble, he was ready. More than ready.

Rourke walked swiftly across the rocky beach, and the older man hobbled over the jagged stones to keep up with him. "Let us turn 'round quick as a flea jumpin' upon a cur." Hollis sent one last, longing glance back to the ship that rolled on the current far in the distance. "I've a bad feeling about this."

"You always have a bad feeling," Rourke countered, tall and strapping in a long surcoat. Deep brown and trimmed in black fur, the coat billowed as he walked without giving any evidence of the hidden pockets deep inside—pockets that held all manner of treasures, tricks, and weapons.

"'Tis better not to wake the demons of the past," Hollis grumbled, nearly slipping as his legs, used to the slippery, oft angled decks of the *Warrior*, had difficulty reacquainting themselves with land.

"And I say 'tis better to claim revenge."

Hollis, pausing to catch his breath, stopped at the edge of the beach. Craggy cliffs rose overhead, stretching upward to the swollen gray clouds roiling overhead.

"Come along," Rourke said, eager to get to the castle.

Hollis struggled to keep up. "Ye lost Bertrice fair and square to Lord Jestin. I was there," he huffed, his voice strained. "Now, that be twenty years ago, 'tis over and done with. There is naught that can be accomplished by trying to best the lord now."

Rourke glowered at the shorter man, and his expression was as thunderous as the swirling waters of the sea.

"Some women ye never forget, Hollis. Ye know this yerself. Some women get into yer blood and burrow deep into yer heart. Ye have no say in it, no means to get rid of it." He glanced at Keegan and laid a big hand upon his son's shoulder. "That's the way of it, boy," he admitted, sadness tempering the rage that had been burning in his eyes. "Stay away from women. All of 'em. They be the curse of each and every man, I tell ye true. When first Eve gave Adam that apple in the garden, 'twas just the beginning of it, to be sure. Just the beginning. Now, 'twas twenty years to this day that I left; 'tis time to fulfill my promise."

Jaw set, Rourke hurried to a path that cut through a small barrier of leafless trees. There the trail widened and joined a muddy, rutted road that wound ever upward to the foreboding castle.

Though the day had barely begun, Rourke's small band was not alone. Carts dragged by straining horses and filled with fine wares inched through the mud. Peddlers swung their whips and cursed their beasts.

Snap! "Hurry along there, Black."

Crack! "Ye can do it, ye miserable, useless piece of horseflesh. Put yer shoulders into it or I'll be sellin' ya to the tanner!"

Women lugging baskets, children clinging to their skirts, soldiers atop fine steeds, huntsmen dragging their early morning kills, all entered the behemoth of a castle through its great maw, where the portcullis, like sharp iron teeth, had been drawn up. Rourke stated his business to a sentry, and though few would recognize what he'd done, he quietly slipped the man a coin or two from one of the many pockets within his robe.

"Ye may pass," the man said, his eyes gleaming, thick fingers surrounding the silver pieces.

Some of Keegan's bravado slipped a bit as he followed his father into the outer bailey of Ogof and noticed the wary sentinels standing guard on the wide curtain wall. Archers and swordsmen, soldiers, knights, and all manner of men who had sworn to defend this monstrous fortress regarded the procession through suspicious eyes.

Keegan doubted if his father had enough coins to bribe them all.

He swallowed back any bit of apprehension.

Nay, he was not afraid.

Squaring his shoulders, he hurried to keep up with

Rourke's long strides and took comfort in the knife strapped to his waist.

There was a rumble behind him, and a woman shrieked and jumped.

Hoofbeats, fast and furious, thundered through the gate.

"Halt!" a guard shouted.

Whirling, Keegan leaped. A sweating horse and rider flew past.

"God's teeth!" Hollis cried, scrambling out of harm's way.

Laughter trilled from the rider as the bay jennet, dark legs flashing, nostrils distended, ears flattened, bolted into the inner bailey. Astride the galloping beast was a girl, skirts bunched to her knees, her head tucked low, her dark red hair streaming behind her like a banner.

Awestruck, Keegan could only stare.

The horse was wet, breathing hard, its chest splattered with the same mud that flecked the girl's oval face. Her skin was white, her small jaw set, her eyes flashing pure devilment. She pulled back on the reins. The bay slid to a stop, and the she-devil hopped lithely to the ground.

Leaning forward, she patted the jennet's wet shoulder affectionately, and Keegan felt a tightness in his chest, a swelling in his breeches. " 'Tis a fine horse you are, Shamrock," the girl said as the mare tossed her head. Flecks of lather speckled the horse's dark coat.

Breathless, her cheeks rosy, her eyes as blue as a summer sea, the rider swiped her sleeve over her face.

"What were ye doin' takin' the mare out so early?" a man admonished. He was crippled up and barely as tall as the girl, but he took the reins with curled fingers and clucked his tongue. "The lady, she'll not be happy."

Laughing, the redhead winked. "When is she ever? 'Tis not Fawn's nature." Wiping her hands on her skirt, she ignored the fact that she was being watched. "See that Shamrock is cooled, Del, and given extra oats as well."

The old man wavered. Frowned. Slid a worried look at

the mare. "Farrell will report your takin' of the mare to yer father, I'm afraid."

"Let him."

"But he be the stable master, and—"

"And he cannot tell me what to do." She shook her mane of tangled red curls, and a precocious smile curved her small pink lips. "Asides, this will give him something to stew over."

Del snorted. "And stew he will, mark my words." He wrapped the reins around his gnarled fingers and, clucking to the horse, ambled off. The woman-child cast a look in Keegan's direction, paused but a second, arched one arrogant eyebrow, and then, as if he was of no interest whatsoever, turned on the heel of her muddy boots and half ran through a gate toward the center of the keep.

Keegan could barely move. She was, without a doubt, the most beautiful girl he'd ever seen. A vision of innocence and mischief.

"Come along," Rourke prodded, his expression darkening as he caught his son's fascination.

Hollis sniffed as he surveyed the interior of the castle. "'Tis bigger than I thought." The grooves furrowing his brow deepened. "Lord Jestin has done well."

Rourke shot him a look that silenced the older man as they strode through the very gate where the girl had disappeared. Keegan, his father's mission temporarily forgotten, trained his eyes ahead to catch another glimpse of the fiery-haired girl.

"Holy Mother," Hollis whispered once inside.

Men shouted orders, women chattered, and the smells of smoke, dung, and the sea blended together. Hammers rang, the skeps in the windmill whooshed, a potter's wheel creaked, and dogs barked over the hum and bustle of people working. Boys stacked firewood. Girls hung laundry. Young children scattered chicken feed or gathered eggs. The tanner was scraping a bear's hide clean, the blacksmith's bellows hissed and puffed, while a mason's chisels cut stone and women toted buckets of water toward the kitchen.

From the corner of his eye, through the knots of workers, Keegan spied the girl trying to shove her tangled hair into a circlet and veil as she hurried toward the chapel. At the door she smoothed her skirts, took a deep breath and, frantically making the sign of the cross over her small breasts, cast a glance over her shoulder. Her gaze collided with Keegan's again and his heart stopped.

She didn't move for a second. Blue eyes narrowed appraisingly. Keegan couldn't breathe.

Without a word, she dashed inside.

Absurdly, Keegan wanted to follow her, took a step in that direction, then felt a hand on his shoulder.

"Careful, lad," his father warned.

The door of the great hall opened fast, banged against the wall.

"Rourke!" a man's deep, resonant voice boomed from inside the great hall.

"Christ Jesus," Hollis whispered under his breath. "'Tis the devil Jestin himself."

Dressed in polished boots, thick breeches, and a tunic lined in silver fur, the lord of Ogof strode onto the top step of the keep. Barrel-chested, with fiery hair stuffed under a hat, he oozed authority. His expression was harsh, his jaw as hard as the very stones that had built this castle. "So ye've finally returned, have ye?"

At the sound of his voice all work in the castle ceased. Hammers stilled, the blacksmith's forge was forgotten, chisels and files were set aside.

Suddenly silent, the air in the bailey seemed to thicken.

A prickle of apprehension caused the hairs on the back of Keegan's neck to rise.

Rourke squinted up at the baron. "Aye, Jestin. I've returned. As I vowed."

"'Tis too late."

"Never. We agreed. Twenty years."

The lord's face folded in upon itself. " 'Tis too late if it was wanting to see Bertrice again, you were. She's dead. Been gone five years."

Rourke paled, his knees seemed suddenly about to give way, and his mighty shoulders slumped. Not a sound was issued from the crowd that had circled around. " 'Tis a lie ye speak." Rourke's voice was a whisper.

"Nay. 'Tis true."

The wind blew as cold as Keegan had ever felt.

"For the love of God," the captain said in a low voice filled with despair. For the first time in his life Keegan saw his father sketch a quick sign of the cross over his chest and close his eyes. Seconds passed, then slowly, as if somehow finding a new sense of purpose, Rourke managed to straighten his spine. "My . . . my condolences."

"Accepted." Jestin cleared his throat. "I've a new wife now." Gesturing toward the open doorway, he motioned with his fingers, and a proud, pale woman, her abdomen huge with child, appeared. She stood next to her husband. Fair-skinned and radiant, she linked one arm through his. "This be Fawn," Jestin said as Rourke frowned, and somewhere far off a sheep bleated. "She's the lady of Ogof now."

In his peripheral vision Keegan saw the red-haired girl slip out the door of the chapel. Yanking at the circlet, she moved silently and swiftly across the dead grass to stand near a doorway at the side of the keep. At the sight of the pale-haired woman standing next to the lord, the corners of the girl's mouth turned down.

"Lady Fawn, this be Captain Rourke." Jestin introduced them.

"M'lady." Rourke, ashen-faced, managed a stiff bow.

She nodded slightly, a smooth, smug smile stitched tightly to her lips. "Welcome, Captain," she said, though her eyes belied her civility. Cold and calculating, they regarded Rourke and his small band of men with an icy consideration that chilled Keegan's blood.

Rourke studied the ground for a moment, then slowly

raised his gaze to meet that of the lord of Ogof. He cleared his throat. A vein throbbed over one eye. His hands clenched. " 'Tis sorry I am about Bertrice, Jestin. I loved her true."

The lord's lips flattened as the first drops of rain began to fall from the heavens. Lady Fawn's eyebrows elevated just a fraction, as if she'd heard new gossip that she could use to her advantage at a later date.

"Since I be here already, I see no reason why ye and me, we can't have another toss of the dice," Rourke suggested as a pig squealed from a pen somewhere.

Raindrops began to fall more steadily, splashing against Keegan's head and running down his neck, sliding from the roofs and puddling on the ground.

Jestin shook his head as the peasants and servants gathered around. "There is no point to it now."

"Are ye no longer a gambling man?" the captain asked.

A pause. Jestin chewed the corner of his lip.

"Mayhap your new wife disapproves," Rourke suggested.

The baron's spine stiffened. Red eyebrows slammed together. "I do as I wish, but 'tis busy I be."

"Too busy for a quick game?"

Jestin cleared his throat, caught a disapproving glance from Lady Fawn, then disregarding her, said, "And what would be the stakes?"

"Oh, we will start small." From one of the many hidden pockets within his surcoat, Rourke withdrew a thick pouch that jingled and chinked invitingly. "Just a few coins, but . . . if it pleases ye, we could raise the stakes a bit after a game or two, just as we did before."

"And what would you have to offer?"

Rourke hitched his head backward in the direction of the bay. "If ye come up with somethin' interestin', I've got me ship I'd be willin' to wager."

Nay! The *Warrior* was their home.

Hollis lost all his color. "Do na be teasin'," he warned the captain in a harsh whisper. "Jestin, he hates ya sure, fer

Bertrice loved ye once. He'd take yer ship without thinkin' twice, he would, and then where would ye be? Where would the boy be?"

"I'll not lose," Rourke insisted, then more loudly, "Have we a bet, then, Baron? What would ye put up?"

"Not my castle, you know that." The lord's eyes narrowed as he looked west and, as if he could see through the curtain wall and watch the *Warrior* rolling on the gray waters of the bay, a greedy, lustful expression took hold of his features. "Ye'll wager yer ship?"

"Aye. What have ye to put up?"

The baron's gaze landed full force on the captain. "I'll make it worth yer while, Rourke, if we get that far."

"I would not trust the captain," Lady Fawn admonished, touching her husband's arm again.

"Nor would I, but 'twould be good to best him." Again Jestin's gaze narrowed on his old foe. "Then, in with you and we'll see if luck is on yer side this time." He snapped his fingers, servants scurried, and within minutes the captain, Hollis, Keegan, and the few other men who had rowed ashore were inside the great hall, the two old adversaries seated at a scarred trestle table, a wooden cup rattling with dice, mazers of wine at their fingertips.

Rushlights and candles glowed from sconces, a huge fire crackled and popped in the grate, hungry flames licking logs that glowed red, while men and servants shuffled around, searching for a better view.

"Saints be with us," Hollis whispered as a crowd gathered around the game.

"Tell me of Bertrice," Keegan demanded.

The old man scowled so deeply that ridges appeared in his brow. "She was beautiful and sinful. Your father was in love with her. So was Jestin. She . . . ach, she flirted with both men, used one against the other, fanned the fires of this rivalry, let me tell you." Hollis sighed and shook his head as the dice rattled like bones in the hull of a ghost ship. "So finally, when she could not make up her mind, twenty years ago this very night, the two men threw the cups. With each toss of the dice the winner banished the loser to a year away from the woman who would be his bride. The game went long into the night, but as dawn approached, your father had lost not only his money but his woman, and twenty years of life that could have been here. 'Tis then he took to the sea forever."

"Why have I not heard this before?" Keegan demanded.

"Because the captain wished it so." The old man laid a hand on Keegan's shoulder. "Women, they be the bane of a man's existence."

"And how would you know?"

The old man snorted. "All men who have lived beyond their youth know."

Keegan asked no more but watched with the others. Pages poured wine. Lady Fawn, her once serene face drawn into a mask of silent condemnation, sat at her husband's side as the stakes were raised quickly. Merchants, peasants, even the priest, a potbellied man who rubbed his rosary beads nervously, huddled near the gaming table.

Keegan stood close enough to see the sweat on his father's brow, the determined gleam in his eye. This was not mere sport. Nay. The tossing of the dice ran much deeper than simple gamesmanship. A tic above the lord's eye was proof enough that each man felt the same prideful need to win. Both men drank and gambled, and for a while they both won, but as the hours passed and the stakes increased, slowly Jestin's winnings mounted. He beamed and ordered more wine; Rourke frowned, counted his money, and tossed back mazer after mazer as more men—soldiers, merchants, visiting lords, and servants trying to look busy with their tasks—surrounded the table.

Keegan was jostled and pushed.

The stench of sour ale mingled with the odor of smoke and roasting meat wafting in from the kitchen.

"Out of me way, lad," a bear of a soldier with foul breath

and a sheathed sword ordered, elbowing Keegan away from
the table.

"Aye, let me have a look," another insisted, one hand on
the hilt of his weapon. He was as large as the first, had no
teeth, and wore the scars of battle upon his brutish face.
Keegan was elbowed and shoved farther from his father. It
was not a good sign, and the fear in Hollis's eyes for once
seemed well founded. Rourke had drunk far too much, was
reckless with his bets, and Jestin's well-armed men were
edgy and alert.

The coins on the table were piled high, and Jestin, with a
flip of his wrist, threw the dice. As the cubes rolled out, he
let out a whoop, and Fawn's place face split with a wide, relieved grin. "Beat that if ya can," the lord crowed, pounding
a triumphant fist on the table. His eyes gleamed, his face
ruddy. A buzz swept through the crowd, and Rourke took up
the cup, rattled the dice, and threw them across the table. A
poor toss. He rolled again. No good. Keegan's heart nearly
stopped, for in this game the third toss was the last.

Swearing under his breath, Rourke threw again.

The cubed and marked pieces of bone rolled to a stop.
The roll was better but not enough. The captain had lost.

Rourke's massive shoulders slumped. He swallowed
without a sip of wine.

Keegan bit his lip.

"Christ Jesus," Hollis whispered as Jestin, his cheeks
puffed by a self-satisfied grin of victory, leaned across the
table and scraped all his winnings across the table toward
him.

"So ye've come to me door just to be beaten again," Jestin
gloated, and several of the servants started back to their duties. Keegan's heart was hammering. Why had his father
lost? It was unlike him. And unnecessary. "You're like a stupid cur, you are, Rourke, never knowing how to stop the
beating." He laughed, and most of the men joined him.

Rourke mopped the sweat from his brow, settled back in

his chair, and scowled. His color was high, his eyes dark with shame and rage. "We not be done yet."

"Nay?" Jestin said, and downed his mazer, then clapped his hands while a page hastily refilled the empty cup. "Face it, man, your luck's run out if you ever had any. Which I doubt." More laughter rolled through the cavernous room.

"I've still got me ship."

The crowd stilled.

Keegan's heart leapt to his throat. *Not the* Warrior. Surely his father had brought up the ship only as a joke.

Hollis stepped forward and, placing a hand on the captain's sleeve, whispered loud enough for Keegan to hear, "Nay, Rourke, this bet, 'twould be no good. Let us be off, now. Ye came, ye had yer chance, but 'tis over."

"Shut up, old man." The captain fished inside his tunic and retrieved the title to his ship, a faded yellowed scrap that he slowly unrolled. "I'll wager the *Warrior*, but ye've got to come up with more than a pile of coins."

Jestin eyed the ownership papers. "Ye be sure of this, Rourke?"

"Nay, he's not certain," Hollis said, "Ye can see he's in his cups and—"

"What have ye got?" Rourke demanded.

Their eyes locked, and Jestin's mind was made up. "Give me but a minute," he said, and took his leave. In the time he was gone, Hollis pleaded with Rourke while Keegan, eyeing the restless crowd, worried about his father. The castle dogs, two gray, speckled beasts, watched his every move through suspicious gold eyes.

"Think, man," Hollis pleaded. "The *Warrior*, she be all ye have in the world aside from yer lad. What happens to Keegan if ye lose her?"

"I won't."

"Ye've said that before, but—"

"Enough!" *Slap!* Rourke cuffed the old man across his face. Hollis stumbled backward. Didn't so much as whimper. Just held his jaw.

"Don't—" Keegan jumped forward. Never had he seen his father strike the older man.

"Nay, lad, do na interfere," Hollis warned, holding his chin with one hand and stretching his arm outward as if to stop Keegan from tangling with the man who had sired him. Rubbing his jaw, he said to Rourke, " 'Tis mad ye be, Captain."

"Go to hell," Rourke growled.

"Oh, I be already there," the old man said, "all because I've followed ye."

" 'Twas nothing I asked of ye!" Rourke tore his eyes away from the wounded man and watched as Jestin and a solitary soldier, a swarthy, muscular man, returned.

"Will this do?" Jestin asked as he sat in his chair and opened his fist. Resting in his palm was the finest gold ring Keegan had ever seen. It glittered in the firelight, and the huge stone that was set into the heavy prongs winked a vibrant, seductive blue.

"Sweet Jesus."

"Not the stone."

Several men gasped. The room went silent. Was it reverence that reverberated through the whitewashed walls, or foreboding?

Two stumbled backward quickly.

Hollis swore under his breath. "By the gods, 'tis the cursed Dark Sapphire."

The man near him swallowed—whether in lust or fear, Keegan knew not which. "Holy Mother protect us."

" 'Tis said the owner will have good luck always," Jestin said, but Hollis shook his head violently.

" 'Tis cursed," he whispered loudly in the captain's ear. "Ye know as well as I do, 'tis the Dark Sapphire of Ogof." Hollis's thin skin was drawn tightly over his skull. "The jewel brings its owner not luck but damnation. 'Tis the downfall of men, and kingdoms and armies."

Rourke's eyes thinned. His lips flattened. " 'Twas Bertrice's ring."

"Once," Jestin admitted. "I gave it to her. 'Tis the Dark Sapphire of Ogof."

"But it was to be mine," Fawn said swiftly. "Do you not remember, husband? You promised me the gem."

"If you bore me a son, which you have not."

Tears sprang to her eyes. "I am with child now! 'Tis but a few weeks until the babe be born, and he will be a strong, fine son to you, the boy you have always wished for. No longer will Sheena be your only issue." She reached for her husband's arm, her fingers curling in the fabric of his sleeve. "Do not risk the ring."

He yanked his hand away. "If I win, I'll name the damned ship for you, and we will still have the ring."

"But—"

"Hush, woman!" He held the ring beneath the captain's nose, and the room was silent as a tomb. "What say you, Rourke?"

Keegan's father regarded the gem as if he couldn't draw his eyes from its seductive blue brilliance. He was not alone. Many within the thick walls of the keep were in awe of the sparkling stone. Rourke swallowed hard. "Aye, 'tis a bet," he said, and placed the *Warrior*'s title on the table, securing the curling edges with a candle. "But not just the ring. The money as well."

"So be it." Jestin slapped the ring atop the ragged, faded papers, shoved the pile of coins to the center of the table, and settled back in his chair. In the hushed room the blue gem glimmered.

Eerie.

Dark.

Tempting.

Rourke picked up his cup.

"The ring is not yours to give!" a strong feminine voice— one that Keegan recognized—accused. "'Twas my mother's!"

Keegan's eyes were drawn to the girl with the wild red

hair as she pushed her way to the table. Insolence held her chin high. Anger sparked in her blue eyes.

"Did she not ask that it be given to me when I marry? Is that not what you've told me again and again as I grew up?"

This girl was the lord's child? With her impertinent grin, wild hair, and smudged dress? "It was never to be given away. Not to her," she insisted, eyeing Fawn, "nor him." She pointed a condemning finger at Rourke.

" 'Tis mine to do with as I please," Jestin said. "I need not answer to you."

"But—"

"Oh, for the love of Mary!" Fawn said in great irritation as she motioned wildly to an aging serving woman. "Zelda, please take her to her chamber and see that she causes no more trouble!"

"Do not even try it," the girl spat.

Fawn looked at her husband, silently blaming him for his daughter's impudence, then wiggled bejeweled fingers impatiently at the maid. "Just get her out of here. Now."

Zelda nodded, attempted to do as she was bidden. Lanky and gaunt, she was as tall as most men but ungainly as well. Though she gave chase to the nearly grown girl, she was no match for the lord's daughter. The girl was as clever and agile as she was speedy. She darted through the throng as quickly as a mouse scurrying through sacks of grain. Sidestepping a page, she slipped around a column and ducked behind a curtain.

The older woman lost her, but Keegan followed the redhead's every move with his eyes. Aye, she was a sassy, impudent one, bound to give her father and whatever man dared try to tame her trouble. But she was as fascinating as the blue stone in the ring.

"Roll!" Baron Jestin ordered. Uninterested in his saucy daughter's antics, he turned his back to the stir and eyed the ownership papers of the *Warrior* with more than a trace of avarice.

Rourke shook his head, sat back in his chair as the room grew still as the middle of the night. " 'Tis your turn."

"So be it."

Keegan drew his eyes back to the table. Again a hush swept through the room. All his father owned in the world was at risk along with a pile of coins and a ring the likes of which few men had seen, a stone whose facets reflected blue crystal brilliance in the hundreds of candles that illuminated the great hall.

" 'Tis a fool Lord Jestin be," one man, a merchant from the looks of him, whispered to another. He leaned heavily on a cane of polished wood.

"Aye, but this be not about the gem," the other said. Dressed in deep forest green with a thin beard, he rubbed the back of his neck. "Nor the ship."

Keegan, standing near the two, his heart drumming in his eardrums, strained to listen. His nerves were frayed, his stomach clenched.

"Bertrice of Llwydrew," the first man said, as if just now remembering the events of twenty years ago.

"Yes, Bertrice. A beauty like no other. Blessed with eyes the color of the sky and the reddest hair ye've ever seen." The man in green lifted one hand and fanned his fingers at the memory of the winsome Bertrice's tresses. "It seemed to catch fire in the morning light."

Just like her daughter's, Keegan thought, realizing that this girl was the daughter of his father's love.

"Who knows what she thought of Jestin and Rourke's wager over her? Or the fact that Jestin won."

Keegan listened for all he was worth.

"And Rourke took to the sea, he did. Swore he'd never marry. Had himself a bastard or two, methinks."

The top of Keegan's ears burned, for he knew little of his own mother—a tavern wench who hadn't wanted to be bothered with a child. He had no memory of her, and whenever he'd asked, his father had grown silent and stern. Even old

Hollis, whose tongue was never still, could not be cajoled into speaking of her.

The two men moved on, and Keegan wove through the crowd to stand behind his father. It wasn't like Rourke to lose; not only was he clever but crooked as well. A black-heart who shamelessly drank and smuggled, Rourke was also a cheat who, if the situation called for it, would do anything to win.

Today was no exception. 'Twas hard to spot, but Keegan's trained eye had caught Rourke's sleight of hand more than once. In a game where a man was given three tries to best his score, Rourke had slowly lost. A few times Keegan was certain his father had switched the dice, but with each bit of trickery, the captain had not won. Now Keegan understood why. Only when the stakes were high enough would his father take advantage of his opponent.

Feet shuffled in the rushes. Servants peered through the curtains. From the corner one of the castle dogs growled, as if the shaggy cur could feel the tension in the room. Faces were strained, muscles taut, eyes focused on the battered planks of the table.

Side bets were being waged among the soldiers and peasants who had gathered.

"A sack of grain on the lord," one man with crooked teeth whispered to another.

"Amen to that. I'll put up me best mule on the captain there."

"'Tis a fool ye be, Luke, but I'll not be arguin' with ye. I could use me a new ass."

Keegan swallowed hard, and as he found a spot behind his father's shoulder, he noticed the lord's red-haired daughter on the far side of the table, partially hidden in the shadows of a curtain. For a second she caught his gaze, and a hint of a smile brushed her lips. Though she didn't speak, he felt that they shared a secret together amid the crowd and the thickness in the air.

His head pounded and he bit his lip.

The dice rattled. "'Tis now the time ye will rue your wager," the lord said.

Keegan dragged his eyes back to the game.

Jestin tossed the cubes onto the table.

The bits of bone rolled to a stop.

A wide, self-satisfied smile stole across the baron's ruddy face. He snagged up two of the cubes, threw them again, then nearly leaped in the air when they landed beside the others. "Beat that if ye can! I need not another roll."

Keegan gulped. The baron's score was high, nearly impossible to break.

"I'll give it me best shot." The captain was solemn, but in his eyes there was a glitter of hatred that rivaled the gleam from the blue stone he sought to win.

He shook the dice in the cup.

Conversation stopped.

All eyes followed the snap of his wrist.

Thwap! He dropped the cup onto the table, then poured out the tumbling bits of bone.

The first toss was no good.

Rourke grabbed the dice again. Rattled them hard. Slapped down the cup.

Smack. Again the pieces of marked bone spilled onto the planks.

Once more the score wasn't enough.

Jestin let out a breath of air, and to hide his smile, he took up his cup, threw back his head, and drained his mazer. The soldiers of Ogof hooted and clapped each other on the back. Fawn sighed. Laughter rippled through the great hall.

Rourke snapped up the cup in a deft motion that defied most gazes, but Keegan saw the trickery as the new dice fell from his father's sleeve and the old ones were stashed within a hidden pocket. Easily. Perfectly. Seamlessly. Rourke gave the cup another shake. "May luck be with me," he whispered fervently.

Whap! The cup hit hard on the table. The dice tumbled rapidly. They rolled the length of the table to land directly in front of the Lord of Ogof. And they spelled his doom. Fawn gasped, looked about to faint.

"Christ Jesus," one man whispered.

"The captain won!" another, a man who had bet on Rourke, cried. "Can ye believe the luck?"

Jestin's jaw slackened.

"There ye be!" Rourke's smile belied his deceit. Half standing, he reached forward to scoop up his winnings.

Keegan's fingers sought the handle of his knife. Surely it wouldn't be this easy.

"Nay, Captain," Fawn said. She'd turned the color of milk without any cream. "This . . . this . . ."—she pointed at the table where the game was so recently played—"is not right!" She turned accusing eyes upon her husband. Her voice was an octave higher than it had been. "Surely, you couldn't have lost the ring."

"'Tis done," Jestin said with a scowl.

"Nay. It cannot be so." Slowly, she turned her head and her eyes fastened on Rourke. "He cheated," she said without much conviction. "No one could be so lucky. No one."

"It seems I was."

She wasn't about to be dissuaded. "Didn't—didn't you see him cheat, Sir Manning?"

"That I did, m'lady," the brute of a knight beside Jestin agreed without a moment's hesitation. The smell of a fight charged the air. Swiftly, Manning unsheathed his dagger.

"Nay!" Keegan cried, but the warrior was lightning quick. The blade glinted in his hand. He slammed his wicked little knife down into the back of Rourke's hand. Pinned it flat to the table.

Blood spurted. Rourke roared in pain. Coins clattered to the floor. "Bastard," the captain hissed.

"Ye should never have tried to cheat!"

Stripping his knife from its scabbard, Keegan sprang forward.

A soldier with foul breath pushed Keegan. "Get back, boy!" Holding Keegan on the floor, he managed to scoop up a fistful of the scattering gold. Swords rattled. Women screamed. Men grabbed their weapons. Others scrambled for the coins. The captain reached for his own blade with his free hand.

"Kill the bastard," someone commanded.

"He tried to trick the lord."

"Nay, 'twas a fair game."

"The dice were weighted," Jestin snarled, throwing the bit of bones onto the floor. He reached for his sword. "You always were a filthy, lying cur, Rourke. 'Tis a blessing Bertrice never had to lay with the likes of you!"

Reeling free of the big man, Keegan sprang at the baron. His fingers coiled around the hilt of his knife.

Crack! Pain exploded behind his eyes. His knees wobbled.

A huge arm threw him to the floor, where he sprawled upon the rushes. A soldier stripped him of his weapon, slashing his arm as he tried to roll away.

"Father," he cried, but his voice was drowned by the crowd. With horrified, blurry eyes he watched as Rourke struggled against the blade impaling his hand on the table.

"This'll teach ye for not playin' fair," Sir Manning snarled, holding fast to his knife so that the captain was nailed by his own flesh. Rourke writhed. His weight pulled over the table. Blood and coin and candles fell to the floor.

Hot beeswax from the candles sprayed Keegan's arm. Flames from the fallen tapers found the dry rushes and raced, crackling in deadly brilliance along the floor. Keegan's heart raced. Fear throbbed through his bloodstream.

"Fire!"

"Bloody Christ, get the pails. We needs water here!"

"Fire!"

"For the love of God, get water!" Smoke billowed through the keep.

Women shrieked, men grunted, swords clanged, bodies crashed into each other.

"Call the guards," Fawn screamed above the din, but the

soldiers were already filling every inch of the smoky hall. Fire snapped, racing up the curtains. Sparks ignited the tapestries. Keegan struggled to climb to his feet.

"Let there be no blood spilled," the fat priest ordered, choking, but it was too late. Soldiers swarmed through the castle, and Rourke's few men, though struggling hard, were bested.

The papers declaring Rourke captain of the *Warrior* crackled as they caught fire. People ran in all directions. Babies cried. Water was thrown from buckets, and Keegan, struggling to his feet, fell against the table and saw the ring. Glowing with an eerie brilliance, it had slipped to the floor.

"The sapphire! Get it," Fawn screamed through the thickening acrid haze.

A woman's dress caught fire. She screamed and fell to the ground, rolling out the flames. Smoke clogged Keegan's lungs and filled the chamber.

Keegan grabbed the gem.

"Take yer soul to hell, Captain," Jestin roared, and from the corner of his eye, Keegan saw the lord lunge at his father.

"Nay!" Keegan cried. Horror pounded through his head. He was too late. With a primal yell of triumph, Jestin rammed his sword through Rourke's chest. Blood gushed from the wound. Rourke screamed in pain. The blade protruded through his back.

"Noooo," Keegan screamed, horrified. He tried to reach his father, was pushed down again by the crowd. No! No! No!

With a groan Rourke slumped to the floor. His eyes threatened to close, but his gaze fastened on his son. "Run, Keegan," he ordered weakly, blood oozing from his lips. "Save yerself. Oh, Christ . . ."

"No!" Keegan cried again, barely able to breathe. Flames raged in the curtains, blackened timbers creaked ominously, and Keegan was sure he'd entered a portal of hell. Nearby a man howled in pain, and not far away someone was sobbing through strangled prayers. "Nay, Father—" Tears streamed down his cheeks, and his throat was raw, hot with smoke and utter defeat. "I cannot leave you." His father, his brave father, couldn't be dead.

"Get out!" Hollis cried as he was dragged away through a wall of smoke and flame. "Run! The devil be after ye!"

"Shut up, old man!" Manning kicked past a dying soldier, his eyes narrowing on Keegan.

"No, oh, nay!" Again Keegan struggled to his feet, was knocked down, and as Manning swung his sword, Keegan caught hold of one meaty arm, raked the ring down already wounded flesh, and was flung across the room, the gem still clenched in his bloody fingers. "Meet yer doom," Manning yelled, raising his sword high as Keegan slithered along the floor, past burning tables and slain warriors, toward a corner. But the big man, swinging his deadly blade, stalked him. "Come here, boy," Sir Manning ordered, blood trickling from one eye. "There be no escape."

The tiny knife in Keegan's boot pressed hard against his flesh. He reached down, pulled out the weapon, was ready to lunge at the black knight but waited, his chest on fire, his head throbbing. When the murdering bastard was close enough, Keegan would leap to his feet and slice Manning's thick, ugly throat.

Through the smoke the big man trudged. Timbers groaned. People screamed. Keegan's fingers tightened over the hilt. *I'll kill you, come on, just come on.*

"Watch out!" a woman shrieked as a horrid rending sound nipped through the hall. The walls quaked.

Crash! Thud! A huge beam collapsed. In a cloud of dust it bounced and landed between Manning and Keegan.

"Get the boy!" Manning yelled, blocked by the burning timber.

Another beam groaned, threatening to give way.

Smoke and dust obscured Keegan's eyes, but he scrambled through the rushes, crawling backward as more timbers gave way and stones began to tumble from the walls.

Water from buckets splashed. Flames sizzled.

"Come with me." A voice—the woman-girl's voice—commanded.

His eyes burned and he couldn't see, but he felt her warm fingers nearly circle his wrist.

"Hurry!"

Scrambling to his feet, he ran blindly, stumbling forward, led by her hand as they dashed around corners and through a maze of smoke, crumbling stone, and flames.

"Duck."

"What?" He ran smack into a wall.

"Through here! Now!"

"But—"

"I said, bend down!" she yelled, and he obeyed, coughing, still clinging to the damned blue ring in his free hand while the fingers of his other were twined with hers. Through a hallway and another door that led to the chapel. "This way. Hurry! By the gods, do you want to be burned alive or kilt by Manning's blade?"

Running swiftly, she led him through another door. Faster and faster, down steep stairs that led to a dark chamber that smelled of death, where the sounds of the screams and fire were faraway, muted, and the scrape of rats' claws more defined. Slipping a key from her pocket, she unlocked a thick barred door and dragged him through. Once they were on the far side, she kicked the door closed. The lock clicked into place.

"Now, follow me." She, feeling along the narrow hallway, ran easily onward. The floor was moist, as if it were earthen, and slanted downward. He stumbled. She held him up. They ran as if Satan were breathing down their backs.

Unable to see her, he clung to her hand, trusted her. Around a sharp corner, through another door where the smell of must and decay entered his nostrils, he kept up with her, though he felt as if he were treading where no man had dared walk for centuries.

"Come along! Hurry!" she insisted, and still the floor

sloped downward, steeper and steeper, as they were forced
to slow to a walk. Another doorway and he smelled salt air.
The temperature dropped and the sounds of voices, of fear,
the smell of smoke, had disappeared.

"What is this?" he asked. His voice echoed. Was it his
imagination or could he hear the distant roar of the sea?

He felt one wall with the knuckles of the hand that held
the cursed gem. It felt moist, cool, hard as granite.

"For the love of Morrigu, run! I lead you to safety."

"There be none."

"Come *on*!" she urged, and he smelled the ocean. "There
be steps here. Be careful."

Not steps, but crumbling stairs that were slick and cold,
yet Keegan hurried. The roar of the tide swelled louder in
his ears, and the smell of salt air cleared his head. Slowly he
saw a bit of light that became brighter as the stairway
opened onto a vast underground cove. A rotting dock jutted
into the deep chasm, and a tiny rowboat undulated with the
movement of the tide.

"What is this?"

"There be no other way back to your ship. Sir Manning
has killed the man who was guarding your rowboat and
claimed it for Ogof. 'Tis only a matter of time, once the fire
is put out, before the army will take over your father's ship."

He hesitated, bit his lip, and eyed the small boat and the
cave's entrance to the open sea.

"Why did you do this?" he asked, looking at her for the
first time since they'd reached daylight. Her face was
smudged, her fine dress torn, her hair more tangled than
ever. "Why did ye save me?"

"Because I want you to take me with you," she said
earnestly.

"But you be the daughter of the lord."

"Aye, but not of Fawn. She—she is a witch." As if she expected him to disagree, she grabbed his mantle in desperation. "You must help me leave this place."

Keegan hesitated. What would he do with the girl aboard

the *Warrior*? If he made it to the ship. Here she was a rich man's daughter. On the sea she would be at the mercy of the men. No longer would his father steer the helm. Nay, he could offer her nothing.

"I cannot."

"You must." Her face fell, and for a second she seemed crushed. It was all he could do not to wrap his arms around her.

Something in Keegan's heart tore. "'Twould not be safe."

"But I would be free."

"I think not."

A look of hard determination crossed her features. She dropped her hands and glared at him. "Listen, boy, take me with you, or I myself will take you back to the soldiers and my father." To prove her point, she pulled a small knife from her pocket and waggled it under his nose.

Keegan nearly laughed, but she was serious, her chin thrust forward, her small pink lips compressed. So full of life. So demanding. So spirited. So much trouble.

"Well?" she said. "We have not much time."

"No, girl, we do not," and for the life of him, Keegan didn't know what possessed him, but he swept her and her silly little knife into his arms and kissed her hard on the lips. She gasped, tried to draw away, but instead dropped her weapon and sighed. Deep inside, he felt a new fire burn through his blood. In his breeches his manhood swelled and throbbed, and for a second he thought of nothing else but kissing her and touching her and . . . and . . .

He stopped then. Stepped away, stared into her suddenly glazed eyes, and took a deep breath. "By the saints," he whispered, then ran, down the slippery, rotting dock, to the small craft that looked as if it might sink at any minute.

She let out a yelp and followed him, but he was fast, untied the boat, and shoved off. The current did the rest, pulled him out to sea so quickly that she couldn't jump on board.

"Curse you, boy!" she cried, stomping an angry foot in frustration. "Curse your soul to hell!"

"It's already there," he said, unable to call up a smile.

"Morrigu and Pwyll, hear my prayer against this son of the devil who would abandon me . . ." She raised her fists, and though he could no longer hear her voice, he was certain she was calling up all manner of spirits to arrest him. He took to the oars and refused to look at her standing at the dock, for there was something dangerous there, something that was far more frightening than any of Lord Jestin's soldiers. It had nothing to do with demons and curses but with emotions he'd heretofore not known.

The brave, impetuous girl had touched his soul somehow, and that would never do. Her kiss lingered on his lips, her curse ringing in his ears. He finally glanced over his shoulder as the tide swept him out to sea, and he saw the *Warrior* riding high above the waves. No, he had no time for a woman.

"There he be!" a hard voice yelled, and as he glanced toward the beach where his father's rowboat had been dragged, he saw three soldiers. An archer took aim and shot.

Thwang!

Keegan threw himself to the bottom of the boat.

Ssst!

The arrow hissed over his head. He flattened to the tiny craft's ribs. Prayed. Didn't move for heart-stopping minutes, but the little boat was drifting down the shoreline, out to sea, far from the *Warrior.* He had to get to the ship. Holding his breath, he sat upright, lifted the oars, and fought the sea.

He threw his back into the effort, saw, from the corner of his eye, another deadly missile sizzling. He flinched. Not quickly enough.

Thud!

Sharp and hot, the arrow's steel tip pierced his clothes and skin, buried deep in his shoulder, burning like a flaming coal. Blood trickled from the sound. *Thwack!* Another shot aimed over the waves.

Hot pain exploded in his chest. His body jolted.

The world seemed to topple and spin.

Sky and sea became one.

The boat rocked wildly.

Keegan fought the pain, battled the blackness that threatened him. He tried not to give in to the seductive sleep that would dull the ache in his body and soul.

But he failed.

As he slipped beneath the gentle cover of darkness, his mind swam with vibrant thoughts of the plucky red-haired girl and her kiss—still warm upon his lips. 'Twas his first and, it seemed, 'twas destined to be his last.

Chapter One

Aboard the **Dark Sapphire**
Off the coast of North Wales
Summer 1380

*B**am! Bam! Bam!*

"What the bloody hell?" Keegan growled from his bunk.

"Captain. I hates to disturb ye, and ye know it, but there's trouble afoot. May I have a word with ye?"

Keegan opened a bleary eye. His cabin, lit only by a single candle mounted in a lantern hung near his bed, flickered and swayed with the roll of the sea.

"Captain! Can ye hear me? 'Tis Hollis and I hate to wake ye, but I needs speak with ye."

"Trouble?" Keegan repeated, his head feeling as if it might split wide open.

"Aye!"

"Pirates?" God's eyes, Hollis was always conjuring up the devil, certain there was a horrid looming disaster afoot. The old man seemed certain the *Dark Sapphire* was cursed to her very keel.

'Twas enough to try a man's patience. But then, he'd saved Keegan's life. Hollis was, and always had been, loyal and true. But a pain in the backside.

"Nay, Captain, there be no pirates," Hollis yelled.

"Are we taking on water? Is the ship sinking?"

"No, but—"

"Are the men planning a mutiny?"

"Nay, nay, not that I'm aware of, Captain, but—"

"Then go away." Keegan rolled over in his small bunk and jammed his eyes shut.

"Nay—"

"Leave me be!" He was cross and had no time for the old man's pointless worries.

There was a pause, then Hollis's nasal whine yet again. He wasn't a man to give up. "If ye'd please jest let me have a word with ye, Captain Keegan . . ."

"Bloody Christ." Snarling at the intrusion, his head thundering from too much ale and too little sleep, Keegan tossed back the fur covers and, without bothering with his dressing gown, threw open the door.

There was a gasp—for a second Keegan thought it sounded like a woman's voice—from the dark stairwell. But that was impossible. There were no women aboard, and they'd set sail three days earlier. A gust of bracing wind cut through his skin. "What is it, Hollis?" he demanded as his eyes adjusted to the darkness. "And whatever it is, it had better be good."

"Oh, sweet Jesus, Captain, if ye'd be so kind as to cover up—" Hollis's round face was illuminated by a lantern he'd hung on a hook near the door. Above his scraggly beard one cheek bore four red welts that had been scratched deep into his skin, his sparse hair stuck out at all angles, and one of his eyes was nearly swollen shut.

"What the devil happened to you?" Keegan asked as he noticed the rope, a thick coil that wrapped around Hollis's hands and trailed behind him and ended with a knot over the bound wrists of a captive.

A woman.

A dirty, bedraggled mess of a woman, but a woman nonetheless. *Jesus Holy Christ, where did she come from?*

"Tell your man to untie me," she ordered, tossing off the hood that had covered her head. Wild red hair caught in the candle glow as it framed a smudged face with high, prideful cheekbones and fierce blue eyes that cut him to the quick. Perfect teeth flashed white against her filthy skin. For a heartbeat he thought he knew her. There was something about her that instantly triggered a dark, forgotten memory that refused to spark. Nay, 'twas impossible. "I am not a slave! Nor will I be treated as one!"

"Who the hell are you?" He ignored the unlikely thought that he'd met her before.

"She's a stowaway, that's what she is."

"I asked her." Irritated, Keegan leaned a scarred shoulder against the door frame and folded his arms over his chest. "What's your name?"

Aside from the howl of the wind and the roar of the sea, there was only silence. The bit of a woman had the audacity to hold his stare, and there was something in her eyes that gave him pause—something that tugged at the corners of his memory yet again. Had he seen her somewhere? Defiantly she raised the pointed little chin of hers.

"She ain't sayin' Captain," Hollis finally offered. "I found her in the hold, hiding behind the ale casks." He cleared his throat and shifted so that his shadow fell across Keegan's bare loins.

Keegan didn't give a damn what the woman did or didn't see. "What were you doing in the hold?" he demanded of the scruffy, prideful wench. "For that matter, what in God's name are you doing on my ship in the middle of the night?"

"Hidin', that's what she was. And up to no good, let me tell you," Hollis answered in his raspy voice. "Nearly tore me apart, she did. Clawed and hissed and spat like a damned she-cat. This one's the spawn of Lucifer, I tell ye. She's cursed this ship, to be sure."

"Have you, now?" Keegan asked.

She didn't bat an eye, just met his gaze with the angry fire of her own. The barest trace of a smile slid across her lips.

"Oh, yes, Captain," she confided in a husky voice. "As surely as the moon rises behind the clouds and the wind screams over the sea." She took a step toward him without a trace of fear. "I be a witch sure and true. I've sent many a fine ship to the depths of a watery hell, and if you do not set me free at the next port, all of the wrath of Morrigu will be upon you."

"Morrigu?" Hollis whispered, horrified, his eyes rounding above his beak of a nose, his skin ghostly pale. His throat worked. "The goddess of death," he whispered.

"Oh, she is much more than that," the woman taunted, turning to stare down the man who had the audacity to leash her. "Fate and war ride on her wings. Destiny is her companion." Despite her bonds, the she-devil advanced upon her captor, and though much smaller than Hollis, she seemed to tower above him as he cowered in fear. "Morrigu's vengeance will be swift and harsh. Trust me. She will have no mercy on you, you pathetic insect of a man, or you, Captain Keegan." Whirling suddenly, she faced him. Fierce eyes, dark with the night, bored into him. Red, wild hair caught in the wind. "This ship and all those aboard will be doomed to the most painful and vile of fates if I but say so. Death will be a blessing."

Keegan laughed despite his headache. She seemed so certain of her gifts of death and pain. "Will it, now?"

"Do not mock me!"

"Oh, wench, I would not," he lied, but couldn't stop the smile he felt slide across his chin. "Curse away," he said, unable to hide the amusement in his voice. He motioned toward the decks with one hand. " 'Twill not be the first time the *Dark Sapphire* has been damned."

She flinched a bit at the name of the ship.

"Nay. Do not!" Hollis's voice squeaked as he spun on a heel, his terrified gaze landing full on Keegan. "Be ye losin' yer mind, Captain? We . . . we wish not the wrath of the fates upon us. Morrigu, do you not know of her power, of her wrath, of her—"

". . . hold upon you?" Keegan demanded, tired of the game. "Even though you somehow managed to bind the witch's hands? Why has Morrigu not saved you, wench? If she be so powerful, why are you tied like a dog?"

The woman's expression was pure cunning. "For she is patient, Captain. Unlike mortal men."

Laughter erupted at the top of the stairs. Several deck hands coughed and snorted.

So the woman had already caused a stir among the men. 'Twas no surprise and yet a problem that irritated Keegan. His crew was a randy lot without much conscience or many scruples. A woman cast among them was certain to cause jealousy and trouble. Mayhap old Hollis wasn't so far off from the truth—that this wench would bring nothing but disaster to the ship and the men aboard her.

Keegan's amusement disappeared. He glowered up the stairwell to the darkness where the faces of his men were hidden. "Every one back to his watch or work, and you"— he fixed his eyes on Hollis and hitched his chin toward the cabin—"bring her inside."

"Nay!" She threw herself backward, and the rope slipped through Hollis's fingers. He toppled to his knees as Keegan snagged the leash and wrapped it skillfully around his palm.

"Do not bother fighting," he warned the arrogant bit of womanhood. "There is no place to run."

In the weak light her expression changed. Fear, though fleeting, darted through her eyes, and an expression of defeat crossed her features, only to be quickly replaced by steadfast determination. Holding her head high, she followed him as he tugged on her tether and led her into the small confines of his cabin.

Dusting off his breeches, his pride completely undone, Hollis followed, barely sliding through the door as Keegan slammed it shut. From the corner of his eye Keegan noticed that the woman was assessing every square, naked inch of him. Worse yet, it was having an effect. His damned manhood, so long dormant, was responding.

His teeth ground in frustration. Just what they needed—a damned woman with her talk of spells on the ship.

Turning his back to his new prisoner, he dropped the rope and plucked his mantle from a hook near his bed. Deftly he threw the cloak over his head and didn't bother with the laces.

"Leave us," he ordered Hollis, who was planted firmly in front of the door. "Wait. Get some water—enough for the lady to drink and wash with." Beneath her grime he noticed a spark, a flicker of intelligence. "And have a tankard of ale as well as bread and meat sent up."

Hollis's bushy eyebrows shot upward. "You want food?"

"For the lady."

Hollis made a disparaging sound deep in his throat. "Water be precious. There be little aboard."

Keegan sent him a hard stare. "Water and soap. Aye, bring soap as well."

The woman stood stiff as a broomstick.

"But—" Hollis attempted to protest.

"Do it! Now." Keegan threw the man a look that could cut through steel.

"As you wish." Hollis, with his rapidly bruising cheeks nodded, though he glanced at the woman as if she truly were a curse come to life.

"Be quick about it, then. My guest waits."

"Guest?" Hollis repeated.

"She'll be staying here. With me."

"Nay!" She turned on him so swiftly her black cloak whipped about her legs, parting enough to allow him a glimpse of her dress. The fabric had once been a silvery gray but now was splattered with dark stains.

"You have no choice." Keegan rubbed the back of his neck and looked down upon her, for she was a mite of a thing, all bravado and little flesh. He glanced at the door through which Hollis was quickly disappearing. A salty breath of sea air seeped inside. "Well, that's not quite true," Keegan amended, rubbing his jaw thoughtfully. "If you would rather, you could take your chances with the rats and the crew, but let me warn you, lest you decide too quickly. The men who serve me have only one virtue—they are loyal to me. I ask no more of them. I know naught of who they really be or of what they have done to make them want to work here. They could be honest seamen or they could be cutthroats or thieves, traitors or debtors, murderers or worse. I know not. I care not. As long as they give me an honest day's work and remain true to me and this ship, I ask no questions."

"Ah, Captain, 'tis a fine assemblage of men you've gathered," she mocked, but beneath her show of courage she was not so brave. He noticed that her throat worked, and she sneaked a worried glance at the doorway.

"There's nowhere to go, you know. Now that we know you be on board, you cannot hide. You either stay here in the cabin with me, take your chances on deck or in the hold with the men, or dive into waters that are cold as ice and filled with all manner of creatures." He sat on the edge of his bed.

Her lips pinched in a display of defiance, and he could imagine the wheels turning in her mind as she conjured up some ridiculous means of escape.

"So now, woman, 'tis time you told me who you are and why you are hiding in my ship." He reached forward and she, who had been bracing herself against the sway of the carrack's floorboards, nearly jumped out of her skin. "I'll not harm you. Well, at least not yet." He took her hands in his, and when she tried to resist, to pull away from him, his thin patience snapped. "Do you wish these bonds removed?"

She froze.

"I thought so. Be still." He started untying the knots, keeping his eyes on his work though her breasts were heaving in front of him and through a gap in the laces of her cloak he caught a glimpse of white skin and the dusk of cleavage. Again his manhood responded, growing thick, hard, and needing relief.

Setting his jaw, he ignored the sensation; 'twas foolish to even think of it.

"Now," he said, his head bent over his task. The light was poor and Hollis's damned knots had swollen tight. "Who are you?"

A moment's hesitation. "Victoria."

"Victoria?" he repeated, knowing it to be a lie. "From where?"

"Rhydd."

"So far inland?" He glanced up at her, noticed the blanching of pale skin beneath a layer of mud and grime. She nodded, red hair seeming to catch fire in the candle's glow.

"Where did you board my ship?"

She bit her lip.

"Not from Rhydd."

"Nay. I—I got on at Gwagle—"

"Why?" The knot was loosened and the loops of rope fell away. Swiftly, she drew her hands from his, rubbing her wrists and sneaking a longing glance at the door.

Hollis, grumbling under his breath, returned with a large platter upon which was balanced a small pitcher of water, tankard of ale, crust of bread, and several strips of dried venison. A cat slithered between his boots, nearly tripping him.

"Damned beast," he growled, "Go after the rats, would ya, now?"

The creature let out a pitiful cry before slinking from the cabin.

"Just set everything there," Keegan ordered, motioning to the bedside desk. Hollis was quick to do his bidding, adding a bit of soap and a cloth from his pocket to the tray he set on the small table. With a disapproving look at the captive, he made a quick sign of the cross over his chest and, mumbling about sea witches and hexes, slipped through the door.

It closed tightly behind him. The woman—Victoria— started. No, now she was not so bold.

Rubbing his whiskered chin thoughtfully, Keegan leaned

over the table. "If you got on the *Dark Sapphire* in Gwagle, you've been with us for three days." Again she flinched at the mention of the ship's name. Now, why was that? "If you boarded earlier, then it's been longer still. You must be hungry, thirsty, and would probably like to clean yourself." He paused, picked up a piece of venison jerky, and took a bite. She followed him with her eyes. Aye, she was starving, just too damned proud to admit it. Her small shoulders were squared beneath the muddied finery of her cloak. At first he'd thought her an alley wench, a poor woman, presumably a whore, but that was before he noticed the fur lining her mantle and the embroidery that was visible on her dress when she moved. This woman was no pauper. She carried herself with a regal bearing and looked haughtily down her small, straight nose, though she was in no position to argue with him.

Keegan chewed thoughtfully and tapped the remainder of his portion of smoked meat against his cheek. "So what have you to say for yourself . . . Victoria?" Waiting, he took a long drink from the tankard. Again she watched his movements. "Why did you steal onto my ship?"

Victoria gritted her teeth. Her stomach rumbled, and her mouth was dry as parchment. Lord, what she would do for a swallow of water or ale. But she couldn't tell this devil of a captain the truth. She couldn't confide in anyone and expect to live. Her skin itched, her muscles ached. Shuddering inwardly, she remembered the past three nights of hiding aboard this ship, listening to the sound of tiny, scurrying claws, feeling the rats climb over her feet, across her shoulders, or through her hair as she nodded off. Even now, just at the thought of the vermin, her skin crawled.

"You're running from something," he decided, his eyes narrowing in the frail light. Another bite of jerky. He chewed deliberately. "What is it?"

" 'Tis not your business."

"You're aboard my ship. Without my permission." Another precious swallow of ale. "Seems like that makes it my business."

"I'll—I'll pay you for passage." The ship rocked slightly, the candle flickered.

"With what?"

"When we dock, I'll make arrangements to see that you're compensated," she insisted.

"How?"

"'Tis not your worry."

"'Tis precisely my worry." Frowning, he offered her the tankard. "How do I know that I can trust you?"

She held the cup in both hands, took a long swallow, felt the cool ale slide down her throat, and forced herself not to gulp it all down so fast she would vomit. Slowly, she lifted the metal tankard from her lips. "You know not that you can put your faith in me, of course, but I give you my word."

"Your word?"

"Aye." She took another swallow, and he shook his head at the folly of it all. She pinned him with her gaze. "I promise," she said slowly. "I will pay you and well, Captain. Of that you can be sure." Her mind was reeling, her thoughts pricked with fear. She had not known the name of this ship when she'd boarded or that of the captain. Could it be? Could this strong, strapping man be the boy . . . ?

His gaze raked down her body, and she was well aware of her sorry state, the rips and tears her mantle had endured as she'd raced through underbrush, the tiny scratches on her face and hands, the blood staining her skirts . . .

The moments dragged by.

She forced her mind to the present. This man Keegan held her fate in his callused hands.

Her pulse raced anxiously.

Outside, the wind moaned as the ship rocked.

"We dock in a week's time, Victoria," he finally said, his gaze assessing her reaction. "You have until then to convince me that you have a way to pay me for my inconvenience, that you are not on board to steal from me and that at the time we lay anchor there will not be authorities ready to storm the boat and search for you." He leaned closer to her, and she saw that his eyes were the same steely color as the sea in winter.

"There will be no trouble," she lied.

"We'll see." He stood, towering over her, and she noticed his bare legs, all sinewy, tough muscle and dark hair. She kept her eyes averted though she'd witnessed his sheer nakedness only a few minutes earlier, had surveyed strong back muscles covered with tight skin that bore the marks of floggings, old scars that had never faded. And then there was his manhood; she'd glimpsed that as well, though she'd studiously avoided staring at the juncture of his legs.

Once she'd been curious about men.

But no longer.

Never again.

"Eat." He nudged the platter toward her. His teeth flashed white in the depths of his beard.

Her stomach grumbled, and it was all she could do not to eat greedily. The bread was dry and hard. Delicious. The jerky was tough and salty. It tasted like heaven. Never had she been so hungry.

"Why were you hiding in my ship?"

She nearly choked on a bite of bread.

"As I said, 'tis my guess that you were running from someone." The *Dark Sapphire* pitched and rolled. "Probably the soldiers." Her back stiffened and he nodded, "Oh, yes, they were there at Gwagle. I met their leader, Sir Manning of Tardiff . . ." His eyebrows drew together as he considered the name—as if it had some significance but was lost on him. Sheena's heart turned to ice. "He was searching for a woman, a murderess. But this woman's name was Sheena, not Victoria."

Suddenly her appetite disappeared. Her stomach threatened to give up everything she'd just swallowed.

"It seems this Sheena was recently married and killed her husband, the Baron of Tardiff. She then stole some of the jewels from Tardiff's treasury." Sheena began to shake inside. *Be calm, this is but a test, one you must pass.*

"This murdering wife, she led the soldiers on a merry chase. They tracked her to Gwagle only to lose her again." His lips pursed and he pointed at her skirts. "Now *Victoria*, your dress, beneath your cloak, appears stained with blood." He leaned closer to her. "A bit of a coincidence, wouldn't you say?"

She set aside the tankard, gathered her strength, and though the tip of her nose was mere inches from his, met his gaze steadily. "All I ask of you, Captain Keegan, is safe passage. I said I would pay you and I will, so, please, give me the same respect you bestow upon the men you hire. Inquire not of my past. Ask only that I be loyal to you, and hold me to the bargain we have struck."

"You are in no position to bargain," he pointed out.

"But you agreed." She saw hesitation in his eyes and something more, something indefinable. Again she was set upon by the unsettling feeling that she'd met him before, long ago. The name of the ship should have been warning enough. But was it possible, was this surly Keegan, the upstart of a boy she'd saved—the handsome, cocky bastard who had allowed her to save his life, only to kiss her and leave her stranded in the cove? But that was impossible. That boy had been killed. She'd seen his death with her own eyes.

"'Twould be a mistake to cross me," he was telling her.

"As it would be to cross me."

The hint of a smile touched thin lips surrounded by his dark beard. "Is that a challenge, lady?"

"'Tis a fact."

His gaze traveled to her mouth. "Is it now?" So close she could see the streaks of blue in his gray eyes, she was, for a second, lost in his gaze. He suddenly straightened and she swallowed hard. If he wasn't the boy—then who? A man so like him as to be his brother? His twin? Dear Lord, maybe she was imagining the likeness. The boy was dead. *Dead.*

"Well, Victoria, we shall see." Again he took in her sorry state, and involuntarily she squared her shoulders.

His black eyebrows drew together. "You clothes be dirty and damp. Mayhap you would like to change."

She nearly laughed, knowing she was lucky to have escaped Tardiff with her life, much less any possessions other than the three stolen stones. "I be sorry to disappoint you, Captain," she said, her gaze lowering to his bare legs, "but I am wearing all that I have, which is more than I can say for you."

"You're a bold one for being my captive."

"Ah, so there it is," she retorted hotly, meeting the dare in his eyes with that of her own as the timbers of the ship creaked. "A captive. Did you not tell your man that I was a 'guest'?"

His lips compressed. He looked as if he wanted to step forward and strangle her.

"Or was that just a lie, a reason to keep me here alone with you?"

Shaking his head at her impudence, he bit out, "Be you careful, lady, for that tongue of yours has a way of getting you into trouble." He turned his back to her, kneeling at the side of his bunk. "And it be my guess that you've found enough of that already."

She opened her mouth, then snapped it shut as he pulled out a deep drawer from beneath his bed. Inching nearer to the door, she watched as he rummaged through the garments, obviously searching for something she could wear, though nothing he could own would fit her, as he was nearly twice her size.

Yet he uncovered a bag that was tucked beneath a pair of breeches. "'Twas a good thing I thought better of throwing this into the sea," he muttered under his breath. Withdrawing a large, coarse sack that smelled faintly of lavender, he straightened and untied a fraying drawstring.

He reached inside, and to Sheena's amazement, he retrieved a wine-colored gown embroidered with gold thread.

Without a second's thought he tossed the dress to her, then pulled out another gown, this one deep blue, the sleeves quilted in silver and lined with black fur. "Wash yourself and wear whichever of these you wish," he said, dropping the second gown over the first.

Dumbfounded, she shook her head. "I cannot."

"Why?"

"Because they—they must belong to someone," she said, running her fingers over the plush pile. The dresses were as fine as any she'd ever seen, meant for a lady.

"Aye," he said, his voice without emotion, his expression harsh and dark. "They once belonged to my wife. Now, Victoria, they be yours."

Chapter Two

What to do with the woman? Keegan asked himself over and over again. In the darkness, beneath the rigging and masts he paced as he eyed the slice of moon with a jaundiced eye.

Victoria she claimed to be. Victoria of Rhydd. Yet she was lying, he sensed it. And he'd met her before. The more he'd spoken with her, the more certain he'd been, but where? When? For the life of him he couldn't remember. But wasn't that as it had always been, ever since the dark time?

The soldier he'd spoken with in Gwagle, a knight with hard eyes and severe features, had sworn he was looking for Sheena of Tardiff, a murderess.

Sheena. 'Twas an unusual name. Keegan paused, placed both hands on the railings, and looked ahead, past the prow to the night-shadowed horizon. He had heard the name once before, he was sure of it, but that memory, along with far too many others, had been lost to him. *Sheena*. He rolled the name through his mind, and it evoked a response in him—a mixture of emotions from anger to something akin to love. 'Twas folly.

But not only the name. The woman was familiar as well. Or was she? Sweet Jesus, was he imagining it all? Had she, as she had threatened, cursed him? Had she done so in another time and place?

"Oh, for the love of the saints," he growled. How could he even know if they'd met before? With all the mud and grime upon her, she was nearly disguised, mayhap a tavern wench in finery, or a daft woman of means who had wandered off and boarded the ship by mistake.

Clasping his hands behind his back, Keegan began pacing the deck in agitation, hunching his shoulders against the bracing wind, feeling the salt spray upon his face, spying the great sails billow as the *Dark Sapphire* cut through the inky waters. Silently Keegan swore at the fates that had delivered him a stowaway—a bit of a woman who had the nerve to climb aboard his ship and the impudence to talk back to him. Though he was uncertain that he'd met her before, he was convinced she would bring him nothing but trouble.

Aye, she had to be the runaway bride. The blood stains on her dress were testament enough against her. And her bearing, the way she angled her chin, the fire of contempt in her eyes, led him to believe that she'd been born privileged. He leaned over the railing, his fingers curling over the strong wood. He watched a bank of filmy clouds scud across the thin slice of moon as he considered his captive. He couldn't find it in his heart to think that she had actually slain an unarmed man.

"God's eyes, what does it matter?" She was running from something and, like everything else aboard this ship, would fetch a fair price whether she paid him herself or he was forced to ransom her back to Tardiff—if that's where she belonged. Let her face justice or her husband, if the bastard be still alive and not dead as the soldiers claimed, or whoever bloody well else claimed her.

Keegan had learned long ago to never trust a woman; they were simply irrational creatures whose only purposes were to give pleasure and provide heirs. His own mother was proof enough of that. At the thought of the woman who had borne him, his lips flattened against his teeth. He'd never known her, never laid eyes upon her sorry face . . .

"What have ye done with the stowaway?" Hollis's voice was thin over the rush of wind and the soft moan of the sea. Smelling of ale and cradling a lantern so that the candle within the glass shelter would remain lit despite the breeze that howled off the sea, he sidled toward Keegan and leaned his rump against the rail.

"She is in my cabin."

"Ye trust her there alone?"

"Where can she go?" Keegan asked, but, in truth, he didn't trust her at all; the very fact that she was on board bothered him. "I doubt she'll make her way back to the hold with the rats, and she seems far too cunning to throw herself overboard."

"A pity, that." Hollis was nervous. He gnawed his lower lip and sniffed loudly. "I would not take me eyes off her if I were ye."

"And why is that?" Keegan asked. "What possible damage can she do?"

"She be a woman. Is that not trouble enough? And from her own lips she admitted to being a witch, that she could call up the Morrigu and—"

"Bah! I'll hear no more of this nonsense." Keegan pointed a long finger at Hollis's nose. "That kind of talk is for gossiping old women who have nothing better to do than spin tales of treachery."

The candle's flame flickered, casting tiny golden shadows over Hollis's features. "There be rumors, Keegan. Some of the crew were in the tavern at Gwagle, and while they were drinking ale and flirting with the whores, a band of soldiers from Tardiff arrived. Their description of the husband killer they were chasing is the same as that of the woman. Did ye not talk with their leader yerself?"

"Aye. Sir Manning of Tardiff."

"But dinna let him board."

"Nay. I trusted him not." Keegan frowned.

"Nor would I."

"You know him?"

"Nay, nay," Hollis said hastily, mayhap too hastily. His eyes didn't meet Keegan's. "So what of the woman?"

"She claims her name is Victoria."

"Do you believe her?" There was a shadow of something more than this simple question in the older man's eyes—a shadow that quickly slipped away.

"Nay, do you?"

"No." Hollis shook his head with authority. His sunken eyes narrowed. "And she did stow aboard. She be runnin' from something. Mayhap she sliced the man's throat while he slept, as the soldiers claim. 'Tis more than possible, me thinks. She's not to be trusted, Captain."

"No woman is," Keegan said, "but I doubt she will kill anyone on board."

"Why not? She may well be daft."

Keegan laughed bitterly as overhead the sails flapped with a change in the wind's direction. "Daft?" The ship shifted and pitched, turning into the breeze as the helmsman steered ever northward. "Aye, she probably is, old man. What sane person would take refuge in this ship of cutthroats, thieves, and fools only to hide in the hold with the stench of bilge water and the feel of rats?"

"Oh, listen to ye! Jokin' about it all when I'm worried about the ship and the men aboard her."

"You're only worried about your own sorry hide," Keegan said as Hollis's candle died and the older man cursed.

"Hells bells, Captain, if all I cared about was me own fortune, ye'd not be here yerself, now, would ye?"

"Nay, I suppose not." Keegan slapped Hollis affectionately on his stooped shoulder. If not for the ancient one's true heart years ago, Keegan would died alone in a tiny boat. But the old man had saved him from a warrior's arrow, stayed with Keegan during the weeks it had taken to heal, been at his side as he'd lain on a pallet, unaware of the world around him. 'Twas true: Keegan owed the old man his life.

"And the men, they be a restless lot. She may be no beauty, that one, but it matters not. A skirt is a skirt to many of 'em." He sniffed loudly. "I'm just askin' ye to be careful with the stowaway. She's touched by the devil, that one is."

"I'll see to her. Rest easy, old man. I thought she needed some privacy to wash up a bit and change."

"Change?" The old one lifted a bushy eyebrow and coughed. "Into what? Breeches?" Hollis threw up an age-spotted hand. "So now she's going to look like one of the deck hands, is she?"

Keegan snorted as he thought of the wench and the cleavage he'd seen as she'd leaned toward him. "If she be mistaken for one of the men, Hollis, then we've all been at sea far too long."

Mentally kicking herself, Sheena considered escape. Of course there was none. She'd trapped herself aboard this ship in the middle of the sea, with a brooding, dark captain whom she didn't trust for a second—a man whom she'd met before. She was certain of it. But how was it possible? It had been years but . . . was it reasonable . . . had her eyes betrayed her that day? Had that horrid, Judas of a boy somehow survived? This hard-edged captain with the black beard, wide shoulders, and gruff voice, could he be the wounded son of a captain she'd helped escape from Ogof so many years earlier? If so, why hadn't he remembered her? Oh, if he be the same rogue who had left her in the cove that day when she'd risked her life for his, he would not think anything of betraying her yet again and turning her over to Sir Manning. At that thought her stomach soured.

She worked feverishly, stripping off her mantle and gown, then ripped out the hem of one sleeve and removed the jewels she'd hidden there. For a few seconds they winked in the frail candlelight—blood red, brilliant green, and shimmering gold. They had been part of her dowry, the only valuables she now owned, and she wasn't about to lose them. She had no string to sew them into the new gown, and didn't dare cram the gems into some knothole within the miserable captain's quarters for fear of never being able to retrieve them again.

For the moment, lest she be caught with the valuable stones, she wrapped the gems in a piece of cloth from her dress and stuffed them into the toe of her boot. Then she began scrubbing, hard and fast, working up a lather on her face and hands. There was little water, but using it sparingly, she even managed to rinse some of it through her hair before it trickled down her neck, shoulders, and breasts.

Goose bumps appeared on her skin, but she rubbed hard, washing away the dirt, the grime, the blood and the painful, dark memories . . . oh, sweet Mary, the horrifying images that stalked her as relentlessly as did Ogof's soldiers.

"Stop it," she told herself as she rinsed the lather away. "'Tis no good to think of it." As she bathed she again considered escape and found no answer. Until the ship docked, she was a prisoner of a captain she dare not trust. "So be it, then," she murmured and spied the mazer left upon the small desk. Grabbing the cup, she hauled it to her lips and in one quick gulp finished the ale. Then, with an eye on the door, she grabbed the blue gown, tossed it over her head, and felt the smooth brush of velvet over her skin.

It smelled of lavender and was soft as down. Fur lined the collar and cuffs. She laced the bodice, and though the dress was a little too large, it was heaven to have fresh clothes brush against clean skin. Without benefit of a mirror, she finger-combed her hair, then spied her pool of clothes cast onto the floor.

Her dress and mantle were ruined, her chemise and stockings black with dirt. Quickly she searched the pocket of her filthy gown and retrieved her small knife.

The old fool who had stumbled into the hold to tap a cask of ale and caught her dozing had been so startled he hadn't had the brains to search her pockets, thank Morrigu. She thought for a moment and considered the old one who had caught her—was he the same man who had been with the boy? Oh, by the saints, 'twas true. The man had been hauled to the dungeon but had somehow escaped in the confusion of the fire eleven years ago. Had he somehow caught up with the boy, the one she thought was dead, and found a way to heal him? Holy Mother, what was this? Her knees wobbled. What trap had she inadvertently thrown herself into? Had she only known the name of the ship as she'd run up the gangplank, mayhap she would have chosen an alternate means of escape.

But there was none. Even had you known this was the Dark Sapphire *you would have rushed aboard.* "Think not of it now," she warned, and deftly tucked her sharp little dagger deep into a pocket of the dress—the captain's wife's gown, she reminded herself, and one that, from the look and feel of it, had never been worn.

Fleetingly she wondered about the woman who had married such a formidable man, then cast those thoughts aside. "It matters not," she reminded herself.

With the remaining drops of water in the pitcher, she soaked her undergarments as best she could. Using the last bit of soap, she scrubbed until her fingers were raw and she heard the sound of footsteps on the stairs outside.

Sheena froze for a second. "Sweet Mother, help me."

The captain was returning.

Or was it another of his men?

She lifted her hands from the wash. Her stomach tightened as she slipped a hand into her pocket and her wet fingers surrounded the hilt of her knife.

The door swung open.

With a rush of cold wind that caused the lantern to flicker, Captain Keegan with his damnable broad shoulders, beard-darkened jaw, and suspicious gaze ducked inside.

Sheena felt more than a moment's fear. In her lifetime she had been frightened of little, but this man, with his harsh expression, mirthless laughter, and haunted eyes scared her.

She had met him before; now she was certain of it. But either he had forgotten that horrid tragic day, or he was keeping his knowledge to himself.

His hair was black as midnight, his skin nearly bronze, his eyes the color of steel. He was angles and planes, tight skin stretched over bone and sinew and muscle. She doubted many men were bold enough to cross him.

"Well, well, well," he said, smoldering eyes assessing her slowly from the top of her damp hair to the toes of her boots where her jewels were lodged. One of his eyebrows cocked. "Lady Victoria."

"I did not say I be a lady."

"You did not have to."

"And how would you know?" Did he remember?

He grinned, a wicked slash of white. " 'Tis evident."

Her spine stiffened and she hiked her chin upward before she realized that in so doing she'd proved his point.

Sheena's heart raced, and she felt as naked as if he'd actually seen her without any clothing whatsoever. He closed the door slowly behind him. The latch fell into place. She nearly jumped out of her skin.

The cabin seemed suddenly close and far too small for the two of them. The floor rolled with the tide, and Sheena, balancing herself against the gentle rock, couldn't take her eyes off this man, could barely breathe.

"For the rest of the journey," he said slowly as he appraised her, "you will remain at my side."

"Your side? Why?"

"For your own safety."

"What care you about that?"

"Not much," he admitted, his lips pursing. "Just protecting my investment."

Her blood ran cold. "Your investment?"

"Aye, you have agreed to pay me when we dock. How you will accomplish this, I know not and I care not. If you do not pay as you have promised, I will be forced to call upon the soldiers of Tardiff; it seems there are men who are searching for you, men who might pay well to have you returned to them."

"You would ransom me?" Disappointment tore at her soul. The candle in the lantern flickered. Why had she considered him the least bit different from any other man she'd ever met? Had he not left her once before, shown his true side then, when he was little more than a lad?

"Aye, m'lady." He nodded and glanced at her one last time. His eyes darkened a bit. "Now climb into the bunk."

"What? Think you that I will gladly warm your bed, then you be sadly mistaken." Dear Lord, her heart was pounding so crazily, she was certain he could hear it. He, if he be the same man, was the first she'd ever kissed, the only one who had made her blood race wildly, her mind fill with wanton, unthinkable images. "I'll not—"

A strong hand reached out and circled her wrist. "Hush. I mean you no harm," he vowed, his face so close to hers his breath raced over the skin of her cheek. She noticed the shading in his gray eyes—the hard glint of determination. He was not a man who was used to being challenged. "I'll sleep on the floor."

"But I cannot—"

"Do not argue." His fingers tightened. "And do not be foolish enough to think that you might trick me. If you try to escape, remember, there is no place for you to run. Your virtue is safe with me, but I can not promise the same of the men. If you leave this cabin, no place on board will be secure." His fingers tightened, the warm pads pressing against the inside of her forearm, feeling her pulse, which was throbbing in dread. "Not on the deck, or in the hold, or even the crow's nest. They will find you. And you will be sorry."

She swallowed hard.

"Do you understand me, lady?" he demanded, and she couldn't summon enough spit in her mouth to answer. She couldn't imagine sleeping in his bunk, or having him so close. "Do you?" This time he yanked her arm.

Dear God, what did she get herself into by boarding this ship? "Aye," she whispered.

"Good. For I am weary and tired of dealing with half-drunk mates and lying women, so take to the bed, go to sleep, and pray that you find the sense to speak the truth to me in the morning."

Sheena opened her mouth to argue, then shut it quickly. And though it galled her to no end, she moved around the man, who seemed to fill the room with his presence, then sank onto the hard mattress. She expected the captain, despite his promise, to follow her. She was sweating with fear, the fingers surrounding her dagger wet, her grip so tight her joints ached.

She saw him move toward her.

She would not let him touch her, not let him do the unthinkable . . . oh, dear God in heaven, not yet, not here, not with this man, or any man.

All her muscles tensed. Her eyes burned but were dry.

Touch me and meet your doom, she thought silently, though even with her knife, she knew she was no match for him.

He sighed loudly and blew out the candle.

Sheena strained to see, but there wasn't the tiniest bit of light in the cabin.

Dear Lord, please, help me . . .

True to his word, he didn't slide into the tiny space with her. Instead she sensed that he had settled on the floor. At least for the moment, it seemed, the captain had decided to leave her be.

She didn't release her death grip on her dagger, but some of the tension in her body eased. For the first time in three days she was able to stretch out, and her muscles, cramped and aching from too little sleep, relaxed. The ship rocked gently on the sea, and though she tried to stay awake, to be ready should the fierce one change his mind and try to climb into bed with her, she closed her eyes. Exhaustion took its toll. Despite her need to be wary, within a heartbeat Sheena drifted off.

I'll hear no excuses!" Lady Fawn hoisted her considerable bulk from her chair in the great hall of Ogof. The baby, soon to be born, kicked deep in her womb, reminding her of her mission, the urgency of the task at hand as she advanced on Sir Manning, her one true ally, as he warmed his backside near the fire in the great hall. "How could you have let Sheena elude you? For God's sake, she's little more than a child and a pampered one at that." Fawn threw an angry look toward her husband, Lord Jestin, who was no help at all in this matter. He sat in his chair, sipping wine from a wooden mazer while staring at his wife as if she'd gone completely and utterly daft.

It seemed to Fawn that Jestin grew older and fatter by the day, and the man she'd thought she'd married, the strong warrior, was slowly withering beneath his bulk. Fat as he was, he was only a shell of the man he'd once been. Sheena was his firstborn daughter, the only child from his union with Bertrice, his pathetic, sickly whore of a first wife whom he'd loved so fervently that he'd given her a ring the likes of none other. The gem had been worth a king's ransom, and he'd promised it to his second wife. Fawn felt the sword of injustice pierce her heart again, as it had over and over in the years she'd been married to the oaf. Bertrice had died when Sheena was but a girl, and from that point on Jestin had doted on the precocious, snotty child. Jestin had treated Sheena as if she were his son, for the love of St. Peter, as if Sheena were his only heir. He had favored Sheena over his other daughters, the three girls Fawn had borne him in rapid succession, as she was as anxious as he to bring forth a son.

A foolish old man, Jestin had let his firstborn run wild and even allowed her to play with the peasants' children. He'd taught her how to ride and use a bow and arrow. 'Twas hideous, and now he was paying for his mistakes.

All because the fat bastard had never stopped loving his first wife. In the years since Bertrice's death her memory had evolved into that of a saint. A shrine had been placed in the chapel, fresh flowers and candles lit every day. *St. Bertrice*—the wife who had raised her skirts and spread her legs for another man, but Jestin had seemed to conveniently forget all that. Oh, he was getting more disgusting by the day, Fawn thought bitterly, then realized that Manning hadn't answered her.

Were all men imbeciles?

She turned her attention back to her most trusted knight. "How is it possible that this—this snip of a girl has been able to vanish and leave the best huntsmen and soldiers in all of Ogof and Tardiff combined looking like fools?"

"She is either exceedingly cunning or very lucky or both," Manning said, his color high, his eyes, so very dark and wickedly seductive, clouded.

"A clever girl she is," Jestin added, with more than a touch of that galling pride that Fawn found sickening.

"Forget not that she be a murderess!" Fawn whirled on the balding old man to whom she'd given the best years of her life. "If you do not remember, husband, 'twas Sheena who killed my brother, your best friend, the man to whom she pledged her love forever." Tears filled Fawn's eyes, tears of grief, regret, and guilt. Angrily she dashed them away as dozens of candles flickered cheerily. Tapestries draped the tall whitewashed walls, and the scent of dried flowers in the rushes strewn over the cold stone floors met her nostrils, reminding her of all that was hers, all that would belong to her unborn son. This keep, once nearly in ruin from the fire when Captain Rourke had died, was strong again, built to her specifications, the envy of other baronies. And it would be her son's.

Sheena couldn't get in the way.

Sighing loudly, Jestin set down his cup, climbed to his feet, and rounded the table. He placed a calming hand upon his wife's shoulder. "Now, now, do not upset yourself,

Fawn," he suggested, and slid his hand down the smooth wool of her dress to caress the roundness of her swollen belly. "Think of the baby."

"I am!" she snapped back, then caught herself and placed a hand over his. "Please, husband, do not doubt that everything I do, every breath I take, all of my plans are for the child. Our son." She felt the heat of Manning's gaze upon the back of her neck, but refused to glance in his direction.

"'Twill be all right," Baron Jestin whispered, linking his fingers through hers, and she knew again he was a fool, a poor, pathetic man who gambled and drank too much. Were it not for her, he would surely have lost his barony years before. 'Twas she who kept everything running smoothly. Jestin did little more than hunt these days and preside over the peasants' measly squabbles.

"Lady Sheena will be caught," Manning said, and when she looked over her shoulder, Fawn saw jealousy in the set of his jaw. The fire crackled and popped behind him, throwing his magnificent body in stark relief. His tunic and breeches were dirty, still wet from his long ride through the rain, and yet Fawn's heartbeat raced at the sight of him. "This I promise you," he vowed, his gaze holding hers.

"So your allegiance is to me?" she teased.

"The lord, of course," he sneered, but Jestin didn't notice the disdain in his voice. "As I am loyal to Tardiff, so I be loyal here. Have I not been your servant for all these long years?"

"Aye," she said, smiling, for Manning had proved himself time and time again. She felt a ray of hope, but before she could answer, the steward rounded a corner at the base of the stairs leading to the second floor. Wearing his forever dour expression and a brown cloak that had seen far better days, he walked with silent footsteps. "M'lord," he said, and lowered his head a bit. "If I may have a word."

"'Tis late, Allen." Jestin was tired; it was evident in the heavy bags beneath his eyes. How long had it been since he'd seemed a youthful man? There had been a time when he was dashing and proud and filled with a powerful passion . . . but that had been years ago.

"Yes, yes, I know," the steward apologized, hesitating as he glanced at Manning and Lady Fawn. Clearing his throat, he said, " 'Tis a matter of much importance."

"Is not everything?" Jestin sighed and rubbed a hand around the back of his neck. "What is it?"

" 'Tis the cook. He knows not how to use the spices sparingly, nor does he discipline the boys who work for him. There is so much waste and—"

"You deem this important enough to interrupt us?" Fawn asked, stepping toward the rail of a man.

Allen lowered his gaze. " 'Twas the first time I could speak with the baron."

Jestin lifted a once red eyebrow that now bristled with long gray hairs. "I will have a word with him."

"Thank you, m'lord." Allen drew himself to his full height.

"If it is not one thing, 'tis another," Jestin said irritably. As the steward hurried silently out, Jestin offered his wife a smile begging her patience. "This will take only a few moments."

"Aye," she said frostily. "Why you keep him on, I cannot imagine."

"Because, Fawn, he is loyal. He cares. Elsewise why would he bother me?"

"Because he longs for power." Couldn't the old fool see what was so blatantly evident? "As do all men."

"And women. Forget not the ambitions of women." He pushed his weight from the chair. "I will be back."

"Nay," she said hastily. "I am so weary 'tis hard to keep my eyes open. I am nearly finished here, and when I am I will meet you in our chamber." She forced a smile on lips that felt as if they would crack from the strain.

"So be it, and you, Sir Manning, find my daughter and bring her back to me." He hesitated. "Alive and unharmed.

Your men are to find her and escort her to Ogof, but should anyone lay a hand upon her, I will have his head."

"Aye, m'lord," Manning agreed.

With a nod, Jestin followed after the damnable steward. Fawn stilled her tongue until she could no longer hear her husband's heavy tread on the curved stairway and she was certain he was out of earshot. Eyes scanning the dark corners and curtains where servants were known to eavesdrop, she slowly turned to Manning.

"Remember," she said, touching the tall knight on his arm as she lowered her voice. "Sheena may be the lord's daughter, but she is a criminal as well. Not only is she a thief, but a murderess—"

"M'lady—"

"Shh." She placed a finger upon his lips, forcing his silence, as the castle walls could not be trusted. There was forever a twit of a laundress, the silent priest, or a manservant lurking in the corners, hoping to hear a bit of gossip to spread throughout the streets of Ogof. "Remember that above all else." Fawn angled her chin upward to gaze upon Manning, silently daring him to argue with her as she withdrew her finger.

"What I remember, m'lady, is that you and I have a bargain."

"Aye, we do, Manning. We do."

Chapter Three

"**D**amn that woman," Keegan growled to himself. He cracked open an eye. Every muscle in his back ached from his cramped position on the floor by the door. His head thundered from too much ale and too little sleep. Christ Jesus, how had he been cursed with such a bad turn of luck? What fate had he crossed that he now had to endure the next week with the lying chit?

And who the bloody hell was she? He dreamed he'd known her long ago, and in his dreams he saw smoke and fire and a beautiful, headstrong red-haired girl upon a blood-bay horse that reared and pranced to a backdrop of flames. The girl had tossed back her head and reached her small hands to the heavens as if to invoke the spirits, but he'd still had the urge to kiss her as she'd never been kissed before. . . .

He'd awoken in a sweat, the images receding quickly, the mixture of emotions—desperation, fear, and love—ebbing away.

He must've known her. Hearing his spine pop, he rolled to his feet. As the first shafts of morning light pierced through the small window, he stared down at his newfound burden. Fast asleep, breathing deeply, she sighed. Untamed hair fanned around her small, heart-shaped face, where a crescent of fine lashes caressed the tops of her cheeks and her tiny lips parted with each breath. Aye, she was a beauty, despite what Hollis might say, but she was trouble of the worst kind. He knew it in the deepest part of his soul.

He turned away quickly but caught sight of the tops of her breasts rising and falling in a smooth rhythm above the square neckline of Brynna's dress—a velvet thing that she'd never had the chance to wear. Remembering Brynna, he scowled. The woman he'd made his wife had been fair-skinned and even-featured, with almond-shaped eyes that could round in innocence or slit in cunning. With sable-colored hair and an air of mystique, Brynna had been seductive and treacherous.

Not unlike this woman with her strong chin and sharp tongue. One more glance in her direction convinced him he'd seen her before. He just couldn't place where. Or when. His mind clicked back to images of his travels, the towns where he'd docked running the length of Wales. Had he seen her in a market? In a tavern? An inn? On the street?

Was she the Lady of Tardiff? A woman who had slain her husband and robbed him? Never in his life had Keegan been close to Tardiff Hall, though he'd heard of it.

Or did you meet her in the black time—that part of your life you remember not?

Vexed, for he had no answers, Keegan dressed quickly, pulling on breeches and boots, a tunic and mantle. As the mystery woman lay sleeping in his bunk, he walked noiselessly from the cabin. Dawn was just breaking over the eastern horizon, the soft gray of morning parting the mist that rose from the sea. To the east, through the thin veil of fog Keegan spied the coastline of Wales, where the bare mountains of Snowdonia spired upward.

On deck the men were stirring and mumbled greetings as he strode past. Big Tom was already swabbing the deck, his mop moving evenly over the floorboards, Cedric was checking for tears in the mainsail, and a third man, Reginald of Hawarth with his straight back and thin mustache, was on his way to relieve the night helmsman.

None of them was the man he sought, but as he glanced up at the top castle on the foremast, he spied Wart and waved him down. Within seconds the agile little man had shimmied down the spar, swung onto the rigging, and dropped to the deck at Keegan's feet.

"Ye be lookin' fer me, Captain?" Wart asked, his ruddy skin creased, his body tough as old leather. He was a loyal one, Wart was, though his past was as murky as the sea before a storm.

"Aye, I've got a mission for you."

Bushy eyebrows raised expectantly. "A mission, is it?" He glanced to the shoreline barely visible in the distance and scratched his beard with the fingers of his left hand—there were only four. A thick stump was all that was left of his thumb. He'd never explained the loss, and Keegan had never asked.

" 'Tis that why ye've had old Seamus take us so close inland?"

"Yes." Keegan clapped him on the shoulder and together they walked toward the bow.

"It has somethin' to do with the stowaway, I bet. The lady. Ah, but she's a looker, that one. Even in the dark, wearin' rags, a man with any eyes in his head could see she's a beaut."

"Is she, now?" Keegan mocked.

"Don't tell me ye ha'na noticed or I'll call ye either a blind man or a fool." Wart chuckled, and the laughter deepened into a cough that rattled in his thin chest.

" 'Tis said you were once a spy," Keegan said.

Wart stiffened. The smile that had begun at one side of his sharp jaw disintegrated. "I was told when I signed on the *Dark Sapphire* that a man's past was his own." Pale lips flattened over his crooked teeth. "That no questions would be asked about his reasons for joinin' the crew."

"I asked nothing," Keegan said, eyeing the horizon. " 'Twas merely an observation. I need someone I can trust to take a small boat ashore, sell it, gather some information, and meet up with me when we dock at the next port."

"Do ye, now?" Always ready for adventure, Wart notched his chin toward the land. "What kind of information, eh?"

"You're to see if the woman be who she says. Victoria of Rhydd."

"You think she is lying?" Wart's eyes blinked rapidly.

"She is a woman, is she not?"

"Humph. There be no denyin' that, I'm afraid." Wart sighed. "'Tis been a long while since a lady walked these decks." As if he'd realized he'd said too much, he quickly cleared his throat. "Is there anything else?"

"Nay, only the truth." A twinge of conscience assaulted Keegan, but he ignored it. If the woman had lied, then 'twas best that he found out now. "You've heard of soldiers from Tardiff searching for a woman who murdered her husband. Lady Sheena, wife of the baron."

Wart whistled long and low. "The murderess?" he said, new respect in his voice.

"Mayhap. These soldiers, they are willing to pay for her return."

"And you think the stowaway might be that woman?" Wart rubbed his hands, either from the cold sea breeze or the thought of ransom.

"You know me, Wart," Keegan said simply as they reached the forecastle and he glared at the rugged shoreline of the coast, green hills emerging more clearly as the fog dissipated. "I trust no one."

"Especially someone who hides in the hold with rats."

Especially a woman.

Wart winked. "Consider it done, Captain. Consider it done."

Sheena stretched and pulled the coverlet to her chin. She nearly smiled in the warmth of the bed until she felt a gentle rocking and her eyes flew open. Oh, Lord! Where was she?

Not in a bed. Nay, she was lying in a small bunk.

Oh, God.

She remembered. All too vividly.

She was a prisoner on this ship, the very one she'd snuck onto. How had she been so stupid as to stow away on the *Dark Sapphire* with the beast of a captain who was holding her prisoner ? Aye, this morning she was certain he was the boy, and had somehow survived an archer's wound and the stormy sea. Too many facts assured her of the truth. Was not the old man the same who had escaped? Was not the name of this ship the same as that winking blue stone he'd stolen—the sapphire that had belonged to her mother? So he was older, taller, with wide shoulders, muscles, and raven black hair covering his jaw and chin—aye, he was the same betraying beast who had left her to deal with her father's wrath all those years before.

She cringed as she thought of the punishment she'd endured, how she'd nearly been banished, how ever after she'd been at Fawn's beck and call. She'd been imprisoned within the walls of the keep, forced to become a lady, never allowed to ride Shamrock through the surrounding fields, disallowed from the hunt, kept away from playing with the servants' children and, at every turn, Lord Jestin had threatened to marry her off to anyone of his choosing. In the end, he'd waited long and eventually given her to the worst possible choice. She shuddered when she remembered the mockery of a marriage ceremony at Tardiff Hall and the man who thought he owned her and could therefore treat her worse than a slave.

"God help me," she whispered as she thought of her escape and how she'd hidden from Sir Manning's men until they cornered her in Gwagle.

And she'd willingly boarded his cursed ship! She flung an angry fist on the bed as she remembered the horror of the chase through the town's crooked streets, the jangle of bridles, thunder of steelshod hooves, rattle of swords and the mind-numbing fear of being caught by Tardiff's merciless soldiers. All other avenues of escape had been blocked. She'd been forced to board the *Dark Sapphire* and had hidden in the hold until Hollis had discovered her.

Now Sheena was sleeping in the captain's bed. Had she traded one horrid fate for a worse one?

"You had no choice," she reminded herself, and banged her head as she sat up. "Damn." Rubbing the bruise, she climbed out of the tiny compartment and glanced around the room—the harsh captain's private quarters. The candle in the lantern had burned out, but a shaft of light streaming through a small window illuminated the wood-paneled room. A small desk had been bolted to the floor, the narrow bunk surrounded by a few drawers and a cupboard. A cloak and mantle hung from the hooks near the door, and there was barely enough space to turn around.

" 'Tis time to face him," she told herself as she adjusted her wrinkled dress—Keegan's wife's gown. What poor woman had been foolish enough to marry him? Keegan's bride probably had had no choice in the matter. Or else she'd been taken with the beast's maleness.

'Twas not worth worrying over. She prayed the door wasn't locked. She didn't trust the blackheart of a captain for a second and suspected that he would try to jail her. Aye, they had a bargain, but it meant naught. The man was the spawn of Satan, she was sure of it. She yanked the door open.

Mayhap dealing with Tardiff's soldiers would have been safer.

At that thought her blood ran cold, and she climbed the short flight of stairs to the main deck, where the breeze was stiff and smelled of the sea. By some means, either fair or foul, she had to escape. As soon as the ship approached land, she would steal a rowboat and make her way to shore. From there she would take seldom used roads ever eastward. She was adept with a bow as well as a sword, and with the proper weapons she could fend for herself until she came to some obscure village where, using the jewels for money, she would establish herself.

As what?

A seamstress? Nay, her stitches had always been poor and weak.

A midwife? While growing up at Ogof, she had witnessed the birthing of cattle, sheep, pigs, and horses in the stables and fields of the castle, but she'd never seen a baby brought into the world.

A cook ? Or tavern maid? At the thought of serving raucous men, soldiers, tradesmen, peddlers, and merchants anxious to get away from their duties or nagging wives for a few hours, gathered together laughing, telling bawdy stories and trying to get a glimpse under her skirts, Sheena could not hold back a grimace of distaste.

For the moment she would not worry about what she would do once she had escaped this ship. No reason to put the cart before the donkey. First and foremost she had to find a way off the *Dark Sapphire*.

On deck, the wind slapped her face. Overhead, the sails billowed full and the ship cut through the clear blue waters while onboard men of all shapes and sizes scrambled from one end of the decking to the other. Chains rattled, flags snapped, and sailors barked orders at each other. Some of the crew washed the deck, others dumped buckets of bilge water overboard; still others scrambled up the rigging and adjusted the huge white sails, booms and yardarms.

On legs that were far from steady, she picked her way across a grating to the rail. Though the sea was calm, the ship still rocked along with the contents of her stomach.

"Well, look at that, would ya?" a deep male voice said behind her. She didn't bother to turn around, but shaded her eyes with a hand and looked eastward to catch a view of land in the distance.

"That be the stowaway," another man answered in a nasal tone. "Mayhap we should be spendin' more time in the hold with the rats, eh, Big Tom?"

"No tellin' what might happen if we did." Deep laughter rolled Sheena's way. 'Twas all she could do to tighten her jaw and keep from giving the scallywags the tongue-lashing they deserved. Seamen were, in large, a superstitious lot; if they bothered her further, she would cast a spell in their direction and let them discover if there was any power to it or not. The taller of the two was a muscular man with thinning blond hair. His nose was crooked, as if it had been broken more than once, a scar ran from one ear to his chin, and one cold blue eye was slightly larger than the other. He sniffed loudly.

"Outta me way!" a huge voice boomed behind her. She jumped back as a heavyset man lumbered forward with a bucket filled with dead rats. Her nose wrinkled as, with only a second's curious look her way, he tossed the furry carcases overboard. "Who are ye?" His eyes were small and close together, his lips thick around few remaining teeth, his belly protruding farther than his chest.

"She's my guest." Keegan appeared from the other side of the mainsail. Dressed in black, his chiseled jaw set, his eyes narrowing on the crew members, he strode across the deck easily.

Sheena froze.

"And as my guest," he continued, "she will be treated with respect. Is that understood, Maynard?" The wind ruffled his raven-black hair, his jaw was set in stone, his eyes fierce and burning as they pinned the three idle seamen.

"Aye, Captain, aye." Maynard, his head lowering, his tiny eyes downcast, hauled his pail with him and hurried away.

All hint of amusement fell from the faces of the other two men.

"You, Tom, have you nothing better to do than joke here with the lady?" Before the man with pale hair could answer, Keegan added, "I thought you were to help James fix the bilge pump."

Tom's cracked lips pursed, and he seemed about to argue but clamped his jaw shut. Keegan's gaze was already upon the smaller of the two. "Jasper, if I'm not mistaken, you were to take inventory of the casks of wine and ale this morning."

"'Tis right ye be, captain," the shorter man agreed, nodding frantically. One of his eyes drooped. His face was ruddy as if he stood on the decks of this ship in all weather and rarely had use for a razor. Under the captain's fierce glare, Jasper scurried off like a crab seeking a rock for shelter. Tom wanted to argue. His nostrils flared and his fists clenched, but he, too, ducked beneath a shroud, two thick ropes leading from a masthead, and vanished from view.

Keegan's gaze followed Tom as he leaned a hip against the railing. Then, as if satisfied that the sailor had indeed gone about his duties, he turned angry eyes upon Sheena. "As for you, woman, did I not ask you to stay in the cabin?"

"Aye, but I'll not—"

"What you'll not do is argue with me." Irritation laced his voice, and she bristled. Aye, he was an intimidating man, but she'd grown up with bullies, soldiers, and the like. Though Keegan was taller than most men, his shoulders wide as an ax handle, and he carried himself with the air of someone who had given commands all his life, she wouldn't let him order her about.

The ship rose upon a swell, and Sheena fought nausea. She was certain her skin had turned the color of pea soup.

"I needed fresh air." She inched her chin up a tad. "And worry not about my safety. I take care of myself."

"Not on my ship."

"Anywhere."

"Nay, woman, not anywhere. Not here. Not on the *Sapphire*." Irritation tugged at the corners of his mouth. He raked stiff fingers through his hair as he spied a boy of about eleven high on the rigging, hanging onto the main yard. Impish eyes peered through an unruly curtain of brown hair, and a crooked smile twisted the lad's mouth. "Back to work, Bo," Keegan ordered.

"But I be workin'."

"Is that what you call it?" One of Keegan's eyebrows rose in doubt, but for just a second Sheena saw a hint of a kinder, softer man, one with a soul and a sense of humor, behind the captain's gruff exterior. Had she misjudged him? Nay, she had but to remember how he had abandoned her when she had risked her own life for his.

"Aye," the boy answered, his small chest puffed out.

"Well, if you think you will be paid for hanging onto the mainsail as if you were a monkey, then you'll have to think again."

The boy laughed out loud, a bubbling sound that caught on the wind. Beneath the beast of a captain's beard his lips twitched a bit.

"Is that yer lady, Captain?" the impudent lad, leaning off one of the yardarms, asked.

"She is my guest."

"Why?"

"'Tis none of your concern."

"Methinks she be your woman."

"Nay, Bo," Sheena said, twisting her neck to better view the boy. She shaded her eyes against the sunlight dazzling off the sails. "I be no man's woman."

"No?" Obviously he didn't believe her.

"Mayhap you would like her to be yours," Keegan suggested, and from behind the Bonaventure mast there was a rumble of laughter, wheezing chuckles. Unseen eyes had watched the display.

Keegan's expression turned cold. He grabbed the crook of her arm and steered her toward the prow of the ship as it cut through the swells. Steely fingers held her fast. Boots rang on the decking. Overhead the huge sails filled and flapped as sunlight spangled the water. "I'll accept no back talk from you," he said slowly. "Not in front of my men. Not on my ship." He leaned down so that his face was near enough to hers that their noses nearly touched, and she couldn't help but notice the hint of blue running through his gray eyes. "Listen, Victoria of Rhydd," he whispered as her queasy

stomach quivered. "On the *Dark Sapphire* I am the rule. No
one questions me, no one argues with me, no one dares
speak against me. My men are loyal to me, the ship, and
each other. You are but a guest, an uninvited guest at that,
and certainly one who will follow my rules."

"Or?"

"Or what?"

"It seems you were about to threaten me," she said, biting
back hotter, angrier words while fighting the sourness in her
belly and bracing her legs against the rise and fall of the
deck.

"I do not threaten, lady." His gaze drilled deep into hers.
"But I expect to be obeyed. Is that understood?"

Oh, how she would love to defy him, and she would. But
not now. For the moment he had the upper hand. "Clearly."

"Then I will have no trouble from you?"

"Oh, aye, aye, Captain," she spat out sarcastically, her
temper flaring despite her attempts to hold her tongue. Her
head ached where she'd bumped it, her stomach threatened
to disgrace her, the jewels crammed into the toe of her boot
cut into her flesh, and she was angry with herself for ever
climbing aboard this cursed chip. "Or," she said, as if a sudden thought had struck her, she added with mock sweetness,
"mayhap I should call you lord. Or master. Or both?" He gri-
maced, but she couldn't still her sharp tongue. "Is it possible that God Himself takes orders from you?"

"Only when He's aboard this ship, Victoria," Keegan
said, his teeth flashing against his bronzed skin. "But, aye,
then He surely does. And when I suggest He stay in the
cabin, He doesn't argue. I expect no less from you."

She was about to challenge him again, but the fingers
around her elbow dug into her flesh. "Remember, not only
do we have a bargain, but I saved your neck the other night.
If not for your taking safe harbor aboard this vessel, those
soldiers would have found you and don't—" He pressed a
finger to her lips as she started to protest. "Don't even think
of arguing with me. 'Tis of no use. Until we dock, you are

to stay by my side. Once ashore, we'll conclude our business, you'll pay me for my trouble, and then you can be on your way."

For a second she only stared at him. 'Twas all she could do not to rip her arm from his, kick him in the shin, and curse his sorry soul to the darkest depths of hell, but she restrained herself. Instead she yanked her arm from his. Like it or not, for the next few days she would have to obey him; she'd given up all freedom when she'd run up the gangway of his bloody ship. Short of throwing herself overboard, she had no escape.

As if he could read the capitulation in her eyes, he slowly grinned, and for a second the bastard was nearly appealing. Nearly. She smoothed the folds of her skirt, felt the brush of velvet of another woman's dress on her palms, and asked, "Is this how you speak to your wife?"

His smile fell away. A tiny muscle worked in his jaw. "No longer."

"I would hope not."

He looked at the sea for a second. One fist balled up and he let it fall against the railing before his eyes found hers again. She felt a chill as cold as the sea pass through her bones. Pain, quickly disguised, slid through his gaze. "My wife is dead, Victoria," he said through lips that barely moved. "Brynna died three years ago."

"Is there no word?" Fawn asked, tucking a braid behind her ear as she walked through the garden. Marigolds and roses were showing their colors, and she should have found some joy in their beauty, but she didn't. Not today. She felt like an old plow horse as she plodded toward the bailey. Her ankles were swollen, her entire body misshapen, and she was tired of the ungainly weight. Allen, that skeleton of a steward, was with her. He was an odd man, one who made the hairs on her arms stand on end.

"The lord has not yet returned from his hunt," he observed tonelessly.

"Nay, I care not about the hunt," she snapped, her temper quick to fire these days. She watched a thatcher repairing a roof. "I was speaking of Sheena. Has she not yet been found?"

"Sir Manning has not returned, but it has been only four days since he departed."

It seemed like an eternity.

Though Fawn hated to admit it, she missed Manning. She had told herself that she would only use him. He was strong, cunning, and brave, and above all ambitious far above his station in life—the perfect choice to help her with her plans. And yet she was nervous. Anxious. So impatient.

Oh, bother, mayhap it was only her condition. Pregnancy always seemed to cause her brains to curdle a bit. She paused to rest on a bench near the chapel. Bees buzzed through the showy blooms, and the air was heavy with the scents of flowers and spices, as the cook had demanded rosemary and sage be planted in clumps near the kitchen.

From her position Fawn observed a woman retrieving honeycombs from the bee skeps mounted high on one turret. On the flagstaff over the woman's head the standard of Ogof, emblazoned with a blue and gold dragon, snapped in the brisk morning breeze.

Fawn folded her hands over her protruding belly and felt very much like the oldest and ugliest sow in the castle pigsty. The baby moved within her, and she told herself to be patient, that this child was worth every morning of illness, every day that her ankles swelled, every hour of discomfort. This babe, her son, would be Lord of Ogof.

And Tardiff.

Finally.

"The minute there is word, you are to tell me," she said to the steward, who was standing near her, nervously shifting his weight from one foot to the other. Idly she wondered if she was to puncture his veins, would she find blood—or ice water.

"As you wish," he agreed, nodding as he took his leave.

Oh, he was harmless enough, she decided, though she was suspicious of anyone and everyone within the keep's thick walls. No one, it seemed, could be trusted.

Even Sir Manning, a voice inside her head warned, though she ignored it. She motioned to the ninny of a girl who was attending her. "You, Sarah, fix this!" With one chubby finger Fawn pointed at her wayward coil of hair, and the scrawny little maid came over and began fussing with her tresses. "Where is Zelda?"

"She be in the keep, m'lady. She wasn't feelin' well, and she asked me to attend to ye for a bit," the twit replied. Fawn was instantly irritated at the old lady in waiting—she'd never liked her. Never. She'd inherited the dour woman from Bertrice.

"Zelda should have spoken to me herself."

"Aye." Fawn felt a tug on her head as Sarah reattached the braid. "There ye go, m'lady. Good as new," she said.

Fawn opened one eye slowly and the girl's face loomed into view. She could have been pretty, Fawn supposed, if not for large, crooked teeth and a weak chin. Not that it mattered. She was, after all, merely a servant. Beauty would have only caused her pain, for all the men in the castle from the lord to the gong farmer would have lusted after her and taken what they wanted. 'Twas a blessing that the poor girl was homely. "That's all, Sarah. Tell the midwife I need to see her in my chamber."

"Aye, m'lady." With a quick bow the relieved girl slipped quietly through a gate to the outer bailey, and Fawn struggled to her feet. She swatted a pesky fly and lumbered to the chapel, where she planned to kneel and pray just long enough so that the priest wouldn't reprimand her. It was important that everyone within Ogof's thick walls believe she was a loving wife, devoted to Lord Jestin, and devout in her faith.

'Twas a bother, to be sure, but necessary. If all was to go as planned.

Chapter Four

"Have I not seen you before?" Keegan asked as they sat in his cabin, she in the solitary chair at his desk, he standing near his bunk.

Sheena swallowed her crust of bread and told herself to remain calm. So he didn't remember. "I think not."

"Nay?" Frowning, he rounded the desk to look down at her. " 'Tis familiar you be."

Oh, Lord, should she tell him the truth? Did she dare? She drank a sip of ale and set the platter aside. Upon it were the remains of bread, cheese, and dried meat that they'd shared. "How do you mean?"

Gray eyes regarded her with such intensity that she wanted to squirm beneath his stare. She remembered the kiss they'd shared so long ago, the betraying touch of lips that had turned her bones to jelly and caused her heart to pound as quickly as a hummingbird's wings. But that was long ago—before she'd found what brutal savages men could be. "It's—it's as if I've seen you in my dreams," he said, his gaze narrowing and moving from her eyes to her lips.

A rush of heat burned up the back of her neck as the ship rolled lazily and the timbers creaked. Did he remember? Was he but toying with her? "That I do not know. Your dreams be your own."

"Mayhap, but they be bothersome."

She lifted a brow.

"Yea, as you be, woman. Why did you stow away on my ship in Gwagle?"

" 'Tis . . ." She bit her lip and felt the stones in the toe of her boot. She wanted to trust him, to confide in someone, but she didn't dare. Oh, he seemed concerned now, his fierce demeanor slipping to reveal the face of a man who cared, but she knew it to be trickery. Were she to admit—oh, by the saints she would be a fool. " 'Tis difficult to explain a private matter. We had a bargain, you and I," she said, and wondered why the small room seemed suddenly closer still, more intimate. "You promised to ask no questions."

"And you promised to pay me." The mask of suspicion fell quickly back into place.

"Aye." She forced the lie over her tongue. "And I will. When we dock."

He wasn't convinced. She saw the doubt etch lines near his eyes and pull at the corners of his mouth. "I will remember, you know," he said, and her mouth lost all spit. "If I have met you before. I will remember."

And what then? she wondered.

"But for now your secret, whatever it be, is safe." With that, he strode out of the room. Sheena let out her breath. Being so close to him, in constant contact, was difficult. There was no place on this ship to run to, no spot in which to hide. Keegan seemed to be everywhere at once, and though she reminded herself that he was a blackheart, a horrid beast who would sell her as surely as not, she caught glimpses of a kinder man beneath his fierce surface.

She'd watched him with his men, and he was forceful, to be sure. 'Twas his way aboard the *Dark Sapphire* and there was no mistake to be made of it, but he was never savage or cruel as he'd dealt with each man's complaints, or arguments, or laziness. In one instance when she'd been on deck, she'd heard him reprimand a spry man who'd been lounging

against a barrel of tar used by the caulker, who had also
abandoned his task.

"Back to work, James," Keegan had ordered. "And what
the hell happened to old George—he's not yet finished
caulkin' here."

James had scurried to his feet. "I'll find 'im fer ye, Captain," he'd said, and rushed off as quick as his limp would
allow.

Another time she'd seen him approach one of the men adjusting a sail. "Cedric, ye need to be tending that line more
closely. Like so." Keegan had taken over the man's task agilely, his muscles bunching. Sheena had tried to look in any
other direction, but the stretch of his shirt across his shoulders had held her gaze and she'd imagined his muscles beneath the cloth, hard and rippling, covered with smooth dark
skin that bore the scars of ancient floggings. A warm flush
had crawled up her skin, and desire, an emotion she was certain had died within her, had suddenly come to life.

She'd turned away quickly, stumbling over a rope, and
she'd clumsily made her way back to this cabin only to see
her reflection in his mirror. Her cheeks had been rosier than
usual, her eyes wide, and she was sick with the thought that
she'd actually found him attractive. "You be daft," she'd be-
rated herself. "A fool of a woman. Remember, Sheena. Remember who he is."

But the feeling had persisted, and she'd found herself following him with her eyes, watching him deal with each of
his men.

"Jasper, mind that ye don't leave the pulleys to rust. Ye
know better," he'd said, clapping the crooked man on a
shoulder one afternoon.

The very next day, as the *Dark Sapphire* had cut through
the waters of a calm sea, he'd approached the big oaf of a
man whose job, it seemed, was to rid the ship of pests.
"Maynard, check the inside hull for ship worms—we may
need to repair when we get to port," Keegan had ordered, his
black hair gleaming in the midday sunlight. Sheena had

been standing on the upper deck at the time, searching for the coastline of Wales. Her stupid heart had skipped a beat at the sight of Keegan. Wearing a black tunic and breeches decorated in tooled leather, he walked with authority toward Maynard, who was again tossing his kill over the deck rail.

"But, Captain, the rats—"

"You've been doin' a fine job killin' the beasts," Keegan had acknowledged. "A fine job. But them that's still aboard, they be goin' nowhere, and that bloody cat of yours will tend to them while you check the inside of the hull. Take Bo with you. He can scramble around in the small spaces more easily than you. Report to me about the worms, and then, Maynard, you can get back to the rats."

The big, lumbering man had obeyed without any further argument, and Keegan had flashed him a smile, that, though not rained upon her, had touched Sheena's foolish, feminine heart.

And the nights, Lord, the nights were the worst. Knowing that he was sleeping close enough that she could reach down from the bunk and touch him, wondering if he was awake, listening to the sound of his breathing . . . 'twas enough to drive her mad.

"Do not think like this," she warned. "Too much is at stake. He is a man. You cannot trust him." She had only to think of her wedding day to remind herself of the horror of men. She had been certain less than a month ago that she would never want a man again. Whenever she remembered her dead husband she swore all over again to never be with a man. And no man could be trusted. Had not even her father betrayed her?

Sheena hadn't wanted to marry Ellwynn; had fought her father's decision from the moment he'd suggested a marriage to the Lord of Tardiff. . . .

"Nay, Father," Sheena responded when Jestin approached her with talk of a husband yet again. She was in the outer bailey with Bart, Ogof's falconer, at her side, working with a new bird. The falcon, wearing its leather hood, was perched nervously upon Sheena's gloved arm, and she was speaking softly to it, but her voice changed at her father's suggestion.

"I'll not marry Tardiff!" she said, startling the falcon, whose talons gripped harder, wings flapping noisily.

"Ah, Sheena, 'tis time you married. Long past time. Ye be three years past twenty. Ye should have been married long ago and have babes of yer own."

"I be hardly a spinster."

"Nay?" he snorted in disbelief. "Besides, it would be a good match."

"I like him not." The bird cried and attempted flight, but was bound by its tether.

Irritated, Sheena handed the hunting bird to Bart and stripped off her heavy glove. A spring dew collected on the sweet-smelling grass. The sun, shining pale through a thin mist, cast weak rays that warmed Sheena's crown and reflected on the spider webs stretching across the lush blades. Stalking toward the keep, Sheena slid her father a glance as they passed the orchard. Fragrant blossoms hung heavily in the leafy trees. Sheena barely noticed.

"This marriage, it be Lady Fawn's idea," she charged.

"Aye, she thinks 'twould be best for both baronies."

"She wants to get rid of me." Sheena kicked a dirt clod in her path, sending mud and pebbles flying.

"'Tis time her brother married as well."

"He was married before."

"Ah, but poor Lady Alyce passed on."

Sheena shuddered. Alyce had died when she'd been thrown off a horse and her head had struck a rock.

"And now Tardiff is lonely and needs a wife. He be a handsome man, Sheena, with good, profitable keep."

"I trust him not."

"You know him not."

"He be Fawn's brother." In Sheena's mind that alone was enough to condemn the man.

Her father sighed, rested a big hand on her shoulder, and

guided her through the gate to the inner bailey. "I'm think-ing only of you, Sheena," Jestin persisted. Stubbornly she threw off his hand. "Your mother, God rest her soul, would want you married and bearing babes of your own." He sighed, and there was more than a hint of sadness in his aging eyes. "Bertrice was a fine woman, Sheena."

"My mother loved you," Sheena cried, whirling as they reached the steps of the great hall. "She believed in love and would not want me to marry for the sake of convenience."

"Oh, but 'twas not always so. She grew to love me, but the first years of our marriage I think her heart was with an-other."

She knew this. "Captain Rourke," she muttered under her breath, refusing to think of the seaman's dead son who had left her standing on the dock years before.

"Aye. Bertrice was very young. Foolish."

Jestin placed one foot on the second step as the door to the keep flew open and the castle dogs ran out. Barking madly, the two swarmed around her father's boots as the kennel master slammed the door behind him, hurried down the stairs, and apologized.

"Do not worry, they are fine with me," Jestin said. He scratched one behind its lopping black ears while the keeper of the dogs hurried off to the kennels. Jestin glanced at Sheena as he continued, "Bertrice, she never said his name around me, held her head high, and eventually forgot him. In time his image faded and she came to know how much I loved her."

"But Rourke loved Mother. That was why he returned here." Again she thought of his blasted son, the one who had disarmed her with a kiss she had never forgotten.

"Rourke was a fool," Jestin said, his face flushing even more scarlet at the thought of his old rival.

"But Mother loved him as well."

"'Tis something we need to discuss. Rourke was . . . a distraction. Nothing more." Jestin patted both dogs on their heads. One leaped up expectantly. "Down," he ordered. To

Sheena he said, "I was not a wealthy man. Ogof was not nearly as grand as it is now when I courted your mother. I had spent much of my time in battle, but I knew Bertrice would make me a good wife.

"I swore that I would love her and care for her and that in time she would learn to love me as well." He rubbed the stubble upon his chin thoughtfully. "It took time, Sheena, I'll not deny it. There were moments when I thought she would never come to love me, but I was patient and eventually she realized my love was true."

"And what of Rourke?" Sheena asked.

"Bertrice forgot him." He said it with authority, but Sheena noticed the doubt in his eyes.

"I remember not much of her," Sheena admitted.

"Mayhap I should have told you sooner," Jestin said, wiping some mud from his boot on a tuft of grass, "but you were young and it never seemed the right time. Now that you are about to marry, I thought you should know."

"I'm not about to marry anyone," Sheena corrected. "Least of all Lord Tardiff."

"Have you someone else in mind?"

"I have not yet found the man I love."

"Oh, girl." Jestin ruffled her hair as if she were a tiny child. "This is what I am trying to tell you. Love comes slowly."

"Has it come for you and Lady Fawn?" Sheena demanded.

Her father's expression turned guarded. "That is different."

"How so?"

"I—I needed a wife and a mother for you."

Sheena let out a disgusted puff of air. "She is no mother of mine."

The door to the great hall swung open again. Fawn stepped out of the keep, radiant in golden silk. The Lady of Ogof was followed by her three daughters, towheaded stepping-stones. Mary, the eldest with buck teeth and pale

eyes, was twelve years younger than Sheena and a prissy
thing who was forever sniveling and spying upon her older
half sister. Ann, the middle daughter, was quiet and aloof,
while the baby, Lynna, was a playful cherub who brightened
upon spying her half sister.

"See-Na! See-Na!" she cried, scrambling down the stairs
and running on short, chubby legs toward her. Grinning,
Sheena bent down, picked up the imp, and twirled her in the
air. Lynna giggled and screamed in delight. Her cheeks were
flushed, her blue eyes bright and happy. "More!" she cried
when the spinning stopped.

"Careful," Fawn reprimanded. "Don't get her dirty—oh,
Sheena, look at you." Frowning in disapproval, Fawn pried
the reluctant two-year-old from Sheena's arms. "Your
clothes are a disgrace, and your hair, for the love of St.
Peter, look at it." Her lips tightened as if pulled together by
a purse string. "And you, Jestin, should not be condoning
this behavior. Sheena is a woman now, soon to marry my
broth—"

"Nay, I will not marry Lord Ellwynn!" Sheena glared at
the older woman.

"Of course you will," Fawn snapped, then turned accusing eyes upon her husband. "This is your fault for letting her
run wild and treating her as a son. She thinks she has a
choice in the matter."

"I do—"

"Hush! I'll have none of your back talk!" Fawn glanced
around the inner bailey, where within the stone walls the
peasants and servants had stopped their tasks. The dyers
tending their vats in a nearby hut were looking up from their
work, and the candlemaker had come to the door of his hut
to see what was happening. Even soldiers on the wide curtain wall were peering down at the inner bailey.

"There is to be no more discussion," Fawn ordered.
"Come, girls, and you, Zelda," she added, snapping her fingers at the maid, "See to Sheena. My brother visits tonight."

"Nay!" Sheena's heart dropped.

"Go, daughter," her father said, and she noticed a tinge of regret in his words. "We'll talk later."

"There is nothing more to discuss," Fawn insisted as she gathered her brood, including a fussing Lynna, and returned to the keep. Mary cast a superior look over her shoulder and smiled as if she enjoyed seeing Sheena put in her place.

Sheena wanted to protest wildly, but the harsh slant of her father's jaw convinced her any further argument would be futile. He had set his mind, and at Ogof his word was law— as long as his wife agreed.

Not for the first time in her life, Sheena was embarrassed to be his daughter.

Who was she? Keegan scowled in the darkness. Bits of memory, snatches that didn't quite fit together, pierced his brain. Had he not seen her astride a dark, sweating horse as it raced across a meadow? Had he been in a town where she, mischief dancing in her eyes, had pulled on a circlet and dashed into a cathedral? Was there not a time when she had taken his hand in a dark place that smelled of the sea, drew him to her, and brushed her lips against his? Had she not teased him with a blue stone, holding it before his face only to snatch it away? Were these pictures in his mind, so vivid and real, naught but dreams? Christ Almighty, was this the first vestiges of madness?

He gazed up at the coming stars. Nay, he was not daft, but something was amiss. If only he could remember. Could he have met her in the dark time—the span of months where he was little more than a lad, the time that he had no memory of but had been regaled with time and time again? 'Twas the time when his father had been killed by his old enemy. Keegan had been there, at Ogof, but remembered nothing from the time the ship had laid anchor in the bay until long after, when his wounds had healed and he'd awoken to learn that his father, the only parent he had ever known, was dead.

Even now when he remembered awakening to the sight of Hollis's gaze, he felt a coldness deep in his soul. "Father?"

he'd choked out through lips that were cracked and dry. His voice had not been his own, had sounded even to his own ears as if it were echoing through a long, dark tunnel. His head had thundered in pain, and Hollis's words had echoed through the anguish.

"I'm sorry, lad, but do ye not remember? The captain, he was killed."

"Nay . . ."

"Oh, son, 'tis only ye and me and whatever we can scrape together."

He'd fallen into the darkness yet again and then had awoken days after without much memory but with a new, heavy pain that weighed on his heart and burdened his soul.

So how then would he have met this woman? *How?*

His back teeth ground together, and he told himself it didn't matter. Within a few days' time he would be rid of her and be a richer man. And yet he couldn't help listening for her tread upon the decking, glanced far too often over his shoulder to see if she was nearby, looked forward to the nights when he could gaze upon her in slumber even though his shaft was hard and thick and painful.

Aye, 'twould be good to get rid of her, whether she be Victoria as she claimed or Sheena as he suspected.

"Be ye a witch?" Bo asked as Sheena walked up the steps from the captain's cabin. The boy was lugging two pails, one filled with dead fish, the other empty. Sheena was grateful for someone to talk to, even if the subject was a little difficult. The ship was confining, and there were always men about, eyes following her every move.

Then there was that blasted captain, calling her Victoria, acting as if he'd never laid eyes upon her before the night she'd been dragged to his cabin by Hollis, and questioning her as if he truly had no memory. The sooner she was able to escape the *Dark Sapphire*, the better.

"If I were a witch, do you think I'd tell you?" she teased the scruffy-looking boy.

He eyed her suspiciously. "Nay, I'd be bettin' that ye'd cast a spell on me."

"Better be careful or maybe I will," she said, and laughed at the thought.

He didn't share her amusement. "Old Hollis, he be sayin' that ye have some kind of"—he thought for a minute, pulled out his dagger, and waggled it in the air—"some kind of power to call up the gods of the ancient ones."

"And what do you think?" For some reason she wasn't angry, just amused. Dragging in a breath of salt-sea air, she rested her arms on the top of the railing and eyed the horizon, searching for any glimpse of land.

"Mayhap." Bo plopped himself down, one leg stretched in front of him, his back braced against the railing, and pulled a fish out of his pail. As he looked up at Sheena through a shag of brown locks, he slit the fish agilely, slipping a sharp dagger through its skin near the tail and cleaving the flesh to the gills. "I heard ye sayin' ye could cast spells meself that first night ye were found." With a smug smile he added, "I sees more than they all know. Most of the men, they think me slow . . . but I be smart as any of 'em," he said proudly, and she wondered that anyone would mistake his youth for dim-wittedness. "I seen ye cursin' the captain on the first night when old Hollis found ye in the hold. Ye were callin' up the Great Mother—Morrigu—and ye asked her to doom this ship and all of us aboard."

She arched an eyebrow as she glanced down at him. "I only said it was possible."

With quick fingers and his well-honed blade, he scraped out the innards of the fish and ripped out the gills, dropping the guts into his second bucket. The herring's carcass was tossed back into the first pail. "Hollis, he's convinced ye be the daughter of the devil, and he's been bendin' the captain's ear."

"Has he? Hmm. And what did the captain say?"

"He laughed."

So the man did have a sense of humor, even if it was at Sheena's expense.

"Hollis has been sayin' it to the men, too. He's certain ye are here to damn us all. And half the crew—Seamus, Jasper, Cedric, and the lot—they believe him."

Sheena didn't argue against the old man's warnings about her, for if the men feared her, or her wrath, they would leave her be. Or so she hoped.

"So, are ye gonna chant a spell, call up the ghosts of the sea to capsize the ship so that we can all be eaten alive by sea serpents?"

Sheena smothered a smile. "I've been giving it some thought, aye."

The boy's eyes narrowed suspiciously on her. A gust of brisk wind caught her hair and brought a soft salty spray to her face. Overhead clouds gathered, their dark underbellies warning of a coming storm.

"So, Bo, what do you think?"

"Oh, I be sure you're a devil-woman," he said with a quick nod, "but I'm not afeared of ye."

"Nay?"

His smile was bold. Cocky. "Because I be able to take care of meself. I kin wield a blade as well as Big Tom and I'm quicker." He snorted. "The others—they know not what I see, what I hear, what I know." He held his dagger aloft, and a few rays of sunlight piercing the clouds gleamed against the sharp blade. "Ye want to know why I be so certain you be a witch?"

"Oh, please," she mocked, "tell me."

"Because ye've cast a spell upon the captain."

"A spell?" She glanced down at him, certain she would see mockery in his boyish face, but Bo nodded curtly again, as if agreeing with himself.

"Why else would he allow a woman on board?" Bo grabbed another unfortunate, but already dead, fish and sliced its belly evenly with his sharp little knife.

"Captain Keegan knew not I boarded."

"But he did na toss ye overboard when he found ye, did he? He didn't make ye walk a plank, as he said he would if ever a woman stepped on the ship."

"Has he done it before?"

"I donna know."

"If he tossed me overboard, Bo, I would surely drown or . . . or be swallowed whole by those horrid beasts of the sea—the serpents. Is that what you want?"

He thought for a second, the point of his knife nearly touching his chin. "I was but makin' an observation, lady. The captain, if he be true to his word, he should have wanted ye dead fer trespassin' and stowin' yerself away. So that the men know he means what he says." He yanked the gills of the herring, and again slippery organs spilled into the bucket. With a smack the second fish joined the first, and within a split second a third herring was in one of his hands, belly exposed, glassy eyes seeing nothing as Bo's wicked little dagger cut into it. He scowled to himself. "I dinna say I wanted ye dead."

"I should hope not," she said, then cocking her head to one side asked a question that had been with her ever since the first night of her entrapment in Keegan's cabin. "What of the captain's wife?" she asked, and Bo became silent as he quickly dispensed with three more fish.

"I'll not cast a spell on you if you tell me," she said, prodding the boy. He was chewing one side of his lip as if deliberating how much he should confide in her.

"I knew her not," he finally said. Again he tossed a cleaned-out fish into the rapidly filling bucket and snagged up another in his deft hands. "And ye did not answer me question."

"What question was that?"

"What have ye done to the captain to keep him from throwin' ye overboard?"

"Nothing," she hedged, for she didn't want to think of the bargain she'd agreed to the night she'd been captured.

Bo snorted in disbelief as he grabbed the final herring and

cleaned it swiftly. With one eye peeking upward through the shaggy strands of hair, he appraised Sheena with a look that called her the liar she was. He tossed the last fish back into the bucket. Its scales glimmered silver in the faint beams of sunlight that filtered through the clouds. "For you, the captain, he goes against his own rules, ye know."

"How so?" she asked, leaning over the rail and searching the depths of the ocean with her eyes. A salty breeze lifted her hair as she tried not to show too much interest in the blackheart of a captain, the man who had betrayed her years before yet acted as if he remembered her not. Was he blind? Or baiting her? She was not sure of his intentions, and every time she was around him, she was on edge. Nervous. Off balance.

"He always said there was to be no women on board. None." Bo's lips pulled into a thoughtful scowl. "And there never was one."

"Never?"

"Nay."

"Not even his wife?"

"I said I dinna know her. Asides, she be dead," the boy said without a bit of sympathy. He hopped to his feet, grabbed the pail of entrails, and tossed the contents overboard.

"I know, but when she was alive?"

"She never stepped foot on this ship." Big Tom rounded the foremast. "And well she shouldn't!" He was carrying a coil of rope over one of his massive shoulders, and his expression, as ever, was harsh, his eyes as cold as a winter sea. How long had he been within earshot? Sheena's cheeks reddened as she thought of her questions about the captain.

Tom snorted and spat over the railing. "Women have no place on the sea, and that one, she was a lyin' whore. There be no mistake about it. Killed herself when the captain found her with another man, she did."

Sheena didn't believe the huge man for a minute.

"Carryin' a babe at the time." His nostrils flared, and he

hitched the rope higher over his shoulder. "Spoilt she was, but sly as a fox. As beautiful as ye be with a heart as black as the devil's own. Any man who saw her wanted her. Including the captain."

Footsteps rang on the deck behind her, and she knew in an instant that Keegan was near. Her heart sank. Embarrassment stained her cheeks.

"Bloody hell," Bo whispered as he stared over her shoulder.

"Bo!" Keegan's voice heralded his approach. The boy straightened and picked up his catch. "The cook's lookin' fer you."

"Aye, Captain," the boy said, then cast Sheena a glance that warned her to keep what they'd spoken of between them. Then, his hair flopping in the wind, he scurried down the stairs to the lower deck.

"And ye, Tom, have ye naught to do but gossip like an old woman?" Keegan demanded. His expression was unreadable, his eyes dark.

"Ye have no gripe with me, Captain."

"Then why are ye not mindin' the jibs?"

"Because I see no reason for it," Tom said, standing his ground. "Where are we goin' Captain? Why is it ye've taken us so far off course?" Tom's eyes narrowed on the horizon, and he spat on the deck. He pointed toward the east. "Where is the coast land, eh, Captain?" A few sailors inched closer.

Keegan's lips tightened. "We be this far asea because of the shoals, Tom," he said with little patience.

Wiping his nose with the back of his hand, Tom shook his head. Two men who had been adjusting the sails stopped their work.

Keegan's patience was stretched thin. A muscle leaped in his jaw. The muscles at the base of his neck bunched, and he looked as if he wanted to pummel the bigger man with his bare hands.

The ship rocked, timbers creaked, and chains rattled as crew members looked on. The smell of a fight was heavy in the salty air, and Sheena knew, that at the root of it, she was the cause of all the dissension between the men.

"'Tis the woman," Tom charged, voicing her own dread. Thud! He dropped his coil of rope.

Sheena wanted no part of being any reason for Keegan's men to challenge him. Right now she needed him and . . . and, truth to tell, she hoped no harm would befall him regardless of their pact.

From the stairway Hollis appeared, his hood blowing off in the wind, his old eyes taking in the scene unfolding beneath the huge billowing sails.

"She's been distractin' ye, Captain, as she has many of the men." Tom hooked a disparaging thumb toward Sheena. "The sea be no place for a woman, a ship no home for a witch."

"The lady has nothing to do with the course we take."

"Nay? Well, I say she's cursed this ship by castin' a spell of doom over it and addling yer mind."

Hollis frowned and shook his head. "Enough of this—" he ordered, but Keegan paid him no heed.

"Tend to the jibs, Tom. Worry not about the stowaway."

Tom's face reddened and he motioned to the older man. "Hollis, there, he agrees with me, no matter what he be sayin' now. And so do Maynard and Seamus. Ye've not been the same since the old man found the witch in the hold and dragged her to yer cabin. She's cast a spell over ye, Captain, I swear it."

"And I say you're wrong. She is my guest. Nothing more."

"Or yer whore," Tom said under his breath.

Sheena's back stiffened. "I be no man's whore," she vowed, her fists clenched as she took a step forward on the slippery deck. Outrage and indignity burned through her blood. "Not the captain's. Not any man's. As for spells, mayhap you should be careful lest I cast one on you."

"Enough," Keegan said, but Sheena wasn't finished.

She'd endured much already, and she wouldn't let any of these thugs and cutthroats intimidate her.

"Now, what is it you'd like, Tom, eh? There be spells that make a man blind, or kill him dead, or shrivel his manhood to the size of a babe's finger or—"

"I said enough!" Keegan growled, glaring at her with a gaze that was sure to cut through stone.

"But—"

"Cast whatever bloody spells you wish, Victoria, but do it quietly, alone, in my cabin."

"Careful, Captain, lest I turn my magic on you." A gust of wind slapped her in the face, tore at her hair, but she didn't move as the ship turned into the wind.

"Try it," he suggested without a drip of humor in his voice.

"Nay!" Hollis cried as other men looked up from their work. Keegan rounded on Tom.

"Back to work. All of you." Keegan's jaw was granite. The skin over his face had stretched tight, and deep grooves surrounded his mouth. "As for you, Tom, I warn you, never speak of the lady again lest you do it with respect."

"Bah!" Again Big Tom spat, this time on the deck. "Things are not as they should be, Captain Keegan, and ye know it. We be off course and Wart be missing. What of him?"

The wind shifted. Keegan pinned the big man with his eyes. "I sent Wart ashore a few days past. He took a rowboat and will meet us at the next port."

What was this all about? Who was Wart?

"Why?" Tom demanded, and Sheena realized the answer even before the next words were spoken. "Because of the whore?" Tom asked, cocking his head toward Sheena in disgust.

Keegan lunged forward, his fists curled, his shoulder muscles tight as if he was ready for battle. He stopped short of grabbing the taller man. "You treat the woman as a lady, Tom. Or ye will have to answer to me. Now, go about your duties, and be quick about it or you and I, we'll settle it another way."

"Ye would fight me?"

"'Tis your choice."

Jasper, Reginald, and Seamus gathered on the deck, witnessing this hint of mutiny. They looked at each other, then Tom.

Time froze.

Keegan didn't move.

The sails snapped.

Tom's thick lips curled into a sneer, and Sheena was reminded of the castle dogs, how they crouched and glowered when they'd been cornered and expected a beating from the kennel master. Tom's gaze never moved from Keegan. "Ye be the captain only because ye cheated a man out of this ship in a game of chance," he snarled, rounding a bit, looking for a place to land a blow.

Just like his father before him, Sheena thought, swallowing hard. Had not Keegan's father, Rourke, nearly lost his ship, the *Warrior,* in another game of luck? Instead of winning, he'd given up his life.

"Every man on board knows it."

"'Tis of no matter, Tom," Keegan said, moving with the other man. "Whether I bought this ship, stole it, or built it myself, I still be the captain." Every muscle in Keegan's body was tense, the cords in the back of his neck standing at attention. "And you, Tom, along with the rest of the men, are to obey me. There be no questioning my authority. Ever."

"Then ye be a fool."

"Mayhap."

Tom's gaze darted around the deck, and for a second Sheena expected him to throw a meaty fist in Keegan's direction.

He hesitated, then growled, "It be not worth the trouble." Backing off, he sent a glare of pure hatred in Sheena's direction before spitting again. Finally, he reached down to pick up his coil of rope, tossed it over his shoulder, and strode off, lowering his head as he ducked beneath the mainsail.

"Now, Victoria," Keegan said slowly as he turned to face the bane of his journey, "never are ye to—"

"Captain!" Hollis picked his way across the deck and cast a worried glance at Tom's backside as the big man disappeared behind the rigging of the foremast. "By the saints, Tom, he's always sayin' things he should na. But he means it not. 'Tis his temper only."

Keegan didn't comment.

"Ye know this, Keegan. He's always spoutin' off, now, but he's proved himself true."

Keegan glowered irritably at the older man. Tom's words had cut deep, for what he wanted to do right now was grab the sharp-tongued woman, haul her down the stairs to his cabin, and lock her away where she was out of sight of the men and could not cause any more trouble. But he had to deal with the old man. "What be on yer mind, Hollis?"

"'Tis Seamus. He's ailing and needs be relieved of his duty. It seems he drank too much ale yesterday."

"Come along, then." Keegan strode toward the short stairway leading to the lower deck, where Seamus now guided the ship with a whipstaff.

Seamus barely glanced in Keegan's direction as he approached, nor did he look at Victoria, as the fool woman had come to the helm with him. Keegan's lips tightened over his teeth. He'd known she would cause more than her share of trouble, and he'd been right. Blast her and her damned beauty.

From the corner of his eye Keegan noticed James, who sat with his back against the wall as he repaired a large net. Smothering a grin, James nudged Jasper with his elbow. James's mouth curved into a crooked grin as he whispered into the other man's ear. Jasper barked out a laugh, and Victoria visibly stiffened. Her shoulders squared, her chin lifted proudly, and for just a second an image tugged at the corners of Keegan's memory—a picture of a younger woman, nay, a girl. But before he could quite grasp it, the recollection slipped away. Yet again. But he would remember. Soon. He sensed it.

Her cheeks were flushed in embarrassment, her lips compressed, for she knew that, as Big Tom had voiced, some of the men believed her to be warming Keegan's bed. Well, so be it. Whether she realized it or not, she was safer with him than locked away in the hold.

However, he thought with more than a trace of irony, mayhap Hollis had been right this one time. Perhaps he should have taken the woman ashore the minute she'd been dragged to his cabin.

"Captain," the helmsman greeted Keegan as he approached. A tall, gaunt man with a scraggly brown beard and tired, lifeless eyes, Seamus was holding onto the whipstaff as if it alone were holding him up. His cheekbones were visible beneath skin that was tinged a sickly green.

Keegan minced no words. "Hollis here says you want to be relieved of your duty."

"It might be best, aye." Dead eyes flicked toward the captain. "For now. 'Tis sorry I be, but—" He cleared his throat and looked guiltily at the floorboards.

"Off with you," Keegan said brusquely. He took command of the whipstaff, the long pole attached to the tiller that guided the ship. To Hollis he said, "Find Cedric."

"Aye, Captain, that I will."

"And take the lady with you," Keegan ordered.

Sheena opened her mouth to argue with him, but changed her mind. "I need not an escort," she said instead. She made her way to the upper deck and felt the jewels pinching her toe. She needed to get off this cursed ship and soon. Keegan was not all he seemed. Did he really not remember her? Should she tell him that they'd met before?

She arrived at the cozy little room she shared with the brooding captain, and she collapsed onto the bunk, nearly banging her head, and threw one arm over her eyes. Oh, he was a shameless one, Keegan was and yet . . . a part of her found him fascinating. "Then 'tis a fool you be," she told herself. "He's no more charming than a wolf about to slaughter a lamb!"

Why had he sent the man—what was his name— Wart—ashore? Wart? What kind of name was that? Where had he been sent—to Tardiff? Ogof? Her heart froze. Would Keegan double-cross her, knowingly keeping her captive to sell her back to the men who were chasing her down?

He had no scruples . . . or had he?

Had he not stood up for her on the deck less than an hour before? Had he not taken that horrid Big Tom to task? Not that she couldn't have dealt with the man herself, but the captain had stepped in.

'Tis only because of your bargain, she told herself, but frowned, for there was something about the rogue of a captain she found intriguing.

What was wrong with her? She knew him to be a traitor. Had he not proved that years ago? She couldn't trust him, wouldn't. Nor, even if he held up his end of their pact, could she honor her bargain with him.

At that thought she felt a pang of true regret. She removed her boot slowly and pulled out the stones. They winked in the frail light from the lantern—brilliant, sparkling gems in the dark room. She wondered about the dark blue stone he'd taken—the most valuable of her mother's jewels—the cursed Dark Sapphire of Ogof. Had he sold it and bought this ship, naming it after the stolen gem? Did he still own it? Was it hidden somewhere in this prison of a ship? Or had it been lost in the sea years before when she'd thought he'd been killed in that tiny boat—the one she'd given him?

"It matters not," she reminded herself. As soon as the ship was near land, she would escape and leave Keegan with his mysterious past and seductive eyes behind her.

And then what will you do? Once you flee the Dark Sapphire *and are on land again, what then?*

Mayhap you should go home, Sheena of Ogof. Somehow

you must elude Sir Manning's men, sneak into the castle, and find your father alone. Explain to him what happened on your wedding night and then accept whatever punishment he metes out.

She swallowed hard, sat up, and looked into the mirror at her reflection. She was suddenly pale, for the thought of facing the hangman wasn't pleasant. She'd never been one to run from a battle, was usually bold to the point of impudence, and wanted to return to Ogof to explain herself.

Don't do it. 'Twill be certain death, one part of her mind admonished. *But the truth needs be told; leave your fate in the hands of your father. Trust in him. He's a fair man,* the other part of her brain disagreed.

She stuffed the stones into the toe of her boot once again and considered her future. Only two things were certain: She had to escape the *Dark Sapphire* and elude the soldiers of Tardiff. Then she would decide if she would run and hide for the rest of her life, be forever wary, continually look over her shoulder, or return home to her father's brand of justice. "God help me," she whispered, not for the first time, though she expected no answer to her prayer.

Chapter Five

"Say it not," Fawn warned as she lay on the bed in her chamber. She wore only her chemise while the midwife Maven, an aging crone with little sense of humor and a reputation Fawn wasn't certain she believed, poked and prodded with spotted fingers, then shook her head sadly as if there was not the slightest chance of an easy delivery.

"'Tis sorry I be," the midwife admitted sadly as scented tapers, smelling of a mixture of pine cones and acorns, burned beside the bed.

Zelda, her maidservant, stood near the grate, waiting with infinite patience, holding Fawn's clothes while the midwife took her sweet time with the examination.

"Tell me not that the boy is not in position." Fawn was in no mood for bad news. Anxious and edgy, she awaited word from Manning about Sheena. How had that twit of a girl eluded the best men in Ogof for so long?

Maven pursed her already wrinkled lips as a small fire hissed from the grate. Tapestries adorned the walls, and fresh rushes, scented with rose petals and lavender, had been strewn over the stone floor. But today, with the feel of a storm in the air, Ogof held no warmth, no joy for Fawn. Coupled with everything else, the midwife's dour expression was all the more irritating.

"What? What?" Fawn demanded, eyeing the woman who was supposed to give her good news—only good news.

"You told me not to say, m'lady, but the babe, be it boy or girl, has not yet turned. If it does not—"

"*He*. If *he* does not," Fawn corrected, sitting up in bed and yanking down her chemise over the protrusion that had once been a waist so small a man's hand could span it easily. "'Tis a boy I carry. Forget that not."

"Aye," the woman said, though from the shadows in her eyes it was obvious she still had doubts. Fawn didn't. Secretly she'd ridden to the edge of the forest where the fortune-teller Serena dwelled in a crude hut.

Serena had placed warm, knowing hands upon Fawn's naked belly and, closing her eyes, had told Fawn the truth—that the child inside her womb was male, was destined to rule and would be as strapping, cunning, and fierce as his father. Serena had said that the child had all the qualities of his ancestor, Llywelyn the Great, and Fawn believed every word. Serena's prediction was a good sign, to be sure.

"If *he* does not turn, the birthing will be difficult," Maven said softly. A breath of wind rushed through the open window, and the embers of the fire flared and cast shimmering golden shadows on the whitewashed walls.

"I have born three babes." Fawn snapped her fingers at Zelda as she stood. The older woman was quick to help her don a green tunic and darker surcoat. "And aye, their births were not pleasant, but not so difficult, either." With Zelda's help, Fawn adjusted the tunic, frowning as she had to stretch the fabric over her distended belly.

"This child is larger."

"'Tis not a simpleton I be," Fawn shot back, angry at the tight fit of her gown and the fact that the midwife should bring up her ever increasing size. "Boys often are." Fawn managed a smile despite the old woman's concern. Discomfort aside, this birth would be a blessed event, the likes of which Wales had not seen since the Llywelyn himself had been brought into the world. Jestin would be proud.

But then, he was a fool.

"But, m'lady, sometimes, if the babe does not turn and is born back end first, even if it—he—survives he may . . ."

"May what?" Fawn snarled. "Tell me not that he would be crippled or . . . or . . ." Dread froze her heart. "Or that he might be born an idiot, for that is blasphemy, Maven. Do you hear me? Blasphemy!"

"I said it not."

"Good." Fawn would not worry about the midwife's concerns. "'Tis up to you to see that the babe is born healthy. I trust you are able to do it."

Maven chewed her lower lip. "I have lost only three in all the years that I've birthed babes, m'lady."

"And this one will not be your fourth," Fawn insisted. She grabbed the midwife's gown, her fingers curling in the worn fabric. "Remember that this child is destined to rule not only Ogof but Tardiff as well. Now, be off with you!" She released the wretch and heard the sound of thunder cracking over the distant hills.

A storm was brewing.

As the midwife, hunch-shouldered and grim, scurried out of the room, Fawn glanced at the window. Why had Manning not returned with news of Sheena? Absently she touched her belly and felt the child growing within her kick. Hard. Ah, he was a warrior, this one. Very soon she would have a son. And then, by all that was holy, that old man of a husband of hers owed her a jewel, and not just any bauble, oh, no. She expected a ring with a stone as awe-inspiring and dazzling as the Dark Sapphire of Ogof had been—the treasure he'd bestowed upon his first, pathetic wife. Nay, whatever prize he gave her, it would have to be *more* valuable than that damned ring.

Sheena tossed and turned on the bed as the wind howled across the ocean and the ship pitched wildly. She couldn't sleep, though it wasn't because of the roll of the sea; she'd become used to the rise and fall of the ship as it cut across the waves. Nor was it from worry about being captured by Sir Manning and his army of thugs. She felt safer aboard the ship than she had on land. But the captain, she found him disturbing, and though she reminded herself that he'd betrayed her once before, that he was only keeping her on board because it spelled a profit for him, she felt herself melting where he was concerned. Not only was he strapping and handsome, but she'd seen beneath his gruff exterior another man, one who might just have a soul.

"Do not even think it," she worried aloud, tossing off the covers and wondering when he would return to the cabin. *If* he would return. She was becoming charmed by him and had even pretended sleep to watch him remove his tunic and breeches, though in the dark she'd seen very little of him aside from corded muscles and a swirling mat of black curls upon his chest. All else was lost to her.

"And a good thing," she muttered, feeling guilty for taking the space where he was to sleep. He deserved better—or did he? Just then she heard his boots ring on the steps outside. Her silly heart jumped, and she bit her lip as he threw open the door and strode inside. His clothes were wet, his hair in damp ringlets, the smell of salt upon his skin. The lantern had burned low, and Sheena, careful not to bump her head, climbed out of the bunk.

"What's this? Can you not sleep? 'Tis the storm. Do not worry, it will be over before morn."

"Nay 'tis not the weather," she admitted, realizing she was wringing her hands and willing them to stop. "I can take your bed no longer." She stood and the ship pitched again. She nearly fell against him, but caught herself and stood toe to toe with him in one of his wife's dresses.

"Why not?"

"'Tis not right." She shook her head proudly. "Though you call me your guest, I was uninvited and I—I . . ."

Her words faded as she realized he was staring at her with his damnably gray gaze that had somehow scraped against her soul. Rainwater ran down his chiseled face and down his neck. Her pulse throbbed in her throat, and she was suddenly tongue-tied. He was far too close, and she remembered all too vividly how it felt to have him kiss her so many years ago. The tiny room seemed to shrink even farther, the flickering light from the lantern casting golden shadows on the dark wood walls and defining the hollows and planes of his face.

"I—I will sleep on the floor."

"I have not asked it."

"I know, but 'tis your bed and, as you so often remind me, your ship." Unexpectedly she'd felt her cheeks warm.

He hitched his chin toward the bunk and sighed. "Now, Victoria, I be weary." His voice was low. Intimate. "Take the bed."

"Nay, I—"

"Do not argue with me."

"But—"

"Oh, for the love of the saints." Quick as a cat springing, he grabbed her by the arms. His fingers tightened. His eyes glowed with the reflection of the candle. "Must you always defy me?" Sheena's blood spurted hot through her veins. She swallowed hard as he slowly pushed her backward the few feet to his bunk. Her calves brushed up against the hardwood frame.

All time stood still. The ship rocked. Somewhere overhead footsteps could be heard and the masts creaked. "Christ Jesus, what is it about you?" he demanded, shaking her a bit. "Why is it that I feel I know you?"

She swallowed hard. Should she tell him? Or would opening the gates to his memory bring with it all manner of demons from the past?

"Get into the bed, Victoria. Now." His mouth drew downward, brooking not a solitary argument. "Alone."

"I do not want—"

"Then I will be forced to sleep with you. Would you prefer that I share the bed with you?"

"*What?*" she cried, her voice low and raspy at the thought

of him lying next to her, his body pressed intimately to hers in the small bed. "Nay, I'll not . . ." She gulped, and his gaze was drawn to her neck, watching the movement at the hollow of her throat. She felt dizzy and the roll of the sea only intensified the sensation.

He said nothing, just stared. So near. So distant. And yet she detected a yearning deep within his soul. Felt his desire as well as her own.

"Test me not, Victoria of Rhydd or Lady of Taradiff or whoever it is you be," he whispered in a voice as raw as a winter wind.

She didn't budge, just stared at him in the dim glow of the lantern and licked her lips nervously. The fingers over her arms dug in, and he drew in a swift, whistling breath.

"Either you are an innocent who knows not what she does, or an accomplished temptress who is testing me. Now, woman, get into the damned bunk before I throw you into it." She inched up her chin but didn't have the chance to rebuff him, for he said, "If you defy me, I swear, I may do something I will forever regret."

She didn't ask what he meant. The air was thick with lust and longing, nearly crackling with a need she never thought she would feel. For once she held her tongue, and clearing her throat, she lowered herself onto the bunk. Quivering inside, she closed her eyes and listened as he strode out of the cabin and the door shut with a thud behind him.

"Oh, God, no," she whispered, feeling a deep, dusky ache in the most intimate part of her. Denying the sensations of wanton lust even as they assailed her, she curled her fingers in the coverlet, tried to close her mind to the thought of him without his shirt and breeches, and ended up lying awake half the night, calling herself a thousand kinds of fool because a wayward part of her had found his threat appealing.

God forgive her, after all she'd been through, she wanted Captain Keegan both in body and spirit. Tears sprang to her eyes, but she refused to cry. Not for him. Not for any man.

She forced herself to sleep, reminded herself that she

would want no man, and she dozed all the while the ship fought the waves. Time passed. The captain didn't return. She must have fallen asleep, for suddenly she was startled awake. There was a cry—or was it only the moan of the wind?

She slipped out of the warmth of the bed and felt an instant chill. Again the cry. Not bothering with her mantle, she opened the cabin door, where rain lashed from the night-dark heavens. The ship listed to one side, then shuddering, righted itself and, barefoot, Sheena fell against the cabin wall only to hear the cry again.

"Hello!" she yelled, climbing the steps.

"Help me . . . oh, please . . ."

She sprinted onto the deck. "Where are you?" she screamed, her voice snatched by the wind as it shrieked through the masts and the *Dark Sapphire* bobbed wildly. 'Twas as if Satan himself were at the helm.

"Here! Help."

Was it Bo's voice? Heart pounding, feet sliding, she dashed through the rain and the darkness, bending under the boom. "Bo! Where are you?" she cried. Oh, for the love of God, answer!"

"Here!" he screamed as the boat rocked and pitched. Sheena's body slammed against the mast. Pain shot through her. Icy rain pummeled her from above. The wind roared and shrieked as she peered into the darkness, straining for a glimpse of the boy.

"Where?"

"Here! Up here!" And then she saw him, a small boy caught in ropes that had tangled in the wind. His dark contorted shape was barely visible against the huge white sails rippling in the wind.

"Hang on," she screamed, and, fearing he might lose his grip at any second, began climbing in the darkness, her toes curling over the wet, swollen ropes, her fingers clawing ever upward. The drenched dress was a dead weight, dragging her ever downward, her hair blew in front of her eyes, and her fingers scraped against the rough cords until they were raw. She forced herself upward. "Hang on."

Bo was caught, dangling half upside down. Somewhere below she heard voices, men shouting as the crew tried to keep the unsteady boat afloat.

Keening wind filled the sails. The ship rocked. Sheena's hands bled. The boy was a dozen yards above her. "Can you see me . . . Bo!"

He didn't respond. His face was white as death. *Oh, God, was she too late? Had he somehow hung himself on the rigging? Had he tangled himself in the complex network of wires, pulleys, and ropes?* "Bo! For the love of God, can you hear me?"

He was closer, only half a dozen yards. Just a little farther. The *Dark Sapphire* shuddered suddenly. Waves crashed over the deck. The wind shrieked and the huge ship listed so far that one of Sheena's legs swung free. Closing her eyes, she clung to the rough ropes, sending up prayer after prayer as men below worked to right the ship. Fear constricted her heart, and she was shaking with the cold. She stretched. "I'm—I'm almost there!" she yelled through teeth that chattered and bargained with God for Bo's young life.

"Lady . . . Lady Victoria," he cried and she was grateful for the sound of his voice.

" 'Twill be all right."

"I got meself tangled up. The wind . . ." He tried to sound brave. "I slipped and a pulley hit me . . . and somethin' must've torn and—"

"And we're going to get you down. Right now." Oh, Lord, she sounded more confident than she felt. Slipping one leg through the netting so that she would not fall, she worked with the twisted ropes that bound him, her frigid fingers forcing the frayed cords apart. "Come on," she said. "Easy, now."

As he was freed, he began to move much more agilely than she. "Come on, hurry," he said as the wind tore at her and the rain blurred her vision.

She followed more slowly, careful as she descended, her stomach jolting each time the ship rocked. Her dress was matted against her body, her hair sodden, her flesh chilled to the bone. Her hands were scraped raw on the slippery, coarse ropes. Her shoulders ached, and she bit her lip to keep her teeth from chattering like a ninny.

"Hurry," Bo yelled, seemingly well.

She was halfway down, lightheaded and frozen, when she felt a strong arm surround her.

"'Tis no witch you be," Keegan said, grabbing her and holding her close, his breath warm against her frigid skin. "But a foolish, foolish woman." She was too exhausted to argue, too grateful for his strength to disagree. She wanted to collapse against him, but clung to the ropes high above the deck. "Now, let's get down from here."

"Who's . . . who's at the helm?"

"Seamus. Worry not." With one arm on the main cable and the other around her, he half carried her ever downward, his feet sure, his muscles tight. She wrapped an arm around his neck, felt his warm, wet body pressed tightly to hers. His face was tense against the rage of the wind, but he never faltered, never said a word. Within minutes he'd stepped onto the deck, still carrying her as if she weighed nothing.

Maynard stood near the main mast. "Ye saved Bo's life," he muttered, his voice barely audible over the wind.

"Nay." She shook her head as Keegan carried her toward the stairs. "I helped him."

"No. Ye saved his life." Big Tom agreed, and the surliness that had been his constant companion was no longer with him. The boat listed again, and Keegan barked orders at his men.

"There be work to do!" A cable snapped. The ship pitched wildly. "Get Jasper and James. Someone has to fix the rigging. Now!" he yelled as he carried her across the uneven deck. The two men scurried away, and Sheena struggled to stand on her own feet.

"Do not struggle, little one. I'll carry you." With surprising tenderness, he carried her into the cabin and set her carefully onto the bed.

"Where's Bo?"

"With Hollis. Worry not for him," Keegan said, pointing a finger at her soiled dress. "Take that off before you come down with chills."

"I—I'm fine." She tossed her hair from her eyes and wiped her face with her hands, only to wince in pain.

"Are you?" He bent down and held up one of her hands, exposing the cuts and scrapes in the candlelight. Her fingers were raw, bleeding. "I'll send someone with warm water, soap and a cup of wine."

"Do not bother—"

"'Tis none." He strode to the door, then paused, his great shoulders sagging a bit. With a glance over his shoulder, he said, "'Tis true. For once Maynard was right. You saved Bo's life. And now I must see to the helm." With that, he was gone, and Sheena had no thoughts of disobeying him for the first time since she had been dragged on a leash into this very cabin on the night she'd been discovered. Tonight, as the *Dark Sapphire* battled the storm that still raged, she sank backward onto the bunk. There was no fight left in her.

The maid was a comely wench if ever there was one, Wart thought as he sipped dark ale from his bench at the tavern. Her hair was braided into a long plait that fell over one shoulder and was the color of wheat at harvest time. Sky blue eyes, a pert little nose and, above the neckline of her dress, white breasts like pillows, soft and beckoning. A man could smother between those inviting mounds, and ah, what sweet death 'twould be. She moved between the tables, avoiding the patrons' hands, for many a man too far in his cups was willing to risk a slap for a chance to pinch her fine arse swinging invitingly beneath her skirts.

"Lizzie, girl, another drink," one man yelled over the noise. Wart guessed him to be a merchant of some sort by the finery of his garb.

The girl picked up a tray of cups filled by a birdlike woman with wrinkled skin who opened casks, brought out steaming platters of food, and anxiously counted the coins that the lass collected. As dried up and drawn as Lizzie was ripe and young, the old hag watched the tightly packed room with eyes that missed nothing. Conversation buzzed, bawdy jokes were passed, raucous laughter vied with the clink of cups, and the struggling strains of a musician who plucked at his lute and sang in a thin, wobbly voice could hardly be heard over the din.

Wart sat and listened. From what he understood, a small army of men had stopped at the inn, soldiers from the south, just the night before.

Lizzie delivered to the merchant a cup of ale, then worked her way down two plank tables to the corner that Wart had occupied for most of the evening.

"Will ye be havin' another cup?" she asked in a voice that was like a songbird. It brought back memories of Wart's first love, a girl who had sworn her heart to him, only to marry the son of a farmer her parents had chosen—his cousin Peter.

"Aye, if ye be pourin', Liz."

She giggled, though he suspected that her flirting wasn't because she was interested in him. Nay, he knew he wasn't a handsome man, but he paid well for his drink, and she sparkled and laughed and brought a bit of joy into his tired, jaded heart.

"And how did ye lose yer thumb, eh?" she asked.

"Defending a pretty lass's honor," he lied. The incident that had cost him partial use of his hand was not worth telling. He motioned her closer. "Ye say there were soldiers in here just last eve?"

"Aye. Half a dozen of 'em, I'd guess. All asking questions, they were." She filled his mazer and, leaning over, offered him a long look at her breasts. Wart's old, lonely member rose in his breeches, and he resisted the urge to shift on the bench.

"What were the soldiers doin' here?"

"Oh, they be searchin' for a woman. A lady, methinks."
She lingered, anxious to pass on a little gossip.

"A lady?" Wart feigned surprise.

"Mmm. Lady Sheena of Tardiff." Lizzie leaned ever
closer, and the faint scent of honeysuckle tickled his nose.
"The knight who be in charge—Manning, they called him—
said she killed her husband!"

"Nay."

"On her wedding night." Lizzie moved her head up and
down slowly.

"'Tis hard to believe."

"I heard it from the knight himself." Clucking her tongue
and shaking her head so that her braid brushed the tops of
those supple breasts, she added, "Can ye imagine? She bein'
a lady and he bein' a lord. Stabbed him, she did, nearly gutted the poor man."

"Mayhap he did not please her," Wart said, then took a
long draught. "It takes skill, ye know, and patience as well.
Not all men be able or willin'."

She didn't so much as blink; nor did she blush.

"Lizzie! Make haste, will ye?" the old shrew behind the
counter yelled. Oh, she was a nasty one, that. With a shrill
voice, beaklike nose, and tiny eyes that sparkled suspiciously, she slammed a tray upon the counter. "There be
thirsty men here!"

"Aye." Lizzie started off, but Wart was quick and grabbed
her wrist. "These soldiers, were they headin' north?"

"I did not hear." She glanced nervously to the counter,
where the nag was watching with her tiny, hawklike eyes.

"Lizzie!"

Wart released her; there was no more she could tell him.
He would locate the encampment, listen to the men himself,
and then have a word with Sir Manning, find out exactly
who the knight was searching for. Victoria of Rhydd or
Sheena of Tardiff, it mattered not to him.

He left some coins and a piece of his heart with Lizzie,

then walked outside to a night as dark as death and prayed that he'd find the army from Tardiff soon. He'd been too long on the land and was itching to return to the *Dark Sapphire*. He missed the smell of brine and the feel of the ship as it cut through the night-black waters. 'Twas a feeling like no other, a freedom he missed sorely. Despite all the fetching maids in Wales, Wart had learned long ago not to trust them. Now and forever his only true love was the sea.

The ship was too damned small, Keegan decided as he walked to the prow and took in a great lungful of bracing night air. Grand as she was, the *Dark Sapphire* was far too confining. All because of the woman. No matter where he turned, Keegan saw Victoria, and when he didn't, he couldn't help but look for her. Christ Jesus, he wished she'd never boarded the ship, never stowed away. And yet if she hadn't, would Bo be alive this day?

Last night, as he'd held her tight while helping her down the rigging, his memory had flared, and he thought he'd been near to her before, holding her close, running through the darkness . . . and yet just as he was certain the image would come into sharp focus, it had slipped away from him again. Much later, after his watch, when the storm had abated and he had returned to the cabin just before dawn, it had taken all of his willpower not to join her in the bed. He'd ached to touch her, to feel her warm skin against his cold flesh. She'd been in peaceful repose, her red hair fanned around her face, the sweep of her lashes and parted lips as seductive as a siren's call.

Oh, she was a distraction. Not only to him, but to the men as well. All of them. Jasper was completely smitten, and even Big Tom, ever since she'd risked her life for Bo, had started following her with his eyes. Bo, of course, had been won over. Only old Hollis was still wary, and even his harsh attitude against her appeared to be softening. "She be a witch, I tell ye," he still proclaimed, but Keegan had caught the old man speaking with her, even cracking a smile and showing off his snaggled teeth when she spoke with him.

Nay, it wouldn't be long before every man on the ship was besotted with her.

He leaned against the bowsprit that held the jibs in place. It jutted over the night-dark water above the figurehead he'd had specially carved after Brynna died—that of a solitary wolf with painted eyes that were gold as a summer sunrise.

Keegan had always felt at home on the sea, but now he was restless. This night was no different from every evening when he thought of the woman sleeping in his bed. 'Twas all he could do to withstand the temptation of returning to his cabin, locking the door behind him, and sliding under the covers to lie with her. He'd caught glimpses of her in the night when she'd moved on the bed and the candle in the lantern had burned low.

He hadn't been immune to her allure, though he'd gritted his teeth and dragged his gaze away from the curve of her spine, the slope of her shoulders, even a firm, small breast with its button of a nipple that had been exposed for a brief second as she'd rolled over on the bed—*his* damned bed.

The fires within him burned, for it had been long since he'd been with a woman. Too long. And the other night, when she'd defied him by not taking the bed, it had been all he'd been able to do to stride out of the cabin. He had spent the next three hours looking out at the sea, his hands clenched, his mind burning with the want of her.

Last night, with her hands bleeding, her sodden dress molded to her body, her tiny lips chilled, he had forced himself back to his duties.

Now at just the thought of her, his manhood swelled uncomfortably. He stared up at the inky sky, millions of stars winking overhead. The moon was full, casting a ribbon of light on the rippling waters, but his thoughts were far from the beauty of the heavens. No, his mind would not waver from the seductive image of the woman lying in his bed.

Who was she?

What was she running from?

Was she a pampered lady who had actually plotted to kill her husband?

And why did he have the feeling that he had known her once, long ago, that she remembered him? Worse yet, he suspected Hollis was keeping something from him as well. The old man had trouble hiding his true feelings and was holding tight to a secret. What the devil was it?

Questions, like a flock of hungry gulls after a single dying crab, kept circling and wheeling through his mind. Why was he certain he'd seen her before? That red hair, those blue-green eyes, so bright and deep. Bloody hell, why couldn't he remember? "Blast it all," he growled, drumming his fingers on the smooth wood of the bowsprit as he glowered into the starry night and listened to the wash of water against the *Dark Sapphire*'s hull.

He wondered how much ransom he could demand for Victoria and felt a jab of guilt, for she had shown true bravery when she'd saved Bo.

The air stirred, and he sensed a presence before he heard the light tap of boot heels against the decking. Glancing over his shoulder, he saw her, a small thing with wild hair and skin that seemed as white as alabaster in the moonlight.

"Did I not tell you to stay in the cabin at night?" he growled as she approached.

"I could not sleep." She tossed her hair over one shoulder rebelliously. God's teeth, what would he do with her? "Remember, Captain, I be not your prisoner."

He snorted. She was an impertinent thing. And beautiful. Damnably beautiful.

Her eyes slitted in the darkness, and she reached up to twine her fingers in a shroud stretched to the rigging. "Are you afraid that if I walk around the ship I might uncover your secrets?" she baited.

He didn't respond.

"'Tis too late. Some of your men have loose tongues."

"Especially if they be threatened by witchcraft."

Her lips pulled into a little smile. "Mayhap."

"And what have they told you?" He crossed his arms over his chest and leaned back, telling himself that whatever she'd learned, it was of no consequence.

"I know that you be a thief."

He frowned. Didn't say a word.

"And a smuggler. I was in your hold."

He lifted a shoulder and tried not to stare at the hollow of her throat, a seductive, dusky indentation above the tops of her breasts. He clenched his teeth so hard they ached.

"So what is it you carry on board?"

"Other than sharp-tongued stowaways?" he asked.

"Aye." She chuckled. "Tell me, Captain Keegan, what is it you hide?"

"If you found my hiding spots, then you found what was in them. You tell me."

She frowned. Tapped her fingers on a pulley. "They be empty." Lifting her eyes, she stared straight into his, and his gut tightened. He wanted her—God, forgive him, but he wanted her as he'd never wanted another woman. "But they not be empty for long, me thinks," she guessed, hitting too close to the truth. Stepping closer to him, so close he felt the heat of her body, she looked up at him with her incredible eyes, and it was all he could do not to wrap his arms around her, drag her up against his body, and kiss her until they were both breathless. "What is it you do on this ship? What are your secrets, Captain? What is it you're hiding that is so important that you refused to let the soldiers on at the last port?" she asked, unwittingly tempting him.

Without thinking he grabbed hold of her arm. "Whatever be my secrets, they be mine," he said, his fingers circling her wrist and feeling the leap of her pulse. "Mayhap I should remind you that I be not the one running from the law, little one." Her muscles tensed beneath her sleeve, and yet he didn't release her. "As for the soldiers, I allow no one on my ship I do not wish aboard." Roughly he yanked her closer to him.

"Except stowaways, and then I throw them off at the next port. In your case I made an exception."

"Because I promised to pay you."

"A promise you cannot keep." He tried not to notice the way her bosom rose and fell with her breaths, or the curve of her lips or the fire in her eyes. She was a stowaway, nothing more. Nothing!

"You have to have faith, Captain."

"Blind faith."

"Aye. You will be rewarded for taking me safely to shore."

"Empty words, Victoria. False promises." His fingers dug into her flesh as the wind snapped in the sails. "Let this be a warning. If you lie to me, if you treat me like a fool, I will not rest until I have chased you down."

"And what?" she threw at him. "What would you do to me then?" Her head inched up mutinously, and her lips quivered in rage. "Threaten me not, Captain," she advised as his blood, suddenly hot, began to pound in his ears. "Just trust me."

He gazed into her eyes a second too long, and rashly, without thinking, he dragged her against him. " 'Tis not your position to make demands of me, lady."

" 'Tis not yours to order me about."

"I be the captain."

"And I be your guest. Is that not what you told your men?" she challenged, her eyes bright.

He could not resist her. She was as hot as the sun and cold as the sea all at once, her gaze promising him heaven while her lips condemned him to hell.

"And yet you treat me as if I was a prisoner!"

"Are you shackled?" he demanded.

"Nay, but—"

"Chained?"

"Not by iron links."

"Held under lock and key?" He lowered his face, stared deep into those night-dark blue eyes.

She swallowed hard, looked down at his mouth. "Nay," she whispered so softly he barely heard the words over the rush of the wind filling the huge sails and driving the ship through the inky waters.

"Are you not given food and water, precious as it is?" She was quivering now, and she bit her lower lip. "Have I not clothed you, given you my bed, and kept you safe?" He felt her stiffen, her spine become rigid. "And yet you not only disobey me but accuse me of holding you hostage when you, *you*, lady, stowed away on *my* ship, hid in the hold and took refuge here. 'Tis only by the grace of God and my patience that you are safely aboard. We dock in two days' time. Until then I order—nay, I ask—you to obey the laws of this ship and my commands."

She wanted to argue; he saw it in the defiant twist of her neck and the set of her shoulders, but when she opened her mouth to speak, no words flew out. Instead she clamped her jaw shut for a second, as if choking back the words she so dearly wanted to say. Glowering up at him, she finally said, "No man has the right to tell me what I will do. But as we have a bargain, I will try to hold up my end. I will do as you command, and in the end, believe me, Captain, you will be paid for your trouble. 'Tis all that you want."

"Oh, no, lady, 'tis wrong you be," he said, desire pounding through his bloodstream. "There is much more I want from you. Too much." Damning the consequences, he cupped her head and stared deep into her eyes.

As his brain screamed that he was making a mistake which would waken the dogs of hell, he fell victim to temptation and kissed her. Hard, hungry, demanding, he slanted his mouth over hers. The feel of her skin was pure magic. It awakened in him the long dormant feeling of youth. He groaned, expecting her to pull away or to slap him soundly across his chin. Instead she didn't move for a second. Then her lips slowly parted.

Deep inside he throbbed. A memory sizzled through his brain.

His tongue slid easily between her teeth, and the taste of her, the feel of her body as he dragged her still closer, brought his damned manhood to further attention. By the Gods, he wanted her. His body ached to claim her. His brain was in flames, his mind spinning with erotic images and more—in rapid fire succession the hidden doors to his mind were unlocked. Click. Click. Click. Her tongue flicked against his, sending shivers of want through his flesh. His arms wrapped around her tightly, and he kissed her hungrily, anxiously, as the night wind swirled around them and the sea splashed upon the ship.

Drawing back his head, he saw the slumberous passion in her eyes, felt her quiver, knew in an instant who she was.

"Ogof," he whispered. "You're the girl. You, Victoria of Rhydd, are Sheena of Ogof." He remembered their last bittersweet kiss and how he'd left her alone to face her father after she'd helped him escape. "So why are you here aboard my ship?" he asked, holding her at arm's length and staring into her eyes. "For sanctuary or for vengeance?"

Chapter Six

Sheena's mind spun as the *Dark Sapphire* cut through the dark waters and the moon climbed higher in the sky. How could she tell him the truth? Confide in him? Trust him? She struggled for an answer and found none.

"Tell me, Sheena," he said, her name rolling off his tongue as the sea breeze ruffled his hair. Strong arms held her so close to him she was certain the breath was being pressed slowly and ever so seductively from her lungs. "You are that imp, are you not? The daughter of Lord Jestin."

"A-aye," she whispered, barely able to think. So he knew who she was and the fire in his eyes was a cold, hard flame of accusation. Yet he didn't release her. Her heart was racing, her skin flushed and heated, yet the night wind felt cool against her cheeks. *God help me.*

"And you were married to Tardiff."

She gulped.

"Slayed him?"

She closed her eyes as the horrid images assailed her in rapid-fire succession, memories from which she wanted nothing more than to escape. But they chased her down, were relentlessly shadowing her with the pain and torment of her wedding day and night. She shivered, shook her head and tried to pull away from the captain's embrace.

"What?" he asked and his muscular arms seemed sud-

denly sheltering rather than imprisoning. One hand brushed
the hair from her eyes. "What happened, Sheena?"

Something inside her broke when he said her name again.
Trembling, she bit back a sob and tried to speak, but her
throat was swollen. Tears, those horrid, relentless drops that
she'd sworn she'd never again shed, burned in her eyes and,
as if he somehow understood her pain, he folded her tight
against him.

"Ah, 'tis a beautiful liar you are, Sheena of Ogof," he said
and kissed her forehead. She closed her eyes, refusing to cry.
She wouldn't allow herself to be duped by this small, un-
characteristic display of tenderness from a man she knew to
be a Judas. *Nay!*

She tried to wriggle away. " 'Tis . . . 'tis something of
which I cannot speak," she said, her voice lower than it
should have been.

"You brought danger to the ship and my men," he said.

"You bring it yourself."

"Aye." The tenderness in his voice disappeared. "But
never have I crossed Sir Manning again. Mayhap, 'tis time."

"Nay, we . . . we must . . . escape him."

Keegan snorted. "Think you he will stop?" Slowly he
pushed her away, his big hands covering each of her shoulders. "He will chase you to the ground, Sheena. Mark my
words. Either he will capture you and drag you back to
Tardiff, or die trying."

Her knees weakened for she knew Keegan spoke the
truth. "Then I must evade him. I must be more clever than
he." The thought was daunting, but not impossible. Refusing to be beaten, she tossed back her hair and lifted her chin.
"I will not give in."

One corner of Keegan's mouth lifted, as if he found her
bravado amusing. "I'm afraid you have more spirit than
brains."

"You should know," she tossed back. " 'Tis a trait you
seem to have honed to perfection."

He laughed then, the deep timbre of his voice rumbling

over the flapping of the sails and the rush of wind. "Nay, m'lady," he said, releasing her. "Not a trait, I fear, but a curse."

"Then we both be damned."

"There be no doubt." His smile fell away and again she was staring into those intense eyes. "Now, be off with you before I do something we both will not want to face in the morning."

For once she didn't argue. She had but to think of his kiss and realize should she stay much longer she would find herself in deep, deep trouble. Her blood pounded through her veins, her heart clamored as if a thousand steeds were galloping through it, but she somehow managed to turn on her heel and run across the ever-undulating deck. Her boot heels rang against the steps as she hurried down the short flight of stairs and hurled herself against the door of the cabin.

Once inside, she drew in several calming breaths, touched her so-recently kissed lips and wondered why this man, this vagabond captain could evoke such passion in her. Why was his kiss forever impressed upon her mind? Just as that cursed touching of lips while on the slippery dock all those years ago had left her weak, senseless, her silly mind swirling with wild thoughts, so had this kiss stolen all rational thought from her mind.

She flung herself on the bunk—his bed—and closed her eyes. But the smell of him was in the small cabin and the taste of his skin was still on her lips.

Oh, what a fool she was. She curled a fist and pounded it impotently against the coverlet. God in heaven, why had she challenged the brute of a captain? Had she not learned her lesson about men? And now Keegan knew who she was. Once his mind had cleared, he would certainly now deliver her to Manning, for he knew that she'd lied to him and would surely realize that there would be a ransom paid for her.

Oh, 'twas a trap she'd thrown herself into. She wound herself in the covers and squeezed her eyes shut.

But she wanted him. As a woman wants a man. Idiot that she was, lying under the covers fully clothed, knowing he was somewhere on this ship, she yearned for him.

Are you certain, Sheena? her mind taunted. *Think hard. Do you really want to share this bunk,* his *bed?*

"I don't know," she said aloud, jumping at the sound of her own voice. Only a few weeks ago she'd been certain that she wanted no man to ever touch her again, that her marriage had destroyed any desire she had.

It was an ominous fateful day when Ellwynn of Tardiff arrived to claim Sheena as his bride. The sky was dark as night, thick, swollen clouds threatening rain as Tardiff, dressed in a blue tunic and dark breeches, sailed through the gates of Ogof upon a galloping black stallion. Servants scattered, chickens squawked and flapped out of the way, a peddler yanked hard on the reins of his stubborn mule as the steed barreled into the inner bailey. Girls who had been carrying pails of water let go of their buckets and jumped from the horse's path. Boys hauling firewood to the kitchens nearly let go of their kindling. Aye, the bastard acted as if he were the lord of this very keep.

"You there, page, tend to the horses and be quick about it," Tardiff yelled to Paul, a young, shy boy. As the boy approached, Tardiff hopped off the wild-eyed steed's back. The horse reared and snorted, and as Ellwynn slapped the reins into the frightened boy's palm, the destrier bowed back its great head. The reins nearly slid from Paul's hand, and it was all he could do to handle the beast.

Sheena observed the wild entrance all from her window. Looking down at the bailey, she cringed at the sight of the man to whom she was unwillingly betrothed.

A dozen soldiers, all on prancing, high-strung beasts, escorted Ellwynn. Dressed in the bold red and yellow of Tardiff, they surveyed the keep and walls of the castle as if they were spies—enemies rather than allies.

Sheena's skin crawled.

Though Tardiff was a handsome man, he was perhaps too much so. His brown hair gleamed with red streaks; his face was chiseled, his jaw square as if it had been hewn by a master mason. On the steps of the great hall he stood proudly, hands on his hips, cape tossed over a shoulder as he surveyed the bailey with a practiced eye.

"Brother!" Fawn cried, streaming out of the great hall as if she could not wait for him to be announced. "'Tis grand you look."

"And you, too, Fawn," he said with considerably less enthusiasm. Though she flung herself into his arms, Ellwynn appeared embarrassed at her display. She wrapped one arm through his, and they walked together to the garden that was located just below Sheena's open window. Their voices, lowered so that the rest of the castle could not overhear, rose on the slight breeze, allowing Sheena to catch each word clearly.

"My men have traveled far. Some are hungry, some need women, and all are thirsty."

"They will be seen to," Fawn assured him, nodding her head rapidly as if in full agreement.

"I knew I could count on you." The Lord of Tardiff laughed, and it wasn't a merry sound. Sheena resisted the urge to spit on him. "So, now, sister, where is the girl who is to be my wife?"

Sheena's stomach turned sour. *Wife.* Oh, sweet Mother Mary, no!

"Come in, come in," Fawn insisted brightly. "She's waiting for you." Suddenly realizing that some of the kitchen maids who had been gathering eggs had stopped to stare at the visitors, Fawn snapped her fingers and commanded abruptly. "Back to work. All of you!" The silly girls nearly dropped their baskets as they dashed off to the kitchen.

"Some of the servants and peasants here appear lazy, sister," Ellwynn observed, peeling away from Fawn's arms and eyeing the blacksmith's and candlemaker's huts where children kneeled and played in the dirt. "It surprises me that you would allow this here in your keep."

Fawn's expression turned to ice. "'Tis the baron. He is too soft with them."

"'Twill come to no good. Servants are like dogs and should be treated as such. Rewarded when they please, beaten when they do not. I see no scaffolding for a hanging should there be need of one, no peasant in your pillory, no example set."

"As I said, my husband is aging. He lacks . . . discipline."

Sheena's blood congealed. Though she did not like her stepmother, she had believed that Fawn loved her father.

Fawn sighed loudly and linked her arms with her brother again. "Come in and see the girls. You will be surprised at them. They have grown much since the last time I brought them to see you. And you've never met the baby, little Lynna—"

"'Tis only Sheena I wish to see," he cut in with irritation. "Your daughters are fine, Fawn, to be sure, but I want to see my bride." He laughed wickedly. "She's a beauty and a fiery-tempered lass, is she not?"

"Sometimes too much so."

"Then I shall just have to tame her, won't I? After all, I be baron."

There was a moment's hesitation, and Sheena felt a short burst of hope that her stepmother would caution the bastard to treat her well. But, of course, Fawn only laughed and said, "Oh, would I were a mouse in the corner to witness that. The girl has been a thorn in my side since I came here. Even after that nasty business with Rourke, when she helped the bastard's son escape. Jestin punished her, but in the end, it was just as before. Jestin spoils her and treats her as if she were his son."

"That will change," Ellwynn decreed, and Sheena, her cheeks hot, again thought she might lose everything she'd eaten that day. "I promise that. After the wedding, when you next see your stepdaughter, she will be meek and obedient.

I look upon her as a challenge, Fawn, and I will break her spirit."

"We'll see."

"Oh, sister, I rarely lose. This you know."

"Oh, yes, brother," Fawn said with a slight edge to her voice. "For you are the Baron of Tardiff." There was a bitterness in her words that Sheena had never heard before. "Come in, come in. There be food and drink aplenty for you and your men. Sheena will be pleased to see you."

"Nay, I think not. If what you say be true, she will not be anxious to meet a man who intends to bend her will to his own."

"She will get used to it," Fawn predicted.

"Or regret it." He laughed, and Sheena thought it the most wicked, disgusting sound she'd ever heard.

In the forest off the main road, Wart lay on his stomach. The ground was cold, his blood warm from a few too many cups of ale, his skin scratched from crawling through briars and brush to stare at the encampment of Tardiff's soldiers.

Lanterns glowed within the few tents crowded in a small clearing, and a campfire, flames crackling, sparks rising to the sky, burned bright. Soldiers squatted near the ring of stones surrounding the fire as they tended the quail and rabbits that sizzled on a spit. Wart eyed the charred meat hungrily. He'd spent more time drinking than eating in the past few days. His stomach rumbled in empty anticipation and his mouth watered. Yet he didn't move, forced his muscles to freeze as surely as if he were a stag who recognized a hunter's spoor.

The soldiers of Tardiff were a sorry lot in Wart's estimation, a scraggly bunch of men who grumbled, and told bawdy jokes that barely brought a chuckle. Warming themselves by the fire, they rubbed their hands and passed a jug of ale or wine between them. For the most part they groused like a gaggle of unhappy fishermen's wives.

Still he waited, his ears straining, hoping he could hear

what he came for without having to approach anyone. From what he'd gleaned, more than a few of the men considered themselves on little more than a fool's mission. They were anxious to return to their families at Tardiff Hall. The names they said were unfamiliar to him: Ellwynn, Fawn, and Jestin—somehow linked. There was talk of murder as well, for the lord—Ellwynn of Tardiff—had been slain by his wife. Few seemed to mourn his passing; most considered him a cruel, useless ruler.

"A bastard if ever there was one," one man with patchy red hair and a pointed nose sniffed as he tore off a piece of charred rabbit, then sucked the bones.

"Aye, mean as a wounded bear, he was," another agreed. He was a portly man with thick arms that bulged as he cleaned his few teeth with the tip of his dagger. "Always kickin' the dogs or whippin' the horses when they be spent."

"Worse than that. He enjoyed wieldin' his power over everyone," a third man, a quiet man who sat cross-legged and stared straight at the spot where Wart lay hidden, admitted. "Baron Tardiff, he had his eye on me daughter, he did, and Kate and I we were afeared he would call for her one night. I thought I might have to send her to live with me sister up ta Twyll, but afore we found means to get her there, he was kilt." The quiet one took a swig from the jug that was being passed, then wiped his mouth with his sleeve. "Good riddance to him, I say."

The wind rustled through the leaves overhead. "So Lady Sheena, she did ye a favor," the round one said.

"Aye, that's what I be thinkin'."

The flap of the largest tent was flung open, and the leader, an ox of a man with a hateful expression and eyes as dark as pitch, strode into the campfire's light. He glanced up at the heavens and frowned. "A storm be brewin'. Christ A'mighty, will nothin' go right?"

"Mayhap this mission be doomed, Sir Manning." The hawk-nosed one spoke up and, as if his muscles were sore, rubbed his forearm with his opposite hand.

"Doomed?" Manning asked, his voice as loud as thunder.

"Aye. The old ones at Tardiff, they claim the Lady Sheena, she be a witch. Is it not possible she cursed us all?"

"You feel cursed, Leonard?"

Somewhere in the distance an owl hooted softly and the wind rushed through the branches of the trees overhead.

Several men shifted uncomfortably as Manning strode toward the fire and loomed above Leonard.

"I repeat only what I heard. Many think Sheena be a witch."

"Gossip. From old women. Nothing more." Manning's suspicious gaze swept the area around the campfire where the men squatted and crouched. "Do any of you others feel as Leonard? Cursed? Doomed?" Before anyone answered, Sir Manning dragged the naysayer to his feet, twisted his arm hard. The man squealed as his shoulder popped from its joint.

"For the love of God, leave him be!" the round one cried, on his feet in an instant.

"Now, I'll hear no more talk of doom or witches," Manning snarled. "There be no dissension in my camp."

Wart was thankful for his nasty little knife hidden deep in a pocket. Sir Manning was a bully, a man who forced obedience by fear, a man who would have no compassion for the woman, if indeed she was Sheena. Two men went to rescue the writhing soldier, forcing his arm back in its socket, and Wart crawled back to the spot where his horse was tied. He didn't want to turn the woman over to the beast who led this band of soldiers, but 'twas not his decision. He would ride to meet up with the ship and warn the captain.

Silently he untied the nag. Some unseen rodent stole through the underbrush in a hurry. Wart didn't move. His ears strained to hear. A twig snapped. Scrabbling for his knife, Wart spun. But it was too late. The tip of a soldier's sharp sword found his midsection.

Wart froze.

"Who be ye?" the soldier asked, his voice echoing over

the wind. It was a voice that stirred unwanted memories. Wart gulped.

"Warren . . . Warren of Halliwell?" the soldier demanded, giving his weapon a little nudge. "And what be ye doin' spyin' on Sir Manning?"

"Oh, nay, I weren't spyin'," Wart lied, wishing he could wrap his fingers around the hilt of his knife, but the point of the sword held him at bay. "I did go up and look, fer I'm hungry and weary and—"

"And ye be a liar, sure as I can tell. I've seen ye before, years ago, Wart. I was there the night ye lost yer thumb. The night ye tried to rob me of me finest horse."

"I—I know not of what ye speak," Wart lied, feigning innocence.

"Do ye not recognize me, Warren? Yer own flesh and blood? I be Peter. The man who married your woman? Remember?" Wart's knees turned to water. "Now, be ye called Warren or do ye still go by Wart, eh? Even if ye seem to have lost yer memory, I haven't."

Wart's heart plummeted. He'd hoped he'd been mistaken. God's teeth, what bad luck!

"Do ya not see that I'm yer cousin?" The pressure on the sword increased, slicing menacingly through Wart's tunic just as the first fat drops of rain fell from the night-darkened heavens.

"Come with me, Wart. I think ye have something to say to Sir Manning." Peter's voice was smooth as warm pudding. "And if he don't kill ye fer spyin', believe me, I will."

Chapter Seven

So the stowaway was Sheena of Ogof.
And, no doubt, Sheena of Tardiff, the woman accused of slaying her husband.

Hiking his mantle more firmly around him, his back pressed against the cabin door, one leg bent at the knee, the other stretched in front of him, Keegan tried and failed to sleep.

The memories were too vibrant. 'Twas as if, in that one kiss, the floodgates of his brain had opened and all the pieces of his life that he'd forgotten rushed forward in a swift, mind-spinning current.

The images were disjointed, but he remembered his father and the crushing grief at the vision of his death. Clearly Keegan recalled the journey to Ogof, his father's mission, the despair at the loss of Bertrice, the rattling dice cups and the fire. But more distinctly, more defined, were his images of Sheena, her red hair streaming behind her as she rode a dark horse as if racing the very wind, the mischievous grin as she, forcing a circlet over her head, ducked into the chapel, and her insistence on saving him from certain death as she'd tugged him through the dank corridors to the cove. But the most brilliant memory, the one that was wedged deep into his brain, was that kiss on the rotting dock, the chill of the air, the warmth of her lips against his, the magical touch and feel of her. He scowled as he thought of abandoning her, of catching a glimpse of her disappointment, the anger as she invoked the furies against him. Only moments later he'd felt the sharp sting of an arrow. He'd given up consciousness with the warmth of her lips still lingering on his.

"Bloody, bloody damn," he growled. And now the girl was a full-grown woman. Sleeping in his bed. And a murderess? A woman capable of slaying her husband? Had it been an accident? How had she come to kill him, if indeed she did? At the thought of the lord he felt a burning jealousy. Who was this man who had won her hand only to have it turned against him? Why had she agreed to be his wife, to obey and honor and love him, then end his life?

It made no sense. Would a woman who was a cold-blooded killer risk her own life not once but twice that he knew of? Not only had she saved him at Ogof all those years before, but she'd climbed the shrouds just the other night to rescue Bo, a boy she barely knew.

No, he wouldn't believe her to be a calculating killer. There had to be more to the tale, more than he'd pieced together from his dealing with . . . His guts knotted. *Manning!* The brute who had pinned his father's hand to the table with his dagger and had tried to kill Keegan. *Manning* was leading the search party. *From Tardiff?* Had the dark knight somehow changed his allegiance?

A thousand questions seared his brain. Some Sheena could answer; others the old liar Hollis might be able to explain. Anger tore through Keegan's veins when he thought of the aged man: Hollis, who had nursed him back to health; Hollis, who had sold the *Warrior* to buy this ship; Hollis, who had dragged Sheena to his cabin on a tether and insisted she was a witch. What was it that the old man feared from her?

Keegan rested his head against the door and stared upward to a pitch black sky where no stars were able to shine through the heavy clouds. Kissing her again had unlocked his memory, aye, but brought with it grief for a father who had died young, new unanswered questions that haunted him as surely as ghosts, and the vibrant images of a sprite of a girl that he'd left to her own fate.

Mayhap he should never have kissed her again. For now the wanting was only worse. Even as the night sky threatened to pour, he was thinking of the sweet, sensual pressure of her lips again.

The mere thought of kissing her caused his manhood to rise and his breeches to become too tight. He imagined the feel of her skin against his, and the hard swelling between his legs began to ache. "Stop it," he muttered to himself, pulling his mantle tighter and attempting to force his thoughts from the woman as the sky opened.

The wind was up, the sails full as the helmsman tacked over the swells. Angry whitecaps rose on the sea, and the *Dark Sapphire* pitched and rolled as she headed ever northward. Soon they would dock, Wart would return, and Keegan would determine what to do with the stowaway.

'Twould be a blessing.

Or mayhap a curse, his traitorous mind taunted. *Could you give her to the soldiers of Tardiff if her life was threatened? What if she did kill her husband, what then? Many of the crew had no doubt done the same, and yet you do not hand them over to the authorities, not even if they have a price upon their sorry heads. And what of Hollis? He's the one member of the crew who is certain of her guilt, the one who refuses to trust her at any juncture. Aye, Hollis knows more than he's said all these years, allowing you to live in the "dark time" when your memory was lost to you.*

Well, the old man had much to explain, Keegan thought, huddling against the rage of the storm, watching the sails bulge and flap as the wind rose. As rain lashed his face, chilling his skin, he considered the warmth of his cabin, just on the other side of the door. Sheena was within—warm, inviting, seductive. And deadly, he was sure of it. She was like a sweet-tasting poison, a slow but oh-so-tempting death.

Gritting his teeth, he silently vowed to himself he would not touch her again. Never.

He had but one more day until they docked, when they would meet up with Wart, and then what? Hand her over to Sir Manning?

How in the name of heaven could he release her to Manning? How would she ever find justice?

And, blast it, he was attracted to her. More so now that he had remembered who she was. Beyond reason.

Aye, she had a sharp, wicked tongue, and he'd experienced more than once the bite of it. Nonetheless, for a reason he refused to contemplate, he looked forward to the sight of her each morn, when her fiery hair was tousled, her eyes still slumberous, her lips spreading into a yawn and her arms stretched over her head as she awakened. He enjoyed her banter and wit, saw that she wasn't afraid of the men, all of whom were now half in love with the witch—well, except for Hollis, of course—but even he was thawing to her appeal while Keegan himself, the man who had told himself all women were the ruin of man, dreamed of making love to her. With each night his thoughts of her turned dangerously erotic.

God's eyes, he would love to strip her bare, cup those firm breasts in his hands, and enter the sweet, wet warmth of her. He would make love to her for hours, until they were both spent and sweating, gasping in each other's arms.

"No!" he growled under his breath as the wind shrieked and the ship bobbed. The rain was unleashed in a torrent, pouring, sheeting, blurring his eyes, stinging his face, and running down his neck. His mantle was soaked, his skin raw and chilled. Not that he cared. He'd been long on the sea, had spent many stormy nights wondering if his vessel would survive a tempest's fury. To this night the *Dark Sapphire* had not let him down.

Lightning split the sky and thunder pealed loudly across the water. Stretching, Keegan climbed to his feet and made his way to the helm, where Henry, the strongest helmsman on the ship, was holding fast to the whipstaff. "I'll finish your shift," Keegan offered, for the man was tired of facing into the storm. There were walls around the helm and a roof that overhung the window, allowing the helmsman a view, but in a tempest such as this, with the shutters open, the wind and rain pelted in.

"Nay, Captain, I can handle her—that is, if the tiller holds true," Henry said. He hazarded a quick glance in Keegan's direction. "Ye're wet as if ye've been swimmin' in the sea. By thunder, Captain, ye best be dryin' yerself out."

"That I will, Henry, after you get a bit o' rest," Keegan insisted, and took over the helm. Few of the men were sleeping this night. Old Hollis found his way to the small room and prayed that they'd be safe, Bo huddled in a corner and tried to act as if he wasn't afraid of the storm, and even Big Tom passed through, eyeing the whipstaff as if he expected it to break in Keegan's hands.

"'Tis a rough one, this," Hollis said as thunder cracked and the helm shifted. Keegan set his shoulders into holding the ship steady. His muscles strained and ached. The ship stayed true.

"We've been through worse."

"But the lady, she hasn't," Bo said. "Is she all right?"

"She'll be fine," Keegan muttered, though he wondered himself.

"Do not worry about her," was Hollis's advice, and he pulled nervously on his beard. The old liar. What other secrets was he keeping? The need to demand answers was strong, but Keegan would not do so with so many crew members about.

"If ye be asking me, I say she's the reason for this storm," Hollis continued.

"Because ye think she be a witch?" Bo asked, then snorted in disgust. "If anything I think she be an angel."

"Be ye in love there, boy?" Jasper said, then went about his business as Bo shot him a look guaranteed to kill. He'd been right, Keegan thought bitterly. Most of the crew were besotted with the woman.

Including you, fool that you be. He shoved that wayward concept aside and with boots planted on the slippery decking strained to keep the *Dark Sapphire* on course.

Henry relieved him just before dawn, but still the storm raged. Cold, furious waves sprayed over the sides of the ship while the wind roared with a voice as deep as if Satan himself were cursing the heavens. Bracing himself against the gusts, Keegan made his way back to the cabin and considered the woman. Was she sleeping through this storm, or was she huddled beneath the blankets cringing in fear? He thought most likely the former, for she didn't scare easily, not even when she'd been little more than a child. Nor did he imagine her holding herself for fear of losing the contents of her stomach, for Sheena had grown to be a worthy sea woman, if there be such a beast, in the past week. Aside from her gender, she was like the men aboard this ship, running, hiding out. The crew of the *Dark Sapphire* were men without pasts, men who had bargained for their lives and agreed to stay aboard or pay to be shipped to a far-off port, far from their mistakes. Keegan had enough cargo—fleece, wool, and twine—to satisfy any officials who demanded to board, but there was a false bottom in the floor of the hold and a space beneath where three or four desperate men could hide. 'Twas a bit of irony that Sheena, had she approached him and paid him for his trouble, could have hidden safely aboard.

As it was, he was caught between trusting her for the fee she offered him and turning her over to those who were looking for her to collect the reward he was certain would be offered by the soldiers of Tardiff. *And Manning!*

For the first time since he'd become captain of this ship he doubted himself, wondered if there was money enough to send Sheena to her fate. Surely he'd saved many a murderer from the gallows before, why not trust the woman? Her money was just as good as any man's.

Lightning forked in the dark heavens. 'Twas a night not fit for man or beast. Rain poured from the sky to run down his cheek. Cold wind sliced through his clothes. His blood was ice.

He shouldered open the cabin door, intent upon having words with the woman, but the sight he beheld stopped him in his tracks. She was sitting on the floor, her eyes closed, her lips moving, the folds of the burgundy-colored dress spread around her like a blood red pool. Murmuring words he didn't understand—was it a spell? Quickly, nearly losing her balance, she scrambled to her bare feet.

"Captain," she said, obviously embarrassed that he'd caught her chanting to whatever pagan gods she believed in. "I—I thought you were steering the ship."

"I was."

She seemed nervous, mayhap because of the storm. Anxiously she glanced at her boots.

The boat shuddered and pitched. She started to fall, caught herself.

"Why are you not in bed?" he asked.

"I couldna sleep—oh!"

Again the ship rocked. Hard. Her feet slipped. Thunder cracked. The ship lurched again. Arms flailing, she toppled forward. Instinctively his hands shot out. He grabbed her around her small waist, held her fast against him.

For a heartbeat she didn't move. Nor did he. She smelled faintly of lavender, her wild hair brushed his chin. Even through the folds of velvet he felt her flesh, heard her catch her breath quickly. She was light in his arms . . . warm. Oh, so enticing. She looked up at him with blue eyes that seemed to see beyond the man to the boy who had kissed her with ardor only to betray her. Her teeth sank into her lip, and Keegan groaned inwardly, for all sense was surely fleeing him. The thought of kissing her lips, touching her white skin, of watching as her pink nipples buttoned beneath his fingers was more than he could stand. Images of making love to her, of kissing her navel and searching out the nest of red-brown curls that surely guarded her womanhood and hid the most delicate parts of her scorched his mind. His frigid blood heated. His pulse throbbed.

"Sweet Mary," she whispered, swallowing hard as those erotic eyes held his.

God help me, he thought as his arms tightened around her. She didn't push him away, yet didn't cling to him as the *Dark Sapphire* steadied. Slowly he released her, but not before the touch of her, the warmth of her body, the scent of her, had burned deep in his soul.

Christ Jesus, how he wanted her. The bed would be warm, her body hot, their passion as wild as this very night. In the light from the lantern he saw that her cheeks were flushed. In the hollow of her throat her pulse pounded.

"The storm will pass." Forcing himself not to reach for her again and tumble onto the bunk with her, he shoved his wet hair from his eyes, strode to the small window, and searched for signs of the coming dawn. The ache in his loins was nearly unbearable.

"If we do not capsize first."

"The *Sapphire*, she's as seaworthy as the best." He glanced back at her and was surprised to find no fear in her gaze. The girl he'd kissed on that rotting dock was a fearless one, possessed of a restless, adventurous spirit. "Worry not." As he peeled off his wet mantle, he noticed she averted her gaze. At first he thought she was embarrassed that he was stripping himself of his sodden clothes, but there was more to her discomfort, it seemed. Suddenly, as if snapped out of a trance, she hurriedly reached for her boots.

"You need not leave." He hung his cloak on a peg, and drips of water puddled upon the floor. "Go back to bed."

She blanched. Her spine stiffened as if a rod had been jammed up it. She began stuffing one foot into a boot. "I will."

"In those?" he asked, eyeing her as she forced the leather up the smooth curve of her calf. He couldn't drag his eyes from her.

"In—in case I needs get up and it be dark and I cannot find them. The deck be too wet to go bare of feet."

"The deck be too wet to walk about it at all." As if she hadn't heard him, she plopped down on the edge of the bunk and bit her lip as she tried to yank her boot higher, though it seemed stuck.

"What were you doing in here?" He motioned toward the center of the wood-paneled room where she'd been kneeling.

"Praying, of course." She looked up at him with luminous eyes, and his gut tightened. Again the ship rocked. The lantern flickered. Sheena nearly lost a boot.

He braced himself. "To Morrigu?"

"To whoever will listen," she tossed back defiantly. The room seemed to grow smaller still, and his mind was filled with thoughts of kissing her and the temptation of her perfect lips.

"Go to bed, Sheena."

"I said—"

"Leave off your boots, throw the covers over you, and go to sleep."

"Why care you what I do?"

"Because, lady," he said, crossing the short distance quickly and grabbing her by the forearms and hauling her to her feet once again. "I be a man without much patience, a man who has been to sea far too long, a man who, like the rest of the men on this ship, would like to bed a woman."

"And—and that be me?"

"Is there another woman aboard?" Her arms were supple and firm beneath his fingers.

"Nay, but if there were . . . ?"

He steeled himself, for he knew that other women had not affected him as this one had. In all his life no other woman had somehow reached beneath his skin and delved as deep as this stowaway of a female had. "Aye," he lied. "No woman would be safe."

Her chin inched up a bit. "I'm not afraid," she asserted, though her eyes betrayed her.

"Then you're foolish."

She stood with such defiance, it was all he could do not to toss her onto the bed and make love to her for the rest of the passage. She managed a humorless grin. "I have prayed to the Great Mother for my safety."

"'Tis of no matter who you pray to. I care not, be it God Himself, the Holy Virgin, or the pagan idols of the old ones. But be warned, Sheena," he cautioned, pointing a long finger at her nose. "I'll not have you chanting and casting spells where the crew might see you."

"Nay?"

"My men, they're superstitious, and . . ." Sweet Jesus, he couldn't look into those night-darkened eyes and not ache for her. His throat was suddenly dry, his groin tight as saddle leather. "They needs have their wits while manning this ship and . . . and I'll not have them distracted . . ."

"You think they be distracted by me?" she asked with feigned innocence. Oh, she was a wicked one, and as the single candle in the lantern cast her face in pale, golden shadows, he remembered the scamp of a girl, his enemy's rebellious daughter who had pleaded with him to take her away from Ogof.

Desire throbbed in his skull. "The crew would be diverted from their tasks by you or any woman."

"As you be?"

"Do not test me."

"I try not." And yet her lips twitched in mocking amusement.

Despite the storm, aside from the fact that she, for all he knew, was running from the gallows, laughter sparked in her night blue eyes. And it was as if they were the only man and woman alive on this storm-tossed ocean, the only two souls in all the known world.

"You be a liar." His hands clenched tightly on her forearms.

"As are you, Captain." Her face was turned up to his, and for the second at least she appeared to have forgotten her blasted boots. Was her smile an invitation or accusation? A temptation to heaven or certain passage straight to hell?

He wanted to shake some sense into her, to make her realize just how dangerous teasing him could be. Instead, without regard to reason, he lowered his head swiftly and placed his eager mouth over hers. Again he felt the sweet torment of her soft lips pressed to his. He thought she might draw back and slap him, might fight and pull away. But she yielded easily. Her mouth opened in silent invitation.

His mind screamed that he was making a mistake he would take with him to the grave, but he gave no heed. He was chilled to the bone, his flesh wet with the clothes on his back, desire pounding a hot tattoo through his brain.

His blood thundered, his skin ached with want, and as he felt the seductive pressure of her lips against his, he forgot every last reason why he couldn't make love to her. His arms surrounded her, and he felt any remaining trace of her resistance melt, her knees weaken, and a sigh, soft as a sea breeze escape from her throat. From that second on, he was lost to her.

Desire drummed through his blood.

As his body pressed urgently against hers, he imagined stripping her bare, kissing her in every dimple upon her skin, making her tremble with the want of him. Hunger raged, his manhood throbbed, and he twined his fingers through those fiery strands and kissed her as if he would never stop.

Sheena gasped, his tongue slipped past her teeth, and she closed her eyes, wanting more. She told herself that she had no choice, for she had to distract him, to take his mind off her boot where the jewels were hidden. Kissing him was only a ploy, or was it?

As her blood heated, she trembled deep inside. Passion as hot as a smith's forge, and an emotion she'd been certain she'd never feel again, trapped her. Through her dress she felt his hands, strong, rough, anxious. Her resistance crumbled to dust.

She tasted the raindrops on his skin, smelled the salt air mixed with the pure male scent of him, felt hard, strident muscles straining through his wet clothes, and wanted him. Oh, dear Lord in heaven, how she wanted him.

His tongue circled and stroked, flicking against the roof of her mouth, causing her blood to sing through her veins. Never had she felt such elation, never had she tingled so with desire, never had she flirted with such certain disaster, for lying with this man, giving herself to him, could only cause heartache, only bring pain.

Think, Sheena, think. Do not cast off your virtue so easily. Do not fall victim to his sweet, hot seduction. Kissing him is madness! 'Twill only bring you agony most vile. Remember that bastard Ellwynn and how he used you! For the love of all that is holy, Sheena, stop this now!

Before 'tis far too late.

And yet she couldn't. Wouldn't. Captain Keegan was not the spoiled Lord of Tardiff; nor did he try to hurt her. There was no pain, only pleasure, oh, such sweet, delicious pleasure. Sheena's eyes closed. Keegan's hands moved anxiously against her back, bunching the fabric of her dress only to smooth it again, causing goose bumps of desire to rise on her skin, awakening a hot yearning deep within the most feminine part of her.

She lifted her arms, linking them around his neck, pushing her body ever closer to his, until the dampness from his tunic soaked her dress. The heat between them, white-hot and pulsing, caused steam to rise. Her breasts ached to be touched, her heart thudded wildly, and deep inside she hungered with a newfound want.

"Sheena," he whispered. "Sweet, treacherous woman." He pulled her hair and kissed the crook of her neck.

"Ooh." She tingled and lolled her head back, wanting more, so much more. Though she knew she was wading into a dangerous, seductive whirlpool from which she might never swim away, she gave herself completely.

His weight was welcome as it forced her onto the bed. Clinging to him, she felt the bittersweet ache of passion pulse through her blood, sighed desperately as his fingers loosened the lacing at her neck.

"Sweet, sweet lady," he whispered, his lips kissing the corner of her mouth, her eyelids and cheeks before dropping lower. "This be a mistake." His breath brushed warm across her neck and the tops of her breasts.

"Aye." Was that her own voice that sounded so breathless?

"One you may regret."

"No . . . yes . . ." she rasped, unable to heed anything but the hot tide of passion roaring through her blood. Her fingers curled in the bedding as he lowered himself and kissed her neck and shoulder as the laces loosened and the bodice of her dress inched downward, over her shoulders, past her breasts. Cool air caressed her skin, only to be followed by the warm, gentle persuasion of his lips.

Think, Sheena, think. Do not lose your head. But it was too late. The velvet slipped over her flesh. He kissed the tops of her breasts. She squirmed, feeling a hot, desperate ache forming deep within her. The ship rocked, the storm pounded the old timbers, but inside, Sheena was melting, wanting, writhing.

The dress lowered farther and he traced a path with his tongue, sliding along the slope of her breast to a nipple, hard and waiting. Sheena gasped as he took the little bud in his mouth, kissing, touching, laving the nipple while her back arched.

More, she thought impatiently, *I want more,* and as if he understood, he took her other breast in his hand and caressed it, gently at first and then more roughly as he suckled. Her blood was on fire, her mind no longer questioning. Her fingers felt the cords of his neck and drove through his hair. With a growl he ripped off his tunic and was upon her, hard,

sinewy muscles running across his shoulders and down the
flat plane of his abdomen. She ran her fingers down his
arms, felt his strength, heard him sigh into her skin. "'Tis a
witch ye be, Sheena," he whispered, his breath rolling across
her fevered flesh. "For you have beguiled and vexed me and
enraptured all my men." His tongue traveled lower and her
lips murmured in pure pleasure as he pulled the dress over
her hips and down her legs.

Sweet Mary, she was hot. Even as the boat swayed and
the rain lashed the cabin, her blood was near boiling, desire
pulsing through her veins. He kissed her navel and she
bucked upward, surprised as his big hands caught her, held
her in the curve of her spine, and he buried his face in the
curls at the juncture of her legs. Fiery as a dragon's breath,
the air from his lungs raced through her thatch to the sensi-
tive skin guarding her womanhood. She wriggled, and he
kissed her hard, his tongue teasing and playing with the
most secret part of her.

As if of their own accord, her hips lifted, and she opened
to him, twisting, giving him more intimate access, her mind
spinning with the wonder of his touch, the storm within her
as violent as that blowing across the sea.

Pressure. Hot and sweet. She was moving, closing her
eyes, rocking, harder, faster, feeling his warm, wet touch
until at last a dam gave way and with a cry she convulsed,
breathing hard, not understanding what had happened.

Her skin was wet with sweat, her heart a drum, her breathing as ragged as if she'd run a hundred miles and yet . . . she
glanced up, saw him unlacing his breeches, and the back of
her throat was suddenly without moisture. The breeches fell
to the floor and she saw his manhood, stiff, hard, thick as he
reached for her again.

With strong arms he drew her to him, kissed her urgently,
and she tasted herself for but a second as his tongue found
and mated with hers and her fingers touched the sinewy
strength of his shoulders and arms. Again she felt the
warmth, again her blood fired, and as he touched her, she re-

sponded, her body still tingling from before, her mind spinning with wanton images of lying with him. The ship creaked and rolled, the bedcovers fell away, and Keegan, dark, mysterious Keegan, kissed her neck and shoulders. Rough, callused hands cupped her breasts, anxious lips kissed her face, hard knees spread her legs as her mind spun. "Please," she whispered, wanting more of him, arching upward.

"Ah, woman, ye vex me," he said, as if admitting weakness, then his lips found hers. She felt him nudge against her, caught her breath as he thrust hard.

She felt a moment's hot pain, gasped, and cried out as his shoulders flexed, and he began to move, slowly at first. She caught his rhythm, rising to meet each of his long, deliberate thrusts, closing her eyes and mind to everything as he began to sweat and breathe as if he couldn't drag in enough air. Faster and faster, as if the ship were spinning in a moon-spangled sea, whirling feverishly.

Hotter and hotter. Time stopped. Sheena closed her eyes, dug her fingers into his flesh as he moved ever more quickly. Sweating, catching his tempo, her mind whirling with flashes of light until she couldn't think, couldn't breathe. The universe was centered in the joining of their bodies, of their spirits. "Keegan," she cried, her voice ripped from her throat.

Her body jolted.

A hot wash of liquid fire exploded behind her eyes. She screamed as she touched ecstasy, her mind no longer with her body.

Keegan threw back his head. Through bared teeth he let out a primal roar somewhere between pleasure and pain.

He collapsed upon her, his skin wet with perspiration, his weight flattening her breasts, his breathing fast and shallow. "By . . . by the gods, woman," he gasped, holding her close, his breath ruffling her hair, "what am I going to do with you?"

"'Twas just what I was thinking," she teased, though as

she realized what she'd done, she felt a tinge of sorrow, for now, certainly, she would have to escape. And soon.

"You were a virgin," he said, and she froze in his arms. "So now the question is, who are you? The woman the soldiers are looking for, a murdering bride who did not lie with her husband? Sheena of Tardiff?"

"It . . . it matters not," she said, but as the warmth of love-making faded, she heard her own lie.

"Then tell me . . . oh, for the love of Mary." His entire body tensed. His arms tightened to iron bands, as if he suddenly realized the calamity of lying with her. As if, despite what they had just shared, he intended to turn her over to Sir Manning and the soldiers of Tardiff. "Do not lie to me any longer," he ordered, and his voice was suddenly cold as the sea. He glared down at her, and even in the shadowy, flickering light from the lantern, she saw realization and condemnation dawn in his steely eyes.

"'Tis time you told me the truth, Sheena," he said, and all the warmth that had been in his voice had disappeared. "Did you marry the Lord of Tardiff only to kill him on your wedding night?"

Chapter Eight

Sheena swallowed hard. Suddenly she felt foolish. She tried to roll off the tiny cot, but Keegan held her firmly beside him, the length of his naked body brushed up against hers, the springy curls of his chest hair tickling her breasts. "Did you kill Tardiff?" he repeated.

Oh, God. She managed to look up at him, this man who had so recently become her lover. "'Tis said you ask no questions of a man's past when they board."

"Aye."

"And yet you make demands of me."

"Because you did not come aboard honestly, now, did you? And you answered not my question." Steely fingers manacled her wrists. "Are you Sheena of Tardiff?"

"Aye." She nodded, unable to lie a second longer.

"So you married the Baron of Tardiff, then sent him to his grave before he bedded you."

She bit her lip, fought against the terrifying, ugly images that crossed her mind. "There was more to it than that," she admitted, and felt him tense beside her.

"How?"

"He . . ." Oh, God, she would not shed a tear for that bastard who had been her husband, *would not!* "'Twas the wedding night. He, uh, he drank much and . . ." Shivering, she willed hot tears backward, forced her mind to view what had happened as if to someone else, not her. ". . . he tried to bend my will to his."

"You would not take to his bed."

"Nay, I—I was there. I was . . . willing to do what I had promised, but . . . I loved him not. He was my father's choice, the brother of my father's wife. And when we were alone . . . he wanted me to do more than . . ." Her voice faded and she avoided Keegan's eyes. "Tardiff was drunk. He had a knife and brought another woman in, a serving girl. . . . She was Tardiff's lover, and he wanted the three of us to . . ." Shuddering, she sighed, her voice aquiver, Keegan's eyes intense and dark. Unreadable. "I objected and he pulled out his dagger, laid it upon my throat and . . . and I disobeyed him."

Keegan's eyes swept to her neck, and he touched the scratch now nearly healed with one finger. "He did this?" His voice was low. Ominous.

"Aye."

"Anything else?"

"He dinna get the chance," she said, biting her lip and looking away.

"But he threatened you?"

"Promised to cut me if I did not do everything he ordered. We struggled. Fought. I—I was able to wrest the blade from him."

"So you stabbed him." His voice was without condemnation.

"If I had not, he would have done the same to me," she said, not expecting Keegan to believe her. "If not for Fannie, the serving girl, I do not think I would have been able to escape. She helped me and . . . I fled Tardiff Hall."

His hand cupped her naked shoulder, and he forced her to meet his night-darkened gaze. "You did not go back to Ogof?"

"Nay." Sheena shook her head, heard the rush of the wind and the roar of waves battling the *Dark Sapphire*'s hull. "As I said, my father's wife, she is the Baron of Tardiff's sister."

"Lady Fawn," he said as if drawing up an image of the cold, calculating woman.

Scowling darkly, not releasing her, Keegan let out his breath. "So you ran away because you killed your husband and were worried for your life?"

"Yes. There are those who would see me hanged."

"Including your father?" he asked, his jaw tightening as he remembered the man who had slain Rourke so callously. It was all clear to him now, that dark time when he'd been half-besotted with a fiery-haired girl who had helped him escape.

"Mayhap," she said as his grip relaxed, and she, desperate to get away from him, from his bed, from their so recent lovemaking, tried to roll away. He would have none of it and suddenly was upon her, pinning her to the bed with his body. "But—until a few moments ago, you were a virgin. Do not try to lie to me," he said. "What of your husband?"

"We fought before . . . before 'twas done," she said, shuddering at the memory and feeling ashamed as she lay naked with this man, one who was not her husband, one she did not love . . . or could she? Oh, 'twas foolish to think of it.

Bam! Bam! Bam! "Captain? Be ye awake?" Hollis yelled, pounding his fist upon the door.

"Go away."

"But Henry. He needs yer help at the helm."

The ship shuddered, old timbers moaned, and Keegan, swearing under his breath, released her. He rolled off the bed and yanked on his breeches quickly.

Sheena reached for her dress as Keegan crossed the small space and threw open the door.

"What of Henry?"

"He's tired, methinks, or mayhap has been in his cups too much," Hollis said as Sheena swiftly squirmed into the wine red velvet. Keegan was large enough to block most of the door with his body, hiding her from view. If the old man caught a glimpse of her, he was wise enough to hold his tongue.

"Bloody Christ!" Keegan snapped up his tunic and mantle.

"I tell ye true, Keegan, the ship will capsize."

"Not this night. Tell Henry I'm on my way."

"Aye," the old man said, and was out the door.

Keegan whirled on Sheena. "You," he said as she slipped one leg from beneath the bed and reached for her boots. "Stay put."

"But I—"

"Do not argue with me." His eyes flashed and he grabbed his wet mantle. Quickly donning the cloak, he found his boots and pulled them on. "This cabin. 'Tis the safest place for you."

"But I might help."

"You'd be in the way. I need concentration, as do the crew. There be not time for"—he motioned with his hand by his head as if he could not find the right word—"for any interruption." Then he straightened, reached for the door, and paused again. His broad shoulders slumped a bit, and he sighed. "Please, Sheena. Do not leave. 'Tis only that I fear for your safety."

"How noble you be," she mocked, unable to keep her tongue still as the great masts creaked and the wind shrieked.

"Do not test me, woman, I have no time for it." Then he was out the door. It slammed shut, leaving Sheena alone in the bed, listening as his boots rang up the stairs. She counted to ten, then, convinced he would not return, she swung out of bed, tightened the laces of her dress and yanked on her boots. The stones were still tucked inside one, cramping her toes, reminding her that she had little time. If they were to dock the following night, she had much to do.

Once the storm abated, *if* it let up, she would leave the vessel and take her chances alone. The ship would be close to shore and she could lower a rowboat and make her way to land. She felt more than a little tug of regret at the thought of leaving the *Dark Sapphire*, for she had felt an awkward peace aboard the ship, a sense of safety as she'd realized that the soldiers of Tardiff could not discover her as long as the ship was at sea. Asides, she would miss Bo and Jasper and Seamus . . .

And Keegan?

Oh, God, yes! He was gruff, harsh, seemingly unforgiving, a man she'd sworn she hated, couldn't trust. She tossed a glance at the rumpled bed, still smelling of sex. Fool that she was, she knew she'd long for him with all her body and heart.

Angry at the turn of her mind, she gave herself a swift mental kick. This was no time to be maudlin or sad. Just because he'd bedded her was no reason to trust him. Had he whispered that he loved her? Or even cared for her? Nay. He'd mentioned some fear for her safety, but she doubted it was for any other reason than he intended to sell her back to Manning or demand payment from her.

Love?

Never. Captain Keegan knew not the word.

She paused, touched the fine velvet of his wife's dress, and her heart twisted. Mayhap he had once loved, but 'twas another woman, a woman who had betrayed him.

Oh, fool that she was, her heart ached for him, though there was no time for it. She had to plot her escape and make it good.

And it had to be soon.

The ship pitched, masts groaned in the wind, and rain flailed the decks and hull. Sheena sent up a quick prayer for safety of ship and crew. Once the storm receded, she would leave the *Dark Sapphire* and the demanding captain behind.

Her throat tightened at the prospect and she called herself every kind of fool, for she was beginning to care for the brute who steered this ship, the man who had left her standing alone once before.

She gathered up her few belongings and hurriedly finished dressing. Knowing that once she escaped the *Dark Sapphire* she would never see Keegan again, she felt a moment's chill.

Stupidly, her heart tore a bit. She glanced at the bed where they'd so recently made love. Keegan was a bastard, true, a blackheart whom she couldn't trust, and yet a part of her wanted to feel his strong arms surround her, wanted to kiss him and taste the salt water on his warm lips, to lie with him again and experience the thrill of his skin rubbing against hers.

But it could never be.

Theirs was a few short hours of desperate passion, nothing more. She found her mantle, threw it over her shoulders, and fought this newfound and unlikely sadness.

She had thought after her horrid, agonizing wedding night that she would never want a man to touch her again. The memory of that horrible night lingered with her still. . . .

Sheena whispered her vows in front of Father Percival at Tardiff Hall—removed from those that she loved. There was an underlying malaise within the recesses of the dark, unhappy keep, a chill that danced upon Sheena's neck as she knelt and forced out the horrid words of obedience and commitment. Sheena felt the discontent as she suffered through the knowing glances cast her way, witnessed the nudges of elbows of the soldiers of Tardiff Hall, and realized that they were sharing a joke at her expense. Though Tardiff had raised his cup to her at the meal after the ceremony and had demanded all of the servants obey her and treat her as a lady, she had caught him winking at a large-bosomed serving girl. The lass had swallowed a smile and blushed to the roots of her hair.

Sheena had been mortified, but the worst was yet to come.

That night, after her father and Fawn left Tardiff, she and her new husband were alone in his chamber. Sir Manning, a

gift from Lady Fawn, was posted as a sentry on the other
side of the door to the lord's chamber, but Sheena held no illusions that the dark knight had been left to protect her as
much to see that she did not escape. The surly knight had
been her shadow in the days before the wedding. Otherwise
she would have fled Tardiff and its lord.

Ellwynn closed the door with a thud. Turned the lock.

Sheena, shivering inwardly, swallowed back her fear and
told herself there were worse fates than submitting to her
husband. 'Twas a man's right and, she'd heard from the gossiping old women as they'd shelled beans or pared apples, it
could be very pleasant. Sheena had seen dogs and horses
mate. She'd known some of the laundry maids at Ogof who
had giggled and told stories of the thrill they'd experienced
kissing and loving a man. But to her, with the Baron of
Tardiff, the thought was vile.

Tardiff crossed the room, where a fire was dying in the
grate. "Come here," he demanded as he stood by a large bed
covered with the skins of animals. Throughout the room
small indentations held candles that burned weakly, tallow
dripping down the wall. Two windows were open, but no
breath of wind stirred the single tapestry draped over the
bed.

She hesitated.

"I said, come here," he repeated, and his words seemed to
echo against the coved ceiling while the red embers of the
fire glowed brightly. His voice was calm, and he spoke as if
to a slow-learning child. "And when I say those words, you
reply, 'Yes, my lord,' and do my bidding. 'Tis the same
when I command you to do anything. Your response is 'Yes,
my lord.'"

"Nay," she said, shaking her head. "I'll not—"

"Come here, *wife*."

She froze.

"Remember, 'Yes, my lord.' And then you do my bidding," he repeated with slow patience.

Anger spurted through her veins. "And when I ask you to do something, will you say, 'Yes, my lady?' "

His eyes flared with silent fury. "Do not make me angry," he warned.

"Then do not order me about as if I were a slave."

He glared at her. One of his nostrils drew up a bit. "Do not make me come after you or you'll regret it. Come, Sheena. Now."

She glanced at the door.

" 'Twould be foolish," he cautioned, "and to no avail. This is my castle. My men stand guard and do as I tell them. As you will. Now. Come *here*." With one long, arrogant finger he pointed at a spot on the floor just in front of him.

Clenching her teeth, knowing that to say anything further would infuriate him and only cause her pain, she approached.

"That's better." His eyes slitted and he appraised her. "Now, take off your clothes."

She froze. "But—"

"Do it, Sheena, and do it quickly. I want to see you naked." His lips barely moved when he spoke, and drops of sweat beaded his forehead, slipped through the strands of his hair.

Throat dry, again she glanced at the door, locked and bolted, with Sir Manning posted on the other side. With fumbling fingers she removed her belt and gown, tossing them onto the rush-strewn stones of the floor. She wanted to die, to save herself this humiliation, but death was far from her, it seemed. Shivering, she stood in her chemise and felt as if the entire castle could see her. Tardiff smiled coldly, then motioned with his finger to her chemise. "That as well. Get rid of it."

Gritting her teeth, Sheena obeyed, letting the lacy undergarment slide down her body to pool on the rushes and leave her naked as the day she was born. Though mortified, she managed to stare straight at her tormentor.

His smile was pure evil, made all the more sinister by the

dying light. "I see I have bargained well." He twirled a long finger in the air, motioning for her to turn before him. "Aye, ye be a nice piece of flesh, wife. You will suit me well. Stay." He walked to the fire, where on a small table three mazers of wine were waiting. Sipping from one, he paced the room slowly, his eyes turned in her direction, watching her intently as if searching for flaws and imperfections. "Your father assured me you were a virgin."

She elevated her chin and glared at him, refusing to answer.

"Are you?" He took a long swallow from his cup.

"Are you?" she tossed back before she could think twice.

"Mind your waspy tongue, woman, or you'll pay for your impertinence." He swirled his wine. "But nay, wife," he said, and she cringed at her new title. "I assure you that I am quite skilled in the art of lovemaking. You will be well satisfied."

She didn't respond, just held her ground, squared her bare shoulders, and tried vainly not to tremble. Though patience was not in her nature, she had learned to watch and wait, her father stressing that biding one's time was considered a virtue whenever she accompanied him on a hunt. This night she felt as if she were the prey. But she would wait. Smoke curled up from the nearly melted candles, and the fire gave off a soft hiss.

Sheena's nerves were strung tight, and she prayed she'd find a way to get through the long night ahead. Mayhap the baron, who seemed so fond of wine, would be well into his cups tonight and fall asleep.

She could only hope.

Plucking a small bag from the table, Ellwynn winked at her, then poured out its contents. Vibrant gems gleaming red, gold, and green sparkled in the firelight as they tumbled to a stop.

Her heart was wrenched as she recognized her mother's jewels. "Nay," she whispered.

"Part of your dowry." Ellwynn sighed as he fingered the

stones. "A pity the blue one's missing. 'Twas the most valuable of the lot, worth much more than these three together. But your fool of a father lost it in a game of chance, my sister claims." He dribbled the jewels through his fingers. "But this be payment enough, I suppose." He held the gold stone aloft and stared at its many facets. "Asides, it was rumored to be cursed, not that I believe in such things."

Sickened at the thought that her father had given her mother's precious stones to this beast, she dragged her eyes away. As if satisfied with her reaction, he finished his wine, set down his cup, and clapped his hands. "Page! More wine."

With a creak, part of the wall opened up, and through a hidden doorway a page appeared carrying a vessel. He was a gawky boy who averted his eyes as he hurried through his chore. Sheena, burning with embarrassment, turned her back to him and silently wished the horrid man who was now her husband would drop dead in the rushes.

She felt rather than saw the boy leave the jug, then retreat through the hidden doorway.

"Be you embarrassed of your body?" her new husband asked.

"Nay, but neither do I display it!"

"That will change. You have no reason to feel any shame. You are, I assure you, genuinely perfect. As beautiful as any of the stones that were given me for taking you off your father's hands."

She wasn't warmed by his compliment, only sickened. "I will not allow—"

"Lie down on the bed!" Tardiff ordered, cutting off her protests. She heard him loosening his belt. Her stomach clenched, and she slowly sank onto the bed. *It will be over soon, this act of lovemaking, though no one would think of love at this coupling.*

"You can watch me undress, wife," he invited, and she heard him removing his clothes. She didn't move, but he walked in front of her proudly, like a strutting peacock.

Though he sickened her, she raised her eyes to his and re-fused to show him any sign of weakness. He had already discarded his tunic and was unfastening his breeches. All too soon they fell to the floor and he was naked, too. Inside, Sheena shuddered in revulsion. He was a tall, muscular man, strong, but with the hint of soft flesh about his belly—the suggestion that he would someday soon run to fat.

He was carrying his cup and tossed back his wine in one swift motion. "Now, wife, we have business, you and I."

She steeled herself. "Be ye ready for me?" he asked, and when she didn't reply, he laughed as if at a private joke. "Well, ye will be." Calling over his shoulder, he yelled, "Fannie, girl? 'Tis time."

From the hidden doorway a woman appeared. Sheena re-membered her—Zelda's daughter. Zelda, who had served Sheena's mother, then Fawn when she had married Jestin. Fannie had been sent to Tardiff to punish some minor wrong Fawn had claimed Zelda had committed. For a second Sheena felt relief—mayhap Fannie would take her place—but knew it was a false hope.

With nary a glance at Sheena, Fannie swallowed hard, crossed the rushes to the naked lord, kissed him soundly on the mouth, and squealed when he grabbed one of her but-tocks through her skirt and pinched hard. "Like that, do you, wench?" he asked, his eyes gleaming with a malevolent light as he looked past her shoulder to Sheena on the bed.

"Aye, m'lord," Fannie said, though her eyes seemed to have no luster.

"What is this?" Sheena demanded as the lord guided the girl to the bed.

"Fannie will be joining us."

Sheena's stomach roiled. No matter how distasteful she found Ellwynn, she had never expected this depravity.

"Nay." Sheena spat the word. "'Twas bad enough that I was to lie with you as your wife, but I'll not share the bed with her and you and—"

Smack!

The flat of his hand slammed against her cheek.

Her head snapped back from the blow. Pain exploded behind her eyes. She stumbled backward. Tasted blood. Before she could defend herself, Tardiff lunged. The weight of his body forced her onto the bed. "I've had enough of your arguing with me at every turn," he growled, his eyes dark with hate and more—lust and arousal.

"Get off me."

"Not until I've had my way, wife!"

She struggled. Slap! He hit her again. Pain ripped through her.

"Nay." Fannie was shaking her head, holding her arms tightly around her. "Do not hurt her, m'lord, please."

"Stay out of this."

"But—"

"Or you'll get some of the same," he yelled, his face red, a vein pulsing in his forehead as he pinned Sheena to the bed.

"But she's just a girl."

"She's my wife," he snarled, holding Sheena down as she struggled to free herself. She fought from instinct, kicking, clawing, writhing. The more she fought, though, the stronger and more determined he became. His member was swollen and stiff and rubbed anxiously against her abdomen as she tried to push him away from her.

"Oh, I knew you'd have fight in you," he said, panting and sweating and reeking. His eyes gleamed. His mouth pulled back in an evil, ugly grin. "I'll show you what it is to serve a husband." He forced her knees apart with his, and she closed her eyes, told herself to let it happen but couldn't. She twisted, trying to throw him off, but he was too heavy, too intent.

"Fannie," he ordered. "Come here."

"Oh, no, m'lord, please. The lady, she is not yet accustomed to this." Then to Sheena she pleaded, "Please, lady, do not fight him."

"I'll have no back talk from you," Ellwynn snarled, turning his head a fraction and glowering at the serving maid with his hateful eyes. He was panting, tiring. " 'Twill be your turn to please me as well, and you'd bloody well do my bidding or I'll turn you over to my men and they be not as kind as I."

Tears filled Fannie's eyes. "A-aye, m'lord," she said meekly. The fire popped and somewhere far away, on the other side of the door, a dog barked.

"That be better." Ellwynn's horrid gaze returned to Sheena. "Now, wife, beg me to take you."

Sheena stared up at him. Clenched her jaw. Felt blood dripping from the corner of her mouth.

"Now."

"I'll beg nothing of you," she vowed.

He grinned. "Nay? Oh, woman, be careful." He was enjoying humiliating her, and at that second she hated him more than any man on earth. Positioned above her, his stiff cock brushing her naked belly, he reached under the bed with his free hand and retrieved a knife, a bone-handled dagger with a hideously curved blade.

"Now, wife, you will do my bidding," he warned. "Or I will be forced to use this." The blade winked in the candlelight. "And I would hate to."

"May your soul go straight to hell," she replied, refusing to stare at the horrid knife.

His muscles flexed and his nostrils flared in rage. "Oh, I intend to, wench. And I'll take you with me."

"I be already there," she swore. She saw the blade move and she reacted, drawing up her knee. Fast. Hard. To connect with his groin.

Ellwynn roared in rage and pain.

"Oh, merciful God, no," Fannie whispered. She gasped in horror, and Sheena tried to slide away as the Baron of Tardiff howled in pain and his body coiled around his groin. Rolling back and forth, swearing loudly, he clenched himself together in agony.

"Now, ye've done it," Fannie whispered, her eyes round

in horror as she backed away from the bed. "He'll kill us both."

"Not me, he won't." Sheena sprang from the bed, ran to the door, and pounded with her bare fist on the thick oaken planks. "Sir Manning! Open this door at once. The baron is ailing!" she cried, intending to run past the sentry when he opened the door.

With a roar Tardiff exploded from the bed. "You foolish piece of flesh," he said, flying across the room and throwing himself at her.

She ducked, but he was quick, grabbed her by her hair, and flung her against the wall.

"Ooof." She slammed against the lime-washed stone. Every bone in her body was jarred. A table toppled, candles fell to the floor.

She tried to scramble away, but he threw her against the door.

Bang!

Her head cracked hard against oaken planks, and he pinned the length of her body with his.

"I will have you, wench, and you'll never forget this night. Never forget that I own you." Behind him flames crackled in the rushes.

"You'll have to kill me first."

"So be it." He lifted his hand, and she saw the ugly knife, curved and raised. Her heart pounded. There was no escape.

"Oh, sweet Mary," Fannie whispered. "Look what's happened here!" Quickly she poured water from a pitcher on the rapidly spreading fire, sending steam and smoke toward the ceiling. "Do not hurt her, m'lord."

"She deserves it."

"But not the knife." From the corner of her eye Sheena saw the woman make a quick sign of the cross over her naked bosom as smoke hung low in the air. "Not the knife, please."

"Lord Tardiff! Be ye all right?" Manning yelled from the other side of the door.

"Leave us!"

"But there be smoke and sounds of a fight and—"

"Leave us!" Ellwynn thundered, the cords in his neck rigid. Quickly he placed the knife near Sheena's throat, and she felt the sting of its blade as it broke her skin ever so slightly.

"Oh, sweet Jesus," Fannie whispered. "Nay . . . oh, nay . . ."

Sheena, Tardiff in tow, inched toward the hidden door. Nervous sweat gleamed on her body, blood dripped from the shallow cut, fear consumed her while the smell of smoke and burnt tallow was heavy in the air.

"By all that is holy and all that is not, I curse you, Ellwynn," she said, holding his ugly glare with her own, but her hands were working, fingers creeping along the wall to an indentation where a candle was burning. "Not only God but the Earth Mother as well shall condemn you."

"So you'll use your witchcraft, will you? We shall see." He shifted. The blade flashed. Sheena spat hard. "Wha—" In the split second that he jerked back, she reached for the candle, grabbed it, and jabbed it in his bare, sweaty abdomen.

Hisssss.

"Aaaaagggghhh."

The smell of burning flesh and hair filled the air. He dropped the knife. The candle fell away.

"I'll kill you," Tardiff screamed, writhing in pain. Sheena wasted no time as he jumped at her. She fell to the floor, hot rushes burning her skin, her fingers curling over the bone hilt of the weapon.

"I'll teach you to—"

She whipped around and without thinking plunged his own knife into his side. Blood spurted from the wound. Tardiff's face blanched. He bellowed in pain.

She ran, stumbled, ran faster. As he fell to the chamber floor, collapsing in a pathetic heap, blood pooling around him, she snatched up her clothes and fought the nausea that burned up her throat. *You've killed him! Merciful God in heaven, Sheena, you've murdered your husband, the lord.* Staggering on legs that threatened to give way, she made her way to the hidden doorway, where Fannie, quivering, her eyes wide and disbelieving, waited.

"Oh, my God, oh, my, God . . . oh . . . Run," the serving girl cried. "Run as far as you can, for this one, if he lives, he'll hunt you down like a stag in the forest and kill you sure. And—and take these . . ." She stuffed the stones into Sheena's outstretched palm, closed the door behind them and, using a hand against the wall for guidance, took off at a dead run, leading Sheena down a curved stairway. Tears ran down Sheena's cheeks though she felt no sorrow, her bare feet scraping against the floor. She and Fannie careened down the corridor, stumbling, falling, scratching themselves as they heard the squeal of terrified mice racing away. At the main floor there was a fork in the tunnel. "Wait." Fannie slipped through a door and returned quickly with a burning taper. "Go that way," she said, "it leads beneath the portcullis and into the moat. Oh, by the gods, ye're bleeding."

"I care not." Teeth chattering, Sheena threw her dress over her body. She had to get out. To find freedom. To put as many miles between her, the dead baron, and Tardiff Hall as she could.

"Then be off with ye. Take care and God speed, m'lady," Fannie whispered, biting her lip and choking back tears. "I—I must go back and sound an alarm, for if I don't, if—if I do not, the lord will kill me as well."

"Thank you," Sheena said. "You didn't have to help me—"

"There be no time for this. Run! Go! Now."

Sheena didn't argue. Shivering with fear, she drew on her boots.

Through the tunnels, cupping the candle's weak flame, praying she would be able to escape, she ran until she reached a door, unlatched it, and smelled the moat in the darkness. She could not see it was so dark, but she sent a prayer toward the heavens and jumped, not knowing if she would live or die.

"You knew who she was," Keegan finally accused, manning the whipstaff. His fingers curled over the long rod attached to the tiller, and he strained against the bucking of the sea. "You knew she was Sheena of Ogof."

Hollis was the only other person in the room besides Bo, who was huddled in the corner and sleeping despite the turbulent, raging waters.

"Why did you not tell me?"

"I thought it best," the older man admitted. "And when I first came upon her in the hold, I dinna know."

"But you did soon after."

"Aye." He rubbed his balding head and bit his lip.

"You claimed she was a witch."

"I wanted ye to stay away from her." He steadied his legs as the *Dark Sapphire* shuddered. "She be the daughter of the man who kilt yer father. She be the one ye left when ye escaped Ogof. She has reason enough to hate ye, Keegan. I trust her not."

Keegan's teeth clamped together, and he steered the ship against the thrashing power of the black water. His muscles ached and strained, and yet he sensed the storm calming, felt the tiller respond. "I never knew you to lie to me, Hollis. I did not expect it."

The old man had the decency to cast down his eyes. "'Twas a mistake. But since you remembered not, I thought it best." He lifted a shoulder and sighed.

"You were wrong."

"Mayhap. But she's cast a spell on ye, lad. She cursed ye, she did. When ye were near death and not awake, healing from yer wounds, ye flailed and cried out, talking of her and the curse. I was sure ye were about to die, I was. Because of her. I tried to tend to ye, to comfort ye, but 'twas as if ye had no mind. I believed she'd damned yer soul to the devil and that was why ye were not wakin' as ye should."

"I believe not in curses."

"Then ye be a fool," Hollis insisted. "And ye did then, when ye were lyin' on the bunk, sweatin' and swearin' and callin' out fer help." His old hands lifted upward. "Rantin' and ravin' ye were, as if Satan himself had taken over yer soul." Sighing, Hollis worried his cracked lips with his teeth. "And then, after all this time, she appears here on the ship, hidin' in the damn hold, the daughter of the man who kilt yer father, the woman who swore vengeance against ye. If not the spell of a witch, then that of a beautiful woman. They have ways of turning a man's head, of telling him what he wants to hear, of getting what they want. She has no reason to love ye, Keegan. Nay, she has all the more reason to despise ye."

That much was true, though Keegan still didn't believe that Sheena had cursed him. "What other secrets are you hiding?"

"None," the old man said so swiftly, Keegan knew it to be a lie.

"Nay?"

"I'm tellin' ye true—"

"What of my mother?" Keegan demanded, thinking back to other times he'd been certain the old man was altering the truth. "Each time I ever spoke of her, you held your tongue, but there was something in your eyes, I know it."

Hollis scowled, picked at his beard.

"What?" Keegan insisted, fury burning through his blood. "What is it you are keeping from me?"

Studying the floor, the old man shook his head slowly, as if arguing with himself. "Lorinda . . . she was my sister."

For a second Keegan didn't move. The whipstaff shuddered. "You lie."

"Nay. 'Tis true. She—she was always a wild one. She met yer father, got with child, and me own father threw her out." Guilt filled his ancient eyes. " 'Twas because of me that she came to meet Rourke; 'twas after Bertrice."

Stunned, Keegan sucked in his breath, held onto the long

pole attached to the tiller, as if he intended to break the damned thing. "You're tellin' me that you be my uncle," he accused, suspicion evident in his words.

"Aye. 'Tis true."

"And yet you never told me."

"Nay."

"By the gods, Hollis, I should throw your miserable carcass overboard." He seethed as other questions blazed in his brain. "Lorinda." He would not think to call her Mother any longer. "Be she alive?"

Hollis shook his head. "Nay. She died long ago, before Rourke was killed."

A dozen emotions he'd never felt before assailed him as he steered the ship. "How?"

"Ye do not want to know—"

"I do! Tell me." He threw the older man a hard, unforgiving stare and would've shaken some sense into him if he'd dared to release the whipstaff for a second.

"She married a farmer, worked herself to the bone, and took ill the first winter. Died within a fortnight." Hollis frowned. "I was at sea with Rourke and you at the time. Didn't find out that she'd passed on until the next spring."

"So you stayed with my father because of me?" Keegan asked, his mind searching for answers.

"'Twas one of the reasons."

"And the others?"

"'Twas fond I was of your father. And you. And the sea."

"You're scared to death of the sea."

A strange smile played over his lips as Keegan strained against the bucking of the waves. "And yet I love it, I do."

Keegan wiped one hand on his breeches. "Lorinda. Did she ever ask about me?"

Hollis hesitated. The wind shrieked. Keegan felt a bitter disappointment even before the answer.

"Nay."

So that was it. Keegan felt a loss that he would not consider for a mother's love he'd never known. But he'd survived and he would not grieve for a woman who bore him in shame and gave him away. Hollis headed for the door, but Keegan, arms straining, had more questions. "Be there other secrets ye keep, old man?" he asked caustically, his eyes narrowing into the rush of air that swept through the open window.

"Nay."

"No?" Keegan didn't believe him. His mind was spinning with questions that had been unanswered since the dark time. "What of the ring?"

"Ring? There be no ring," Hollis replied, but something flickered in his gaze.

"The ring with the Dark Sapphire of Ogof, the stone you were certain was cursed. What happened to it?" A wave splashed over the deck, the ship shivered. Keegan gritted his teeth.

Hollis bit his lip, glanced up, and Keegan braced himself for yet another lie. "I sold it."

"You sold it? A ring with a stone that valuable?"

"Aye." He nodded, scratched his balding pate, and said, "I barely escaped with me own life, there at Ogof. Had it not been for the fire and the confusion and the lucky fact that the guard who was hauling me off to the dungeon was scared for his child's life, I would have died. Heard her cryin', the guard did, and released me for a minute. I made it to the shore, and while the other soldiers were hurrying to the castle to put out flames, I stole the rowboat we came in on, and found you. Bleedin' to death from arrow wounds ye were and clutching that damned stone as if it were blessed from God. When I finally got ye back to the ship—"

"The *Warrior*," Keegan said, remembering his father's craft and the man who had so bravely manned her, the captain who had been both father and mother to him. For this parent he still grieved.

"As I said, for the first few weeks it was nip and tuck, didn't know if ye were gonna pull through, in a deep sleep ye were—rantin' and screamin' about the curse. I spoon-ladled ye soup and cleaned yer wounds, but I feared that Jestin's army would be after us, so after a week or so, I sold the boat to an Irish sea captain and bought another—this one." He patted the walls with a loving hand. "Used the money from the *Warrior* and the Dark Sapphire as well."

"Who bought the ring? What was his name?" Keegan asked suspiciously as he realized how easily the old man had lied to him over the years. For love? Or for his own gain?

"The owner of this boat bought the cursed gem, I'm tellin' ya. A man who said his name was Kroft, but I be doubtin' that, though I never called him on it. We both had something to hide, he and I. Fer all I knew he was a pirate and had stole this ship. As for the Dark Sapphire, it belonged to Ogof. So we asked no questions and the trade was made. I renamed the ship, just to remember, and set to sea. Ye awoke a week later, but ye didna remember anything. Not the battle, the fire, the stone, yer father's death, not even the girl who helped ye escape."

"Sheena," Keegan said softly, scowling as the lanterns bounced shifting yellow shadows on the walls. The smell of the sea was everywhere. His thoughts turned toward the clouded time that had been hidden from his memory, so long forgotten. He held firm to the whipstaff, fighting the pull of the sea and the strength of the wind, using all his muscles as he guided the ship through the rough water. His shoulders and arms ached from the task. Despite the icy breath of the wind, sweat sprinkled his brow, slickened his palms, and ran down his spine. Gritting his teeth and throwing his back into his work, he wondered what would happen when they docked. He only hoped that Wart was waiting for them and had news of Tardiff's soldiers.

"I dinna want to deceive ye, Keegan."

"But you did."

"Aye." Hollis nodded sadly, though Keegan doubted the old man's show of remorse. He'd had plenty of time to undo his untruth and confide in Keegan. But he hadn't. Hollis's secrets regarding his mother, Sheena, and the Dark Sapphire of Ogof had been locked away for too many years.

Keegan's eyebrows drew together and he turned his concentration to steering the ship. Little by little, as Keegan refused to think of the woman who had borne and abandoned him, or the girl he'd later betrayed and was now his lover, the storm slowly abated.

Old Hollis, curse his story, lying hide, was right about one thing, though: Sheena was far more trouble than she was worth.

Or was she?

It occurred to him that he was beginning to fall in love with her, and he quickly banished the thought. Love was only for fools. He'd learned that lesson all too well years before at his wife's hands.

Never again would he fall victim. *Never.*

Baron Jestin of Ogof rolled over and reached for his wife. Though Fawn was heavy with child and refused him these days, he had need of a woman. He was anxious, his cock stiff with want, his mind worried. There were many troubles within the castle walls. The steward was forever prattling that the cook was skimming spices from the larder or that the candlemaker was behind, forever in his cups, or some other bothersome concern. Lately there had been trouble collecting wood-penny, agistment, and chimiage. The peasants were cutting firewood, grazing their animals, and carrying goods through the forest without paying the proper taxes.

There had been a restlessness within the castle walls since Sheena left, a cloak of discontent that covered the keep, and Jestin felt as if he could trust no one.

Worst of all, there was another worry he'd been carrying around with him for the better part of a week. 'Twas his piss. Ah, there had been a time when his stream had been strong as a stallion's, and clear; then it had grown weaker and murkier, though he'd ignored it. Now, however, 'twas often black with blood, and he wondered if he was dying. Rotting from the inside out. He'd not yet called the physician, for he did not want to face the truth, should it be so. Asides, the scrawny, balding man would do nothing more than apply leeches to his body to draw out the bad blood.

Jestin decided he was losing enough as it was.

Whatever was wrong with him was his own secret, one he would share with no one.

Fawn's side of the bed was empty. Cold. As was the woman herself. He knew she was fidgety and uncomfortable; the baby was due shortly. Another girl, no doubt. No matter how loudly his wife proclaimed that she was carrying a son, Jestin had sired only daughters. Sheena, the three he fathered with Fawn, and four others that had been conceived when he was away from the castle. All girls. No boys.

None of them were anywhere close to Sheena. Oh, he'd tried to love his other children, at least the ones that were legitimate, but Fawn's issue were petulant and wily creatures, all with big, haunted eyes, milky white skin, pouty little lips, and weak chins. They were a sorry lot; all three of them tied together could not hold a candle to Sheena. Or Bertrice—now, there was a woman. One worth fighting for. Even killing for. Not so Fawn.

Bertrice.

He closed his eyes and remembered the only woman he'd loved. She had been big-bosomed and big-hearted, a beautiful girl with a lilting voice, lustrous red hair, and fetching eyes that had promised him so much.

As they had promised Rourke.

Bertrice's father had been eager to marry her to a lord, and then she'd met the sea captain and lost her heart. Aye, she'd slept with him and had not come to Jestin's bed a virgin, but he'd loved her with all his heart. And even though he'd had to win her hand in a game of dice, he'd never regretted it; even now, when Fawn's sharped-tongue barbs were cast at Bertrice's memory, he had but to walk to the shrine in the chapel and feel the peace of her spirit.

She'd never brought up Rourke again. Once she and Jestin were married, she had not mentioned the fact that Rourke had promised to return in accordance with the terms of their first bet.

Jestin was thankful that she hadn't lived to meet the captain again. He'd lived every waking moment in fear that she would desert him.

Ach, the troubles he had. To think so many envied him being baron. His head pounded with his worries, and his member was so hard it ached. Fawn would not accommodate him. He thought of a serving wench who could handle his needs, a girl who worked in the kitchen with high, firm breasts, teeth that overlapped a bit, and a sparkle in her green eyes whenever she offered him more wine. When he'd teased her, she'd flirted outrageously, and once when she was serving jellied pigeon's eggs, she'd fed him right from her smooth hands. Then as he'd chewed, she'd licked her fingers provocatively. One by one. He'd never bedded her, had tried to remain true to his wife, though he wondered why.

Fawn was not the kind of woman to trust. He'd known as much when he married her, and yet he'd needed a mother for Sheena and a wife who would bear him an heir.

Ah, Sheena. His heart was heavy whenever he thought of his firstborn, and as he slid to the side of the bed and shoved himself to his feet, he felt a jab of remorse. He should not have insisted she marry. Aye, she was well past the age and had refused all suitors, but he missed her terribly and now there was all that trouble at Tardiff.

So where was his wife? He listened to the sounds of the castle starting to stir for the morning, but the door to his chamber did not creak open. Nor did he hear Fawn's tread in the hallway. She'd changed and become different with this pregnancy. She was far more distant and much moodier, forever running to that odd fortune-teller, Serena. Mayhap Fawn was right; mayhap she was carrying a boy child—that would explain the difference in her temperament. Or, mayhap something else was bothering her, something he sensed but didn't really understand—trouble on a larger scale.

His damned shaft throbbed, and he thought if he couldn't mount his wife because of the babe, at least Fawn could offer her hands and mouth as comfort.

But it was evident she was not returning, and despite the chill in the air, his manhood was hard as ever. 'Twas a joke. He was still always ready to bed his wife, and yet when he relieved himself, that same organ of which he was so proud, the one that ensured he'd sire heirs, would offer up colored piss to remind him of his own mortality.

With a grunt he threw on a fresh tunic and breeches and wished his throbbing member would wilt. Grabbing his quiver and arrows, he found the green mantle he used for hunting, as it always assured him of good luck, then walked into the hallway where the guard was dozing. As the door to Jestin's chamber thudded shut behind him, the soldier awakened with a start.

"M'lord," the flustered man said. "Good morning and—"

"Tend to your post," Jestin barked as he strode to the steps usually trod upon only by servants. Every so often the baron took the back staircase just to keep the lazy ones who idled near the windows on their toes.

Outside, it was still dark, the moon high in the sky, no streaks of dawn yet visible. Stars blinked through a haze of clouds, and the bailey was coming alive and filled with the scents of cut hay, salty air, and a lingering fragrance of roses from the garden. Boys were drawing water and carrying firewood; the armorer was sharpening spears and lances by the light of an early morning fire.

'Twas a peaceful time of day, though 'twould soon pass as the cook would be rising, the guards changing, the portcullis raised. The windows of the baker's hut already glowed from the fire where he baked the castle's bread. Overhead, the sweeps of the windmill whooshed. Jestin looked up as a bat flew by.

He ducked, crossed himself, and hoped that seeing the

black creature was not a sign of bad luck. As he passed the
well a rooster crowed and the dogs, ever ready to put up a
ruckus, howled.

"Shut up, ye miserable curs," the hound master snapped,
then, upon spying the baron, managed a gap-toothed smile.
"Are ye goin' out huntin' this morn, m'lord, and will ye be
needin' the dogs?"

"I'll not need the dogs today," Jestin said, shaking his
head. "Another time." As the first shafts of morning light
pierced the thin haze he strode to the chapel and peered inside. Father Godfrey was at the altar, praying, not even lifting his head as the door opened. The candles flickered at the
shrine for his first wife, and he sent up a silent prayer. But
Fawn was not in attendance, and Jestin was beginning to
doubt her. Forever claiming to be praying for the unborn
babe's health, or stopping off at the stables to check on the
horses, or walking through the garden, Fawn avoided his
questions as to her whereabouts. The feeling that she was
lying to him bothered him again, like a slowly festering
wound.

Closing the door, he turned and walked quickly to the stables, where the stable master was ordering boys about. A
gruff man with an odd-shaped head—the result, gossip said,
of his mother being kicked in the belly when she was about
to delivery. Whatever the reason, Farrell was an ugly man
with one side of his face mashed in. Angry at the world in
general, he had a unique touch with the steeds.

"You there, Will, haul the water and be quick about it!
The pails be in the corner." As the first boy grabbed two
buckets and hurried toward the well, Farrell grabbed the
other one and boxed his ears. "And you, Nate, where 'ave ye
been these past two days?" He tweaked the boy's ear, and
the lad let out a howl that rang through the bailey.

"'Twas me mum. She was feelin' poorly and needed me
help with the twins."

"Bah." Farrell spat on the ground. "The next time ye pay
yer mom no mind."

"But me dad is dead and—"

"And the lord's horses still need tendin' to." He twisted the upper part of Nate's ear, and the boy let out a pain-filled shriek. Several horses whinnied and snorted nervously.

"Ah, ye cry like a woman. Now grab a shovel and clean the stalls up right quick. Then, once yer finished with that, pick up that pitchfork and start givin' 'em hay."

"But the gong farmer, 'tis his job to clean the dung," Nate complained, fighting tears and rubbing his ear.

"Not today, it ain't," Farrell turned from the lad and dusted his hands. "Ah, m'lord, I was expectin' ye. Got yer steed all saddled, I did." He snapped his fingers. "Nate, get the baron's horse and be quick about it."

The boy hurried the length of the stalls, unlatched one, and led Banner out. A spirited gray, the stallion's ears were pricked forward, his nostrils flared.

"Ye'll not be takin' anyone with ye?" Farrell asked, rubbing one of the horse's shoulders with his big hand.

"Not this time." Jestin swung onto the saddle.

"Same as the lady," Farrell said, his crumpled face frowning a bit. "I told her I did not like her riding out alone. Even though it be near dawn, there be pickpockets and thieves about. A fine lady like her, full with child, aye, she be an easy target," he said, lifting the eyebrow of his good eye.

Jestin's jaw turned to steel. "When did she leave?" he asked.

"Not even an hour ago, maybe less."

"Did she say where she was going?" Jestin hated to ask, realizing the deformed stable master was enjoying the fact that he had a bit of knowledge over on the Baron of Ogof.

Farrell shook his misshapen head.

"But she was alone?"

"Aye. Since Sir Manning was given to Tardiff, she rides alone."

"He was her personal guard," Jestin said, rankled by the undertone in the man's voice but ignoring the suspicions that had begun to germinate in his mind—suspicions he'd told himself were unfounded.

"Aye, and she be missin' him." Hearing the implication in his words, Farrell added quickly, "Manning, he watched over her."

"And was paid to do it." Irritated at the horseman's suggestions, Jestin picked up his reins and clucked to his mount. Banner took off at a trot, anxious to run to stretch his legs.

Jestin needed some time alone with his thoughts. He leaned forward. The horse's strides lengthened. As he neared the main gate, the baron shouted to the guards barely visible in the pre-dawn light.

"You there, let me pass."

"Aye, m'lord," a man's deep voice yelled back. He bellowed orders to someone in the gatehouse. Within seconds, groaning and clanking, the portcullis was raised. Jestin, still simmering at the insinuation of the damned deformed stable master that he might have been cuckolded, kicked Banner in the flanks.

As they passed through the gates, the stallion stretched out, easing into a gallop, his hooves flinging mud, his ears pricked forward.

Jestin guided his mount along the road running parallel to the coastline. Faster and faster until tears stung his eyes and the rutted lane curved upward through the forested hills. Rather than ride to his favorite hunting spot on the ridge, he veered south along a beaten path beneath a canopy of leafy branches. A stag leaped out of the underbrush and sprang over a fallen log, disappearing deep into the forest. Jestin didn't give chase. Barely noticed. His bow, arrows, and quiver were forgotten. He had a new purpose as he rode.

He intended to find his wife, and he wouldn't rest until he did.

Chapter Nine

"Tell us where the woman is," Manning demanded as he pulled off a glove. In the dirt by his feet, coiled like a snake ready to strike, was a whip. "Or, my friend, I assure you, you'll regret it."

"I know not." Wart was sweating, stretched between two men in the clearing, where the fire burned low and the first hint of morning light was visible above the lacy branches. They had been at this for hours—accusations from the dark knight, denials from Wart.

"Ach, you be a fool." Manning picked up the whip and shook the sinister loops free. "Peter here says he knows you as Warren of Halliwell, that you be his cousin, isn't that right?"

"Aye," Peter said, his eyes narrowing on Wart. "And a thief he be, though I be ashamed to admit it. Robbed everyone in town including the baron, stole horses from him and then poached in the forest. Some say he was even a spy. Warren, he be the rotten apple in the family, fer sure. Caused his parents nothing but shame, he did. His old father, he disowned him."

Manning smoothed the whip with his fingers. "Then he's a wanted man with a price upon his head."

"Aye, the Lord of Halliwell would pay well for his return."

"What have ye to say to these charges?" Manning asked.

"Peter's me cousin, aye, and he be a liar. From the time he was a lad he couldna tell the truth." Wart spat out the words though fingers of fear were clutching his heart, making it difficult to breathe. He'd been flogged before, knew the bite of a whip against his back and hated it.

Manning fingered the whip thoughtfully. "It matters not what ye be running from, but 'tis important that you tell me about the lady, Sheena of Tardiff. I know she boarded the *Dark Sapphire*, ye see. I have men posted at all the ports, and one saw her climb the gangplank, so all I want from you is the name of the ship's next port."

"I know not. I told ye I was not aboard any ship."

Manning sighed impatiently, deep grooves visible around his mouth. "Several of my men disagree. They saw you in the tavern the night we chased the lady into the town, and later one man witnessed that you boarded the ship."

" 'Twas not me."

"Liar," Peter accused. High overhead, hidden in the branches a crow let out a throaty caw. "I saw ye with mine own eyes, though I could not believe it."

"So, tell me," Manning said, obviously straining to keep his patience under rein, "where is the *Dark Sapphire* going to dock? We know her route was northward, we've checked along the seacoast in the towns where she stopped. I've spies at each village so I will find out the truth, but 'twould be easier and less painful for you if you were to give up that information now."

Wart snorted. "And then ye would let me go free?"

"You would stay on, as my guest, of course . . . until we locate the lady."

"I tell ye, I know nothing about the ship or a woman who boarded."

Manning's eyes gleamed malevolently. All his civility disappeared in an instant. " 'Tis your memory that's the problem, man, and I intend to improve it."

Wart braced himself, felt a tingling in his arm.

The dark knight smiled without a hint of mirth. As his men circled around, grinning and wagering on how many lashes Wart could take before he could no longer stand, Sir Manning drew back a huge shoulder slowly. "Turn him 'round," he ordered in a voice that echoed through the trees. Those holding Wart did as they were bid.

Wart closed his eyes. Waited. Sweated. Felt a shift in the air. With a horrifying hiss the whip sizzled through the air. Snapped beside Wart's head.

Crack! It sounded like thunder. A flock of startled quail flew upward in a whir of wings.

Wart steeled himself and turned his head to call over his shoulder, "Ye may flog me within an inch of me life, but I cannot tell ye what I do na know." He had trouble breathing, and his arm, held by one of Manning's oafs, began to feel numb.

"We'll see." Manning's voice was smooth was oiled leather. "Take off his shirt," he commanded, and in an instant, too quickly for Wart to break free, his tunic was ripped over his head.

Wart stared into the forest, and deep in his chest he felt pain, sharp as a pick cutting through his breastbone. He sagged. His captors forced him to his feet.

"I see this is not the first time ye've been punished," Manning observed as he noticed the old welts scarring Wart's back. "I would have thought you had learned a lesson."

"A stupid one he is," Peter said. "Thick-skulled as any mule."

Some of the men laughed. Wart gasped.

"He's afeared, he is. Look at him," one man chortled. But Wart could not respond, couldn't think. His chest was exploding, his lungs gasping.

"He's about to piss 'is breeches."

"This be your last chance, Wart. If you do not want to add to those scars and then, once ye're flogged, taken back to Halliwell to face the charges against you, I suggest you tell me about Sheena and the *Dark Sapphire*."

Wart held his silence, felt the other man's anger rising.

"So be it." Manning's voice was a death knell.

Snap!

The whip bit into his back like a viper. He flinched. The men held him upright. He couldn't breathe. Blood thundered through his ears.

Crack! Again. Pain ripped through his flesh.

"What say you, Wart?"

He closed his eyes. Tried not to think of the sting. Of the pain. *Help me. By the gods, I'm dying.*

"Fine, then." Some of the laughter from the men died, and the whip sliced open more of his skin. His back was on fire, as if he'd been stung by a thousand wasps. Squeezing his eyes shut, bracing himself against the next blow, Wart sent up a prayer to a God he'd long before forsaken, and before the whip sliced through him again, his entire body shuddered and he felt his soul slipping away from him as blackness, more friend than foe, overtook him.

Lying upon a small table in the hut, Fawn waited as the cherub-faced seer touched her stomach with gently probing fingers. A fire burned brightly in a small grate, and a few candles gave off a golden glow. Several chickens walked along the dirt floor. Fawn, though trying to remain calm, felt impatience grab her.

"Well?" she demanded when the woman with one blue eye and one green didn't say a word. A mottled cat slithering along the wall hopped imperiously to the windowsill and began washing itself. "What of the babe? Is he all right?"

"What does the midwife say?"

"Oh, her," Fawn snorted with disdain. "Maven's an old crone who has not a good word to say to anyone."

"She told you the babe was breech, did she not?" Serena removed her hands from Fawn's naked belly and, before Fawn could protest, deftly picked up a kitchen knife and sliced off a small lock of Fawn's blond hair.

"Nay!" Fawn's hand shot to the tresses of which she was so proud.

"I need this." Serena held the bit of hair up to the candle-light. "You wanted my vision, did you not?"

"Aye, but . . ." Fawn was in no position to argue. "Just don't take much."

"I have all I need." She rubbed the pinch of pale tresses between her slim fingers and eyed each separate blond strand.

"What does that midwife know, anyway?" Fawn complained, her back nearly breaking on the planks of the table. "Maven's a fool. I don't know why my husband keeps her. The same with that old, useless Zelda. What a pathetic excuse for a lady in waiting she is." Fawn shuddered inwardly at the thought of the serving maid with her haunted, deepset eyes. The woman never smiled. Never. 'Twas as if she had an inner poison running through her blood. Especially since Fawn had sent Zelda's daughter, Fannie, to be a kitchen maid at Tardiff. But Fawn had no interest in having the pretty young maid at Ogof.

Mayhap Zelda would die soon. Fawn could only hope. She felt the same for the ancient midwife. Maven would surely leave this earth before too many seasons passed. Now, if Fawn were baron, both of the dried-up old hens would be cast out. . . . Ah, well, that would not happen for 'twas her curse to be a woman and put up with and pretend to be subservient to the men who ruled. 'Twas enough to curdle the contents of her stomach if she thought too long and hard on it. Instead she pretended obedience.

'Twas hypocrisy, to be sure, but she'd learned long ago she had to be coy and cunning. Smart and beautiful were not enough. She'd once been outspoken and had only earned herself a slap from her mother and worse from her ogre of a father. Gryffyn of Tardiff had liked nothing better than to lift her skirts and punish her with his huge hand. He had often times hit her hard enough that her bottom had been sore for days. But it was a lesson well worth learning, for now she was about to earn the spoils of her pretended obedience.

Rolling ponderously to her side, she sat up with effort and felt dizzy for a minute. The hut was small and dark, filled with creatures and drying herbs that hung from the rafters. Chicken dung stained the floor and windowsill. Above the door, nailed to the dark wall, were the talons of a hawk, the bleached skull of a stag, and a rusting horseshoe.

"Do not tell me there will be trouble with this birth," Fawn cautioned Serena, for though she desperately sought the truth, she was tired of Maven's gloomy predictions. "I have borne three babes easily."

"But they were different," the woman said thoughtfully as she crossed the small space to the fire and tossed in Fawn's lock of hair. The embers sizzled angrily and foul-smelling smoke curled upward. Serena slowly shook her head.

"You mean because this time I am carrying a boy child," Fawn guessed, though she felt a drip of ice water in her blood as the sorceress's expression turned dark as midnight.

"Nay."

"But 'tis true, this one is different," Fawn insisted, an inner fear nearly strangling the words in her throat. If this child be a girl, oh, nay, she would not even think such heresy.

"'Tis not the babe's sex that concerns me," Serena said, turning from the fire to stare at Fawn with silently accusing eyes.

"Then what?" Fawn slid into the mantle she'd borrowed from an unknowing maid. 'Twas nearly dawn, and she needed to return to the castle. Already she was forming a lie for her husband, that she had visited an ailing woman who needed comfort.

"The babe be not Lord Jestin's."

"What?" Fawn gasped in horror. Her hand flew to her chest with feigned indignance, and warmth swept up her pallid cheeks. How had this woman divined the truth? "'Tis a vile lie you speak, sorceress. Of course my husband is the sire."

Serena studied the wisps of smoke as they disappeared up the charred stone chimney. "Nay, m'lady. This child be sired by a warrior—a fierce one at that."

"The lord is—was . . . a warrior of great renown."

"But he be different. The father of this babe is a warrior who has not yet gotten what he strives for, a man who lusts for more power, a soldier who has recently spilled blood or killed in battle. The lord has not seen war in many years. This warrior wants more and will stop at nothing, even bedding the wife of the baron, to get what he wants. This be the man who is the father of your babe."

"You know this not," Fawn insisted, though she was turning to jelly inside as she edged off the table.

"You come to me for the truth." Serena's expression was without judgment as she leveled her steady odd-colored eyes on Fawn, her voice low but unbending. "You pay me to tell you what will be and I do. Now you would lie to me?"

Fawn felt a knife of desperation slice into her soul. Her throat was suddenly dry as if she'd swallowed sand. "Nay . . ." Abruptly she was anxious to leave, and she delved into a small leather purse, found a silver coin, and left it on the table where she'd so recently been examined.

Outside, hoof beats thundered.

Serena's head snapped up. Fear pulled at the corners of her mouth. Hissing, the cat leaped to the floor and scurried off to hide beneath a stack of wood. A horse snorted. A bridle jangled.

Damn! Fawn's eyes scoured the little cabin for a means of escape. No one could find her here. No one. She started for the door, but it was too late.

"'Tis your husband," the seer declared, still studying the flames.

Fawn's heart dropped. "No, he would not—" Oh, God, was it possible? Serena was not just telling the future, she was warning Fawn. The fortune-teller stepped to the window and peered through the slats of the shutters.

With the telltale sound of a man dismounting a steed, boots landed on the earth outside the door. Heavy footsteps approached.

Frantic, Fawn searched the small hut for a hiding space or a back door or any way to escape facing her husband. There was none. Asides, 'twas too late. Her mare was tethered outside, and there was little doubt the lord had not recognized her horse.

Bam! Bam! Bam! A huge fist pounded on the old timbers. Fawn's bones jarred with each horrifying knock.

"Open up," Jestin roared. "I know you be in there, Fawn. And you, witch woman, if you want not to be dragged back to the keep and tried for heresy, you'll not hide my wife!"

Fawn wanted to melt into the floor.

"I tell you true," Serena said, unshaken by the fact that she was being threatened. "You be carrying a boy child and his birth will be difficult, for he has not turned."

Fawn reached for the door handle.

"And, lady." Serena laid a hand upon the rough wool of Fawn's sleeve. "Your babe was conceived in lust by a dark, angry soldier who would slit your throat as easily as lie with you. Be careful."

"Nay, nay, you lie," Fawn insisted, jerking her arm away, her heart as cold as death with fear. "Shh. No more of this."

"Oh, for the love of St. Andrew!" A boot crashed into the door. The oak bolt shivered. Wood splintered. "Open up! Fawn, I know you're in there."

"Wait!" Steeling herself, Fawn lifted the bar with trembling hands and opened the door to find her husband, his face flushed and livid, his lips tight over his teeth, fury emanating from every pore of his body, glaring down at her in a pyre of self-righteous fury.

"And what be you doing here, wife? Tell me true," he demanded. A vein bulged in his forehead, and his gloved fists opened and closed as if he would like nothing more than to wring her neck.

Fawn drew in a deep breath and formed a lie, but no words escaped her lips. Pain ripped through her body. As excruciating as a stallion's kick to her abdomen, the agony robbed her of her breath. Her knees buckled. She nearly fell to the dirt floor. "Oh, God," she cried, closing her eyes and counting her heartbeats as the sharp agony slowly waned. Sagging against the doorway, she closed her eyes. "It matters not now, Jestin," she said as she gasped for breath and felt a rush of water flow from between her legs. "The babe—your son—is on his way."

Sheena slipped through the door of the ship's cabin and slowly climbed the stairs. The storm was behind them, the water still uneasy, the sky beginning to lighten through a thin mist. She'd rested, never slept and knew that she had to make good her escape before Keegan returned.

Though the wind no longer shrieked across the water, the air was cool and heavy with the smell of brine. The deck was slick and dark, the great masts spiring upward as the *Dark Sapphire* held a steady course.

Somehow she had to get off the ship. Now. While no one was watching over her. Before Keegan returned and she willingly fell into bed with him all over again. Oh, how had she been so foolish as to have made love to him, the boy who had abandoned her, a captain of a smuggler's ship, the man who was secretive and dark one minute, kind and engaging the next? Why did her inner soul scream that she was falling in love with him when she knew him to be a rogue and a blackheart, a man whose life was the sea?

"Because you be an idiot," she growled at herself, and refused to think of the painful emotions burning deep in her heart or the pleasant soreness between her legs. 'Twas daft to have such feelings, and she had no time to worry over them.

Stealing across the deck, she heard voices. Through the

shadows of dawn she made out two figures, men who stood near the bow. Though she could not see their faces, she heard their words.

". . . you think the storm was not some kind of spell?" Tom asked, his meaty hands curled over the rail as he stared into the coming morn. The *Dark Sapphire* rocked as if in protest.

"Nay." Jasper shook his head, his hands moving frantically as he spoke. " 'Twas but a storm, a bad one, but only a storm. I do not think ye can blame the lady or any kind of witchcraft for the rise of the wind or the anger of the waters. Only God Almighty controls that, and ye'd be smart to pay it heed."

"A woman aboard a ship is a curse," Tom insisted, though he seemed confused, his thick eyebrows drawn together as he battled inwardly against all he had held true. " 'Tis known by all good men of the sea." Tom spat into the water as a gust of wind pressed his mantle to his body. "I know she saved Bo but . . . did she not sneak on board and try to hide? Did she not threaten to curse us all? Did not the captain send Wart to find out the truth about her? And by the gods, did he not become smitten with her, same as the rest of the crew?" Tom's voice was filled with worry. "Even Maynard is besotted. And the captain. He not be thinking straight. He's in love with her, plain as I'm tellin' ye. I can see it in his face, the way he looks for her, watches her when she be not lookin'. And that's what I'm tellin' ye, Jasper, no one but a witch could burrow into Keegan's heart."

Sheena didn't move. Her ears strained to hear over the wind, and she bit her lip. Was it possible? Could Keegan love her? Oh, nay, 'twas only Big Tom worrying aloud. He was a man who didn't trust any woman.

" 'Tis full of it ye are," Jasper argued. "The captain, well, aye, I've seen him look at the woman with longing, but he'll not put any of us in jeopardy. Wart's gone, true, though I do not know why. But I do na think it has anythin' to do with the lady."

"Bah. Then 'tis a fool ye be, Jasper. I overheard the captain and Wart talkin', I did. And Keegan, he sent Wart to find out if she's that woman Tardiff's army is lookin' for. The one who kilt her husband. Captain Keegan, he wants to know if there's a price upon her head and how much it be so that he can ransom her."

Sheena's heart dropped.

"Would he do that if he was in love with her?"

"He wasn't at the time. Now 'twould be different."

Or would it? Sheena wondered, refusing to think of their lovemaking. Would Keegan give her up to Manning, though he knew the dark knight was brutal? Had he believed her when she'd confided to him about her wedding night, or had he thought her a liar? Did she mean nothing but a few coins to him? Sadness pierced her soul, though she told herself to put it aside, forget Keegan, and make her way off this cursed ship. She couldn't take the chance of trusting him. 'Twas a mistake she'd made once before.

"Keegan knows not what love is." Tom reached for a length of chain. "He dinna know his mother, and that wife of his betrayed him at every turn. He would not trust another woman, nay. That be why I say he be under a spell."

"A spell not strong enough to keep him from ransoming her back to those who be lookin' for her?" Jasper snorted again.

"Ach, I know not. But 'tis plain enough to me and every other man on this ship, Captain Keegan's not the same as he was before he met the woman. And even if she did save Bo's life, she's still treacherous, I tell ye. Mayhap more so as we all want to trust her. She did not come aboard and hide in the hold if she wasn't."

"A pity that," Jasper agreed. "If she be runnin' from somethin', I say she has a good reason. 'Tis not as if the rest of us don't have our own shadows chasin' us."

Big Tom shook his head. "But none of us jeopardize the safety of the *Sapphire*. We've all pledged to protect her. With the lady, 'tis different."

"Let's not be condemnin' her just yet."

"I'm just tellin' ye what I think."

"Well, we'll see, now, won't we? We dock in a few hours."

A few hours? She had only a few hours? And then what? Face Sir Manning? She glanced across the choppy water to the dark coastline, nearer than it had ever been on this journey.

The wind kicked up, and whatever further conversation the two men engaged in was lost to her ears. Not that it mattered. She knew only that she had to leave. She couldn't risk being dragged back to Ogof by Sir Manning and his army of cutthroats. Nor did she want to give Keegan a chance to betray her again.

Determination filled her soul. She could not run forever. Nay, she needed to face her father again, but she had to do it alone. Not as Sir Manning's prisoner. At the thought of the dark knight shackling her, humiliating her, leading her back to Ogof with her hands bound, she felt sick. 'Twas time to return. On her own. She would ride into the castle not a prisoner but a free woman determined to see her father. No longer would she run and look over her shoulder and hide like some night creature afraid of the light.

As damp strands of her hair blew across her face in the salty breeze and the prow of the ship knifed through the gray waters, Sheena realized she could not stay here with Keegan a moment longer. Whether he intended to turn her over to Manning or not, the truth of the matter was that she could not risk falling in love with him.

"Fool," she said under her breath and edged around the mainmast to look to the east and spy the shoreline not far off. Stealing the boat would be difficult, but she had to try. She waited until Jasper and Big Tom disappeared into the hold, then sneaked to the side of the ship where two rowboats were fastened down. Murmuring a quick prayer that she wouldn't be discovered, she untied the heavy ropes with nervous fingers.

"Give me strength," she prayed under her breath, hoping to lift the small craft, but it was heavy, barely moved as she pulled on its prow. *You can do it,* she told herself, trying again, muscles straining, but the damned rowboat didn't budge. Biting her lip, she stepped back and looked for a tool, a board, anything she could use to pry the boat away from the deck and into the sea, but there was nothing except for the pulleys and chains, which would cause too much noise and take too long. She reached into the boat, grabbed hold of one of the seats, and felt the old wood give.

The sky was getting lighter. She was running out of time. She heard men's voices and the shuffling of boots upon the deck. "Come on, come on," she said, trying yet again, her fingers wrapping around the nearly broken seat, her jaw set, her muscles straining. The boat didn't move, not one bloody inch. *Damn!* Clenching her teeth, her hands bleeding, she pulled once more. The seat creaked. She yanked. Wood splintered and the seat broke off in her hands.

Sweating, her muscles aching, she knew she had no chance with the fool boat. Nay, she would have to find another way. She looked up at the rigging, but found no salvation in the tall masts stretching up to the still, dark heavens. The sails were of no help. She quickly eyed the deck, found nothing to help her. "Bloody hell," she muttered. Determined to find a way off the ship, she leaned back against the railing.

"Ye need to rest." Hollis's voice rang over the decking.

"Aye, and I will." *Keegan. Lover. Traitor. Judas.* She scooted behind the stairwell as he approached. "But only for a few hours. Wake me before we dock."

"That I will," Hollis promised. "Do ye think Wart will be waitin'?"

"I hope so."

"If anyone can find out the truth, he will," Hollis said. "And he'll find out where the soldiers are, how big the army is, and what price is upon the woman's head—what ransom will be paid."

Keegan didn't argue.

So he would give her up. Sheena's heart sank as if it were tied to an anchor. Why would she think differently? she wondered as she hid and the two men passed. Had he not as a boy kissed her and then left her on the dock? Was this not the same? Only this time he'd done more than kiss her, he'd made love to her before offering her up to her enemies. A pang of disappointment knifed through her.

Well, he could curse and rot in hell for all she cared, she told herself.

But she could not stay on deck any longer. She had but a few minutes, then surely Keegan would find she was missing. All hell would break out. She had no doubt that Keegan would lock her in the cabin until they docked, and then, oh, dear God, would he really turn her over to Manning?

She couldn't risk it. She heard the door to the cabin open. She looked toward the shore, barely visible through the thin mist, but close enough to give her a chance. Without another thought she tossed off her mantle, hauled the broken piece of bench with her, and climbed to the deck.

"Bloody hell. Where is she?" she heard Keegan say, then, more loudly, "Search the ship!"

Swallowing back her fear, she climbed onto the railing and, before she thought twice, clutched the board to her chest and jumped.

Heart in her throat, she sailed through the air. Feet first she plunged into the swirling, icy water. Bam! Her chin hit the hard wood. Pain shot through her jaw. Her mind spun. Down she went, deep into the frigid darkness. Cold as ice, the salty water filled her mouth and nose, clutched at her dress and boots, dragged her downward into the darkness. Her lungs burned. She kicked, hard, upward, where there was so little light.

Her chin ached, the black waters swirled around her. Thoughts of all manner of horrid sea creatures, the very beasts Hollis claimed existed, tumbled through her mind, but she struggled hard, kicking, clinging to the damned piece of wood. *Don't worry about sea serpents,* her mind taunted, *you'll drown or freeze first.*

Her lungs were on fire. She kicked harder. Against the sea. Through the clinging folds of her dress. Ever upward. Her mind spun. Just as she thought she would lose consciousness, her head broke free and she gasped, choking, coughing, kicking madly away from the ship, which loomed much too near. The coast seemed miles away, a dark shadow stretching impossibly in the distance, but she hung onto the board for dear life, forcing her legs to move while the drag of the sea insisted on pulling against her.

Her boots were waterlogged, the stones still jammed tightly against her toes, the long skirt of her dress an anchor, but Sheena was determined to break free and return to Ogof to face her father and whatever brand of justice he would mete out.

Unless the cold sea claimed her first.

Never!

She kicked hard, clung to the board, and headed toward the rugged shoreline. The waves crashed over her, salt water drenched her and clogged her throat. Her mind spun and her body felt as if cold, sharp needles were piercing her skin.

Still she kicked.

Her legs were numb when she first heard her name, lost in the moan of the wind and the crash of the surf.

"Sheena!"

Oh, no. Her throat clogged as she recognized Keegan's voice screaming above the wind.

Go to hell, she thought, squeezing her jittery jaw shut and forcing her heavy legs to move. Tears sprang to her eyes. She saw something—another shadow on the water's surface.

Another wave crashed over her. The board slipped from her fingers. *Nay, sweet Mary, No!* She scrambled, tried to hold the slab of slippery wood, but the angry tide stripped the board from her frozen fingers.

Another wave pounded her. She screamed, swallowed

water. Her body flopped forward, closer to the land. Choking, salt water burning her throat, she surfaced. Her arms flailed. Treacherous, foaming water was everywhere. Above. Below. She bobbed up again, spat salt and seaweed. Shivered. Again she was dragged under. Her foot scraped something. A rock. She tried to stand, only to be hurled forward.

Bang!

Her head crashed hard into the jagged rock hidden beneath the water's swirling surface.

Pain exploded behind her eyes.

Her body was tossed as if she were a rag doll. Her arms and legs were useless, the pain in her head blinding. One leg scraped against rough hidden shoals. She gulped water, spewed it up and then swallowed more.

Somewhere there was sky—the pale light of dawn visible in short flashes. Her arms wouldn't move. Her legs were dead. She caught a quick image of the shore, so far away, much, much too far. She would never be able to reach it.

Her body failed her. She couldn't move.

As the water dragged her under she thought of Keegan—tormentor, lover, blackheart. She would never see him again.

All was lost.

Chapter Ten

"Man overboard!" a deep voice boomed across the deck of the *Dark Sapphire*. "Get the boats! Hie! For the love of Christ! Man overboard!"

Keegan's heart plummeted to his knees. *Sheena!* He knew in an instant she'd either fallen or jumped overboard into the swirling, icy depths. Why? God in heaven, why? He raced to the edge of the ship and stared through the rising mist, searching for any sign of her. His gaze roved the sea, hoping to spy her struggling in the gray waves.

"Who?" Bo asked, sliding down the foremast and scrambling over the rigging to land at Keegan's feet. His face was ashen with fear, his mop of hair flat and wet from the mist.

"I don't know," Keegan lied.

"Would ya look at that? Someone ripped apart the rowboat! For the love of Mary, who would do such a thing?" Jasper muttered as all the deck hands scurried, like rats seeking higher ground on a sinking ship. Seamus unlashed one of the rowboats. Tom was working on the other. But Keegan was immobile, his heart dark with dread, every muscle in his body tense, as he squinted into the half-light of dawn.

"Where's the lady?" Maynard demanded.

"In the captain's cabin," Bo insisted.

"Nay." Keegan admitted what he most feared. "She's missing."

The boy blanched even whiter. Chains rattled as a row-boat was lowered.

"What the devil do ye think ye're doin'?" Hollis was beside him in an instant. "Ye can't go jumpin' in after her, Keegan. Think. If she wants to kill herself, well, so be it, but nothin' will be helped if you drown as well."

Ignoring the older man, Keegan kicked off his boots.

"Think, man," Hollis insisted, grabbing hold of the sleeve of Keegan's tunic. "There be no reason to—"

Keegan stripped off the damned tunic, climbed onto the rail, searched the deadly whitecaps, then dove.

"Nay!" Hollis cried.

The sea came at him like an angry, frigid mistress, full of fury and wrath, devouring him. Ice water hit his skin. Salt spray filled his nostrils. He dived deep into the darkness, then kicked upward to the surface, where the roiling water had not an ounce of mercy.

"Sheena!" he screamed. Gray light stretched over the waves. "Sheena, by God—" But his voice was lost over the roar and rush of the sea tumbling ever toward the shore.

He treaded water, turning in a wide arc, squinting toward the shore. His teeth began to rattle with the cold, but inside he was on fire with anger and fear. God's eyes, how could she have been so foolish? The ocean was a sure tomb, a watery grave.

His heart wrenched in a newfound pain. He'd lost a wife already, and though he'd loved her once, that love had been tarnished and betrayed, but this—this feeling of sheer panic and desperation was new to him. It tore at his soul, played havoc with his mind, screamed through his body.

She couldn't be lost. *Couldn't!*

He would find her if it took his last dying breath!

"Sheena!" he screamed again. "Sheena, oh, for the love of God, answer!"

He strained to hear, over the wild thudding of his heart and the crescendo of the sea endlessly pounding the shore, but the only other sound he heard was the clank of chains, the call of voices from the ship urging him to swim back to the safety of the *Dark Sapphire*, screaming for him to wait for the rowboat that was being launched.

Still he swam, keeping his head above the waves, choking on gulps of cold, salty water, feeling his hope ebb as the minutes passed. Why did she fling herself into the sea? Not to kill herself, nay, she was too strong of mind for that, but to escape him and the uncertainty of the docking.

Bloody Christ, it was his fault.

Her death would be because of him.

"Noooo!"

His throat closed as he thought of their lovemaking, so recent, so warm, so filled with passion.

"Sheena! For the love of God, answer me!"

He prayed, his body growing numb, his jaw quivering. For the first time since the dark years, he prayed as he tried to stay afloat, his eyes ever searching.

Please, Father, if you're listening, save her. Take me, but, please, see her safely to the shore and far from the horrors of Tardiff.

Shaking, teeth chattering, breath short and fast, he felt his muscles rebel. He'd had little sleep, had manned the helm and fought the sea most of the night. In the hours he was to rest, he'd been with Sheena—hotblooded virgin. Murderess. Thief. Liar. Stowaway. Lover. His mind spun and he called her name until he was hoarse, and when he opened his mouth, no words came.

He was cold to his bones, yet he felt nothing in his arms and legs. 'Twas as if they were not attached. Water sprayed in his nose, and he coughed as he rotated slowly, scanning every inch of the horizon as he fought the urge to close his eyes.

"There he is!" Hollis's voice came as if from a distance over the dull roar that invaded his mind, penetrated his soul. "Row. Faster. Holy Father, he's about done in. Bloody fool." Keegan tried to swim closer to the shore, but the rowboat was upon him and strong arms surrounded him.

"Nay . . ." he croaked out, his world upside down, his only intent to save the woman he loved.

"Pull him in." Hollis's disgusted voice again. "I'm tellin' ye, I'm sick to death of savin' his sorry skin, I am. But do it and be quick about it."

Someone—no, not one but two big men—dragged him into the small craft and dropped him into the bottom as if he were fish caught in a net.

"Now, row back to the ship. Quickly," Hollis commanded, his voice brooking no argument. The tiny boat moved, tossed about, but Keegan didn't care, couldn't lift his head.

"Captain, stay with us!" Who was that? Seamus?

"We're losin' him, sure." Another voice far away, as if Jasper were at the far end of a long tunnel and calling to him. "Captain, ye'll be all right."

Cold. It was so damned cold. Shivering, clutching himself, thinking of making love to her . . . over and over again . . .

"Where's the lady?" Was it Bo's voice raised in fear? "We cannot go back without her!"

"Row!" Hollis ordered again. "Bloody Christ, men, throw yer damned backs into it!"

"But we cannot leave her!"

"Enough! Shut up, Bo, and row, for the love of God. She's dead already most likely."

"Nay, we must find her, we must—"

There was a scuffle of sorts, and the boy was yelling, screaming, kicking, the boat pitching. Keegan's mind faded in and out, taking him to another time, long ago, on the dock in the cove when first he'd kissed her. *Sheena, oh, love, you were the first . . . and the last . . . And I failed you yet again. Again he was fifteen, full of piss and eager for adventure. Again he was in a bobbing craft fighting for his life, certain that he would never see her again. He felt the sting of the arrow, the curse of her words . . . the pressure of her sweet, sweet lips to his.*

"We'll all drown, you little bugger," Jasper was saying. Or was it Jasper? Keegan could no longer tell. "Now, forget the lady. What's done is done. It's the captain we've got to save."

Keegan tried to argue but only coughed. Didn't know where he was, didn't care, but the weight on his heart, heavy as an anchor, wouldn't leave, trapped the air in his lungs, reminded him that he'd let her go, lost her, the one woman he'd loved. . . .

Someone, Keegan couldn't tell who, threw a heavy wool mantle over him and he lay, shivering, coughing, certain Sheena had died. Because of him. Guilt burrowed in hot, painful holes through his brain. 'Twas his fault she'd jumped, his fault she was now at the bottom of the sea. 'Twas his destiny to forever fail her.

The boy was crying, soft, muffled sobs, and the small boat rocked over the water. Keegan tried to fight the urge to give in to sleep, to the welcome, mind-numbing blackness that threatened him. He was the captain. He had to man the ship. He had to find Sheena, be she dead or alive. But the fight was out of him, and the blackness was soft and seductive, a spell of tranquility that was cast upon him, rolling like the tide and drawing ever closer, blocking out all hint of light until he fought no longer and willingly gave himself up to the peace of unconsciousness.

"Do not push!" Serena ordered as Fawn lay on her small bed amid the chickens and drying herbs in the fortune-teller's hut. Jestin paced through the small shack, his hands clasped behind his back, his eyes averted as if seeing the birth of his own child were unclean. Instead of being a part of the birthing, he glowered into the fire, watching as the embers burned low, the flames reflected in his eyes.

Pain cleaved through Fawn's body. She was being ripped in two, torn apart. Sweating, silently cursing, feeling the horrid pressure with each cramp, she clenched her fists and tried not to cry out. This pain, 'twas worth it. For her son.

The next baron, not only of Ogof but Tardiff as well. Aye, she would endure anything for the boy.

"Breathe slowly, do not push."

"I'm not!" she snapped, angry at the fortune-teller, though the woman was but trying to help her bring the babe into the world. "I—I have had three children. Never had I had such horrible . . . oh, sweet Mother." She began to breathe in shallow little bursts of air, braced herself. Sheer agony screamed through her again, blinding, shrieking pain. "Ooohhhh, bloody hell!" she cried out. "By the gods, what's happening?"

Serena, that fool, was at the foot of the bed, attempting to help with the baby, but her quiet words and steady hands were not enough. Something was wrong. Horribly, painfully wrong.

Sweat poured down from Fawn's forehead, drenching her hair, soaking the bedclothes. Blood and water soiled the bed, and yet the babe did not come. "Call for the midwife!" she demanded.

" 'Tis too late." Serena's face pulled into a tight pucker of concentration, as if it had been drawn by an invisible and worried string.

"But something's amiss, I feel it, oh, oh, ooooooo!" God in heaven, she couldn't endure much more of this. Each second felt like an eternity in hell.

" 'Tis not right," Serena said nervously.

"Make it right!" The Baron of Ogof turned on his heel. "No son of mine is going to die before he's born. You bring him into this world healthy and robust!"

"Aye, m'lord, I am trying."

" 'Tis not good enough to try," Jestin growled. "Do it. Do it now and I will forget that you practice the dark arts, that you cast spells and see into the future and are a heathen. Elsewise, if this babe is not born healthy and strong, I will blame you. And trust me, my justice will be swift and harsh."

Fawn moaned in excruciating agony. Morning light

streamed through the solitary window, and yet the Lady of Ogof was certain she had fallen into the darkest bowels of hell.

Something tore.

"It's near," the seer proclaimed, her face sheened in sweat, worry drawing lines upon her forehead.

"He," Fawn corrected, desperately. *"He!"* The baby was crowning, she was sure of it. Pressure pounded through her body, squeezed her brain. At last. She began to push, her body convulsing, trying to expel the infant.

"Not yet, 'tis not the head . . . nay, do not push!" Serena ordered, but it was too late. Fawn could no longer control herself. Her body worked feverishly to rid itself of the babe.

"'Tis time, Serena," she gasped, and then screamed so loudly several of the chickens flapped wildly in the rafters overhead. The cat leaped through the open window. Feathers drifted downward.

Flesh tore, blood flowed, pain the like of which Fawn had never felt wrenched all of her organs. Certain she would die right there on the table, she moaned pathetically. The seer pressed her hand over Fawn's abdomen, pushing gently, whispering "God help us all" in a voice so low Fawn barely heard the words. Ever so slowly the baby came into the world, buttocks first.

"'Tis a boy," Serena said as the babe let out a lusty cry and Jestin turned to look at his wife for the first time since striding into the small, dirty hut.

"A son," he whispered proudly, his throat catching. A smile grew from one side of his stern face to the other. 'Twas as if heaven itself had touched him, for the adoration on his face was pure, nearly holy. "Thank God." He blinked rapidly against a bath of tears.

"Aye." Fawn managed a weak smile when she saw the dark-haired infant. Red-faced and screaming he was. Oh, the babe was fine and strong and would be as handsome and brave as his sire—a true warrior. "A son." Relief washed over her as surely as if she'd been bathed by a dozen hand-maids.

Her husband, who had been ready to strangle her but a few hours before, was moved to tears. His throat worked and he took his wife's hand in his. His thumb rubbed the top of her palm, and his voice was rough with emotion. "I . . . Oh, wife . . . I have waited long for this moment."

"I as well, Jestin," Fawn vowed. "This one, he be your issue, your heir."

She noticed the cursed fortune-teller stiffen as she cut the cord cleanly, tied it off, and swaddled the babe in an old towel. Serena's lips had tightened, but she kept her eyes averted. She would hold her tongue or lose her life.

"At last." Jestin stared at the red-faced baby as if he were the only child on earth, and when Fawn took her son to her breast, the Baron of Ogof looked on proudly. "We shall name him Daffyd," he said. "'Twas my father's name."

Cuddling the baby close, Fawn shook her head. Wet ringlets fell into her eyes. The babe nuzzled and found her nipple. Latching on, her son sucked so hard Fawn drew in a whistling breath, then said, "Nay, husband, I have thought long on what we should call him. Let his name be as coura-geous as he will be." She smiled up at her husband. "I say we name him Llywelyn after the great one."

Serena gasped, but quickly disguised it with a cough.

"Llywelyn," Jestin repeated, not spying the sorceress's surprise. Thinking hard and rolling the name around on his tongue, he winked at his wife. "Llywelyn of Ogof." He nod-ded, as if liking the sound of it. "Aye, wife. So be it. Lly-welyn he be." Jestin gently touched the babe's head of fine black hair. "He is not fair like our daughters," he thought aloud, and Fawn's heart stopped for a second. "But my father, his hair was dark as well. A strapping man he was, a true warrior as little Llywelyn will someday be."

"Aye," Fawn agreed hastily. She held her boy child close, for he was her promise, her future, her entire reason for liv-ing. This one, he was destined to rule. But not only Ogof and Tardiff, nay, those baronies were not nearly enough. This boy would someday drive fear into the hearts of the English and rule all of Wales.

Keegan's head throbbed, his body ached, and as he opened a weary eye, he knew something was terribly wrong. The ship was still. There was no movement of the sea, but that wasn't what caused him concern. Nay, there was a deeper trouble, a weight pressing hard on his chest.

And then he remembered. With razor-sharp clarity memories of Sheena sliced into his brain, and the painful thought that she'd died in the sea caused him to suck in his breath.

"So ye are alive." Hollis was in the room, braced against the wall, his old, wrinkled face illuminated by a single candle in the lantern. "I thought ye might be stirrin' soon."

"Where are we?"

"We've docked, Keegan. The ship is sound. We've cargo to unload and some to take on, but we've done nothin' yet. We were waitin' fer you to wake up."

"You might have waited a long time," Keegan observed, realizing he'd been close to death as he sat up and the headache thundering behind his eyes worsened. He looked past the old man to a hook by the door where a dress hung—the blue velvet that was to have been Brynna's but Sheena had worn. He remembered seeing her for the first time in that gown, her red hair tumbling in soft curls to the shoulders, her eyes as blue as the plush fabric, her shoulders stiff with indignity. There had been other times as well, when she'd stood on the deck and the wind had billowed the skirts, or when she'd been undressing, unlacing the bodice with her back turned to him and he'd seen the slope of her shoulders, the curve of her spine, once, the dimples just above the cleft of her buttocks . . .

"What of Sheena?" he asked, ignoring the pain pounding at his temples and blazing in his muscles.

"She was lost."

"Her body?" he asked, his heart heavy with denial.

Hollis shook his head, his old speckled pate reflecting the lamplight. "Nay. We found no trace of her."

Keegan hadn't expected any better and rubbed a weary hand over his face. He felt a hundred years old. The heaviness in his chest pressed hard against his heart. Never in his life had he known such sadness, such grief. Not even when his father had been killed. This loss was deeper and, he knew, more dangerous, for it played with his mind. Though he'd grieved Rourke's passing, he'd been a child mourning a parent. 'Twas a different agony from this; he now felt that he'd been clawed and gutted from the inside out, that the wounds from which he bled were invisible but carved deep into his soul, far deeper than the pain inflicted by the sea.

He forced himself to his feet and was light-headed but for a second. "Let us start unloading," he said without any enthusiasm, with no speck of life, but another thought struck him. "What of Wart? Has he boarded?"

"Not yet."

"How long have we been docked?"

"Six hours."

"And he has not come aboard?" Keegan asked. 'Twas odd. Wart was loyal and true, had never once been delayed. Though he loved a good pint and a coy smile, Wart had put duty before pleasure many a time. He frowned, glanced at the older man. " 'Tis unlike him."

"Aye." Hollis hesitated. He looked at his fingers for a second as if he was troubled but could not easily voice his concerns.

"What is it?" Keegan demanded, rubbing a temple.

"There be another . . . situation."

"What?" Keegan wasn't interested. He found his mantle, hung near Sheena's dress, and as he reached for it, his fingers brushed against the soft fabric. An image flashed behind his eyes, and he saw her as he had the last night they were together, when he'd given in to his desire for her, kissed her and ended up making love to her in this very cabin. He remembered her lips, rounding with surprise as he'd entered her, the hunger of her kisses, the firmness of her breasts, snowy white and tipped with perfect pink nipples. . . . Sweet Jesus, how could he miss her so badly?

Throwing on his mantle, he forced himself to dispel her image, for 'twould do no good to dwell upon it. She was gone. Lost at sea. Driven to her own death because of him.

His jaw clenched so hard it ached. "What else is wrong?" he demanded, reaching for his boots.

" 'Tis the soldiers from Tardiff. They want to board and search for Sheena."

"Bloody Christ. Already?" Keegan, ready for a fight, grabbed his dagger and tucked it into his belt.

"They were waiting."

"How did they know we were to dock here?"

"I know not."

Angrily Keegan pulled on his boots. "They be relentless."

"Their lord was killed."

And Sheena died as well. His throat grew thick.

"Sir Manning, he awaits ye."

"Does he?" Keegan's smile was without any humor; his head pounded and his blood knew a new vengeful lust. Aye, he would love a fight. His fingers curled over the hilt of his blade, and his muscles bunched in anticipation of battle with the man who had chased Sheena to the ground. He'd love to strangle Manning's thick neck.

"He wants to search the ship. He's brought a sheriff from the nearest keep with him."

"All well and good," Keegan agreed with more than a trace of sarcasm. He flung open the door of the cabin and stormed up the short flight of stairs to the deck. The brutish knight had already boarded, and along with a small band of his men was a fat, surly-looking man who glared at Keegan.

But Keegan's gaze was centered on Sir Manning. He'd aged over the years but was still as dark and swarthy as he had been on the day that he'd pinned Rourke's hand to the table, nailing him to his fate. Aye, a beast of a knight. Tall and thick-chested, strong as an ox with black hair and a

cruel mouth, he seemed as anxious for a fight as did Keegan.
"We needs search your ship, Captain Keegan," Manning
stated flatly. "We have reason to believe that Lady Sheena of
Tardiff is on your ship, and she is to be returned to stand trial
for the murder of her husband, the baron." His chin hitched
toward his companion. "I've the authority of—"

"Then do so," Keegan invited without a smile, his aching
muscles tense, ready to lunge if the chance arose. "There is
no woman aboard. I harbor no criminals. But search quickly.
We have much to unload and cargo to take on. Two of my
men"—he glanced around to the crew, most of whom had
gathered on the deck beneath the masts—"you, Seamus, and
Hollis as well as myself will accompany you."

"Ye need not bother," Manning said.

Keegan knew his grin was pure evil as he watched Manning's expression turn cunning. The promise of a fight
crackled through the air and Keegan embraced it. " 'Twill be
no bother," he assured the man who was now and forever his
enemy. "No bother at all."

Sheena's head throbbed, her body ached, and the world
swam before her eyes. Where was she? What had happened?
Why did she feel as if she'd been trampled by every last
steed in the stables of Ogof?

"She be comin' 'round, Freddy," a woman said, and
Sheena tried to open her eyes but couldn't.

"Is that right?" A man's voice. Nasal, disapproving.
"About time. I was sure she was dead."

"Near enough. 'Ere ye go, missy. Open up." Sheena felt a
spoon pressed to her lips, and then a bit of salty fish broth
slid over her tongue to her throat. "Come on, eat a bit, won't
ya, girl? 'Tis good fer ye, a bit o' soup."

The man snorted. Feet shuffled and somewhere not far
away pigs grunted.

Sheena opened one eyelid with effort. The dim light in the
room pierced right to her brain. "Oohh," she whispered, and
slammed the eye shut again.

"Now, come on, will ye? Try again, missy. 'Ere ye go." Another drop of soup slid down her throat, and her memory unlocked. She'd escaped the *Dark Sapphire*, jumped into the sea and thought she was drowning. Somehow she must've survived, for if this was God's idea of heaven, he had a very large sense of humor.

Again she opened an eye, and this time her blurry vision focused on the kindly, fleshy face of a woman dressed in drab brown. Tiny eyes at odds with an oversized nose peered back at her. A wide grin, showing off spaces where several teeth were missing, stretched from one plump, vein-riddled cheek to the other. "There ye are . . . see, that wasn't so bad, now was it?"

Sheena stretched, tried to sit up, felt another rip of pain sear through her head, and froze.

"Take it easy, now, lass. Ye've been through a lot, ye 'ave. Me husband Freddy hauled ye out of the sea jest as ye went under. He was out fishin', he was, and pulled ye into his boat."

"That I did. Took ye to the beach," the man agreed. "Laid ye on the sand, but ye didn't move, just lay there like a one-legged crab all curled in on yerself and bruised from 'ead to toe."

"Aye," the woman agreed. "Half dead ye were, but he carried ye here and I've been tendin' to ye ever since."

For the first time Sheena realized that she was in some kind of rough dressing gown, lying on ticking that covered a pallet spread upon the floor. Her dress and chemise were hung on a cord near the fire, pools of water shimmering on the dirt floor beneath the sodden clothing. Her precious boots with their hidden treasure were nowhere to be seen. Panic shot through her cold blood.

"Nay," she cried, pushing up to a sitting position despite her throbbing head and scanning the small wooden building with a fireplace on one end, no windows, but a door that led to what Sheena assumed was a pigsty from the grunts, oinks, and snorts that could be heard through the cracks and knot-holes. "My boots—"

"All of yer things are bein' cared for," the woman assured her. She was holding a mazer of fish broth in one hand and a spoon in the other as she squatted over Sheena. "I washed yer dress and under dress, but methinks they may be ruined by the salt water and rocks. As fer yer boots, we—the husband and I—we polished them. Found yer jewels we did. Rest assured that they be safe."

Sheena wasn't certain, but she reminded herself it mattered little. She had nearly drowned in the sea, was lucky to be alive, and had Freddy the pig farmer to thank for it, though it appeared he wasn't too happy about having a guest.

"Who are ye, lass?" he asked, his bushy eyebrows drawing together into a thick line over eyes that were more oval than round. His beard was thin, his cheeks pockmarked, his skin boasting a rash. "What were ye doin' in the tide, eh?"

"Hush, she just awoke. She need not answer yet," the woman said kindly.

"That's the trouble with ye, Esme, you be trustin' everyone, takin' in strays we don't need. What if she stole them jewels, what then?"

"They're mine," Sheena said, her throat raw, her words raspy. "They . . . they belonged to my mother."

"And yer name?"

She couldn't trust this man. Though he'd saved her life and dragged her back to his hut, she dared not admit her true identity. Even now the soldiers from Tardiff could be lurking nearby, searching the villages, fields, and forests for her. "I'm Victoria of Rhydd," she said as if the name had rolled off her tongue all her life. "I was traveling by ship and was washed overboard in last night's storm."

"Bless the saints that ye lived," the woman said, crossing herself quickly and slopping some of the broth onto her apron. " 'Tis a miracle."

"Why were ye on the deck in the likes of that tempest?" Freddy asked, eyeing her suspiciously. " 'Ave ye no brains?"

Sheena bristled but held her tongue. Let him consider her a twit; 'twould help her. " 'Twas a mistake," she said through clenched teeth.

"And nearly cost ye yer life."

"But it didn't. 'Twas lucky that ye were out fishin' so early and ye found her, Freddy, but find her ye did. 'Tis God's will that she arrived 'ere." Esme set the mazer of soup on a small table and rocked back on her heels.

"Oh, woman, don't be goin' on about the will o' God to me. I do na believe in such nonsense." He threw up a big red hand and shook his head. " 'Tis not the will o' God that I be raisin' a mean sow and litter of runty piglets. Na, I do na think so and don't be startin' in about God makin' ye barren to punish ye, I'll not hear it." He reached for a ragged hat that hung on a peg near the back door, then glanced over his shoulder. "Unless the good Lord has brought ye to us, lassie, and meant fer me to save ye so that ye could give me one of yer gems. Now, that I'd believe. Maybe he's makin' it up to me that me prize boar, Old Jack, died last winter before he could get the sow with piglets." Freddy's eyes narrowed on Sheena. "Aye, if there be God's work here today, it's to pay me back for years of breakin' me back working the fields, listenin' to the woman here go on and on, and givin' me such poor luck with me pigs." He jammed his hat on his head and walked through the heavy door. "I'll take care of the sow, then I'm off to the alehouse."

Grunts, squeals, and snorts greeted him, and a stench like no other stole into the room. Freddy shut the door firmly behind him, as if to cut off any reprimands from his wife.

Sighing with strained patience, Esme deftly made a swift sign of the cross over her bosom. "He is an angry man, Freddy is," she said simply. "No sons to help him with the farm. Nor daughters." She wrung her hands, then wiped them on her dirty apron and stood. "Sleep now, Victoria.

When ye awake again, I'll help ye wash and then ye'll eat some more to get yer strength back."

Too exhausted to argue, Sheena slept fitfully, dozing in and out. She woke to the sound of pigs squealing or the off-key humming of the big woman as she went about her work, stoking the fire, turning the clothes on the line, baking bread over the flames, or stirring her stew pot—a black iron cal-dron that hung by a hook over the flames.

Hours and minutes blended together. Dreams mixed with what was real, and Keegan the bastard, Keegan the rogue, Keegan her love was ever on her mind.

When Sheena finally awoke fully, she blinked and ban-ished all thoughts of the *Dark Sapphire*'s captain from her mind. Cautiously she raised herself on one elbow and winced at the pain throbbing through her jaw. At least her headache and blurred vision had fled.

"Awake now, are ye?" Esme asked, stirring the simmer-ing pot. "Hungry?"

As if in answer Sheena's stomach rumbled.

The older woman chuckled. "I thought so. 'Tis a good sign, y'see." She found a wooden bowl and ladled some of the stew into it. As Sheena started to get to her feet, Esme shook her head. "No need to get up, lassie, I'll be bringin' this to ya." She rose to her own feet and carried over the steaming bowl. "Can ye take it in yer hands?"

"Aye," Sheena said, and was rewarded with the wooden dish. The smells of fish and spices tingled her nostrils as she began to sip, slowly at first and then, as the warm broth slid easily down her throat, more hungrily. "I'll be gettin' ye some bread to go with that." And within minutes the woman had sliced off a thick slab of wastel and slathered it in but-ter. Sheena bit into the hard bread and thought it the best she'd ever eaten. Esme's graying eyebrows lifted a bit as if she was anticipating praise.

" 'Tis good," Sheena said, nodding and taking another bite. Around the mouthful she added, "Very good."

"Ah, it's nice to have me cookin' appreciated. Freddy . . .

well, he's used to it, 'e is." She glanced at the window and noticed the sky had become dark. "'E's been gone long." One big shoulder elevated a mite. "But 'tis 'is way. Now, I bet you'd like to take a look at yer gems, wouldn't ye?"

"Aye." Sheena nodded and finished her soup. Esme padded slowly to the fire, retrieved the boots, and dropped them by the pallet. "Inside they are both of 'em."

"Both?" Sheena's heart sank.

"Aye. A ruby and an emerald. Fit for a queen, ain't they?"

"Well, yes, but—" Sheena reached into the boot, felt around and pulled out the two stones, one dark green, the other blood red. Her fingers searched the entire toe area but found no other gem. "There were three."

"Three?" Esme frowned, her lips folding out thoughtfully.

"Yes, an emerald, a ruby, and a topaz," Sheena said, her heart pounding. Had the stone dropped from her boot as she'd been tossed in the sea? Had it fallen when she'd been carried here to this hut, far from the beach where she'd washed up, or had it been stolen?

"Freddy, he told me there were two in the boot, and sure enough, when I got ye undressed, I found 'em."

"There was another one. A gold stone."

"Are ye sure, lassie? Ye took a knock on the 'ead fer sure, and there be no other gem lodged in either boot." Sheena reached into the second boot, and, as Esme had predicted, her fingers found only damp leather. The gem was missing.

"Ye could 'ave dreamed up the third jewel," Esme said, and took her soup bowl, unconcerned at Sheena's loss.

"Nay, 'twas in my boot."

"Not when ye got here. Took 'em both off ye, I did. There was only two stones. The red and the green." She squatted down close to the pallet. "Ye be a lucky person, Victoria. Very lucky. Not only did ye survive the storm and the sea, but ye've got two precious gems, more wealth than me or my Freddy will see in a lifetime." She glanced at the window, and worry drew thin lines around her mouth and eyes. "He should have come home by this time. There be much to do on the morrow—grain that needs be cut and more fishin', as he cut his trip short this morn when he found ye in the waves." With a heavy sigh of the truly persecuted, she turned to Sheena. Esme pointed a thick, square-tipped finger at the end of Sheena's nose. "Ye can be thankin' the Lord above that we be honest good people." There was the hint of hardness in her gaze as she stared at Sheena. "Mayhap we should pray together; thank the Father that you're alive, in one piece, and that ye've got your treasure." She made the sign of the cross and bowed her head. From the other side of the plank door a pig grunted and another one squealed.

Sheena didn't argue any further. She didn't know what had happened to the gem, if it had been lost in the sea or stolen by a poor pig farmer, but it was lost to her forever. Esme was right; 'twas fortunate that she was alive.

And then the man she'd pushed out of her thoughts returned with a vengeance, galloping through her mind.

Keegan.

Oh, love. Traitor.

Her heart squeezed painfully, for she knew she would never see him again.

Mayhap it was for the best.

Or the worst.

Chapter Eleven

The farmer was drunk.

And loud.

The most boisterous man in a tavern that teemed with merchants, peasants, soldiers, and the like. A troupe of musicians was trying to entertain. One was plucking dutifully at a lute, another blew into a pipe, while another, a slim woman with a sad face, was attempting to sing a ballad of sorts. But the din of the patrons drowned out whatever sounds they made. The farmer, dressed in tatters, was by far the noisiest of the lot. Laughing and joking, drinking cup after cup of ale, he was working very hard at making an ass of himself.

And Manning was not in the mood for it.

The night had been fruitless. He'd boarded the damned ship with its smug captain and was certain he'd find the woman. Though there were spaces aplenty in the hold to store men or women, he'd found nothing. But the captain's cabin had been a different matter, and there had been evidence of a woman; dresses hung by the door. He claimed they belonged to his wife, but rumor had it she was long dead.

There was something about the man that bothered Manning, something vaguely familiar. The dark-haired captain tugged at Manning's memory, as if the knight had met him before. The ship, too, was a puzzlement. With a name not unlike the damned ring that Fawn had been mewling about for years, the *Dark Sapphire* bothered him. Could it be? He narrowed his eyes into his cup and didn't like the link that was forming in his mind. He didn't like it at all.

He tossed back his ale, then snapped his fingers at a buxom barmaid to refill his mazer. The music irritated him. He drummed his fingers on the long plank tables as the serving girl filled his cup and offered him more than a casual glance at the cleft between those big breasts. Aye, they were inviting, spilling over the neckline of her dress as they were. But he wasn't in the mood for a flirtation or even an attempt to lift her skirts, though he assumed 'twould be easy enough. The girl kept her eye on him and smiled fetchingly, the very tip of her tongue rimming her lips when she caught his glance. Aye, she would serve a man and serve him well.

But Manning had not the time or the inclination.

Where was Sheena? Still aboard the *Dark Sapphire*, stowed in some hiding spot he and the paunchy sheriff had overlooked?

He took a long draught of ale, ignored the serving wench, and half listened to the drunken farmer rave on and on about a turn in his fortune. Probably a man who planted by the phases of the moon.

Blast it all!

"Can I get ye ennythin' else, sir?" the barmaid asked as she rested a plump hip on the edge of the table and spoke directly to Manning. "Somethin' to eat?"

"I be fine."

"Ah, and there be no denyin' that," she said with a smile and a lift of one sultry dark eyebrow.

"You're a bold chit."

"When I have to be." She poured more ale into Manning's near-empty cup.

"Hey! Wench. Over here. We be dyin' of thirst!" the farmer yelled, flagging her and waving her over. The men around him, dressed in filthy rags such as his, laughed raucously. "Another pitcher and one fer me friends."

Manning's eyes narrowed on the man. The farmer was far too generous for his station in life. But Manning could not think on it. Not now. He had his own problems. He was certain Sheena was or had been on the *Dark Sapphire*. There were many secrets hidden in that cursed ship's hold, none of which Manning had uncovered. He'd left the brooding captain and the damned ship, then once out of earshot, had posted a guard. The soldier would hide on the dock and watch, keeping track of anyone who attempted to board or leave the anchored vessel. Manning had also instructed the spy to make note of any large crates or bundles that were roomy enough to hide a small woman. If somehow in his search he'd missed Sheena, she wouldn't get off the ship without his knowledge.

Caught in the turn of his thoughts, he slowly sipped from his cup as the music, laughter, and gaiety danced in the air surrounding him. He couldn't dismiss what was becoming more evident.

Manning was convinced that Keegan was indeed the son of Rourke, the captain who had tried to cheat Baron Jestin years earlier. Though Rourke had died, the boy and an old man had escaped.

With the Dark Sapphire of Ogof.

'Twas blasphemy to name the ship after the stolen stone. Idly, Manning wondered if Keegan still owned the jewel that was rumored to be cursed, the blue stone of such myth and legend. Oh, 'twould be sweet revenge if Manning were to lay his hands on the gem. He would pocket it and never mention the stone to Jestin or Fawn.

But first he had to find it.

Along with Sheena. Scowling, he swirled his mazer and stared at the beer sloshing in the cup. That woman had proven him and his troops to be fools. She'd eluded them, evaded them, and seemed to disappear each time they came close to her. God's eyes, all of Tardiff and Ogof were probably laughing that one small woman could outsmart his army.

If only the ship's spy had lived. Mayhap Warren of Halliwell could have given him some more insight, but the poor sod had decided to give up the ghost before Manning's whip had even started to pry open the weak man's tongue.

Another bad turn of fortune.

"Aye! Fill the cups, that's a girl," the farmer crowed and pinched the wench's butt through her skirts as she walked past balancing a tray holding six cups. She started, squealed a bit, and foam sloshed down the sides of the mazers.

"Are ye sure about this, Freddy?" she asked. " 'Tis quite a few."

"Get on with it." He showed off a toothy grin. "Old Freddy's luck has changed."

"How so?"

Manning shifted, kept the farmer in his sights. The man was well into his cups and swayed a bit, his speech slurred. "Ah, 'tis me secret," he said, then laughed loudly as the musicians started another song.

Manning wanted to cut out the braggart's tongue, then stuff it down his throat. The smelly, filthy farmer was obnoxious.

Laughing loudly, clapping his friends on the back, grinning widely, his pockmarked face beaming as if he'd just struck gold, he settled onto a stool. There were others in the tavern, a sorry lot of peasants who had spent their entire lives scraping out a living from the soil, paying the lord his due, living from one year to the next, and praying the weather held, his pigs, cattle, and sheep had healthy offspring, and that there was someone who was willing to buy his crops and animals just so he could do it all again the next year.

'Twas a pathetic life, in Manning's opinion. But then, he was an ambitious man. Mayhap too ambitious. His arm ached from flogging the unlucky bastard who'd been spying upon his encampment. The one-thumbed man had just up and collapsed with only a few blows. He'd cried out and stiffened, clutching his chest, his knees buckling. His face had twisted in horrid agony, and he'd been unable to draw in a breath. 'Twas as if his heart had just given out. Before Manning had gotten the information he wanted from him. All he had learned was where the *Dark Sapphire* was docked. Nothing more.

"Come on, Freddy, what is it?" the wench asked, trailing her finger around the pockmarked farmer's neck. "What kind of good luck befell ye, eh?"

"Ah, 'twas a gift from heaven. Brought by an angel." The farmer's tongue had been loosened by too much ale and the thought that he might be able to bed the comely serving wench.

"Bah!" one of his friends said. "An angel, ye say?"

"'Tis true." Freddy nodded emphatically as more ale was poured and sloshed. A fire crackled, giving off heat from one end of the room.

"Let him finish!" The bar wench left her hand resting on Freddy's ragged collar. "What angel?"

"Found 'er 'alf dead in the ocean. Goin' down to her death she was when I plucked her up and—"

Manning's ears picked up. He set down his cup. Focused on the filthy man.

"—and so thankful she was fer me takin' her home and savin' 'er life, she gave me somethin'."

"What?" The wench leaned closer, breathed something into Freddy's ear, and the man actually blushed. With stained, dirty fingers he dug deep in one of his pockets and pulled out a stone—a bright yellow stone that Manning recognized. 'Twas part of Sheena's dowry, given to Tardiff from Jestin.

Manning's pulse jumped.

"Oooh, 'tis a beaut," the girl said enviously.

Several of the farmer's friends whispered among themselves. Other eyes watched as well, and Manning thought there was a good chance Freddy's throat would be slit and

his treasure stolen from him before he staggered back to his
hut that night. But Manning would see that it wouldn't happen. Nay, he and his small army would be the farmer's
guardian angels, for they would ensure that he got safely
home.

Once at the farm, they'd remove this stone from Freddy's
grimy fingers, take the others as well, and put that damned
elusive wench in chains before hauling her back to Ogof.

A smile of triumph twisted across Manning's jaw. His
palms sweated in anticipation. Silently advising himself to
be patient, he slowly finished his drink and observed the
farmer through guarded eyes. Finally, it seemed, Manning's
luck was beginning to turn.

"I'll not stay here another second," Fawn insisted. She
was lying in the fortune-teller's bed, and the darkness made
the hut seem gloomier than ever. In the feeble light from a
candle and the dying fire, the bleached bones and talons of
dead animals seemed more sinister than they had during the
day. The hut was filled with the presence of evil and was no
place for a baby, any baby, and certainly not hers—not this
boy child who would, she was certain, someday rule all of
Wales.

"'Tis best for you to rest," Serena said.

"Not here."

"Just until you and the babe are stronger." Her soothing
voice irritated Fawn. How did this woman who had no children of her own know what was best for a newborn and his
mother?

"I needs be at Ogof," Fawn argued, eyeing her husband,
who had spent the day with her, proud as any new father
who had so long wanted a male heir. He could, if he so
deigned, see that she and the child were taken safely back to
Ogof.

Oh, Fawn longed for the comfort and privilege of the castle, for the servants that she usually found dull and lazy, for
fresh water brought to her, a cook's meals and a nursemaid

who would take the baby away when his cries became too much for her. She licked her cracked lips and lusted after wine for her throat, soap and water for her skin, and ointment to be rubbed into her sore muscles. Most of all, she wanted the sense of victory and self-satisfaction that would come when she reentered the gates with this boy child, an heir for Ogof and Tardiff. Her heart pounded with expectation. "I must go home."

"In the morning," her husband promised. "When dawn breaks I will ride to the castle and return with a wagon for you."

There seemed to be no changing his mind. Oh, Jestin was a stubborn one, he was. Fawn frowned, but then remembered her secret. The baby let up a wail. Again. His cry was lusty, it was. Jestin paced and Serena, thank God, held her tongue about the child's sire. What did it matter? Since Fawn was certain that she was descended from the true prince of Wales, it was insignificant that this boy child was not of Jestin's blood.

"All in time," she whispered to the downy head as the baby fussed and coughed, nuzzled at her breast, only to turn fitfully away. The cat slunk into the shadow. The Baron of Ogof leaned heavily against the warm stones near the fire while Fawn tried fruitlessly to soothe the little one. 'Twas as if he were angry for being forced into the world. Or at being in this horrid little hovel. " 'Twill be fine soon, Llywelyn," she consoled, though his continuous howls were beginning to stretch her nerves thin.

Oh, 'twas torture to endure here at the edge of the forest with only the fortune-teller as a servant. As she tried to hold her newborn close, she wished he was not so loud. She was weary from the birthing, yet the lusty-voiced babe would not let her sleep. Fawn tried to console herself with the thought that his cries were an indication of his fierce, strong spirit, but deep inside she prayed that he would quit squalling and sleep.

Only minutes after he was born, Llywelyn had started

crying and had barely stopped for a moment. He'd suckled at her breast, then stopped, screwed up his little red face, and now was fussing at the top of his little lungs.

The blankets over Fawn itched, and she was certain bugs riddled the straw bed upon which she was lying. Her breasts were beginning to fill and she was hemorrhaging more than she had with the girls.

She was hot, threw off the awful blanket, and felt a flea jump against her leg. It was all Fawn could do not to scream in frustration. But somehow she would endure the night. Then she would return to Ogof triumphantly. With her son. The heir to Jestin's barony.

Sheena no longer reigned.

A weary smile stole over Fawn's lips. 'Twas always the same—to get what she wanted in this life, a woman had to sacrifice for a man. Even one who was but a few hours old.

And sacrifice she would.

For this little one would someday prove to be the true prince of Wales—nay, 'twas not enough. Llywelyn would someday throw off the shackles of the English and become the king of Wales.

But why stop there? A tiny smile played upon her lips. This little warrior might just be destined to rule England as well.

"Where is he?" Keegan demanded, his mood foul as he stood on the deck of his ship and his finger curled tightly over the rail. The noises from the town, the turn of cart wheels, whispered conversation, laughter from a pub, all filtered over the steady lapping of the water where the *Dark Sapphire* was anchored. "Where's Wart?" Smoke rolled to the heavens, and patches of light cast from the open windows of some of the buildings gave an eerie illumination to the docks. Gentle fingers of fog were beginning to stretch throughout the town.

"Who knows?" Hollis glanced up at the heavens, with winking stars flung across the dark sky and reflecting in the night-dark waters of the bay. Only the patchy mist rising from the sea dimmed their sparkle. "Mayhap he found a woman or a pint of ale that he could not resist."

"Nay, he would be here." Keegan's body still ached from his ordeal in the water the night Sheena had thrown herself overboard, and his heart was heavy—a weight in his chest. Guilt pounded through his head. If he had stayed with her, or locked her in his cabin, or never been so bold as to have made love to her, she would be alive this night, her blue eyes laughing, her red hair coppery in the dark night, her tongue wicked and sharp as ever. His back teeth ground together as he damned himself to his own private hell and paced the length of the ship, his eyes trained on the docks, where crates and barrels were stacked around great coils of rope and chain. Men walked near the waterfront, some drunk and stumbling, others huddled deep in their cloaks, their voices carrying in the night, their laughter and bawdy jokes ripping over the waves. "Something's happened to Wart," he decided.

"What?"

"I know not, but I intend to find out." With a rush of determination Keegan took the steps down to his cabin, grabbed his mantle, and then made his way down the gangway while Hollis, like an old woman, chased after him, nagging and arguing about his decision to visit the local tavern.

"'Tis not a good idea," the older man advised.

"Never is."

"I mean it, Keegan. Ye escaped with yer life the other night, and now ye be spoilin' fer a fight. I see it in yer eyes, so don't be lyin' to me."

"Then I won't."

He left the old man swearing under his breath and walked swiftly along the piers, where the acrid odor of rotting wood battled the smells of bilge and brine.

Keegan's head throbbed, his stomach rumbled, and the heaviness in his heart refused to leave him. Cramming his fists into the pockets of his mantle, he thought of Sheena.

Had he sent not only her but one of his men as well to an early grave, all because of his fascination with the woman?

"Do not think of it," he reminded himself, his boots ringing on the wooden pier. He felt a vein throb over his eye, and as he passed a stack of crates he thought he saw movement, the figure of a man lurking near a piling.

So now you be jumping at shadows, eh? his mind taunted, but his muscles flexed and he felt for the knife tucked inside his belt as he reached the street. Was it his imagination, or did he hear the soft tread of boots scraping along the cobblestones in his wake? He glanced behind him, saw no one creeping through the thin fog, and frowned to himself.

There it was again.

The sound of footsteps.

But who?

Wart?

Or some other presence? An enemy? 'Twas time to find out. Ducking along a narrow alley, he hurried his steps, now certain he was being followed. A smile of satisfaction curved over his lips for the old man, Hollis had been right. Keegan was spoiling for a fight. And he intended to make it a good one.

Silent as a cat, he moved in the shadows. He passed a tailor's shop, then ducked around a corner. He crossed the narrow alley past a barrel maker's establishment to a stable, where, pausing only to pick up a few pieces of gravel, he lithely swung himself over the gate to land softly on a straw-strewn floor. With a snort, one of the horses sidled away, blowing and mincing nervously as Keegan squatted and peered through the slats.

He didn't have to wait long.

Within seconds a man appeared. Walking so rapidly as to be nearly running, his head swiveling side to side as he searched the darkness, he neared the stables. Though there was little light, Keegan recognized his shadow as one of the soldiers of Tardiff Hall who had been with Manning.

His lips curled and he placed his knife between his teeth.

The soldier's footsteps slowed. He paused at the stable, as if sensing his enemy within the black interior. Keegan felt that tingle of anticipation signaling a fight, the surge in his blood readying him for battle.

Without a bit of noise he flung the pebbles down the street, where they rattled against the cobblestones.

The soldier jumped. He stepped forward again, his attention drawn down the alley. Now! Keegan sprang, vaulting the gate, throwing his body onto the back of the soldier.

"Bloody hell!" The soldier, nearly toppling to his knees, scrabbled for his sword. Muscles bunched.

Keegan's arm surrounded the man, held him fast against his own long frame, caught one of his enemy's hands, and roughly twisted it behind his back.

"Ach! *Awww!*"

In a heartbeat Keegan's blade was at the soldier's throat; the dirty smell of his adversary filled his nostrils. "Drop your weapon."

The sword clattered to the cobblestones.

"Now, soldier, die or speak the truth," he commanded through lips drawn back far enough to bare his teeth.

"Who—what? If it's me money ye want—"

"I have no need of your paltry coins."

"Aagh! Me shoulder. If—if not money, then what?"

"Ye be a soldier from Tardiff Hall."

It wasn't a question, but the man nodded frantically, his skin white in the night.

"What's yer name?"

"P-Peter."

"So, Peter, your leader is Manning, is it not?"

Hesitation. Keegan twisted the man's arm up a notch and pressed the knife closer to his throat. Tendons popped.

Peter yelped. "Aye—aye, Sir Manning."

"Did Manning come across a sailor? A man by the name of Wart?"

Every muscle in Peter's body tightened. His spine was pressed hard against Keegan's chest. "Nay," he said as Kee-

gan twisted his arm ever tighter. The man's voice raised an
octave, and from the sudden rush of stench Keegan thought
he might have pissed himself as well. "Not that I know of."

"You'd remember Wart," Keegan insisted, sensing a lie.
"He be a small man. Moves quickly. Thin brown hair and
he's missing a thumb."

"I—I haven't seen 'im."

"Nay?"

"Nay. I—I would've remembered."

"You'd best remember or I'll kill you sure. Stick you like
a pig and leave you bleeding here in the street." To add emphasis to his words, he wrenched the soldier's arms and
pushed the tip of his knife into his filthy throat. "Tell me!"
He felt the man melt in his arms.

"Ah, ah, Wart, he was spyin' on us, 'e was, watchin' our
camp and I . . . one of the soldiers found 'im and drug 'im
back to Sir Manning," he finally admitted. "Ach, me arm,
ye're rippin' it out of me!"

"So where is Wart now? With Manning?"

Hesitation.

Another touch of the knife. The soldier gulped.

"Nay, nay, Manning he be off to the farmer's hut in search
of the woman."

Keegan froze. His heart nearly stopped. He felt a thrill of
anticipation, then told himself to slow down. Sheena was
dead. Killed in the sea. He took a deep breath, then asked,
"What woman?"

The horse behind him neighed, and the sounds of the waterfront, laughter, music, and conversation drifted through
the narrow alley.

"The lady we be lookin' for. Lady Sheena of Tardiff."

"How do you know this if you've been watching my
ship?"

"I . . . was in the tavern and sent to relieve the first man
who stood guard."

Keegan didn't trust this liar, and yet a part of him was
desperate to believe that Sheena might be alive. Hope sang

through his veins but was quickly tempered by reality. 'Twas a ruse, a carefully laid trap. "Why would Manning think the lady be at a farmer's house?"

"Because the man was drunk and braggin' about a half-dead woman he pulled out of the sea. The farmer, he showed off a jewel he'd found on her. 'Twas a golden sapphire, a topaz, one of the stolen gems missin' from Tardiff Hall."

Was it possible? Had Sheena lived—only to fall victim to Sir Manning? Did she have jewels upon her?

"When did this happen?" Keegan demanded harshly, his pulse racing.

"Tonight. Earlier."

"Where is the farmer's hut?"

"I know not—ah!"

Keegan kneed the man in the kidneys. "Lie no more, or meet your doom."

Peter nearly collapsed. "'Tis the truth, I tell ye. Sir Manning rounded up some men and followed the farmer home. As I said, he sent me to relieve Donald. They took off to the east and left me on the docks to watch the ship."

"They will be back for you?"

"Nay. I was to meet up with them at dawn, at the camp."

"Then you shall, soldier," Keegan said through tightly clenched teeth, "but you'll go as my prisoner. Pray that you've not lied to me or I'll send you to your grave."

"'Tis the truth, I swear."

Keegan wanted to believe him. With all his heart he yearned to cling to a shred of hope that Sheena had somehow survived. "Now you'd best be on your knees, asking God that your leader will trade your life for the woman."

Peter grunted. "Then I be dead. Manning has searched too long and hard for this one to give her up now."

Keegan's blood rushed through his body. His injuries no longer throbbed. Did he dare believe that Sheena was alive? Hope chased the demons of despair from his soul, and yet he could not believe she had survived. "If the woman is Sheena of Ogof, I'll barter for her."

"And you'll lose. This is not a matter of money but of pride. She has eluded him much too long, made him look a fool."

Keegan's grip tightened. He felt the desperate man was telling the truth, or as much of it as he knew. But it seemed that a miracle had been performed by the farmer and that Sheena of Ogof and Tardiff, the woman he loved, was alive. Silently Keegan vowed that one way or another, this soldier was going to take him to Sheena and Keegan would help her escape. If he had to slit this one's throat, or slay Manning in the bargain, so be it. If he had to sacrifice his own life, he would. He would not let her be dragged to the gallows.

"Where does this farmer live?"

"I—I know not. Please, trust me . . . I only know that the army was heading north of town." Peter swallowed hard. "In the tavern they would know where the man is from."

"Then we shall go there," Keegan said, his mind clicking into gear as he glanced back at the stable and the horses within. He had no compunction about "borrowing" a couple, or of stealing a nag or two if need be. Not when Sheena's life was in danger.

He prodded Peter toward the tavern. Devising a plan to help her escape the deadly clutches of Sir Manning, he whispered to the sweating soldier, "You best pray that your leader has a change of heart. And now that your memory has returned, Peter, tell me, where is Wart—at the camp?"

There was a pause, and a chill as cold as death slid down Keegan's spine.

"Nay. Not there."

"Where then?"

"In hell." Peter spat on the ground, and there was a hint of satisfaction in his voice. "Sir Manning did the honors of sending the bastard's soul to the devil."

"God in heaven, forgive me," Hollis whispered as he stood on the bow of the *Dark Sapphire*. The lights of town were fading, Keegan had not returned, and all the sins of the old man's past rested heavily on his aging shoulders. He thought of his foolishness, of his pride, of his reasons for betraying all those whom he'd loved. He'd done it for Keegan's sake, or so he'd told himself, but he could not deny a bit of avarice in his black soul.

"Forgive ye for what?" Bo asked, darting across the deck quick as a frightened mouse.

"Many things, lad, many things." Hollis sighed and rubbed the pain from his hands. These days his joints were swollen and knotted, and he knew he had not many years left on this earth. It was time to make his peace.

"Like what?"

"Ye be too young to understand."

Bo snorted, flipped his hair from his eyes, and squared his thin shoulders. "I be almost a man and tired of everyone talking to me as if I were but a boy."

Hollis chuckled to himself, for the boy's bravado reminded him of Keegan when he'd been but a lad and Captain Rourke had still been counted among the living. Keegan, too, had been full of himself, anxious for battle and thinking no harm would ever touch him. 'Twas foolish, of course. Ach, it seemed so long ago now. "You'll be a man soon enough, boy. Do not hope to hasten it along."

Bo climbed upon the rail and glared at the older man. "Where's the captain?"

" 'Tis a good question ye ask."

"Ashore?"

"Aye, that much be certain."

"Why?"

"He's off to find Wart, though why they be not back by now, I know not." He glanced anxiously at the star-flung heavens, more obscured as the night fog grew thicker, the lights glowing from the town now blurry. " 'Tis a worry."

"All things be a worry to you."

Hollis sighed and he pulled the neck of his tunic closer, as the night was seeping into his bones. "There be much to be concerned about," he admitted, and the boy, tired of talk-

ing in circles, hopped down from the rail and quickly scrambled up the shrouds and rigging to the crow's nest. Again
Hollis glanced up at the sliver of moon barely visible
through the mist, and he felt a premonition of doom. Something was wrong. Very wrong. Elsewise Keegan would have
returned.

Hollis felt ancient, and the old fear that he'd doomed Keegan and his ship, scraped at his soul. Snagging a lantern
from its hook, he used the feeble light from its single candle
to guide him as he descended to the hold, where casks of
wine and barrels of ale were stacked. Rats scurried out of
his path, and he vaguely wondered why Maynard was not
after the bothersome pests. In the war against the beasts,
Maynard and his cat seemed to be losing.

Easing his body behind a post, Hollis reached upward to
an overhead beam where long before he'd whittled out a
hiding spot. Standing on tiptoe, stretching as far as he could,
he felt the top of the dusty beam with his fingertips, found a
tiny nail, and pulled. A small lid lifted and he frowned, for it
was becoming harder and harder for him to reach so high.
He was shrinking, his spine shortening, and soon he would
have to find a new hiding spot for his treasure. Straining, his
fingers delving into the small space, he felt the ring, cold
metal and icy stone. With effort he pulled it from its age-old
niche and held it up to the candlelight.

He'd kept the ring for eleven years, lied to everyone who
asked about it, including Keegan. But he'd never had the
heart to throw the beautiful gem into the sea, though he'd
promised himself he would do it a thousand times over.

But he, like all the men and women who'd owned the
jewel before him, had been seduced by its dark brilliance,
had ignored the fact that he knew it to be cursed, and kept it
hidden from the day he'd sold the *Warrior* and bought the
Dark Sapphire. He'd even named the ship as a reminder to
himself that the ring was hidden in the hold. And in so doing
he'd probably cursed the crew.

He'd vowed to get rid of it, but each time he'd tried, he

had not been able to cast the stone into the sea. Worth a king's ransom, the ring had been insurance against grave financial loss; Hollis had comforted himself with the thought that should Keegan ever feel the pinch to sell the craft, he would be able to spare him the pain, by offering up the stone to save his nephew's ship.

Or had he simply been bewitched and cursed by the gem?

"'Tis a fool ye be, old man," he grumbled, staring into the deadly blue facets of the sapphire. Oh, 'twas seductive as the most comely wench.

Rather than return the ring to its hiding place, Hollis dropped it into one of his voluminous pockets.

Mayhap this night he would have the courage to throw the damned ring off the bow and into the dark waters of the bay.

Chapter Twelve

B oots clomped outside the door. A deep male voice sang, though very much off-key. In the hut, Sheena raised her head.

Bang! The door flew open. Bounced against the wall.

Reeking of ale and dirt, his hat falling over one eye, Freddy staggered in. A gust of wind chased after him, causing the fire to glow brighter.

"Where 'ave ye been?" Esme demanded. She'd been sleeping on a pallet in a corner near the fire, but she was on her feet, her eyes puffy, her hair standing up at odd angles. "As if I didn't know."

"Just 'avin' a pint or two with some friends."

"It's nearly dawn. And ye've got work to do."

"Ah, Esme, ye worry too much." He shut the door behind him and yawned, showing off crooked yellow teeth.

"One of us must."

"'Tis the trouble with ye, woman," he said, and winked familiarly at his wife. "Always frettin' ye be." Stretching an arm over his head, he started undoing the laces of his tunic with his other hand.

Esme wasn't interested in his sudden turn of affection. "The girl here"—she hitched her chin in the direction of Sheena's pallet—"she claims there was another jewel with her, a golden one."

Freddy's eyebrows lifted high over his eyes, and he turned his palms toward the bare rafters as his bleary gaze turned on Sheena. "I found none, lass. Only the two that were in yer boot. If there was another stone, ye must've lost it in yer swim."

"It was with the others." Sheena rolled to the side of her pallet and sat up. "In my boot. Wedged there. I doubt if it would have fallen out if the others were still there."

Frowning drunkenly, his head wobbling, he said, "Well, now, girlie, Esme was with me when we took yer boots off, and there be only the two stones—red and green."

"But—"

"Ye could search the sea yerself," he said, and chuckled as if he found the thought humorous before turning to look at his wife again. Sheena glared at the man who had saved her, knew he lied, though his wife seemed convinced of his integrity. "Did ye tend to the pigs, Es?" he asked, avoiding Sheena's eyes.

"Don't I always?"

"'Tis a good lass ye be, wife," he said, swatting her familiarly on her rear end. "Hardworking and true."

"And 'tis drunk, ye be, husband."

"Aye. That I canna argue." Swaying, leaning heavily upon the big woman, he waggled one index finger in front of her nose. "But I do na beat ya, now, do I? Newton, the carter, he takes a cane to his wife."

"Yeah, and if I were Newton's wife, I'd take worse to him. Come along, now, Freddy. Let's get ye into the bed. Come on, now."

She managed to turn her husband toward the door.

Hoof beats—hundreds of them, it seemed—thundered outside the door. Horses whinnied and snorted. Bridles jangled. Sheena's heart flew to her throat. Boots pounding the earth outside. *Oh, God!* A deep voice echoed through the night. Sheena's blood turned to ice.

Sir Manning!
Nay!

Bam! Bam! Bam!

A huge fist thudded on the door.

Sheena shot to her feet.

"Now, who the devil is that?" Esme looked at her husband, then the door, and back to Freddy again. "Did ye bring home—?"

"Open up, Fred Farmer! 'Tis the sheriff."

"Oh, bloody Christ," Freddy grumbled.

"What is it ye've done now?" Esme clucked her tongue.

Sheena nearly tripped on the folds of the big dress.

"I said, 'Open up.' I know ye be in there. Saw ye enter meself, Freddy, and there's someone here who needs to talk to ye."

Sheena's heart was a drum. "Do not open the door," she ordered, searching for another way out of the hut. She crossed the room in a second, the hem of the rough dress dragging, the dirt floor cool against the soles of her feet.

"Wait a minute—where're ye going?" Esme asked.

Sheena didn't answer.

"Open up! Fred!" the sheriff commanded tersely. "Now!"

"Break it down." Manning's voice again.

Sheena shuddered. Frantic, she had to find a means of escape.

Chickens fluttered, feathers scattered. The cat hissed. Sheena didn't wait. Couldn't. Throwing open the door to the pigsty, she flung herself into the darkness. The stench was overpowering. Her feet sank into the ooze. Her heart knocked, ricocheting through her brain. *Run!*

More pounding on the front door. Men's voices. Angry. Gruff. Demanding. *Dear Lord, help me!* She slammed the door to the sty behind her but still heard the muffled orders and jangle of swords.

Run, Sheena, as fast as you can! RUN!

Freddy called, "I'm coming, I'm coming—"

Sheena stumbled through the muck. Pigs snorted and galloped out of her way.

Ears straining, she heard the front door burst open, bang hard against the wall again.

Her stomach clenched. Fear drove her onward. A sow grunted.

"Where is she?" Sir Manning's voice demanded as she frantically waded through the dung, mud, and straw. "Where, man, tell me now, or I'll slit your belly—Oh, hell. After her!"

Dear God, no, not like this! Piglets squealed around her feet, the sow snorted and oinked, and in the darkness she bumped her head against a beam on the low-hanging roof. Fumbling, she stumbled away from the house. The door opened.

A lantern illuminated the sty, condemning light catching her in its flickering beam.

"There she is! With the pigs," Manning yelled. "Get her. Now!"

"No!" Esme's voice.

Gasping, dragging herself forward, Sheena ducked beneath the overhang of the roof. Her blood was pulsing through her brain, her legs slogging through the ooze.

"Oh, for the love of God," Freddy growled as she dashed toward a short fence.

Soldiers poured into the enclosure. Pigs shrieked, oinked, grunted, and slopped through the slippery mud.

Sheena rolled over the top rail of the fence that separated the enclosure from a field, landed on the far side, and twisted her ankle. Pain shot up her calf. Still she ran, hobbling through the slimy mud and into the darkness. The smell of the sea was heavy in the air. Fog circled her feet as it rose from the cliffs. Gloomy and gratefully dark, the night was illuminated with only a hint of light from a sliver of the moon.

"There! Shit—get out of me way, you blasted beast!" a man yelled from the shed.

A piglet screamed.

"After her!" Manning ordered, his voice deep, resonant and terrifying.

"She's got away—go out the front!"

Sheena's feet slapped the ground.

The forest wasn't far away, she knew, just on the other side of one of Freddy's fields. She ran by instinct, her legs burning, her ankle on fire. The roar of the sea faded, the smell of salt in the air receding as she headed away from the cliffs on which Freddy's hut was perched. If she could find her way into the trees that spread up the hillside, then hide until dawn, she would be able to steal a horse and—and . . . Oh, God, they were still chasing her. She heard the thud of boots, the shouts of men as they spied her. There was a crackle of excitement, a cry of expectant triumph from a soldier. 'Twas as if he felt the blood lust of a wolf after prey.

Help me, Sheena silently prayed, for the thought of being alone with Sir Manning for even a few minutes was horrifying. The man had no heart, no soul. She would not allow him to drag her back to Ogof a prisoner. Nay, if and when she returned to face her father, she would do it on her own. She'd thought of returning to Ogof when she was aboard the *Dark Sapphire*, and now, as she tried to escape, she knew that she would have to someday walk through the yawning gates of the castle.

Someday.

She couldn't think past the moment and the agony in her ankle. Clenching her jaw, she spurred herself onward, ignoring the pain raging up her leg.

The soldiers were closing the gap, breathing hard, cursing her, commanding her to stop, but the forest was nearer as well. Through the mist tall, dark shapes of trees loomed along the field's edge, protective foliage only a few feet away. Her lungs burned, her ankle ached, and the skirt of the huge dress was caked with mud. It tangled against her legs. *Run. Run for your life, Sheena. Do not give up!* Propelled by sheer will, she found a path in the forest and forced her feet forward as branches slapped her in the face, underbrush snagged her clothes, and her feet tripped over roots exposed on the trail. Her eyes attempted to adjust to the stygian blackness, but with only a sliver of moonlight and a few pale stars as her guide, she was running half blind.

Pain burned in her ankle, but she plunged on, upward through the forested hills. Her only chance was to lose her pursuers in the tangle of oaks and pine. She heard no dogs baying anxiously behind her, so there was hope that somehow, with God's help and her own wits, she could elude them. *Hurry, hurry, hurry!* she silently prodded herself. Deeper and deeper into the thicket. The men were farther behind her now, and yet she felt as if someone was watching her, trailing close at her heels, stalking her.

'Twas only her fear that made her think she heard the snap of a twig so close at hand. The voices of the soldiers were at the base of the hill. The trail forked and she bore right, then dived into a thicket, desperately willing her wild breathing to slow. Her lungs were on fire, her ankle throbbed, her mind reeled as she tried to find some escape.

"In the forest! Sir Manning, she's in there!"

"Oh, for the love of St. Michael, how'll we ever find her?"

"It matters not how, just bloody hell flush her out!" Manning commanded.

Sheena cringed at the sound of his voice, fell back against the rough bark of an oak tree. She was sweating, gasping for breath. Her feet were bruised. Her pulse racing.

"Surround the forest," Manning ordered, his voice far too close. "'Tis but a few trees. We'll work from the outside in."

Her heart plummeted. Somewhere in the uppermost branches of a tree an owl hooted. There was no escape if what he said was true, and she had no way of knowing, for this part of Wales was foreign to her. *Think, Sheena, think. Do not give up!*

She backed up a few steps, her thoughts whirling. She had to get away, to find a place to rest, to—

A heavy hand clamped her shoulder. She jumped. Nearly

screamed as another huge hand reached around and covered her mouth.

All was lost.

Her knees sagged.

Mother Mary, help me.

"Shh," her captor whispered against her ear, and for the barest of seconds her hopeful heart leapt as the deep timbre reminded her of Keegan's.

Keegan.

Judas. Blackheart. Lover.

Her soul twisted painfully at the thought of the bastard who had stolen her silly heart. She swallowed hard and turned to look at the beast who held her in a grip of steel. 'Twas too dark to see, and her mind was surely playing tricks upon her. She considered biting his hand, but knew he'd let up a yowl and then all of the cursed soldiers would be upon her.

Somewhere nearby a horse neighed.

Bridles jangled, steeds snorted, and the beams of torches were visible, golden points of light that shined through the branches and vines.

"Be quiet and do as I say." Dear God, he sounded so much like Keegan. Could it be? Nay, nay, 'twas but her willful mind playing tricks upon her.

Slowly he released her. She turned and felt his face with his hands, knew in an instant it was the brooding captain of the *Dark Sapphire*.

Tears of joy filled her eyes.

"Do as I tell you," he whispered in her ear as the soldiers and horsemen surrounded the forest. "We have not much time." He took her hand and together they ran, stumbling, through the low brush toward the sound of a stream that rushed and gurgled through a chasm that sliced between the stands of pine and oak. "Hurry."

She needed no further inspiration. Fear drove her, and she clung to Keegan's hand as the sound of water tumbling and falling, splashing over stones, became louder.

They reached the bank of the creek, and he guided her around a copse of saplings, then stopped short. Even in the darkness she saw the man, lying on the ground and naked as the day he was born. He was wriggling and trying to speak, but his voice was muffled. His wrists tied, his ankles bound, he was a big, dark squirming shadow who writhed angrily and could not speak because of the gag across his mouth.

"Who—?"

"Shh!"

Sheena heard them drawing even closer, men and horses tromping up the hill. The torches flickered and burned bright, evil lights shining in the darkness.

Her heart was thudding, fear racing through her blood, but Keegan's hand on hers was somehow reassuring. He drew her close, and for a split second she thought he would kiss her. Instead he placed his mouth to her ear. "Now, Sheena," he said so softly she barely heard him, "take off your clothes."

"What?"

"Just do as I say. And be quick about it."

Through the brush she heard the soldiers approaching. They were getting far too near. The thought of facing them without any clothing was daunting, yet she threw off the big, dirty dress and shivered in the barest hint of moonlight. Keegan grabbed the soiled garment and tossed her some garb—men's clothes, a soldier's uniform of red and gold—the colors of Tardiff's army. It smelled of urine and sweat. Her stomach turned over, but she closed her mind to thoughts about the allegiance symbolized by the uniform. Fingers fumbling, feet aching, she donned each piece of the hated, wretched colors of Tardiff while Keegan cut the man's hands free and forced the dress over his head.

Seams ripped loudly as the prisoner squirmed, but Keegan prevailed and soon he'd forced the man to stand up in the foul-smelling gown. Rapidly, as Sheena yanked on the soldier's boots, Keegan retied the man's hands behind him, then sliced the rope that held his legs together.

"Come," he said, taking Sheena's hand.

Silently they waded across the stream, where two horses, standing nervously together, their coats wet with sweat, were tied. She touched one sleek neck. "We will use them later, for escape," Keegan whispered in her ear, "but not yet. Now, scream as loudly as you can."

"What?"

"Do it."

Was he daft? "Nay." The anxious horses tugged at their bits, pulled at the reins.

"Draw the men to the prisoner," he ordered.

"But—"

"If you value your life, Sheena, do it!"

The soldiers were closing the gap anyway.

She swallowed back her fear and let out a cry that echoed through the canyon, reverberating against the hills. The horses pulled hard on their tethers. Limbs cracked and splintered.

"Damn," Keegan swore as the beasts broke free.

"Over here!" one man cried.

Clenching her hand in his, Keegan started down the hill on the far side of the creek. *This is madness,* she thought, for the men were approaching, crashing through the woods.

"Hey! I found her!" a soldier yelled not fifty feet away. Sheena's heart was in her throat, pounding in her ears, her body sweating. "Over here! Sir Manning!"

Hooves thundered up the hill, resounding through the gorge. Keegan's fingers circled her wrist, pulling her behind a tree as a laboring horse, running crazily, splashed up the creek. Leaving Sheena at the base of the oak, Keegan swung onto a low branch that spread over the chasm.

The horse drew nearer. Louder. Sheena cowered behind the bole of the oak.

A massive white destrier plunged into view. Hooves clattered, water splashed. The rider upon the steed's back was a huge, hulking man. One hand held the bridle; in the other was a raised sword that glinted in the feeble light. Sheena's heart froze.

"Where?" Manning bellowed from atop the destrier, and Sheena shrank inside.

As the horse galloped beneath the branch, Keegan sprang upon the rider.

"What the bloody—?" Manning cried, startled.

Together, grappling, both men plunged into the creek. With a terrified squeal the silvery white war horse reared, then bolted forward, his hooves slipping as he tore up the bank. Quick as a cat Sheena lunged. She grabbed the animal's reins as the men, splashing and rolling in the water, grappled and gulped for air.

She forced the wild-eyed steed up the bank, trying to calm him as he tried to rear and pull away. Her leg ached, and in the distance she heard men's voices. Through the trees torches glimmered faintly, burning red and gold in the blackness. "Hey! Look at that!" one man with a nasal voice cawed. "The woman, she's tied, she is."

No! Soon the men would discover they'd been duped. She and Keegan were running out of time, yet the two men battled, kicking and throwing punches, rolling through the rapids, gasping and gurgling, trying to drown each other. Sheena longed for a weapon, any kind of weapon, so that she could help.

"Oof."

"Curse you, you bastard!" *Manning's voice!* So close. He was gasping for breath as he and Keegan swung at each other.

A sword flashed in the darkness.

"Nay!" she cried, springing onto the destrier's saddle. He reared, front hooves flaying the air, back legs slipping on the bank. "Come on, you miserable beast." Slapping the horse with the reins, she forced him back into the creek. He took the bit in his teeth, shook his great head. "Come on, come on," she urged.

"Hey! It ain't the woman!" a man yelled from the direction of the cluster of torch lights.

"Who the devil—?"

"Christ Almighty, it's Peter!"

One man laughed.

Another one cursed. "Bloody hell!"

"Hey! Shut up, would ya! What's that I hear? Sounds like a fight . . . Where the devil is Sir Manning?"

Sheena kicked the horse deeper into the creek. In the splash and rush of the stream she saw fists fly as the men grappled. "Here! Over here!" Manning called, yelling to his troops. He stood and raised his sword as Keegan slipped backward, his feet failing him.

"No!" she cried.

"Where are ye?" The soldiers again.

Manning snarled, "Over here—"

The torch lights started moving in their direction. Men shouted. Feet thundered.

The knight swung downward. Sheena aimed her booted foot, kicked hard. Bam! She connected with Manning's jaw. His head snapped back. He fell into the water. Pain exploded up her leg. "Come on!" she yelled at Keegan, offering her hand. He swung up behind her, his clothes sodden, a bloody stain darkening his shoulder.

Pulling hard on the reins, she forced the big horse down the hillside, through the shallow water as fast as the beast dared run. Keegan's arms tightened around her as she guided the steed through the canyon, once again leaving Sir Manning and his sorry group of soldiers behind. The barest trace of a smile came to her lips.

But it was a false sense of victory, for as the creek tumbled out of the forest to slice across the fields, she knew that it was not over. As long as Sir Manning lived, for all the time Fawn was Lady of Ogof, they would chase her to the ground, drag her back to justice, and lie to her father.

She had no option but to return home and plead with

Jestin, tell him the truth about Tardiff. She could only hope that he would believe her.

And what will you do with the captain? her mind nagged as the horse tore across the grassland and the sea roared in the distance.

Keegan's arms tightened around her possessively, and it felt so good to be close to him, to feel the front of his thighs pressed into the backs of hers, to sense his manhood pushing against the cleft of her buttocks through the scratchy breeches. She reminded herself that he'd come for her—risked his life for her. Somehow he'd found her and helped her escape.

She wouldn't believe that he had imperiled his life just for the bargain they'd agreed upon—because of the money. Nay, there had to be more to it than that.

Or was there?

Tonight, as a few stars winked through the cloaking mist and the aches in her body eased, Sheena would not think of it.

For the moment she and Keegan were together.

Chapter Thirteen

Manning, his jaw throbbing, his head pounding, his pride beaten to a bloody pulp, watched as the woman he'd chased for weeks and the captain of the *Dark Sapphire* were swallowed by the mist-shrouded night.

Once again he'd failed.

Once again he'd been made to look like a fool.

In front of his men.

He stood on unsteady feet. The rocks in the creek bed were slick, he felt a sense of dizziness, but worst of all he knew he'd been bested. By a mere woman. And Captain Rourke's rogue of a son.

"Bastard," he spat, feeling no sense of satisfaction. "Miserable cur of a bastard."

As the cold water of the creek swirled over the tops of his boots, a new emotion coursed through Manning. Blood lust. He wanted vengeance and he yearned for it so desperately he would gladly have sold his soul to the devil if only Lucifer had appeared in the fog. With or without the dark prince's help, Manning needed to restore his pride.

Long ago he'd agreed to help Fawn because of his hungry ambition. He'd allowed himself to be seduced by her, had come eagerly to her bed, never anticipating that she planned to get herself with child, that he was merely the sire she'd chosen for her babe.

He'd been unable to resist lying with her. Not only was she beautiful and powerful, but the thought that he was bedding the lord's wife, sometimes with Jestin just one chamber away, had fired his blood. The sense of power he gained was as potent and intoxicating as fine wine and brought with it a need for more. Manning was anxious to drop the trappings of a common man, the son of a blacksmith and a woman he'd never bothered to marry. Aye, he craved more for himself, for his issue. Fawn had been his stepping-stone that bridged the deep abyss between poverty and privilege.

Willingly Manning had done her bidding and held his tongue, smug in the knowledge that he was getting a little back at a lord who didn't appreciate him, a man who had, through no effort on his part, been given a better station in life. But his sense of power had been lessened when Fawn had admitted to being pregnant and that she was going to pass the babe off as her husband's. This son was going to rule Ogof and Tardiff, and if Manning dared breathe a word that he'd lain with her, she vowed she would cry rape and have him hanged, then drawn and quartered.

"Do not let the fact that the child be yours give you any illusions, Manning," she'd cooed into his ear as they'd lain naked, drenched in each other's sweat, upon her bed. "I will keep you well, yes, but this boy must, for the time of my husband's life, be considered his issue."

"And what if Jestin is soon called to meet his maker?" Manning had asked.

"All the better . . . after the babe is born. But hear me well, do not cross me or I will see to your death personally."

He'd stared into her cold eyes and believed every word she uttered as he'd placed strong arms around her neck, thrown her onto that smooth back of hers, and mounted her again, pouring his rage and his seed into her as she cried out and begged for more of him. Later, still gasping, she had promised him a share of her wealth, though she would not say how they were going to get rid of the baron.

Now, as he stared through the gloom, he cursed his fate.

He was forced yet again to return to the woman who controlled his destiny and admit that he'd been thwarted by Sheena. His jaw clenched so hard his back teeth ached, and his fists curled in impotent fury.

No longer was this mission merely Fawn's will. Now 'twas a matter of pride.

He heard his troops approaching and climbed out of the creek, making his way along the bank to the cluster of torches and the sweating faces reflected in their red-gold light. Smoke singed the air, horses snorted and pawed, and the soldiers were gathered around a woman, a big woman—nay, a man dressed in female garb. "Who have you . . . ?" He let his words fall away as he recognized Peter in the ugly frock. "God's eyes, man, what is this?"

"I was tricked," he said, eyes downcast.

"By the captain?"

"Aye." He gulped.

"And you brought him here."

"He nearly ripped me arm from its socket," Peter cried, mortified, then held his tongue, for the excuse was paltry—the cry of an old woman.

Manning's hands itched to strangle the pathetic excuse of a soldier, but he resisted. Hadn't he, too, been deceived easily, his horse taken from him? By the very girl he was supposed to capture? His blood thundered in his ears. Asides, he needed every man; he could spare none.

"Where's yer horse?" one of his men had the audacity to ask. The soldier was astride a black gelding, his face illuminated by the golden glow of the torch. Theatrically, with eyebrows raised and mouth pulled into an exaggerated frown, as if he were truly perplexed, he glanced around, searching for the steed.

"He was stolen," Manning admitted through clenched teeth and a jaw that still throbbed from the thrust of Sheena's boot. None of the soldiers dared say a word. "And since I am now without a mount, I'll have yours."

The man seemed about to argue, opened his mouth, but

looking down at the raw, dangerous wrath in the dark knight's gaze, he snapped his jaw shut and dutifully climbed off his steed.

Manning hauled himself into the saddle, threw a leg over the beast's back, and glanced at the ragtag band of soldiers who were with him. They were all weary of the chase; he saw the defeat in their hopeless, lackluster eyes. "We will not go back empty-handed," he vowed, silently daring any man to argue with him. "Nay. You"—he pointed at a long pole of a man—"will stay near the farmer's house, watch who comes and goes. Sheena might return there." He doubted it, but he could ill afford to let her slip through his fingers again. "And you, Seth, you shall be posted at the ship. The rest of us will try to track down the lady"—he said the word with a sneer—"and we will report to each other. I doubt the captain will go far without his boat." He looked from one tired, distrustful face to the other. "We will catch Sheena and return her to her father. And when we do, each of you will be rewarded. I swear it."

Keegan's shoulder was on fire, pain blazing down his arm as he and Sheena rode swiftly across the night-darkened fields. He gritted his teeth against the pain as the horse labored, long legs stretching over the grass toward the town. Manning's sword had sliced deep, and Keegan wished he'd killed the bastard who had sent Wart to his grave. Guilt burned in his brain, for Wart had been a true and faithful crew member.

But Sheena was alive, and for that he was thankful. He'd been certain he'd never see her again, and to find her alive had been a miracle, had nearly convinced him that God did exist. His good arm tightened around her slim waist possessively, and he wondered what it was about this woman that had made him risk his ship, the members of his crew, his very life for her. Never had he felt this way, not even with Brynna when he was besotted. Brynna had been a beautiful but cold woman who had never been satisfied, who complained of his months away at sea and yet refused to sail with him.

No doubt she'd been lonely, and for that he supposed he didn't blame her for seeking another man's company. But when he'd found her lying in Sir Robert's arms, naked and sleeping in the very bed where they'd first made love, Keegan had turned on his heel and walked out the door. He'd found his solace in the sea and forced her from his thoughts.

Any shame or grief he'd felt, he'd buried deep. No one had seen his pain, and it had lessened.

But when he'd returned and found that she was dead, he'd visited her grave, stood on that hill and looked down at the mound of earth covering the one woman he'd given his name.

"Oh, Brynna, a goose you were," he'd said, his hair catching in the winter wind as it had blown in icy blasts over the cliffs. That she'd been with child had saddened him. Though the babe had not been his, 'twas a shame that it had never been born. Brynna with her sable brown hair, white skin, and eyes as round and brown as a doe's, had been a sad woman who had deserved better than a man who embraced the sea, a girl who hungered for flattery and a man's touch.

They'd both been fools.

Since Brynna there had been no other woman. Until Sheena.

Silently, as her hair brushed against his chest and she leaned over the tiring stallion's neck, urging the destrier ever onward, he cursed the fates that had brought her to him. He'd sworn he'd never let another woman reach into his heart, would hide his soul for the rest of his days.

His mistress had been the sea, and he'd found comfort in her passionate blue depths. Raging tempest or calm, glasslike water, the ocean was his love.

Or had been.

Now, on this dark mist-laden night, with the fullness of Sheena's breasts weighing on his arm, the feel of her buttocks pressed against his manhood, the warmth of her body so near, he wasn't sure of himself.

For the first time in years the captain of the *Dark Sapphire* second-guessed himself. Though he knew he was being foolish, he couldn't stop the emotions that blazed through his soul and tore through his brain. He argued with himself, but he knew he was lost to her. He buried his face in her hair and flexed the muscles of his good arm more tightly around her as he silently condemned himself to the hell of loving her.

Nay, Keegan, the rational part of his mind argued. *'Tis only because you've been long without a woman.*

You'll not feel this way once you set sail again.

She's a passing fancy, nothing to worry about.

You'll soon forget her.

But all his reasons were but poor excuses. He loved her. That was all there was to it, Keegan realized as the horse broke out of the woods and the destrier's strides lengthened over the silvery fields. Like it or not, Keegan, cold-hearted captain of the *Dark Sapphire*, a man who rued the day he'd ever met a woman, was in love with the daughter of his father's murderer.

"Are we being followed?" she asked, daring a glance over her shoulder, and he caught a glimpse of her straight nose, fine lips, and big eyes.

"Nay." Keegan, too, hazarded a look back at the woods, expecting to see the dark shapes of men and horses pouring out of the forest. But so far they were alone.

The horse was laboring, his breathing loud, and Sheena guided him away from the pig farmer's hut and along a rocky outcropping that led past the sea.

"Manning will expect us to go to the ship," she said aloud.

"Worry not. The *Dark Sapphire* was not to wait for me. Hollis is to see that she gets to Drudwy." He felt Sheena relax a bit as she pulled on the reins, urging the tired horse away from the town and into the hills again.

She tried to ignore the feel of Keegan's body against her

but failed. Images of their night of lovemaking whirled through her mind in seductive circles that took her breath away. With his arm around her, his well-muscled legs snug against the back of her thighs, her spine pressed into his chest, the movement of the horse as he galloped brought back wickedly erotic memories she'd tried so hard to forget. In the higher slopes she drew hard on the reins, and the horse, his grayish white coat flecked with lather, slowed.

"Manning will not be pleased that you stole his horse," Keegan observed.

"Oh, but he'll like the fact that you lunged at him from the tree, knocking him into the creek." She smiled at the thought that the cursed knight had been bested.

"Aye, we've given him more reason to chase you down."

"He would have done it anyway." She shrugged, felt his breath against the back of her neck.

"Before, he was doing his duty. Now he will have reasons of his own."

"I care not." Sheena refused to be intimidated by the soldier who, at Fawn's urging, had pledged his fealty to Ellwynn of Tardiff. Aye, Manning was a beast, but she would not live in terror. One way or another, she would return to Ogof. There she would face her father and whatever brand of justice he meted out.

"You canna leave without the captain!" Bo's face turned white as a full moon as he clutched the sleeve of Hollis's old mantle.

"I'm just doin' as he told me." Hollis made his way to the helm. He'd already ordered the men to raise the anchors, but the boy was beside himself.

"We must wait."

"Fer what? Sir Manning and his troops?"

"Fer the captain and the lady." Bo limped after Hollis to the helm.

So that was it. He, along with the rest of the crew, had been edgy and glum ever since Sheena had jumped overboard. Even Big Tom, the cruelest man on the ship, had been affected. More surly than ever, he'd asked about Sheena more than once. Ach, though Hollis hated to admit it, even he missed her quick wit, sharp tongue, and dimpled smile. Aye, she'd gotten past his crusty exterior, though he'd never admit it. That was the problem with women; they had a way of burrowing past into a man's thick hide and somehow finding a way into his heart. Had he not seen it with Bertrice and Rourke and now, again, with Keegan and Sheena. Women caused men pain. Even his sister, Lorinda, God rest her soul, had used Rourke and abandoned her son. And Brynna, Keegan's wife, had betrayed him. Oh, they were a sorry lot, women were, and yet men could not live without them.

Hollis had managed to stay out of a woman's path. There had been one woman when he'd been a young man, but he'd held tight to his heart and, as he'd expected, she'd found another. And now this one, this Sheena of Ogof—no, Lady Sheena of Tardiff—she'd captured the hearts of all the men. And like it or not, Hollis, though he knew better, had not been immune. Witch or nay, she'd charmed him as well.

"'Tis a fool ye be," he muttered under his breath. Worse yet, he was an old fool, one who knew better, who had, during the course of his years seen the ravages only a woman could cause. Wars were waged for women; friends became bitter enemies over a woman's attention. Lives and careers were ruined because of a woman's allure, and if that wasn't a curse, Hollis didn't know what was.

"We must wait longer," Bo insisted, and Hollis jerked his sleeve free of the boy's clutching fingers.

"I said we'll meet up with the captain in Drudwy; 'tis the way he wanted it, and the way 'twill be. Now, off with ye. Go help Cedric mend the sails or George with the caulkin'. There be work to do."

Bo sniffed and tossed his head to rid his eyes of his uneven fringe of hair. "Aye, aye, sir," he mocked, and scurried off with his uneven gait. Hollis was relieved to get rid of him, didn't even run after him and box his ears for his impertinence. The boy was young. Naive. Needed to be seasoned. But at least he was now gone.

Seamus was at the helm. "I don't mind tellin' ya, Hollis, that I don't like this," he said, frowning. " 'Tis too dark to try and leave this bay safely, and without the captain . . ." He scowled.

"Ye know that Keegan always leaves the ship in my charge when he's gone," Hollis said. "And have I ever gone against his wishes?"

"Nay, but—"

"Do ye think I'm stealin' the *Dark Sapphire*, then? Is that it? After I was the one who saved Keegan's life more than once, sold the *Warrior* when he was but a lad, and bought this ship for him? After I kept him from the hangman when the sheriff found out we were smugglin' men in our hold? Would ya think I would be doin' somethin' against the captain's wishes?"

"Ye've had words," Seamus said.

"Ach, 'twas nothing. Now, I've told the hands to lift anchor and raise the sails. Either you steer this damned ship or we'll run aground sure."

"Aye," Seamus agreed halfheartedly, and Hollis, despite his assurances to the crew, hoped he wasn't leaving Keegan without any means of escape if he needed it. The old man feared that taking the ship out to sea in the middle of the night was sending everyone on board to a certain death.

Worse yet, Hollis was worried. Again.

About Keegan and . . . yes, about that cursed woman as well. He'd even replaced the ring in its hiding place, once again unable to toss it into the dark waters of the sea.

Aye, he was a fool of the highest order.

And, for the moment, he was the captain of the damned ship.

Bo dragged his sleeve under his nose and thought of a dozen curses that he'd like to shout at Hollis, the old mule.

Bo wasn't going to take orders from an ancient man who saw sea serpents at every turn of the prow. Hollis was daft and scared, like a feeble old woman. And Hollis wasn't loyal to the captain, that much was sure.

Bo had proof.

Scowling to himself, trying to walk without a hint of a limp, Bo hurried along the decking. He'd followed the old man into the hold on several occasions, and he'd discovered Hollis doing more than tapping into the barrels of ale and casks of wine hidden deep in the ships bowels. No, there was another secret the old man kept. Hidden between the stacks one day, Bo had peeked around and saw Hollis enter the hold, slip around a post, stretch tall, then finger open a little tiny opening. He'd reached inside and, as the rats scurried and squeaked and the ship creaked in the wind, Hollis had held up a ring with a brilliant blue stone. Sucking in his breath Bo had stared in awe at the gem winking blue fire from the candlelight. 'Twas like none he'd ever seen.

"Old goat," Bo now growled under his breath as he tiptoed down the stairs and entered the dark room where Hollis's secret treasure was hidden. Once it became known that Victoria of Rhydd was really the daughter of Baron Jestin, Bo had heard the story of the captain's father's bad luck at a dice game where the stakes were Rourke's ship wagered against an incredible blue stone, the Dark Sapphire of Ogof.

'Twas Hollis's ring, to be sure. And it didn't belong to him.

Climbing onto the casks, Bo balanced carefully so that he didn't slip and have his good leg crushed between the heavy oaken barrels. His fingers scraped along the beam, and he found the tiny peg, lifted it, and with the tip of his finger felt inside the small hole. The sharp stone nearly cut his finger as he scooped out the glittery piece of jewelry, looked at it while the boat started to move, then, nearly dropping his prize between the stacks, pocketed the gem.

It wasn't as if he was stealing it, not really. The ring did not belong to Hollis. It should have been Rourke's, if the story of his death was true. If not—well, he'd think about what he'd do with the ring. Until then it was his.

"There has been no word?" Fawn asked as the damned maid picked up the baby and gently swayed back and forth. Zelda was an odd one, dark and mysterious, but she had a way with children. She had treated each of Fawn's daughters as if they were her own; the same would be true of this son. Though Zelda had protested when Fawn had sent the maidservant's only daughter to Tardiff, she'd finally accepted her fate. And now, because of Fawn's own maternal instincts, and since Ellwynn was gone—oh, she felt a sharp pain at that—she had decided to order Fannie returned to Ogof. The truth of the matter was that Zelda would not last forever and Sarah was a ninny. Fannie would make a good serving girl.

"Sir Manning has not returned. Nor have any of his soldiers." Zelda smiled down at the baby, yet no light of happiness brightened her haunted eyes. But then, it rarely did.

"Has Fannie returned?"

"Nay, not yet. But soon," Zelda said, and there was actually a spark of life in the old maidservant. "Today."

"Good."

"Thank you, m'lady."

Fawn waved a hand in the air. " 'Tis nothing," she said, somewhat pleased to have the old woman's allegiance if only for a second.

With a sigh Fawn set down her mazer of wine and hoped that the warmth she expected to flow through her blood would come quickly. She was still sore, still bleeding, and anxious to be on her feet again.

Lying in her bed, with the fire in the grate burning bright, the rushes clean and smelling of dried rose petals, the tapestries splashing color against the whitewashed walls, her son finally born and secure as the rightful heir of Ogof and Tardiff, she should have been content. Yet she was restless. She sensed undercurrents of trouble within the dark hall-

ways and wide wall walks of Ogof. Even Jestin, despite his
elation with his newborn son, was tense. Distant again.

Because of Sheena.

Damn that girl to the depths of hell.

There was a knock on the door, and Mary, pale hair flying
behind her, burst into the room. "Papa said you were here!"
the girl said, then spying the swaddled infant in Zelda's
arms, walked over to inspect her new brother.

"This is Llywelyn?" she asked. And as she looked at the
boy, her top lip curled and her little nose wrinkled, as if she
smelled something bad.

"Aye, your brother."

Mary didn't bother hiding her disapproval. "He looks . . .
different." Mary was the first to voice what others who had
come to view the infant had said silently. Upon entering the
room, the servants and peasants had been all laughter, well
wishes, and smiles. They'd burst into the chamber bubbling
over with excitement, but upon observing little Llywelyn
they had, to a one, lost their exuberance, their laughter fading, their smiles becoming hard and chiseled upon their
faces.

"Because he's a boy."

"Nay, because he has dark hair and his skin is not so white
and . . . and his face . . . it be—"

"Fine. He's fine," Fawn snapped, refusing to believe even
for a moment that the boy she'd worked so hard to conceive
could be less than perfect. 'Twas true that in the few hours
since her son's birth, Fawn had noticed the difference in
him. He was not as alert as Mary had been after she'd come
screaming into this world, nor were his eyes as bright as
Ann's had been and, compared to Lynna . . . well, Fawn
wouldn't think such thoughts. Each child was different.

"Give him time," Fawn suggested, irritation lacing her
words. "He's only been here a short while, and he was born
in a tiny, smelly hut, unlike you and your sisters."

"Why were you there? At Serena's?" Mary asked, losing
interest in the babe that Zelda so patiently rocked and held.

She flopped onto a corner of the bed. "She's a fortune-teller, right? So why did you want to see her?"

"I don't know," Fawn lied.

"Were you worried about the baby?"

"A little."

"Then you should have gone to the chapel and prayed." Mary nodded and tossed a ringlet of white hair over her shoulder. "That's what you always tell me to do."

"This was different."

Mary didn't argue, but one eyebrow lifted imperiously. 'Twas a pose that reminded Fawn of herself. "He's just another baby," Mary pointed out, and for the first time Fawn considered that her daughter was a little jealous. Not that Fawn didn't understand. Mary would never be the heir. Never favored. Never become the source of hopes and dreams. Never named after a legendary king. The best she could hope for was to marry a rich baron who was kind to her.

'Twas not fair.

Just as it had not been equal when Ellwynn had been born and Fawn had learned the bitter truth that a person's gender was far more important than a person's intelligence.

Men were destined to become leaders. Women were fated to follow.

Unless they were clever enough to manipulate their men without being found out. Oh, one could never let her husband know that she was plotting her own course and using him as a vessel. No. She had to be silent and appear obedient, even witless at times so that the man was assured that he was the ruler, the one making all decisions. Then and only then would a wife's will be done.

Never would she get kind words for her efforts. Nor would she be allowed a shred of glory.

Glory, fame, and wealth were only for men.

Unless a woman moved in the shadows, whispered lies, hid her true feelings, and was ruthless enough to do what had to be done, no matter how distasteful or bloody it was.

The baby started crying again. "He is hungry," Zelda said, walking to the bed.

Reluctantly Fawn opened her arms and, lowering one side of her tunic, held her son close. Her breasts, large and overflowing with milk, ached; the nipples burned from her attempts at feeding the boy. Again he fought her, suckling for a few seconds only to arch his tiny back and wail to the heavens.

" 'Tis fine you be, Llywelyn," she said, though she nearly choked on the lie. Mary hopped off the bed and, with her weak chin leading the way, flounced out of Fawn's chamber.

The horse was spent. Lather foamed against his once white coat, and he was blowing hard as they crested a small hill and came upon a large lake that reflected the stars and a bit of moon. Dawn was approaching, and it was far past time to rest. Every muscle in Sheena's body ached, her spine was stiff, her ankle throbbed.

Keegan, leaning heavily against her, reached over her shoulder and pointed at a copse of trees and outcropping of rock. "There. 'Tis a good place to rest for a while."

With tired arms Sheena tugged on the reins, and the destrier slowed to a walk. Once at the edge of the lake, Keegan swung to the ground and helped her alight as well.

Blood, a dark smear, stained his tunic, but he seemed strong and helped remove the saddle. "I'll walk him a bit," he said. "You find a place for us to rest."

Too tired to argue, she drank from the lake, splashed cold water over her face and hands, then did as she was told, searching beneath trees to find a grassy spot. Keegan led the horse to the water, let the beast drink a few gulps, then walked him around the edge of the lake until the destrier was breathing normally again.

Sheena dug through the compartments in the saddle, hoping to find some food, but there was none. No provisions whatsoever. Ignoring the emptiness in her stomach, she used the saddle as a backrest laid upon the cool ground and closed her eyes but for a minute. She knew that sleep would be impossible, but as she listened to the lap of the water at the lake's edge, she began to breathe slowly. She barely stirred when Keegan, after gritting his teeth against pain as he cleaned the edges of his wound, settled in beside her. She snuggled up to him, whispered something and, sighing, fell into a deep, untroubled slumber.

She seemed younger than her years as she slept, and he smiled as he brushed a lock of her flame-red hair away from her cheek. She was only a few years younger than he and hardly an innocent. He was troubled by the brutality of her husband and what she'd endured, but she seemed to have put it behind her, not unscathed but strong. Aye, she was a unique woman, one not only accused of killing her cur of a husband, but a woman who had outsmarted the soldiers of Ogof and Tardiff combined, a horsewoman whose sharp kick had felled Sir Manning. She'd probably saved Keegan's life, not just tonight but a long time ago when she'd braved her father's wrath and taken his hand to lead him down a secret tunnel to a rotting, hidden dock.

Aye, she was a woman like no other, and as he held her close, he placed a kiss upon her forehead. His heart was tugged. Resting his cheek upon her crown, he listened to the sounds of the dawn. The wound in his shoulder ached but had stopped bleeding. Though he was near exhaustion, his manhood swelled with desire. Fighting the urge to kiss and wake her, to make love to her until they were both lying gasping and breathless, he stared into the sky, where dawn was chasing away the few remaining stars.

The horse, after again drinking from the lake, lay down and rolled, grunting in pleasure, his powerful legs pawing the air until, with a snort, he stood, shook his great head, and began to graze. Mist began to rise off the water, and Keegan, captain of the *Dark Sapphire*, a man who had sworn to trust his heart to no female, knew he would lay down his life for this mite of a woman with the fiery hair and sharp tongue. Never had he felt such a need to protect and possess. Never had he thought of giving up the sea for a woman, but Sheena of Ogof had turned his thoughts around.

His breath feathering her hair, he fell into a dreamless sleep just as the first shafts of morning light began to crawl across the eastern hills.

Hours later Sheena opened an eye to spy a hawk circling high in a cloudless sky. The horse was grazing, and Keegan, his jaw dark with his beard, was snoring softly, his neck at an odd angle, his shirt stained with blood.

He didn't move when she lifted his tunic and scowled at the sight of his wound. It wasn't as deep as she had feared and had already scabbed over, but the flesh around the cut was an angry purple and his chest hairs were matted with dry blood.

She longed to clean the cut, to apply ointment if she had it, but knew he would wake if she so much as touched him. Besides, she needed a few minutes alone in the lake. She was still wearing the soldier's scratchy uniform, and her feet were filthy from running through the pigsty and the forest. Her hair was tangled and clumped, and the lake beckoned.

She slipped away from Keegan and stripped out of the hated, stinking clothes. Kicking off the soldier's boots, she waded into the water. She sucked in her breath as the icy liquid splashed up her legs. Yet it was clean. Bracing. When she was hip deep, she pushed off and swam, dipping her head beneath the surface and feeling the cold water slide over her skin and through her hair. Using her fingers, she combed the tangles from her tresses, wiped the smudges of mud from her legs, arms, and body, then floated on her back and watched the clouds move across the sky just as she had when she was a child. The water chilled her flesh, but her spirit soared, for she was safe and with Keegan, if only for a while.

Lifting her head, she glanced across the water to the grass in the direction where she'd left Keegan. He was missing. No longer lying with his head propped against the saddle.

Her heart stopped.

Fear knifed through her.

Then she saw him emerge from the forest.

Naked as the day he was born. Bronzed skin stretched over hard, sinewy muscles. He stared directly at her, his eyes as gray as the morning dawn.

The back of her throat became dry as a desert wind, for she'd never seen him naked in the light. The blood-crusted gash on his shoulder was only the freshest of scars that were visible on his broad shoulders and wide chest, where a mat of curling dark hair arrowed down a flat abdomen.

Lower still, stiff as a ship's spar, Keegan's manhood rose between hard, well-muscled thighs. Anticipation caused her chilled skin to tingle as he approached and waded into the water. His gaze never left hers and she was suddenly unable to breathe. They had no time to linger, no reason to spend another second here, where they could be discovered at any instant. And yet when he reached her and his arms swept her against him, she didn't protest.

Cold skin suddenly heated. Her nipples were already hard from the frigid water. Her chilled lips met the warmth of his hungrily, anxiously.

With a groan he dragged her closer still. His tongue plunged into her mouth, his lips pressed hard against hers, and he kissed her until her breath was lost deep in her lungs and the liquid fire in her blood spread through her limbs and to that most intimate part of her.

Deep inside she wanted him, yearned for him. Her arms circled his neck as she kissed him feverishly.

You have no time for this, Sheena, no need. This rogue will do naught but cause you heartache and pain. Asides, Manning's soldiers are riding ever closer. Do not dally! Do not tarry. 'Tis suicide.

And yet she couldn't stop. His hands splayed upon her back, the tips of his fingers grazing the valley of her spine. He lifted her to him, kissed one wet breast, and Sheena threw back her head, felt the early morning sunlight caress her skin as his teeth nipped and his tongue licked and his lips sucked.

Her pulse leapt. Thoughts of love pierced the armor surrounding her heart.

"Ah, witch," he said, looking long into her eyes, " 'Tis true that you've cast a spell upon me."

She couldn't help but smile as she stood in the water that reached her breasts. Her nipples puckered in the cool morning air. "Aye, Captain, that I have. And so you will please me, over and over again."

"So I have no will of my own? I am here but to serve you?" he mocked.

"Aye. 'Tis so." She nodded curtly, then laughed aloud, the sound trilling over the ripples of the lake.

He chuckled deep in his throat. "Is that my punishment?"

"Oh, nay, Keegan. 'Tis your reward."

A glimmer of light caught in his eyes. "Then I accept it now." Reaching down swiftly, he placed his big hands around her thighs, lifted her up, and lowered her over the thick rod of his manhood. She gasped, her tender skin hot and cold all in one instant. His mouth claimed hers in a kiss of pure possession, and her legs wrapped around his torso. Slowly he lifted her, only to kiss her hard and lower her again.

Dear Lord.

She cried out.

Again, kissing her, his hands hard, he raised her to the tip of his shaft, only to bring her back to him.

Desire shot through her. She kissed him fiercely, hungrily, and moved against him. Pressing hard, increasing the tempo. She wanted him. All of him. God forgive her, she needed him.

Water swirled around them, churning wildly as her breath came faster and faster. He lifted her up and down in a feverish tempo, moving with her. She couldn't breathe, could barely think. Moaning, clinging to his neck, she moved with him as sunlight spangled the water and a breeze laced with the scents of summer swept across the lake. Hotter and hotter, faster and faster, he moved, his head bent backward as he kissed her, her fingers digging deep into the muscles of his neck.

"Keegan . . . oh . . ." She couldn't speak, could not force any words past her throat.

"Ah, love . . . sweet, sweet Sheena . . ."

The first spasm hit and she jolted. Her body convulsed, the sky and water fused behind her eyes, and her spirit soared to the heavens. She clung to him, held his face against her chest, listened to the pounding of his heart and the slowing of his breath.

Only when she was able to take in air again did he let her slide down, her feet sinking into the soft silt at the lake's bottom, the smooth dirt filling the cracks between her toes. "So, witch, did I please you?" he teased, gasping and smiling with the knowledge that she'd been well sated.

"Oh, nay, Captain," she lied with a wink. "I think you need to try a little harder."

"Do you?" A wicked smile slid across his jaw. "Then so be it." He dragged her to him and kissed her hard. His arms surrounded her, his body enveloped her, and she wanted nothing more than to hold him to her for the rest of her life.

It was insane. Daft. She was laying her heart bare, and yet she had no choice. Foolish or not, she loved him. There was naught she could do about it.

He kissed her so hard that her knees began to buckle, and the roaring in her ears was thunderous, wild, like hundreds of horses' hooves thudding wildly over the hard ground. Pounding, pounding . . .

Every muscle in his body tensed. He lifted his head. Sheena nearly fell into the water. "Keegan—?"

"Shh!"

Then she heard it. The earth was shaking. 'Twas not her heart that was galloping but the sound of dozens of horses approaching as fast as lightning.

"Damn! Come! Now!" Grabbing her hand, he dragged

her out of the water, did not pause to scoop up their clothes, or the saddle, just the bridle as he ran to the steed, which had lifted his great head. Keegan forced the bit into the horse's mouth, buckled the chin strap and, grabbing the reins in one hand, he lifted Sheena onto the stallion's back. Then he mounted behind her and kicked hard.

"Run, you bastard!" Keegan growled.

The stallion bolted, streaking toward the woods. Across the grassland and into the shadows the horse galloped, long legs eating up the ground, strides lengthening. Tears came to Sheena's eyes, blurring her vision. The thickets of oak and pine loomed closer. *Faster! Run faster, you demon!*

Sheena's wet hair unfurled behind her, slapping Keegan's face as he reached around her and kicked hard. Leaning forward over the destrier's massive shoulders, Sheena could barely breathe.

At the edge of the woods, as the great war horse raced into the dark cover, Sheena dared to look over her shoulder.

Manning of Tardiff's army was just cresting the hill.

Chapter Fourteen

"What mean you that he's not here?" Hollis demanded, wringing his hands as he stared into the worried faces of several members of the ship's crew. For the love of St. Peter, where was Bo? A dozen worries assailed him as he paced the deck of the *Dark Sapphire*. The sun was high, a few clouds moving in, but the ship was steady on her course to Drudwy, the sails billowing full.

"I mean, I checked from the crow's nest to the lowest hold. Even the secret compartments, but Bo, he ain't on board," Jasper said, his good eye squinting in the sunlight.

"Saints preserve us." Hollis studied the shoreline far in the distance and clasped his hands before him, rubbing his aching joints and silently cursing the headstrong lad, who was beginning to remind him more and more of Keegan. At Bo's age, Keegan had been full of piss and nonsense, always looking for and finding trouble. Though they were not blood-related, Bo had learned much from the man who had plucked him off the streets where he'd grown up as a pick-pocket and beggar.

"Methinks he got off afore we sailed," Jasper concluded, wiping a ragged sleeve under his nose and sniffing loudly as the ship rolled gently with the tide. "Maynard, he swears he saw the boy scrambling around below decks just before we raised anchor."

Hollis shook his head and felt mist against his bare scalp. There was no turning back, not if he was to meet with Keegan. He made a quick sign of the cross and whispered a brief prayer for the headstrong lad. Truth to tell, there was a hollowness deep inside him, for Hollis had no family but Keegan and considered these men—ruffians, blackhearts, thieves, and thugs though they be—his clan. Brought together by dark deeds of their pasts, drawn by the lure of the sea, a fleet ship, and a captain who asked no questions, the men were like wolves in a pack, each needing the other.

And there were so many terrors in the world. Sea serpents and witches, the devil around every corner . . . Bloody hell, he hoped the boy had enough wits to survive, but didn't believe it for a second.

So where was the bloody pup? he silently asked himself. *Where?* And why had Bo jumped ship?

Because of the woman, his mind taunted. Nary a man on board had been the same since she'd been found and had become a part of their last voyage. Hollis glowered at the lowering sun and rubbed his arms, for he felt a chill as cold as the bottom of the sea. If not for the comely witch who had stowed away, not only Bo but Keegan as well would not now be missing.

"So what're ye gonna do?" Jasper asked, and Hollis sensed the eyes of other men boring into him, expecting him to come up with an answer. George glanced up from his work as he caulked the seams in the deck floor, and Big Tom, checking the rigging, stayed within earshot. Even Maynard, distracted from catching the day's worth of rats, idled near the fore staysail and pretended interest in coiling rope.

"Stay the course," Hollis said, scowling into the wind. The prow of the great ship cut through the clear waters, bearing ever southward. Just as Keegan had ordered. But the weight of the decision burrowed into his conscience, and he feared for the lad's life.

By the saints, if he ever set eyes upon Bo again, he'd grab

hold and hug the boy fiercely. Right before he gave the lad the tongue lashing of his life or strangled him for being a damned, mule-headed fool.

The saddle was his. Manning squatted on the beaten-down grass, ran his fingers over the tooled leather, and narrowed his eyes in thought. Sheena had been here. She and the captain. Clothes were scattered on the bent grass—the seaman's garb and Peter's soiled uniform—and there was evidence that someone had slept under the branches of a tree near the clearing. Yet there was no sign of Sheena, the captain of the *Dark Sapphire*, or Manning's precious destrier, the best war horse in all of Wales. Anger coursed through his blood, and a muscle worked in his jaw. He rubbed his thumb against his finger and thought of all kinds of punishments for the pair if he ever caught up with them.

And he would. By all that was holy and all that was not, he would run the snot-nosed daughter of Jestin to the ground if it took the rest of his life.

Manning had prided himself on his cunning, on his sheer brute strength, on his ability to make men quiver in fear. But dealing with Sheena had been different and far more difficult. The wench had proved to be sly as a fox and twice as elusive.

And damned lucky. Oh, God's eyes, she'd been lucky.

Standing, he rubbed the muscles of his back and kicked a stone into the clear waters of the lake. The wheels in his mind turning, he watched the pebble sink to the bottom, sending ripples ever outward as the sun reflected upon the cool surface.

"There be no sign of 'em," Leonard reported as his eyes scanned the edge of the woods, but Manning didn't trust the whiny man to have done a thorough job. Leonard had been ready to give up this mission before it had gotten started.

"Keep looking."

"But—"

"I said, keep looking!" Manning thundered.

Leonard and several others returned to the forest, presumably to hunt for clues, though Manning suspected there
were none to be found. The damned woman sometimes left
no more tracks than did a ghost.

He spat, studied the countryside and the lake, where a
dozen ducks were swimming, quacking and turning their
tails skyward as they searched for food. Where the devil was
Jestin's wayward daughter? *Where?* She could not have gotten far on one horse with a wounded companion. Manning
spat, wiped his mouth, and didn't say a word. He would
check the town again, and the farmer's hut, the ship at the
dock, and turn over every sorry pebble in this godforsaken
outpost before returning to Ogof empty-handed. At the
thought he scowled darkly, and had any of his men said a
word, he would have cuffed the soldier from here to eternity.

He paced the grass and conjured up excuses to Fawn.
None were good enough. As the sun rose ever higher,
Leonard and the rest of his sorry band returned. Empty-
handed. "We—we searched the clearing here and the under-
growth, but they be gone now. Emberly spied fresh horse
tracks, but that be all."

So why did they ride off and not take the clothes or saddle?

Manning tossed the dirty uniform to Peter, then scowled
at the captain's bloody shirt and breeches. At least he had the
satisfaction of knowing that he'd wounded the bastard.
Hopefully it was mortal. Obviously they'd found new dis-
guises, Manning decided, but why not take the saddle . . .
unless they'd been found out and left suddenly.

By the Gods, it was his curse to always chase that
woman! Even his men were starting to doubt him, and their
spirits had sunk. They'd become a quarrelsome lot, and if
Sheena wasn't found soon, he feared they'd take up arms
against him.

"What now?" one man, a particularly surly knight with
rotting teeth and bad breath, asked. He was lean and anxious, always ready for battle.

"We keep looking."

Peter spat on the ground in disgust. "Where?"

Manning thought for a moment, and an idea that he didn't like much formed in his mind. Mayhap Sheena kept escaping because he wasn't relying upon his brains to capture her. A strong man who had always used his size and intimidation to get what he wanted, Manning expected those who argued with him to become scared, to give up rather than fight him or try to best him, for most men knew he would allow no one to win, he would be relentless in hunting them down. But with Sheena it was different. His size and reputation hadn't been enough to intimidate her into submission. If anything, she seemed more determined than ever to thwart him.

Perhaps it was time to change his tactics, to use his mind to catch her. To that end, he might have to give up some time, but rather than keep running in circles, looking like a fool while hoping to chase her down, it would be better to lay a trap. He reached down, felt the soil, and let it sift through his fingers as he considered his options.

Though he hated the thought of it, he would have to backtrack a bit. Consider her next move. He glanced across the lake to the shadowy forest and scowled. She was always slipping through his fingers like the earth he'd just scooped up. "No more," he said aloud. His fist clenched as if he could grab her.

"No more what?" one of his men asked.

No more will I lose. He didn't answer aloud. "Come," he ordered, throwing himself upon Delwyn's horse and jerking hard on the reins. "You, Seth, grab that saddle and the clothes. We may need them." Kicking his mount, he led his tired army away from the lake and toward the farmer's hut where Sheena had once taken refuge. Mayhap Freddy or the woman had learned of her plans in the time she'd spent there. For a few coins, or to avoid a flogging, many tongues had been loosened in the past. Manning doubted it would be any different with the pig farmer. Asides, he had unfinished business with the man. There were the stones to consider, the ruby, topaz, and emerald Sheena had stolen from Tardiff and Freddy had bragged about at the tavern. Manning could return to Ogof with the gems if not the woman. He clucked to the horse and started off at a gallop.

Within hours, they were upon the farm, a small piece of land wedged between the forest and the cliffs overlooking the sea. Manning spied Freddy in the middle of a field, shaking dried acorns out of a large sack while his pigs snorted and rutted near his feet. He tossed the bag over his shoulder and was dusting his hands when he looked up and saw Manning's army. Immediately his ugly face twisted into a grimace of suspicion.

"What is it you want?" he demanded, walking through the muck to the fence. A pathetic creature in tattered clothes, he used one hand to shade his eyes as he glowered up at the dark knight. "Did you not find the woman you sought?"

"I need the stones," Manning said flatly.

"Wha—?" The farmer's expression changed. His eyes slitted like a cornered dog. He was about to lie.

"I know the gems be here, Fred Farmer, so don't bother attempting to lie to me."

"But there be no jewels."

Manning picked up his short whip. "Think hard, farmer, and lie to me not. That night in the tavern, you said that the girl you found was carrying stones with her. More than the gold one you were crowin' about. I heard ye with me own ears."

The farmer didn't move. Swallowed hard. High color swept up his pockmarked face. "I do na know what ye're talkin' about."

Manning edged his horse closer, held fast to his short whip. "Of course you do."

"I was drunk."

"I saw the yellow sapphire."

"'Twas the only one and I had to sell it and—"

Manning leaped from his horse, vaulted the fence, and

grabbed the poor idiot by his throat. He brandished his crop as if he intended to slice off the lying bastard's tongue. "Lie not to me, Fred Farmer, or I will kill all yer pigs, burn yer farm, and take both ye and yer wife back to the Baron of Ogof. When he hears that ye've lied to me about his daughter and the jewels she left here, he'll send ye straight to the gallows, make no mistake." He twisted the man's arm behind him and heard sinews and tendons pop.

"Ooooh," Freddy cried, falling to his knees. Manning dragged him to his feet again and snapped the crop near his eyes. Still the fool did not say a word.

"Kill the sow," Manning ordered Seth, and the soldier drew an arrow from his quiver, took aim, and pulled back on the bowstring.

"Nay!" The door to the hut opened, and the man's wife, a big woman with a fleshy face and huge nose, hurried out. "I've got the stones, Sir Manning. They be here, in the lady's boot."

"Esme, no!" Freddy's face fell. All his dreams of riches were about to vanish as quickly as they'd come.

The wife was running, ungainly and heavy, holding a small boot outward and shaking it until it rattled. As if she were eager to give up the treasure. Why? Dozens of sows could be bought with but one of the jewels . . . it made little sense unless she was afraid for her life, or that of her husband. Was she so frightened?

Manning released the farmer, vaulted the fence, and snatched the boot from her fingers. He upended the clean leather, and two stones rolled out onto his waiting fingers. Blood red and forest green, they winked brilliantly in the sunlight.

"Well there, see, Fred, ye fergot that ye had these gems, now, didn't ye?" Manning taunted, tucking his riding crop inside his belt. "Mayhap ye should not drink so much."

Red-faced, looking as if he'd been struck by an act of God, the farmer was clutching his arm with his free hand

and trying to hold back the curses that were so obviously close to tripping off his tongue.

The woman was afraid. Her big face was white as death, and a nasty tic was tremoring beneath one eye. Her hands shook as she wiped them on her dirty apron. Manning climbed onto his steed and was about to ride off, but there was something in the air that he felt, something more that he was missing. Aye, he had the stones and they were worth a lot, but the woman . . . she was acting so strangely.

A thought struck him. Hard. 'Twas obvious Freddy's wife wanted Manning gone and fast. As if she was hiding something. But not the stones; she'd given them up easily. Too easily. And not for love of the man or she would have climbed over the fence to his aid, as he looked about to swoon from the injuries inflicted upon him by Manning. Instead she stood on the dirt path leading to the door of her hut—almost as if she were blocking his entrance to her home.

Why?

Was it because she was hiding something more valuable than the gems in her crumbling shack? The air was cool, the sound of the sea beneath the cliffs a steady rush, and yet Esme was sweating, beads running down from her temples. Squinting against the sun, Manning drew his attention to the doorway and thought he saw a movement within the hut.

His heart jolted.

Someone indeed was hiding inside.

A smile twisted his lips, and anticipation fired his blood. Was Lady Sheena so foolish as to return here? Had she no choice? Was it possible she and the captain had been naked—mayhap even coupling—and been startled by someone, only to seek cover in the only place they knew of to find shelter and safety? Or had she returned for her precious stones—the very gems that were now so easily being offered to him?

"Check the house," he ordered Peter and Otto.

"Nay, there is no one," the woman said, frantic, her eyes

wide. She swallowed hard. "Ye wanted the stones and ye have them and—"

Otto, the strongest of his men, pushed her to the ground and, sword aloft, lumbered up the path and through the open door.

Esme would not be detained. She scrambled to heavy feet and ran after him. "Nay, nay, there is no one here. Be off with ye now—"

A yowl erupted from the hut, then swearing and the sound of running footsteps.

"God help us," Esme cried as Peter knocked her to the ground and held her there with his blade pointed at the cleft between her breasts.

Manning's jaw clenched. Had Sheena escaped yet again? How? "Let no one pass!" he ordered curtly. "Surround the house!"

But it mattered not. Within a heartbeat Otto appeared hauling a boy with shaggy hair under his arm. The lad was struggling, kicking, swinging wildly with his fists, biting and writhing.

Blood dripped from Otto's ear.

"Bit me he did," Otto grumbled, his face twisted in pain. "Little bastard!"

"Who's this?" Manning demanded.

"No one." Esme rung her hands nervously. "He be but a boy who is staying with us and helping me husband with the chores."

"But not your boy?" Manning said, frowning thoughtfully, for he thought he'd seen the shaggy-haired lad before.

"Nay, but—"

"Put him down." Manning ordered, and wondered where he'd seen the urchin before. "Who be ye, son?"

The kid started to bolt, but Otto was quicker than he looked and grabbed the kid by his stringy hair. "No, ye don't . . ." he warned, holding the boy at arm's length. "He's a bad un, he is. Nearly bit off me ear and kicked me in the shin, he did. Aimed higher, too. Wanted to catch me in me balls."

"Why?" Manning said.

"I've seen him before," Peter offered with a bit of pride. "He be a lad who sailed on Wart's ship. Ain't that right, boy?"

Still restrained, the urchin spat on the ground. "Leave me be."

"Aye." Manning, too, had spied him crawling up the spars of the ship as well.

"'Tis not his fault. I found him in town and he was asking questions about a captain and a woman who'd fallen overboard from his ship. I asked him here to talk to him, to find out about the lady . . ." Esme's voice failed her and her chin wobbled. "He's but a boy."

"You've not seen the woman again?"

"Nay," she said, shaking her head as her husband collapsed against the fence. "But do not take the boy, please. He be but a child." She ignored Peter's blade and walked to the fence. "We—we, me husband and meself, we could use a child. Love him."

"I be not a child!" the ruffian insisted.

"This one could be worth something." Manning was warming to the idea of a hostage. Someone to barter with. Manning felt the hint of a smile tug at his mouth, though he knew the battle was not over yet. But now he had the stones and the boy. Things were turning around. He smiled into the salt-laden wind. "Let us go to the ship."

The insolent pup had the nerve to laugh. "'Tis too late," he taunted. "She's already sailed."

"With the captain?" Manning's blood burned. The kid didn't respond, just taunted him with his eyes.

"Well, it matters not, because I have spies strung up and down the coastline," he snarled. "Wherever the *Dark Sapphire* docks, I will soon hear of it. The sheriff in town, he will know." The brat spat again. "Bring him!" Manning ordered, and the woman ran after the urchin, shaking her head, a hand to her mouth. Manning ignored her. "If he puts up a struggle, tie him and gag him."

"Nay, please, he is but a boy." The woman was pleading, tears in her big eyes. All this for a child who was not hers. Manning didn't understand. "You can not take him—" she cried, reaching upward, supplicating.

"I can," Manning said with a knowing grin. "And I will."

"What of the sow?" the archer asked, and Manning realized the man was still sighting on the pig.

Manning looked at the miserable farmer slumped against a fence post and his fat, ugly wife chasing after a child she'd never borne. He glanced at the archer, kicked his steed, and said, "Kill it."

If nothing else, the captain was inventive, Sheena thought, shivering as she stepped into a monk's robe that Keegan had stolen from the laundry of an abbey. As easily as a cat, he'd scaled the walls and slipped naked through the stone corridors.

No one had seen him, he'd vowed once he'd returned, and Sheena didn't really care. She'd hidden in the brush, wondering what she would do if he was caught and detained, which fortunately hadn't happened. At least now she had something to wear again, and she threw on the scratchy vestment and pulled up the hood, hiding her hair and partially obscuring her face.

They'd managed to elude Manning's troops by doubling back on their route, passing the abbey, then heading south again, staying along the coast. At a stable in a small town they had traded Manning's distinctive white steed for two skinny mares which the owner of the stables was more than glad to give up.

"Ye've made yerself a fine bargain, Father," the man had claimed, clapping Keegan on his back and all the while having trouble smothering a self-satisfied smile at the deal he'd struck.

"Aye, I think so, and God will reward you in accordance

with your actions," Keegan had replied, sending the stable master's Adam's apple to bobbing rapidly. "He knows your true heart. Bless you, my son."

With that he and Sheena, who had lingered in the shadows and kept her face averted while Keegan spoke with the horse trader, had climbed astride the two sorry-looking jennets and had ridden away.

Sheena had been nervous, forever glancing over her shoulder, but they'd traveled for miles with no hint of Manning's army behind them. They had met other travelers: men and women on foot or horseback, young children often in tow. A band of musicians had passed, as had a peddler with a noisy cart pulled by a team of mules. Not one soldier had crossed their path. Yet Sheena had been wary, her eyes scanning the horizon, her ears straining for the sound of an army. Her hands sweated over the reins as she checked behind them or searched each fork in the road, certain that at any moment the hated knight and his band of cutthroats would appear over the next rise or be waiting to ambush them around the next corner.

Keegan, however, was calm.

She avoided glancing at him, for each time she did, the image of him, naked and strong as he'd ridden with her on the destrier, filled her mind. The few times they'd made love had been glorious, and yet she knew there was no chance of it again; she was about to return to Ogof, mayhap to face the hangman, and Keegan would return to the sea. 'Twas the way it would be, even though she and the handsome, bull-headed captain had argued about it.

Her heart was heavy with the thought of leaving him, but she had no choice. Elsewise she would spend the rest of her life running from the enemy, nervously glancing over her shoulder and watching her back as she was doing now.

And he would forever be the target of Manning's wrath. Only if she gave herself up to her father would Keegan be free. Her throat closed when she thought of the danger she'd brought to him and his men.

Her heart twisted and she sent a quick glance in his direction, catching a glimpse of his angular features and intense gaze. What was it about the man that he was forever in her thoughts? Even now, as she worried about the threat of Tardiff's soldiers, she remembered their lovemaking in the lake and the feel of his slick, wet skin sliding erotically against hers.

Tingling inside, she forced her eyes back to the muddy road, rutted by heavy carts and hoofprints. Each time they had come upon another horseman she had been certain the man was a scout, one of Tardiff's soldiers. But as the hours passed and they neared the town of Drudwy, she felt a sliver of hope that they had evaded the enemy. All the hours spent backtracking and taking side roads and deer paths might have procured their freedom. "Do not count on it," she told herself as more travelers joined them.

She couldn't let her guard down, not for a minute, and there was another problem to consider. Keegan was certain she would sail with him on the *Dark Sapphire,* though she knew she would never board the ship again, never again imperil his crew.

Another thought that had been bothering her surfaced. "Where is Wart?"

Keegan didn't reply.

"You sent him to find out the truth, I heard it myself," she insisted, twisting in her saddle to pin him with her eyes. "Where is he?"

"Dead."

The single word was delivered without any expression.

"How?" she asked, but knew the answer. "Sir Manning."

Keegan's scowl deepened. "He will stop at nothing. No life is sacred." His eyes scanned the faces in the crowd before returning to hers. "You will be safe on the sea," he said again, as if he were reading her wayward thoughts.

"Nay, Captain." She shook her head, for she knew she had to return to Ogof, her home. Alone. "I cannot spend the rest of my life running. Nor can I hide in your ship. Nor . . . Nor can I put any more of your men in jeopardy." Wart had died because of her, and that was the end of it. Bitter cold swept through her bones, for she'd come to care for every man aboard the *Dark Sapphire,* cutthroats or thieves though they might be. She had not known Wart, but mourned his death and felt the stab of guilt that he had died because of her.

"So you would risk your own life?" Keegan asked.

"'Tis my battle and time to no longer be a coward."

"Even if it means facing your death?"

"My father would not sentence me to die."

"You know this?" he asked as they rode through the town gate. "He is not a patient man."

"He is my father."

"Aye and he killed mine."

Sheena lapsed into silence as the horses plodded through the narrow streets. Music and laughter spilled from the open doors of an inn, while a tin smith was offering up his wares and a blacksmith was working at his forge, the bellows hissing, a fire burning bright and hot. Children ran and played, some rolling hoops, others chasing after dogs. Smoke, salt spray, and the smell of fish mingled with dung, urine, and garbage.

On the far side of town was the wharf, and there, among a small fleet of fishing vessels, the *Dark Sapphire* was anchored. A proud smile cut across Keegan's face as he stared at the tall masts knifing upward to the blue, cloudless sky. Her sails bunched upon the yards, the ship was at rest, the smell of the sea heavy in the air. A man was selling fish near the dock, speaking to everyone who passed, offering up herring and cod and crab. His wife sat near him on a stool, gutting the fish and not even looking up to smile as burly men loaded casks and crates onto the other vessels at port.

Keegan pulled on the reins of his mount and reached across to do the same with Sheena's, but as his fingers twined in the leather straps, he froze. Again he looked at his ship, and his smile faded quickly. "Something's wrong," he whispered, his eyes suddenly dark with suspicion.

"What?"

"Where are the men?" His gaze narrowed on the deck of the *Dark Sapphire,* and Sheena, too, searched from bow to stern, seeing not a single member of Keegan's crew.

"Mayhap they are all below deck or in town or . . ." Her voice faded as she felt a presence behind her. The hairs on the back of her neck lifted one by one, and she turned her head, her heart plummeted.

Sir Manning of Tardiff, astride a black horse and proudly wearing the red and gold of the hated keep, was directly behind them. But he wasn't alone. With him the crew of the *Dark Sapphire* filled the narrow cobblestone street. Hands tied, faces drawn, welts visible on some of them, they stood and stared at the ground—Seamus, Jasper, Hollis, Maynard, even Big Tom and the rest. All shackled. All chained. All held prisoner by the rough soldiers of Tardiff.

Sheena's insides congealed.

Manning, dark knight of Tardiff, had won.

"Lady Sheena," he said, his voice rough, his face warm with pride. "'Tis time for you to come with me and face your father, and mayhap your death."

Chapter Fifteen

Keegan's face grew hard as granite as he faced Manning. "I'll take no orders from you. Nor will the lady." He positioned his sorry horse between Sheena's little jennet and the dark knight's steed, but it was of no use. The battle was over. They had lost and Sheena had brought the crew of the *Dark Sapphire* to their certain doom.

Manning's hate-filled eyes were trained on Keegan and satisfaction laced his words. "You, Captain, have no choice."

Sheena's heart ached. She had put these men in jeopardy, had ruined their lives. The battle scars and bruises upon the faces of Seamus, Jasper, even Big Tom convinced her that she had to offer herself up, to save them if she could.

Worse yet, Bo, who had always been so full of life, an imp with bright eyes, floppy hair and a cocky attitude was now beaten, his wrists cruelly bound by thick rope, a gag stuffed in his mouth. His face was streaked with mud, his eyes round with fear, and for some reason, he was being held apart from the others. Oh, God, please don't let Manning hurt the boy. Her throat turned to dust. Somehow, some way, she had to save him. Bo lifted his eyes to meet hers and despite the fear and the tearstains that tracked through the mud, he squared his slim shoulders, silently insisting that he was a man.

"Now, lady," Manning said as his horse stomped impatiently and his weary, angry-looking army surrounded their prisoners. "Finally, you have nowhere to run."

Keegan leaned forward in his saddle. "You have no juris-diction here, so take your pathetic army and leave the lady, my crew and be off or—"

"Or what?" Manning sneered as the fisherman stopped trying to sell his catch and a crowd began to gather. "You're in no position to bargain, Captain. I've spoken with the au-thorities here. I will take these men prisoner as they have aided a criminal, a woman who killed the Lord of Tardiff." Manning's voice was cold as the sea, his demeanor smugly proud. "'Tis finished, Keegan." He snapped his fingers and motioned and his army circled tighter. Sheena's horse minced, as the soldiers crushed closer.

"I'm warning you, leave her be, Manning." Keegan kicked his mount, drew up near the dark knight. His jaw was rock hard, his eyes bright and despite the horrid odds, he seemed ready to lunge at Manning. "Set these men free; you have no argument with them."

"'Tis too late. The sheriff has agreed."

"I will go with you," Sheena began, thinking quickly, knowing she had nothing to barter with other than herself. The smell of a fight was heavy in the sea air and the crew of the *Dark Sapphire*, though a tough bunch of cutthroats, was no match for the weapons and soldiers of Tardiff. "Just let the others go free and I will—"

"Nay." Keegan's jaw was set, his muscles bunched, his eyes blazing. His eyes were trained on Manning, but Sheena saw him size up the crowd, the enemy, the chances of es-cape. . . . "The sheriff has no such authority. You will stay with me."

Manning laughed. "I need no one's authority," he argued. "I've had my men positioned in the towns along the coast, and I've dealt with the law in each." His eyes narrowed a fraction. "I've been chasing the lady for a long time, but now, at last, 'tis done."

Keegan's hands gripped hard on his reins. "Let her and my

men go free, Manning, and the *Dark Sapphire* will be yours."
He hitched his chin toward the ship rolling on the swells and
Manning flicked an avaricious glance toward the great car-
rack with its tall masts and gleaming hull.

"Nay!" Sheena would not have him lose the *Dark Sapphire*. Nor his crew. "This be my battle. I will come with you,
Sir Manning," she said again, tossing off her hood, "and I
will not try to escape, but the crew and ship stay here. With
the captain."

"Oh, lady, you have naught to bargain with." He tossed a
smirk at Keegan. "Nor do you. If I want the ship, I will take
her. As for the prisoners, I will decide their fate. Now, we be
off! Oswald, round up the prisoners," he ordered. "Take the
captain and—"

"Nay, Manning, listen to me. If you let these men go free,
I will come willingly with you, no longer try to escape or
thwart you. But please, I beg you, do not punish them for my
sins," she said again, more boldly as the crowd became
larger, gathering around the soldiers and their prisoners.
Women peered from windows, men stopped their work, the
fisherman's wife let her knife drop from her bony fingers as
she watched the display. Ignoring warning glances from Keegan, Sheena lifted her chin and met Manning's cold glare.
"You have my word that I will do as you bid," she vowed.

"And if I do not grant these criminals their freedom?"

"Then I promise you, I will get away from you and free
these men, and warn my father that you have no honor, that
you killed an innocent man in Wart."

"The spy? Warren of Halliwell be hardly innocent."

Her insides curdled at his arrogance. Keegan seemed
about to leap from his mount and strangle Manning with his
bare hands.

"'Tis not up to you to decide who lives or dies," she said.

"Nay?" Manning snorted. "I think ye should consider
again, *m'lady*. I be here at your father's request."

"I'll deal with Jestin," Keegan vowed.

"Nay!" There had already been enough blood spilled.

"This be my battle." Inching her chin up proudly, she slowly eased her gaze over the faces of each of his soldiers. "If you let the captain and crew of the ship go free, I will also promise not to do harm to any of your men."

Manning laughed and the cold sound sent a shiver straight to Sheena's soul. "My men be strong; they fear not a woman."

"Nay?" she asked, lifting a skeptical eyebrow, though her heart was pounding and beneath her rough garb she was beginning to sweat despite the cold. "Not even if I call up the wrath of Morrigu or—"

"Ach, she be a witch," a woman with a hooked nose whispered, gathering her children close and scurrying away.

"I believe not in your witchcraft," Manning said.

"Nor did Tardiff."

Some of the soldiers seemed to pale a bit. A massive bay sidestepped, his iron-shod hooves ringing on the cobblestones, his nostrils wide. Somewhere a man coughed. The wind kicked up. The crowd stepped back a pace or two and a few of the more pious made a swift sign of the cross over their chests.

"Do not test me," she warned in a low voice.

Keegan tossed off the cowl of his robe as he leaned forward in his saddle, his lips flat over his teeth. "My men remain with me, Manning, and the woman stays as well. As I said, for our freedom, you will be given the *Dark Sapphire*," Keegan insisted and again Manning laughed. This time the sound was pure evil.

"But I already have it, you see." Manning reached into his pocket and withdrew a ring with a brilliant dark stone that gleamed in the afternoon light.

Sheena gasped.

Keegan stared at the ring as if it had been ripped from the fleshless fist of a dead man.

"So you recognize it."

Sheena stared at the gem that had once belonged to her

mother, had been the object of the horrid wager, had been stolen by Keegan years before. "But how——?"

Keegan's gaze, drawn to the stone for a moment, slowly moved with silent condemnation to Hollis. The old man seemed to shrink into his cloak. "You lied?"

Hollis studied the cobblestones of the street. His shoulders slumped and despair edged his words. "I should have thrown the damned thing into the sea years ago."

"'Twas with the boy," Manning said. "But it matters not. I have everything now, and you, Captain, have nothing but false pride to bargain with. Now, there be no time for argument. Half of my men are going to board the ship and you're going to see that they and the *Dark Sapphire* make it safely to Ogof. The boy here"—he motioned to Bo—"will be kept apart, under constant guard and if there is any whisper of mutiny against me, the guard will slit his throat and throw his scrawny body to the beasts of the sea." Bo gulped and Sheena felt desperation the like of which had never before darkened her soul. If only she could save the boy, or Keegan . . . or the rest of the crew of the *Dark Sapphire*, a sorry lot of criminals that she'd come to trust with her life. She glanced at Keegan one last time and her heart twisted with the knowledge that she would never set eyes upon him again.

The boy she had kissed on the dock.

The man she now had taken as a lover.

Manning snapped his fingers, and seven or eight scraggly soldiers, their boots ringing, stormed up the gangway and onto the ship.

"The rest of my men and I will take the lady back overland. Once there, we will meet, and if you've done your part, I will let your men go free." He motioned to the rest of his small army, most of whom were on horseback. "At Ogof, Lady Sheena of Tardiff will be returned to her father, and the ship will become mine. Baron Jestin of Ogof will decide your fate—whether you live or die. It matters not to me." His smile had faded and pure hatred seemed to ooze from his every pore. "Now, that is how it is to be. I grow weary of this chase and will abide no dissent. If you do not agree, I will be forced to kill your men, one by one, and we'll start with the boy here."

"Nay," Sheena cried.

Manning nodded sharply to the soldier guarding Bo. Swiftly the man pulled out a long knife with a curved blade that glinted in the afternoon light. Bo arched his back and tried to fight, but the soldier put the blade to his throat.

"Dear God," Sheena whispered, tears filling her eyes. "Do not harm him." Surely Manning would not slay an innocent boy and yet . . . she knew how cruel a beast he was. She swallowed the lump in he throat. "Take me back, Manning. Leave these men. Please, I beg of you."

"What, woman? No more threats of witchcraft?" Manning asked with a crooked, self-satisfied smile. His gaze moved away from her to Keegan. "So, Captain, what say you?"

Keegan's face was grim. The veins in his neck throbbed, but his gaze was fastened on the blade at Bo's young throat. The boy shivered with fear, and a drop of blood began to ooze slowly from a tiny cut. "Enough!" Keegan agreed, his nostrils flaring, every muscle in his body bunched. "Let the boy go! Now!" His gaze was hard as he turned to Manning. "As long as you assure me of my men's safety and that the woman will not be harmed, so be it. You and I, we'll meet again in hell."

Manning nodded to the thug and the blade was lifted from Bo's neck. "That we will, Captain. That we will."

Anger roared through Keegan's veins. Fury tore at his soul and guilt, a new and ugly companion, sat heavy on his shoulders. His thoughts were dark and vengeful and the fear in his soul, a fear that Sheena would be forced up the steps to the gallows, besieged him, ripping at his mind with sharp, painful claws.

Somehow he had to save her.

No matter what.

Watching her ride away, her wrists bound, her spine stiff

as she sat astride the old mare, had been more than he could bear. He'd pretended acquiescence, taken the helm without argument and steered the ship ever southward while the man who was guarding him began to nod.

The skin was tight and drawn over Keegan's face, his mind turning with plans of besting Manning and saving Sheena, his hands gripping the whipstaff so hard his knuckles showed white as he pretended to comply with Manning's orders. He'd commanded his men to do the same and now, grudgingly, they went about their tasks upon the ship, working under the suspicious eyes of the guards.

They had grumbled and sent scathing glances at the soldiers, but to all it had appeared outwardly that Keegan had complied, that he'd crumpled beneath Sir Manning's will. Some of his own men had looked upon him with disgust, but it had been necessary for the crew to view him with contempt. He had had to appear weak, in order to lure the enemy into believing him to be compliant, his spirit broken, and that he'd lost all fight in him. Bo had been tied and gagged in the hold, one soldier watching him around the clock.

"But why not try to best them," Jasper had complained one twilit evening. "They be a sad lot if ever I've seen one."

"We cannot risk the lady's life," Keegan had replied within earshot of a strapping soldier with a thick, red beard and hands that appeared strong enough to strangle a man and snap his neck.

"We could take 'em," Tom had insisted, his brows drawing together as he viewed Keegan with new eyes, as if his captain had suddenly turned coward.

"I will not put Sheena in jeopardy," he'd said and Tom had spat on the deck, confusion evident on his face.

"This be a ruse," Hollis had whispered to him on the deck near the bowsprit. "I know ye well enough. The rest of the crew they might believe ye to have bowed to Manning, but me, I've known ye since ye were a babe."

"And yet you lied to me about the stone."

"Ach." Hollis had shaken his balding head. "Worry not

about the gem now." His hand had reached out to touch Keegan's shoulder. "I'm on yer side. If ye be plottin' a mutiny against the soldiers, I'm with ye, as are the men."

Keegan's gaze had bored into the older man's. He had sensed a presence hiding behind the mainsail. "I would never put Sheena's life in danger, Hollis. This you know. I will do whatever I must to see that she's safe."

Hollis had hesitated, then his old eyes had sparked as if he understood. "Then, ye be a fool for a woman," he had said, though there was little conviction in his voice.

"Mayhap."

"The men be disappointed in ye."

Keegan had slid his gaze to the sail and Hollis had nodded, as if he had understood all too well that they were being overheard. "Tell the men that they are to follow my example. Everyone's life is at stake. No one is to question my authority."

"So be it. I'll make sure they understand," Hollis had said, ambling off and the shadow, still hidden behind the sails, had snuck after him.

Now, as Keegan guided the ship through the night-black waters, positioning the *Dark Sapphire* at odds with the current, he planted his feet, rolled with the decking and, from the corner of his eye, caught sight of one of Tardiff's soldiers lose his battle with nausea and lean over the railing.

Keegan grinned inwardly as a huge swell raised the *Dark Sapphire* high, then dropped quickly.

"God have mercy," the man guarding him muttered. He was a heavyset man who sweated and smelled sour and like all of the tired foot soldiers aboard had never before been asea. It wasn't only the rock of the ship that caused them to be ill, but the heavy drinking, more than the soldiers could handle on the rough sea, and the food, deliberately tainted as it was, adding to their sickness. By now Hollis had caught onto Keegan's plans and had spread the word to the rest of the crew.

"Can ye na steady her?" the guard asked, his skin a pasty shade tinged with green in the lantern-light.

"I'm trying my best," Keegan lied and caught a glance from Seamus. A smile played upon the seaman's lips. "Mayhap you would like to take over."

"Nay, nay," the soldier said as Maynard stopped by with his bucket of rats.

"Ye called fer me."

"Do not throw the beasts overboard," Keegan said and nodded at the furry, bloody carcasses in Maynard's pail. "In case we run out of provisions."

"We'll not be eatin' rats!" the guard said.

"Unless we run out of food." Keegan's gaze cut any argument from Maynard's lips. "Sometimes we have no choice."

"God's eyes, who would want a life like this?" the guard muttered and Seamus swallowed another smile as he turned away. "The food and this bloody journey give a man the runs, they do."

"I'll give these ones to the cook," Maynard said, lifting a pail.

"Aye."

"Bloody Christ," the soldier muttered, swiping a palm over his brow. "I'll starve before I eat a rat."

"'Tis your choice."

"I-I needs a drink."

"I've already ordered all the casks opened. There be wine and ale enough to last the voyage."

Keegan tacked again and the ship lurched, the pail of rodents nearly slopping its bloody contents as Maynard hurried below decks.

The guard ordered ale and it was brought, but as the wind picked up, keening across the ocean, Manning's men were restless. Some had drunk far too much, others were listless and tired. All the soldiers were anxious to return to land and Tardiff Hall. They knew naught of the sea, nor of sailing ships, and had to rely upon Keegan and the members of his crew to take them back to Ogof.

It was just as Keegan had hoped.

The tired soldiers, weary from weeks of chasing after Sheena, counted upon the fact that Keegan would do nothing to endanger his men, or Sheena. To be on the safe side, as Manning had ordered, they held Bo in the hold, bound and gagged, as insurance. Should Keegan veer off course, or should any of the men not do as they were told, Bo would be killed.

Or so they thought.

But as they fell asleep at their posts or hung over the deck rail and retched, Keegan gave up the helm to Cedric. He feigned sleep on the floor as his guard had taken the bunk. Snoring softly, his eyes closed, Keegan waited, listening, the sounds of his cabin familiar. Of course he was chained. He had been each night, but what the guard didn't know is that the master key to all locks aboard the *Dark Sapphire* was hidden in a space beneath the drawer in his bunk. Tonight, as the wind raged and keened and the boat creaked, the masts groaning, the rigging rattling, Keegan ever so slowly tugged on the squeaky drawer. It seemed to take hours to inch the drawer open far enough that he could stretch his arm over the space that hid his clothes to the little niche in the back. His muscles ached and he bit hard on his lip as the shackle dug into his calf, but his fingers brushed the metal.

The soldier snorted. Keegan froze. Sighing heavily, his jailer rolled over and Keegan snagged the key, hiding it in the palm of his hand. He waited a few more seconds and as the ship listed slightly, found the lock. With a soft click, the shackles opened and he was free.

Taking the sleeping man's sword from his scabbard, Keegan slipped out the door and locked it firmly behind him. Outside the sky was dark, the wind fierce, the air brisk. He moved stealthily through the shadows, past slumbering guards, into the hold where he found Hollis, wrapped in his cloak, snoring loudly, his head bent at an odd angle. Placing a hand over the old man's mouth, Keegan shook his shoulder gently.

Hollis's eyes flew open. He started to struggle, then spying Keegan in the stygian gloom, he climbed to his feet. "I wondered when ye'd come fer me," he whispered as they slipped silently to a spot on the main deck. "Ye've a plan."

"Aye. Pray that it works. You free the men with this." He dropped the key into Hollis's palm.

"And what will ye be up to?"

"'Tis time to turn the tables on Manning's men. We'll set Big Tom free, and he and I will handle the soldiers. Bring them to the hold where you and the others will be ready to lock them in the chains they've used on us." Keegan's smile was pure evil. Hollis cackled. "Come."

Creeping stealthily, they came upon the guard on deck and Keegan lunged forward, wrapped his arm around the brute's neck, and threatened death with his newfound blade. "Fight me and you'll die," Keegan promised. The soldier, weak as he was, put up no struggle. Within seconds Big Tom was free, rubbing his wrists and anxious for battle.

"I knew ye'd find a way to free us," he said. "I never doubted ye for a second, Captain."

'Twas stretching the truth a bit, Keegan thought, but cared not. "First we free Bo, then the others."

In the darkness, Big Tom smiled. "And then the lady? We'll save her as well?"

"Or die trying," Keegan vowed.

"Then, Captain," Tom said heartily and grabbed the soldier's dagger and sword, "there be no time to waste."

"Amen," Hollis agreed as they slunk through the shadows and into the bowels of the ship. *Hold on, Sheena,* Keegan thought, his eyes straining in the dark, his muscles poised for battle. *I'm coming.*

The night was bitter cold with the promise of autumn. No stars dared shine through the fog that crept stealthily over the ground, yet Sheena recognized the road as it turned toward the great gates of Ogof. They had ridden for days, she was tired to her bones, and she felt no sense of homecoming even as dawn threatened to pierce the mantle of fog surrounding the fortress. Nay, all she felt was dread—deep, dark and terrifying. She had barely slept as she'd always been wary, not trusting any of Tardiff's soldiers who had stared at her with a silent hatred. She'd heard them talking around the fire, picking their teeth with the bones of quail and rabbit, grumbling about the chase she'd given them, arguing among themselves if she were a witch, daft, or just a cold-blooded killer.

Manning had barely let her out of his sight and even when she had to relieve herself, a guard stood nearby. 'Twas humiliating and worrisome, though she'd managed to scratch a few runes in the sand and had even offered up more than her share of prayers to God. She had let the men hear her chanting as if calling up the spirits. More than one Adam's apple had bobbed in worry and the men, aside from the guard assigned to her, had given her a wide berth.

All the better. Now, of course, she had to face her father.

Lord help me, she thought, gathering up her courage and forcing her back to be ramrod stiff as she sat astride her weary mount. *And be with Keegan.* For all of this horrid journey, her thoughts had been with that blackheart of a captain, the man she'd sworn to hate, the man she now realized she loved. With every breath in her body she ached for him, for she was certain she would never see him again. *Oh, love, if I had only told you how I felt.* But she had not known, would not admit it to herself. By the gods, she was a fool like no other. And now she would never see him again, might not know if he lived or died.

Torment, dark and desperate, scraped at her soul.

"Halt! Who goes there?" a deep male voice demanded from the top of the tower. Her heart pounded in fear, and though she had pretended subservience, anger burned bright in her mind.

"'Tis I, Geoff," Manning said, his voice filled with a sickening pride that made Sheena's skin crawl. "And I have with me Lady Sheena. Let us pass."

"Aye, Sir Manning! Open the gates!" Geoff replied, his voice filled with relief and jubilation. So this was how it would be. Even those who had known her since childhood would celebrate her imprisonment, mayhap her death.

With a grinding of gears the clanking portcullis rose. Sheena set her jaw and, her hands still bound, rode into the home that she'd known for most of her life. Through the outer bailey where the quintain was at rest, sheep grazed. The gong farmer rolled out a wheelbarrow of muck; peasants carrying sickles and scythes were walking toward the main gate on the way to her father's fields.

As the army rode to the inner bailey, she felt eyes upon her and heard her name whispered.

"So they finally caught up with her," a man murmured as he hoisted a heavy bag to his shoulders. In the darkness Sheena could not see his face.

"Poor lass, she'll be hanged sure," a woman, mayhap his wife, replied. She carried a basket of candles and was walking to the keep. "And Jestin, her father, he be the one who will have to send her to the gallows. By the saints."

Husband and wife hurried on their way, but the word of Manning's triumphant arrival spread, and peasants and servants alike appeared through the mist. She recognized Allen, the rail-thin steward, and Farrell, the stable master, leading a docile horse. John, one of the pages, smiled shyly, blushing as he saw her. His hair stuck up at odd angles and his teeth were crooked and much too large for his mouth. Harold was walking several dogs which began to bark madly and strain at their leashes, sending up a ruckus loud enough to alert the entire castle. The cook, miller, atilliator, potter, all ran from their huts. At the sight of Sheena, eyes rounded, fingers pointed and a few brave souls even smiled, though most stared at her as if she were a heathen. Children cringed and whispered her name. Mothers held their babes close to their breasts.

"By the saints, 'tis the lady," the potter whispered, his eyebrows shooting skyward.

"I thought she'd never come back to Ogof. 'Tis a miracle, it is," Gillian, the spinster, whispered loudly.

"Or a curse," Owen, a mason, muttered under his breath. Sheena looked away, refused to break down. "Look at her. Her hands are tied."

" 'Tis a pity she returns now, with her father as he is."

Sheena's head snapped around. The baron? Something was wrong with Lord Jestin? No.

"Aye. First the sadness of little Llwelyn and now this—his firstborn daughter brought to justice for slaying her husband. 'Twill kill him sure."

A man snorted. "He already be nearly in the grave."

Despite her bonds, Sheena twisted in her saddle and pinned the spinster with her eyes. "What say you, Gillian? What of my father? Be he ill?" Fear gripped her heart.

"Enough of this!" Manning said.

Sheena's wasn't to be put off. Her head swiveled slowly as she eyed the servants and peasants who had gathered. The sun was lighting the eastern sky. "What of my father?" she demanded and there was much whispering between them. Some cringed, others looked away, several looked upon her with pity in their eyes.

"Come. Now!" Manning was impatient.

"Wait! What's wrong with the baron?" she demanded, her eyes sweeping the upturned faces. "Someone tell me."

Jason, the armorer, and a man she knew to be honest as any stepped forward. He sniffed loudly, nodded to her and, swiping his hat from his head, curled it in his fingers. " 'Tis a sad day, m'lady. Lord Jestin, he be dyin', lady. The physician, he's been with him since morn yesterday."

"What? Nay!" She couldn't believe the horrid words.

"I lie not."

"Aye, 'tis true." Father Godfrey hurried along the walk from the chapel, his tonsure visible, his fingers twined nervously within the beads of his rosary. "I was on my way to be with him when I heard the dogs—" His eyebrows lifted as he took in her monk's robe. Frowning at the disrespect and blasphemy, he opened his mouth as if to reproach her, but seemed to think better of it. Cleaning his throat, he said, "Ye'd best hurry, m'lady, for he's not much longer in this world." As if to add emphasis a cock crowed loudly.

"Nay, oh, nay. I'll not believe that my father—" Her voice cracked and she fumbled with the ropes cutting into her wrists and swung one leg over her horse's back.

"Stop! We have no time for this nonsense." Manning wheeled his horse, but it was too late.

Sheena threw her weight to one side and tumbled from her bow-backed mount, stumbling as she landed in the soft grass of the inner bailey. Manning yelled and sputtered, but Sheena ran through the throng, past men and women she'd known all her life. Working at the ropes she dashed up the crumbling steps and threw herself against the door to nearly fall into the great hall.

A fire burned low in the grate and rush lights glowed through the corridors. "Father!" she yelled, her voice echoing as servants and sentinels hurried forward. "Father!"

"For the love of Christ! Stop!" Manning yelled, bursting through the door.

"Please. Do not mock the name of the Son," the priest said, his heavy tread following that of the dark knight. Sheena didn't so much as look over her shoulder.

With Manning and the priest hard upon her heels, she raced up the steps to her father's chamber, pounded on the door with hands that were tied together, then shoved against the door and tumbled into the room.

At the sight of her father, she gasped, her heart squeezing painfully for he lay on his bed, his face pale, his eyes without luster.

"Sheena?" he whispered, his voice rough as a light of recognition flared in his eyes. "Sheena? Girl, is that you?"

"Aye, Father!" Her voice cracked. Stumbling through the rushes, she flung herself toward the bed. Tears filled her eyes. "What is this?"

He snorted through his nose. " 'Tis said I be dyin', daughter." He smiled feebly and lifted a hand. "But 'tis glad I be to see ye, make no mistake." His lips twitched and he blinked against tears but for a second as she threw herself upon his once-strong body and felt his arms surround her.

"Nay, you be not dying. You are but sick and will improve. . . ." She choked back further words and clung to this man who had raised her alone for so many years, until he had married Fawn. There had been times she'd hated him and thwarted him. Had she not betrayed him by setting Keegan free all those years ago? Had she not wanted to leave then when he'd allowed his new wife to order her about? And had he not given her to Tardiff, insisting she marry? She loved and hated this man all at once, yet could not face his death.

Footsteps thundered through the door.

"'Tis all right," Jestin said into her ear, not seeming to notice the others pouring into the room. "I've made my peace."

"Nay, Father, speak not of this." Tears filled her eyes, tears of regret and pain. "I've not made my peace with you, there is much to discuss." Her heart wrenched. Many times she'd cursed him, and just as many sung his praises. She couldn't lose him. Not yet. "I—I—"

"Shh." He patted her hands, then scowled. "You be bound," he murmured sluggishly, then his mind seemed to clear a bit as he touched her head. With a weak snap of his fingers, he glanced at a guard. "Cut these damned ropes upon my daughter's wrists and be quick about it." The man did as he was bid and Manning, who had entered the chamber, dared not argue with the Baron of Ogof. Glowering at Sheena, he stood to one side of Jestin's bed, the fingers of one gloved hand curled tightly over the hilt of his sword.

"What happened?" she asked her father as the guard cut her free. "Father, what happened to you?" She rubbed her wrists but watched Manning from the corner of her eye.

"'Tis only old age, daughter. I be sick for a while. Knew it, I did, but . . . I felt not too poorly. I could still run the castle, still hunt." He looked up toward a window, but she knew his vision was turned inward. "Then the babe was born and there was all that trouble. . . ." His voice faded, and he closed his eyes for a second. Then he cleared his throat, shoved himself up on the bed. As he did, some of his color returned.

"What babe? Fawn's child?"

"Aye. My son—" A catch stopped him from saying more.

"Where is he, this brother of mine?" Sheena asked through her tears and she saw the hint of a grin curve Manning's evil face.

"With the angels," Father Godfrey offered. "He—he was born wrong, never ate and fussed and just yesterday morn . . ." The priest crossed himself. "The babe, he drew his last breath."

"Nay," Manning whispered, his eyes thinning on Father Godfrey.

Jestin closed his eyes for a second, as if the conversation was much too painful.

"Oh, Father, 'tis sorry I be," Sheena said feeling the lack of warmth in this chamber with its roaring fire and torches glowing, where coming death and desperation could not be heated.

"You lie," Manning accused the priest. Rage flared in his eyes and color swept up his cheeks as he approached the man of God. His nostrils flared, his shoulders bunched in anger, and the lines around his mouth were etched deep with hatred. "The boy, Fawn's son, be fit and hale." He stalked toward the priest, the toes of his boots forced against the priest's shoes, his expression warning that he wanted to tear Father Godfrey limb from pious limb. "Say it!"

"Nay." Godfrey shook his head, cast down his eyes, the bald pate within his ring of fine hair dripping sweat and reflecting the firelight. "I cannot. 'Tis a pity, but God's will. I have prayed much for his little soul, a soul brought into the world in a sorceress's hut, where pagan arts are practiced."

"I believe you not, you worm of a priest." He glanced around, his lips flat over his teeth. "Where be Fawn?" Manning demanded.

"My wife. You're speaking of my wife." Jestin's spine stiffened. "Mayhap I should remind you she is a lady."

Why was he so upset? Sheena wondered. 'Twas a pity that the babe did not survive, a tragedy, but never had Sheena witnessed Manning care a whit about man or beast. Yet the child's unfortunate death seemed to make him forget Sheena and his mission of returning her to meet her doom.

"I needs speak to *the lady.* Now."

"You forget yourself, Manning," Jestin said, eyes narrowed now, hand scratching his chin thoughtfully.

"Where is she?" Manning's face had become mottled with disbelief and rage, his eyes mere slits, his hand tight over his sword as he glared down at the priest.

"I—I know not."

"Enough. The babe is dead. That be the end of it—there is nothing more to say!" Jestin pinned the dark knight with his old eyes and some of the fire in his soul. The old warrior he'd once been was visible in his gaze. With great effort he threw his legs over the side of his bed and sat up tall. Pushing himself upward, he managed to stand and straighten his spine. Even in a dressing gown, he was an imposing figure. "I still be baron here. You will not make demands of me, nor my wife."

"I returned your daughter."

"That you did and for that you will be paid and paid well."

"She killed Tardiff."

Jestin appraised the man he'd once trusted with his own life with new eyes. His graying eyebrows drew together and 'twas as if he were putting together the parts of an intricate, bedeviling puzzle. "I will determine her fate. You needs not remind me, Manning. Again, ye've forgotten yer station." He reached for a mazer of water and took a long swallow. "There has been much treachery here," he said as he set the cup down. His gaze swept the room that had filled with soldiers and servants. "Many of you think I already be dead, that I know not of your plots against me, but be warned, I will suffer no treason." His gaze flicked to Manning. "From anyone. Now, daughter," he turned back to Sheena, "tell me of Tardiff."

Keegan oared the rowboat toward the rotting dock in the cove. Much of the pier had disappeared in the past eleven years and 'twas dark as the devil's soul, but using a torch for illumination, Keegan eased the rowboat close to a decaying piling.

After disposing of Manning's men one by one, and seeing that they were locked in the hold, he had anchored the *Dark Sapphire* in the bay and, with Bo, rowed back to this cavern which smelled of decay and mold. The boy had a personal score to settle and though he was not as strong as some of the men, he was small and wiry and sneaky. He'd insisted upon accompanying Keegan to save Sheena and Keegan had decided that he would help rather than hinder him.

"Come," Keegan ordered the boy as they tied the boat to a sagging post and scrambled up the slick, uneven planks. They carried weapons, rope, axes, and the torch, for Keegan knew not if these old corridors would take him to Sheena. His heart pumped in fear and the memory of kissing her here so long ago was vivid in his mind. Dear God, he felt as if he'd loved her forever.

He would find her. Save her. He couldn't fail.

Then there was Manning. Keegan would personally hunt down the cur.

If only he was not too late.

The thought that Sheena might already be in her grave, the victim of her father's cruel justice caused his soul to shrivel. If it be so, he would kill Jestin and Manning with his bare hands, or be sent to hell himself.

He cared not which.

The water lapped with dark calm around the boat. Keegan forced his legs to run up the stairs, to the first cobweb-strewn doorway. He leaned a shoulder against the ancient oak and it held. A kick. Still the old timbers didn't budge.

"God's teeth," he growled, grabbing an ax.

Throwing his shoulders into the blow, he swung hard. Wood splintered. A rusted lock fell away. Keegan stepped into a corridor that was as dark as Satan's heart. His skin prickled as he forged onward, holding the torch aloft, following its flickering, smoky light up the narrow corridor that he prayed would lead to the center of Ogof toward Sheena.

He only hoped he wasn't too late.

Desperately, Sheena grabbed her father's hand. "Before I tell you of Tardiff, please, I beg you, order Manning to release the men that he captured when he caught up with me." She held fast to her father, willing life and fire into his ailing body. She couldn't lose him. Wouldn't. Theirs had been a stormy relationship, aye, but he was the man who had sired her. "Please, command him to give Keegan back his ship and that all the crew be free and—"

"Hush, child. Slow down." Jestin's face had pinched together. "Who is Keegan?"

"The bastard son of Rourke," Manning offered.

"Rourke?" Pain swept through the older man's eyes, but a newfound vigor as well. "His soul now rots in hell as well it should. What has his son to do with you?"

"She's been with your old enemy, m'lord," Manning spat out. "His son somehow escaped during the fire here at Ogof years ago when Rourke was killed. In the confusion the lad stole the ring, the one with the Dark Sapphire of Ogof. For days, nay, weeks now, your daughter has been with the bastard, plotting against Ogof and Tardiff."

"Is this true?" Jestin turned condemning eyes toward Sheena.

"Nay, Father, never have I plotted against Ogof, or you. Ogof is my home."

From his pocket, Manning withdrew the ring. The blue stone glittered in the firelight. "She lies." Manning held the ring aloft so that the gem's deep blue facets winked seductively. Jestin stiffened at the sight of the gem.

"For the love of God, 'tis the Dark Sapphire," Jestin whis-

pered and the servants who had followed Manning inside
stepped backward.

"The evil stone," Father Godfrey whispered.

" 'Twas to be my ring," Lady Fawn proclaimed in a voice
without much vigor as she hurried into the room. Her pale
skin was whiter still, her expression haunted. She wore a
wrinkled gown over her still bloated body and her hair, usually neat, was straggly and unkempt. She stared at the ring
and couldn't muster a smile. Fawn saw Sir Manning and
nearly stumbled. "I heard you had come finally," she said, as
if no one else, not even Sheena was in the room. Her throat
worked and she opened supplicating pale fingers toward the
beast of a knight. Tears filled her eyes and ran down her
milky skin. "Oh, Manning, 'tis sorry, I be. So sorry," she
whispered thickly as Zelda followed after her, then, stood
silent and grim near the fire.

"The babe?" Manning asked, his voice rough. Everyone
within the chamber grew silent.

A strangled mewling noise escaped Fawn's throat. Her
knees wobbled, and for a second Sheena thought she might
collapse. "Llywelyn," she murmured. "Precious Llywelyn.
Your son, Manning, mine, oh, for the love of God, he is
gone. . . ." She crumpled onto a corner of the bed, and
Sheena felt as if she'd been slapped awake. Did Fawn say
that the babe was not her brother? That the dark knight
had . . . ? Bile crawled up her throat, for Fawn and Manning
had betrayed them all.

"What happened?" Manning's eyes held no compassion as
he stared at the woman he'd lain with.

"What the bloody hell is this?" Jestin demanded, but his
wife did not hear, looked only up at the father of her dead
child.

"Llywelyn . . . Oh, merciful God, he . . . was not born
right." She was shaking her head, sniffing, denying the truth,
even as it passed her lips. "I tried, Manning, God knows I
tried to keep him alive, but I could not. One morning he was

gone." Fawn's voice broke and she sobbed, her callous heart broken.

"*His* son?" Jestin growled. "*His?*" He glared down upon the limp creature that was his wife and contempt contorted his features, rage snapped in his old eyes.

"Nay . . . nay . . ." Fawn said, shaking her head as if realizing her confession. "Your son, husband, of course . . . I am grieving . . . confused." Steadying herself on a bedpost, she swiped back the tears from her eyes, and finally the realization that Sheena was in the room pierced her brain. Her countenance shifted abruptly from grief to a slow-rising anger that swept up her pale cheeks in hot flush.

"You," she spat. "Leave the lord be, can't you see . . . that . . . you are the cause of all the trouble. All that has gone wrong here in Ogof as well as Tardiff can be laid at your feet!"

Her voice faltered again and when she turned back to Manning, she again saw the ring in his hand, the Dark Sapphire that she'd glimpsed, then forgotten with her grief. "You . . . you found it?" she whispered in awe, her eyes rounding in disbelief, her sadness vanishing for the moment.

"What of you, Sheena? What have you to say?" Jestin focused on his daughter, his eyebrows lowered, his lips tight as if he were trying to piece together all of the information. "Manning said you were with Rourke's son." Accusation filled his old eyes. Disappointment slumped his shoulders.

"Nay, Father, let me explain."

"Saints preserve us," the priest whispered.

Fawn whirled upon her husband. "She's a murderess. That be all there is to explain," she insisted, her grief forgotten for the moment. "She killed my brother, robbed him of the gems you gave him, then ran away like the coward she is." Fawn's face had transformed from sadness to a mask of fury and hatred. "But 'tis all over, Sheena. All over. Your true colors have been shown and you have proved yourself to be a traitor to your father, Ogof, Tardiff and God Himself."

"Nay, Wife." Jestin raised a suddenly strong hand. "Let us

not be so hasty. There be much deception here, aye, and I think you be at the heart of it. 'Tis you who betrayed me, you who have lain with another man, you who got with child and lied to me of his conception." Blue eyes snapped in disgust. "Leave now before I wring your pathetic neck. I need time alone with my daughter."

"Nay, oh, husband, nay! You have many daughters," Fawn pointed out, stung. "I gave them to you. Think of Mary and—"

"Be off woman, before I kill you here and now."

"Nay, I can't believe that you would." She looked quickly around, a pathetic creature backing out of the room and then her gaze landed full force on the ring again. "'Tis not I who betrayed you. 'Twas your firstborn . . . Sheena is a killer. Do you not remember what she did to poor Ellwynn?" Fawn's voice had raised an octave and she lifted her arms to all in the chamber. "Killed him she did, stabbed him and left him to die on her wedding night."

"I will hear it from her own lips," Jestin insisted. His old eyes found Sheena's. "In all the years I have known her, she has never lied."

"Nay! Nay! Look at her! For the love of God, she be a traitor!" Fawn's thin patience snapped. She leapt up to snag the ring from Manning's hand, curling her fingers tightly around the cursed stone. As if drawing strength from the gem, she advanced with new determination upon her ailing husband. Sheena was poised to fling herself between husband and wife. Manning's hand was on his sword. The priest scrabbled for his rosary and one of the serving girls ran from the room.

Fawn's expression was hard and accusing as she glared at the man who was her husband. "You don't care, though, do you, Jestin? Because Sheena was born of Bertrice, you think she can do no harm," she accused, her lips turning downward as if the taste of Jestin's first wife's name was bitter. "Saint Bertrice, the woman who loved another man, yet married you. Oh, she did no wrong in your eyes and now her daughter, too, is above the law." She pointed a long, shaking finger at Sheena and her voice was tremulous. "But this one, this one, she be a murderer, a thief and a—"

"Nay, Father, listen not to her lies," Sheena said, unable to witness this outrage a moment longer. For months she had run and cowardly not faced the truth or her father. Now she could no longer listen to her accusers without defending herself. "'Tis true I stabbed my husband," she admitted, the painful night screaming behind her eyes. She remembered Tardiff as he was, a cold, cruel beast filled with lust and depravity. But no love. "I killed him because, upon our wedding night he placed a knife to my throat."

"She lies!" Fawn shrieked.

"'Twas not enough for me to take his bed, but he demanded that I share the bed with him and . . . and another woman." She stared at the floor for a second and the room was silent, only the hiss of the fire to be heard. "I could not. Would not. He laughed, then insisted he would bend my will to his with the knife. I struggled and fought, the dagger fell and . . . 'tis true, then I used his own blade against him, and ran. I grabbed the stones and escaped." She lifted her head, met her father's gaze with her own. "Aye, I be a murderer and aye, I be a thief. I make no excuse."

"Lies!" Fawn said, spinning and leveling a hideous, desperate glare at Sheena. "My brother would not do anything so vile."

"Father protect us," Father Godfrey intoned.

"Lady Sheena speaks the truth," Zelda said quietly from her corner. All eyes turned to the old maidservant. The lines around her mouth and eyes seemed deeper in the reflection of the fire. "Come inside, Fannie," she called across the chamber and Sheena's heart froze. Turning toward the doorway she spied the blond serving girl who had saved her life that night. Fannie, hands wringing her skirt, eyes downcast, cheeks flushed with embarrassment, edged slowly inside. "Tell the lord what happened."

Fannie cringed.

"Now, Fannie," Zelda ordered with sudden strength, then

supplicated the baron. "Please, m'lord, listen. My daughter has something she must tell you."

Fawn's eyebrows drew together. "How dare you say anything, you simpleton!" she scolded, advancing upon the maidservant.

"I shall hear this," Jestin said softly.

Fawn raised a hand to slap the taller woman.

"Do not strike her!" Jestin warned. "Or I shall have you locked away. I would hear the girl speak."

The blond girl gulped. Her eyes were as large as goose eggs as everyone's attention turned toward her. "'Tis true . . . m'lord," she whispered, her worried gaze flicking from Fawn to Sir Manning. "I . . . I was there. Sheena wounded her husband on her wedding night because . . . because he wanted her to lie with him and another woman. 'Twas me. I was Lord Ellwynn's lover . . . and he forced me to join them in their chamber so that he could humiliate his new wife . . . break her spirit. But the lady . . . she would not yield, and the lord, he had a knife . . . 'tis as she says."

Tears of shame ran down Sheena's face, though she forced her spine to be stiff, her chin raised.

"Nay, nay, nay!" Fawn screeched, pointing an accusing finger at Fannie. "Lie no more! How much did you gain by warming my brother's bed only to turn on him now."

"As you turned on your own husband?" Zelda asked.

Fawn gasped, sputtering at her lady-in-waiting's damning accusation. "You're a ninny, a simpleton," Fawn spat at Zelda.

"But, m'lady 'tis true. We all heard it, that the babe you bore, the one who is now in his grave, was not the baron's. Did not Serena say so? Did not you yourself admit it just now when you first saw Sir Manning?"

Fawn scowled desperately. "Nay—"

Manning stepped forward, his fingers curling over his sword.

"Sir Manning fathered poor little Llywelyn. I saw him many a night go to the lady's chamber."

"Nay! You lie," Fawn snarled, her face turning the color of old ashes. "You all lie! And you will pay for it." She snapped her fingers at a guard, pointing at Sheena. "Take the traitor and this, this lying servant and her slutty daughter to the dungeons! Now!"

"Wait!" Jestin cried, his voice louder than it had been. He pinned the serving maid in his stare. "You swear this to be true?"

"Aye m'lord, I swear it on the Holy Mother's soul," Zelda vowed as Fawn raged. "And . . . and that is not all. Fannie," she prodded, her voice ringing through the chamber.

Smack! Fawn slapped the taller woman and Zelda's head snapped back. A huge red welt appeared on her cheek. Manning unsheathed his sword.

"Let there be no bloodshed," Father Godfrey insisted.

Fawn's lips pulled back into an ugly scowl. Motioning to Manning, she ordered, "Take them away! To the dungeon."

"Stop!" With more strength than Sheena thought he had, Jestin bent down, reached beneath his bed and slowly withdrew his sword. He held it high, its blade shining gold in the firelight, his bearing reminiscent of the leader he'd once been. Fire burned in his eyes and he swept a long, steady gaze through the chamber. "I still be lord here." His voice was fierce. It resounded against the coved ceilings and bounced from the rafters. "No one will take my daughter to the dungeon. Nor anyone else, unless it is my command."

Fawn stepped forward.

"That includes you, Wife. Did I not tell you that I would lock you away? Do not," he warned. "Do not defy me again. Ever." He pinned Manning in his hard glare and Sheena's heart froze for there was blood lust in his gaze. "Drop your weapon."

"You would stop me?" Manning sneered.

"If needs be."

"Father, please—" Sheena cried, fearful for his life. If only she had a weapon! She glanced quickly about, searching for a dagger, a sword, a bow, anything!

"Do not do anything stupid," Fawn said, closing the distance between her and Manning. "Not here. Not now."

"Get back, you lying whore. I've listened to you long enough," Manning ordered.

"Nay, Manning!"

Smack! He cuffed her hard across the cheek. She stumbled backward, her eyes round with horror, a huge welt forming on her ashen cheek. Manning wheeled on Jestin. "You *m'lord,*" he said, sneering, "are on your way to hell."

Sheena moved, searching for a stone to throw, hot water to hurl, a stick, a weapon of any kind.

"You would kill me?" Jestin asked the man he'd once trusted.

"You are but a feeble old man."

"Be careful, my lord. Sir Manning, he has killed before," Fannie blurted. " 'Twas not Sheena who took Lord Ellwynn's life. Nay. 'Twas Manning. I . . . I saw him thrust a dagger into Lord Ellwynn's chest when I returned to the chamber after I showed Sheena the corridor to the moat." Fanny swallowed hard. "Sheena did not kill the baron. Sir Manning did. At the lady's request."

"Lying bitch!" Manning cried, lifting his sword.

"What?" Sheena nearly lost her footing.

Manning didn't bother denying the deed and Sheena thought she might throw up. She hadn't killed Tardiff? It wasn't her wound that took his life? Tears filled her eyes and she felt an incredible relief, though she didn't have time to think of it. Not now. Not when her father's life was in peril of being taken from him by the very killer who had slain Tardiff, then let her take the blame. And Fawn had been behind it all? The scheming, the plotting, the sheer bloody horror of it!

"Bastard," Sheena muttered under her breath and Manning, curse him, smiled with pure evil.

"You ordered your own brother's death?" Sheena was ready to wring Fawn's pathetic neck. She advanced upon her stepmother.

Father Godfrey shook his head. "Nay, nay. Let there be no more blood spilled."

Fawn began to shake.

"Is this true?" Jestin asked his wife. "You would have your brother killed, then deceive me with a son who was not mine?"

"Nay, Husband. Never." Fawn, pale as goat's milk, shook her head. "I have been faithful to you. I love you, Jestin, and you know this to be true," she insisted far too quickly, her deception and lies propelling her into a last desperate attempt at denial. "If Sir Manning had anything to do with my brother's death, then he will be punished—"

Manning's eyes narrowed. "I'll hear no more of your lies, woman! I've done yer bidding, been yer damned slave and whipped cur far too long. Aye, the babe was mine, and she intended to pass it off as yours until you died. If I ever told the truth, she promised to accuse me of rape." With a snarl, he lunged at Fawn, as if determined to strike her dead.

Jestin sprang, his tired old body responding to the call of battle as he shielded his wife.

Sheena screamed.

Manning's blade swung downward. Hard. Jestin slid to one side, but not before the sword bit into his shoulder.

"Ahhhggghhh." Blood spurted.

"Stop! Do not do this!" Sheena yelled, frantic as she stripped a nearby guard of his weapon, the man paralyzed by the drama unfolding before him. Jestin rounded, his blade sharp and deadly. But Manning was quick, agilely ducking the blow only to face Sheena and her small dagger. "Stop," she commanded again.

Alarm bells clanged, ringing loudly throughout the castle. Footsteps pounded up the stairs. Men shouted and the walls of Ogof shook.

"What is it?" Fawn cried.

Soldiers burst into the room. One of the guards turned, Sheena grabbed his sword, and with a blade in each hand, faced the man who had so ruthlessly hunted her down. "Drop your sword, Sir Manning," she ordered.

From the corner of her eye she saw blood, thick and purple-red oozing from her father's wound. Jestin was unsteady on his feet, yet he held up a hand.

"Do not take him on, Daughter. This be my battle."

"And mine as well," Sheena replied, training her eyes upon Manning's sword hand.

Manning's smile was inhuman and cruel.

"Drop your weapon or die!"

"Sheena!" Keegan's voice rang through the castle. Her heart took flight and for a second she could not think, losing her concentration. Was it possible? Was Keegan here or was her mind playing tricks upon her again?

"Watch out!" Zelda warned as she turned and saw a flash in her peripheral vision.

Manning swung downward, but Sheena dodged to the right, caught a glimpse of Keegan, her beloved, his face a grim mask, his eyes filled with horror, his bow at his shoulder. "Don't!" he ordered the dark knight, but it was too late.

Manning struck hard. Sheena threw herself to the floor and rolled. The blade of the sword cleaved the air to crash against the floor.

Thwang!

An arrow sizzled past Sheena's head just as she covered it.

Thunk! Manning bellowed in rage as the deadly missile lodged deep in his chest. "You sea-loving bastard," he roared, dropping his sword, both hands surrounding the shaft of the arrow.

"Nay!" Fawn screamed as Manning, stunned, yanked at the horrid shaft and sank to his knees. "Murderer!" she cried, turning startled, tragic eyes toward the captain, before reaching Manning, falling to his side and cradling his great head in her arms. Blood trickled from the corner of his mouth and she leaned over to kiss his lips, her own becoming stained. She took the ring from his hand and put it into one of her pockets, all the while wailing, "Do not leave me, Manning, do not!" But the breath rasped and gurgled in his chest as he drew in his final gulps of air.

"You killed him!" As if catapulted, Fawn sprang at Keegan, clawing and scratching and he held her arms a second before the fight seemed to slip from her. Slowly, as she quit struggling, he released her and she collapsed near the slain soldier again.

Keegan went to Sheena and gathered her into his arms. "Sheena, oh, love, I feared that you . . ." He buried his face in her hair and beneath the strength of his arms, she felt him tremble.

"Nor did I believe that I would see you again."

"Oh, God, no," Fawn wailed, still clinging to the dead knight.

"Get up," Jestin commanded and when his wife sobbed and refused to stand, he motioned to one of the guards. "Take her away." To another, he pointed at Manning's carcass. "Clean up this mess."

Keegan's arm tightened around Sheena as Fawn was dragged off her lover. Blood smeared her dress, panic and disbelief in her eyes.

Jestin, weakened, fell back on the bed as his wife was dragged away. "You . . . you don't understand. . . ." Fawn was crying, sobbing, screaming, beseeching her husband with her outstretched bloodstained arms. "I had to do it. You wanted a son and . . . I . . ."

"You ordered your brother killed," Jestin charged, mopping his brow and refusing to look at the woman who'd sworn to love him for all their years.

"I did it only for you. To give you a son." Fawn shuddered and clutched herself.

Two heavy soldiers carried Manning's body away and no one, save Fawn, shed a tear for the Judas who had betrayed them all.

Keegan held tight to Sheena, his lips pressed into her hair, his arms as strong as the very walls of Ogof.

"The lord should rest," Zelda said and Keegan pulled on

Sheena's arm, drew her past the crowd of servants, soldiers, and peasants and into a dark alcove of the hallway. Glances were sent their way and the whisper of gossip followed after them. Fannie could not help but grin and even Father Godfrey smothered a smile as he passed.

"Sheena!" Bo, carrying a thick coil of rope over his shoulder, threw himself at her. "I told him you would be fine," he said, throwing a glance over his shoulder to Hollis, who, with some of the other members of the *Dark Sapphire*'s crew appeared. "But he worries always."

"Bah! The boy exaggerates." Hollis snorted and flicked Bo a warning glance.

"But you do not?" Sheena teased.

"Never."

Keegan grinned and Bo laughed out loud at Hollis's discomfiture.

"This be a grand castle," Bo said, his gaze roving through the corridor.

"The best. And I think if you go downstairs—Oh, wait! Fannie! See that these men are given food and drink and whatever else they desire."

The girl nodded and the cutthroats and pickpockets and thieves who had become close to Sheena followed her until at last, she and Keegan were alone in the hallway. He kissed the crown of her head gently.

"Thank God you be safe," Keegan whispered, his throat thick as the rushlights burned low in their sconces. "I thought I'd lost you."

"And I you," she said sniffing and clinging tight to this man she loved with all her heart. Tears filled her eyes when she thought of how many times she'd nearly lost him, how she'd thought she'd never look upon him, never feel his strength or feel the beating of his heart.

"It won't happen again," he vowed and he cupped her chin with his fingers and tilted her face to his. His lips claimed hers and she sighed against him.

She closed her eyes and for a minute she was a young girl

on a rotting dock experiencing her first kiss, then she was a woman held captive, half in love with a rogue captain and feeling the heat of his body, then she was a free woman, in love with the one man who had claimed her heart. Her blood heated, the castle seemed to disappear until she felt as if she and Keegan were the only man and woman in the universe.

Her skin tingled and deep inside she wanted more . . . oh, so much more.

When he lifted his head, his eyes shone with unshed tears. "I love you Sheena of Ogof," he vowed. "Whether you be a witch or an angel, a commoner or a lady, I swear on all that is holy that I love you with all my heart."

"And . . . and I love you."

His smile was a crooked slash of white. "You'll marry me, then?" he asked, a dark brow cocking as he looked down upon her.

She smiled through a sheen of tears and kissed him soundly on the lips. "What think you?"

"I think we'd best find that priest and have him do the honors now before you change your mind."

"Never will I," she vowed, laughing. "I shall see that you become Lord of Ogof."

"Mayhap we should wait until your father is no longer with us. He might disapprove."

"We shall see," she teased, shaking inside from relief and the ordeal. It was over. Now and evermore.

"Mayhap you, lady, shall be the first and only mistress of the *Dark Sapphire*."

"A woman upon the sea? Is it not a curse?"

"Not when the captain loves the lady," he said.

"Your crew might not agree."

"My crew would rather see you at the helm than me," he said.

"So be it, then."

Again they kissed and again the corridor spun. He held her close, touched her lips with his tongue and she opened to him just as she always had, just as she always would.

"Ahem!"

Her father's voice startled her and she tried to pull away, but Keegan held her fast.

Jestin, with Zelda clucking her tongue and fussing at him to return to bed, glared at his daughter. He shook his head and rubbed his pate. "So this is how it is? You and the son of my enemy." Already his wound had been bound.

She stiffened, but held fast to Keegan. "Aye, Father, 'tis how it is."

"This will come to no good."

"It already has."

He sighed and rubbed his chin.

"Sheena and I will be married."

Jestin's jaw tightened. "'Tis a mistake."

"One I'm willing to make." Sheena notched up her chin. "This time, my husband will be my choice, Father. And you can banish me, never set eyes upon me or your grandchildren, but I hope not. You're ill and I . . . I want peace between you and the man I love."

Jestin hesitated. "'Twill take time and I may not have much."

"Then we will try."

He snorted, coughed and shook his head. "The folly of children," he muttered. "Do what ye will, Sheena. Ye always have. I must attend to my own wife and other children . . . but . . ." He cleared his throat. "Know that I'll never again doubt ye. As fer ye, Keegan, I hope ye're willing to roll the dice with me before I die."

"Mayhap." Keegan eyed the older man suspiciously. "But I will win."

"Will ye, now? That remains to be seen." With a grudging chuckle, Jestin waved them off, then ambled through the doorway and into his room. "I never could tell that girl what to do."

"Nor can I," Keegan admitted.

Sheena giggled, then slid from his embrace and tugged on his sleeve. With a twinkle in her eye, she pulled him down the stairs and through the series of tunnels that he had only

recently run through. Dank and dark, wet and infested with
rats and bats, they led ever downward past the chapel, under
the curtain walls to the cover where the rowboat rocked on
the swells coming in from the sea.

"Well?" she asked when they were standing on the very
dock where they'd embraced so many years before.

"Well, what?"

"Take me with you."

He laughed and through the entrance to the cove he saw
the silhouette of the *Dark Sapphire* riding high on the waves,
sails full, spars cathedral-like as they reached for the heavens. The sun was setting behind the dark ship.

"Only if you agree to be my wife."

"Have I not?" She lifted a dark eyebrow.

"Then, aye, I shall. But first . . ." He held up her left hand
and slipped the ring with the dark gem upon it over her finger.

"But how—?"

"I stripped it away from Fawn. She was so upset, she
barely knew." He smiled slowly. "Remember, lady, I be my
father's son. He taught me much, including his tricks and
sleights of hand. Now, lady, let us start again."

"Aye, Captain," she teased, the stone shining bright upon
her finger. "But how do I know this stone be not cursed?"

"Oh it is," he vowed. "For now you are mine."

"A blessed curse it be," she answered.

"Aye." Arms tightening around her, drawing her near, he
kissed her.

Again.

The world seemed to melt around them. This kiss was as
magical and breath stopping as the first time ever their lips
had met. Sheena quivered inside, longed for more of his
touch, wrapped her arms around his neck, and felt the breath
of the sea against her skin. Here where it all began, they
promised their love would last forever. And as the dark blue
stone glimmered in the night, Sheena silently vowed to hold
on to her rogue of a captain and never, ever, let go.

He was her destiny.

Turn the page for an excerpt from

Lisa Jackson's next contemporary novel

If She Only Knew

Available from Zebra Books

in August 2000

Something was wrong.

  Terribly wrong.

But she couldn't see, couldn't speak, couldn't . . . oh, God, she couldn't move her hand. Was she paralyzed? Dreaming? Trapped in a horrid nightmare? She tried to pry open her eyes but her eyelids wouldn't budge. They weighed a ton and seemed glued shut over eyes that burned with a blinding, hideous pain.

"Mrs. Cahill?"

Mrs. Cahill? Who's that? There was a touch, someone's cool fingers upon the back of her hand. "Mrs. Cahill, can you hear me?" The voice, kind and female, sounded as if it was from a great distance . . . far away, from a spot on the other side of this horrid threshold of pain where it felt like tiny skaters on sharp, pointed ice skates were spinning triple axles on the nerves in her brain. *Me? I'm Mrs. Cahill?*

"Your husband's here to see you."

My husband? But I don't have . . . oh, God, what's happening to me? Am I going crazy?

The fingers were removed and there was a heavy feminine sigh. "I'm sorry, she's still not responding."

"She's been in this hospital over a week." A man's voice. Clipped. Hard. Demanding. "A week, for Christ's sake, and she's shown no signs of recovery."

"Of course she has. She's breathing on her own, I've noticed eye movement behind her lids, she's coughed and yawned, all good signs, all signs that the brain stem isn't damaged—"

Oh, God, they were talking about brain damage.

"Then why won't she wake up?" he demanded.

"I don't know."

"Shit," he muttered, his voice lower.

"Give her time," the woman said softly. "We can't be certain, of course, but there's even a chance that she can hear us now."

Yes, yes, I can hear you, you idiots, but my name isn't Mrs. Cahill, I'm not married and I'm dying from this pain. For God's sake, someone help me! If this is a hospital, surely you have codeine or morphine or . . . or even a damned aspirin.

"Marla? It's Alex," the deep baritone voice said and she felt pressure upon her arm as he touched her. The smell of some cologne assailed her and she instinctively sensed it was expensive. The hands upon her skin were smooth, soft . . . not hardworking hands. Alex's hands.

She tried to remember his face, the color of his hair, the width of his shoulders, the size of his shoes, but she couldn't. His voice brought back no memories whatsoever. There was a faint smell of smoke that clung to him and as his sleeve brushed over her wrist she felt the scratch of wool from the cuff of his jacket. "Oh, God, honey, please wake up. I miss you, the children—" His voice cracked, emotion strangling him.

Children?

No . . . there was no way. This was something she would know. Certainly her intuition, the female animal in her would sense that she had children. Wouldn't she? But then she knew nothing about herself. Nothing.

A cold, sterile horror crept up her spine, overshadowing the pain for a few seconds as she scoured her memory again and came up with not one single recollection of her life.

This is a nightmare. That's the only explanation. It has to be.

Soon she'd wake up, stare into a lover's face or find herself alone in her apartment or house or . . .

"Marla, please, come back to me. To us," Alex whispered gruffly and deep in her heart she wished she felt something, *any*thing for this faceless stranger claiming to be her husband. His smooth fingers linked through hers and she felt pressure on the back of her hand, the pull of an IV needle stuck into her wrist. Dear God, this was pathetic, a scene from a schmaltzy World War II movie. "Cissy misses you and little James . . ." Again his voice cracked and Marla, well, if that was really her name, tried to drag up some tiny bit of emotion from her sub-conscious, a thread of love for this man she couldn't see, didn't remember, but she failed miserably. The void that was her past gave her no hint as to what this man looked like, what he did for a living, how he made love to her . . . surely she would remember that. And what about her children? Cissy? James? No images of cherubic toddlers with runny noses and flushed cheeks or gangly adolescents fighting the ravages of acne flashed through her mind. She had to remember her own kids! That was only natural. Her throat tightened and she felt the sting of tears for the emptiness that was her soul.

Oh, for the love of God, now even *she* was playing her role in this stupid corny movie.

"How long?" he asked, dragging his hand away from hers. "How long is this going to last?"

"These things take time," the nurse replied. "Comas some-times are only a few more hours or . . . perhaps days or even as long as weeks or months or . . ."

"Don't even go there," he said, cutting her off. "That's not going to happen. She will wake up." His voice was like steel. "Marla?" He must've turned to face the bed for he was louder. "Oh, God, Marla, for Christ's sake can't you hear me?"

Again, she tried to move, but couldn't. It was as if she were strapped down, weighted to the bed. Not even one finger could she raise. "I want to talk to the doctor." There was a new force-fulness to Alex's tone. Obviously he was used to giving orders. "I don't see any reason why she can't be taken home and cared for there. I'll hire all the people she needs. Nurses. Aids. Attendants. Whatever. There are servants' quarters in the house and we've got more than enough room for round the clock, live-in help."

There was a long pause and Marla—oh, Lord, why did that name sound familiar and yet didn't quite seem to fit?—sensed unspoken disapproval on the nurse's part. Well, she assumed the woman was a nurse . . . as she struggled to force her eyes open, to move a part of her body to indicate that she could hear and through the haze and pain that were blurring her mind, she understood.

"I'll let Dr. Robertson know that you want to see him," the nurse said, her voice no longer coddling and patient. Now she was firm. Professional. "I'm not sure he's in the hospital now, but I'll see that he gets the message."

"Do that."

"Now, Mrs. Cahill needs her rest."

"In just a minute." Another voice. Elderly. Refined. It floated in on footsteps that were clipped and solid, at odds with the age of the woman's voice. "We're family and I'd like a few moments alone with my daughter-in-law and son."

"Fine. But please, for Mrs. Cahill's sake, make it brief."

"We will, dear," the older woman agreed and Marla felt the touch of cool, dry skin on the back of her hand. "Come on, Marla, wake up. Cissy and little James, they miss you, they need you." A deep chuckle. "Though I hate to admit it, Nana isn't quite the same as their mother."

There was a rustle of clothing, the sound of soft soles padding across the floor and a door opening as, presumably, the nurse left. Marla knew she was alone with her husband and mother-in-law and for a reason she didn't understand, one hidden deep in her subconscious, she felt a chill as cold as death seep through her blood.

"Sometimes I wonder if she'll ever wake up," Alex grumbled. "God, I need a cigarette."

"Just be patient, Alex. Marla was in a horrible accident, and then suffered through the surgeries. She's healing." Another long, serious sigh and a kindly pat of fingers over the back of her hand.

Why was she in the hospital, what kind of accident were they talking about? She tried to concentrate, to think, but the effort brought only an ache that throbbed through her head.

"I just hope that there won't be much disfigurement," the old woman said again.

Marla's insides curdled. She nearly gasped. *Disfigurement?* Oh, God, no. *Disfigurement?* Her throat already parched, nearly closed in fear and her stomach felt as if it had been twisted and clamped with rubber bands. She tried to remember what she looked like and failed. It didn't matter; not compared to mutilation. Her heart was racing with dread and certainly someone somewhere watching her monitors could see that she was aware, that she was responding, but no loud footsteps pounded outside the door, no one yelled, "She's coming around!"

"She has the best doctors in the state. She . . . she might not look like what we expect, but she'll be fine. Beautiful." Alex sounded as if he was trying to convince himself.

"She always was. You know, Alexander," the woman who called herself Nana said, "sometimes a woman's beauty can be a curse."

A bitter laugh from this man who was her husband. "I don't think she'd agree."

"No, of course not. But she hasn't lived long enough to understand."

There was a rattling sound, as if a cart was being rolled past the open door. Other voices, so far away, a buzz of conversation, the soft chime of elevator doors parting, even the tinkle of laughter. She needed to tell them, whoever they were, that they needed to give her something, *any*thing for the agony ripping through her head.

And besides that, she wanted something to help her remember. Her children. Her husband. Her own face. Her life. Right now, she'd settle for any shred of knowledge. . . . Any shred at all.

*   *   *

Whistling sharply to his dog, Nick Cahill cut the engine of the *Notorious* and threw a line around a post on the dock where he moored his fishing boat. "Come on, Tough Guy, let's go home," he called over his shoulder as the boat undulated with the tide of this backwater bay. Rain drizzled from a leaden sky and the wind picked up, lashing at his face. White-caps swirled and danced in counterpoint to the seagulls wheeling and crying overhead. The distinctive odors of diesel, rotting wood and brine mingled in the wintry air of Oregon in November.

Hiking the collar of his jacket around his neck, Nick grabbed his bucket of live crabs and stepped onto the pier just as his dog shot past in a black-and-white streak. A three-legged shepherd of indecipherable lineage, Tough Guy hurtled his body onto the slippery planks and scrambled up the stairs to the parking lot situated on the bluff. Nick followed suit, more slowly, past sagging posts covered with barnacles and strangled by seaweed.

"There's somebody here ta see ya." Ole Olsen, the old coot in the window of the bait shop located at the landing, grunted. He hitched his chin upward toward the top of the stairs but didn't meet Nick's eyes, just kept working at tying a fly, as he always did.

"To see me?" Nick asked. No one, in all the five years he'd been in these parts, had ever dropped by the marina looking for him.

"Ye-up. That's what he said." Seated on his stool, surrounded by lures and coolers holding bait and Royal Crown soda, Ole had been a fixture at the marina for years. A burned-out stub of a cigar was forever plugged into one corner of his mouth, red hair turning gray ringed his bald pate, and folds of skin hid his eyes more effectively than the magnifying glasses perched on the end of his nose. "Told him you'd be out a while, but he wanted to wait." He clipped off a piece of thread with his teeth, turned over a piece of fuzz covering a hook that looked suspiciously as if it would soon resemble a salmon fly. "Figured if he wanted to, I couldn't stop him."

"Who?"

"Never gave his name. But you'll spot him." Ole's eyes finally looked up, focusing over the half glasses. Through the window, his face framed by racks of cigarettes, tide tables, and dozens of flies he'd tied himself, he added, "He ain't from around here. I could tell that right off."

Nick felt a sliver of doom burrow into his heart. His shoulders tightened a bit and Tough Guy gave up a sharp bark. "Thanks," he said to Ole.

"Enny time."

Nick mounted the stairs and walked across a pocked lot where trucks and trailers and campers were parked with haphazard abandon. In the midst of them, looking like the proverbial diamond in the gravel a sleek silver Jaguar was parked, engine purring, California plates announcing an intruder from the south. The engine died suddenly and the driver's door swung open and from within the opulent depths a tall man in a business suit, polished wing tips and raincoat emerged.

Alex Cahill in the flesh.

Great. Just . . . great.

He'd picked a helluva time to show up.

The bad feeling that had been with Nick most of the afternoon took a sharp turn for the worse.

"About time," Alex said as if he'd been waiting for hours. "I thought maybe you'd died out there." He hitched his jaw west to the sea.

"Not so lucky this time."

"Maybe next."

"Maybe."

Alex's intense eyes, so like his own, flashed. "So you're still an irreverent bastard."

"I keep workin' at it." Nick didn't bother to smile. "I wouldn't want to disappoint."

"Shit, Nick, that's all you've ever done."

"Probably."

In a heartbeat Nick decided his mother must've died. For no other reason would Alex be inconvenienced enough to wear out some of the tread on his tires. But the thought was hard to believe. Eugenia Haversmith Cahill was the toughest woman who'd ever trod across this planet on three-inch heels. Nope. He changed his mind. Eugenia would outlive every one of her children, himself included. He kept walking to his truck and slung his bucket into the bed with his toolbox and spare tire. Around the parking lot, a once-painted fence and fir trees contorted by years of battering wind and rain formed a frail barricade that separated the marina from an antique shop that hadn't been in business in years.

Alex jammed his hands deep into the pockets of a coat that probably sported a fancy designer label, not that Nick would know. Or care. But something was up. Something big and the hangover that had been with him for the past few hours wasn't about to let up.

"Look, Nick, I came here because I need your help."

"You need my help? Maybe I should be flattered."

"This is serious."

"I suspect."

"It's Marla."

Son of a bitch. Beneath the rawhide of his jacket, Nick's shoulders bunched. No matter what, he wasn't going to be sucked in. Not by Marla. Not again. Not ever.

"She's been in an accident."

"What kind of accident?"

Nick's jaw was so tight it ached. He'd never trusted his older brother. And for good reason. For as long as Nick could remember, Alex Cahill had bowed down at the altar of the dollar, genuflected whenever he heard a NASDAQ quote and paid fervent homage to the patron saints of San Francisco, the elite who were so often referred to as "old money." That went double for his beautiful, social-climbing wife, Marla. But there had been a time when he'd thought differently, when Nick, too, had been willing to sell his soul for the Almighty Buck. And for Marla.

"It's bad, Nick—" Alex said.

"But she's alive." He needed to know that much.

"Barely. In a coma. She . . . well, she might not make it."

Nick's stomach clenched. "Then why are you here? Shouldn't you be with her?"

"Yes. I have been. But . . . I didn't know how else to reach you. You don't return my calls and . . . well . . ."

"I don't do e-mail."

"That's one of the problems."

"Sure." Nick leaned against the Dodge's muddy fender, telling himself not to be taken in, for his brother was nothing if not a smooth-talking bastard, a man who could, with a seemingly sincere and even smile, firm handshake and just the right amount of eye contact, talk a life jacket off a drowning man.

"What happened?"

"Single car accident," Alex admitted and to his credit he paled beneath his tan. Reaching into his jacket, he found a pack of cigarettes and offered one to Nick, who shook his head, though he'd love to feel the smoke curl through his lungs, and could use the buzz of nicotine.

Alex flicked his lighter and drew deep. In a cloud of smoke he said, "Marla was driving. Over a week ago now. In the mountains near Santa Cruz, a miserable stretch of road. Had her friend, Pamela Delacroix with her." There was a long pause. A heavy sigh. Just the right amount of hesitation to indicate more bad news. Nick steeled himself as a Jeep with a dirty rag top sped into the parking lot, bouncing through the puddles before sliding to a stop near the railing. Two loud guys in their twenties climbed out and opened up the back to haul out rods, reels and a cooler. "Unfortunately Pam didn't make it."

A coldness swept over Nick. "Jesus."

"Killed instantly."

"But Marla survived."

"If you can call it that."

"Son of a bitch." Now he wanted a smoke. Bad. He shoved

his hands into his pockets and warned himself not to believe his brother, not for a second.

"What happened?"

"You mean what caused the accident? Who knows? The police are looking into it. Marla could be charged with negligent homicide, I suppose. I . . . I haven't gotten into the legalities of it all. Not yet. There's been too much to worry about with Marla. This . . . it's been a nightmare. Hard on everyone."

That, Nick believed. If the situation hadn't been grim, Alex would never have made the trip. Hell. Rainwater ran down his face as he opened the cab door and reached inside, found the remains of a six pack of Henry's, ripped one from its plastic collar and tossed it to Alex, then popped the tab of a second for himself.

"If Marla does pull through—"

"If, Alex? *If*? She's the strongest, most determined woman I know. She'll make it. For Chrissakes, Alex, don't put her in the grave yet. She's your damned wife!"

A beat. Unspoken accusations. Memories that had no right to be recalled—dark, seductive, erotic came to mind. Nick's throat turned to dust. The wind slapped his face. He took a long gulp of beer and heard Tough Guy whine at his feet. But his thoughts had already turned that dark corner he'd avoided for years, the narrow path that led straight to his brother's wife. Forbidden images came into play. Taboo pictures of a gorgeous woman with a lilting laugh and mischief in her eyes. He heard the gentle lap of the water against the dock below and the hum of traffic on the highway, the dull roar of the sea pounding the coast on the other side of the jetty, the call of the damned sea gulls, yet nothing was as loud as the thud of his own heart.